I0706447

Mercer

Saint and Sinners

Ruby Vincent

Published by Ruby Vincent, 2021.

Copyright © 2021 by Ruby Vincent
Cover Design: Cover By Combs
All rights reserved. No part of this publication may be reproduced, stored in a retrieval system, or transmitted in any form or by any means, electronic, mechanical, recording or otherwise, without the prior written permission of the copyright holder.
This is a work of fiction. Names, characters, businesses, places, events, and incidents are either the products of the author's imagination or used in a fictitious manner. Any resemblance to actual persons, living or dead, or actual events is purely coincidental.

Prologue

We sat around the living room, the perfect family scene.

Cash typed on his computer while watching the news, switching between screens.

Sinjin and Mercer talked new safe houses and where we'd set up our home. I curled up on Brutal's lap, content as he stroked my hair.

I hummed. "I'm thirsty but I'm loath to get up."

"Don't." Mercer got up, tickling my toes as he passed. "Tea?"

"Yes, please." I wriggled on Baris's lap, feeling his ridge thickening, and earning a smack on the backside for my trouble. I kissed him in apology. The kiss I received in return was not apologetic. I threw my arms around him, getting deep in our make-out session.

"Killian, turn that up," Sinjin said.

"What?"

"The news." Sinjin upped the volume himself.

"—today that they've confirmed the young man killed outside Opium four years ago has been identified as Mercer Santos."

I dropped my feet on the floor. Santos?

"Some may remember the headlines following this grisly murder. A man was stabbed and then the body disfigured to prevent identification. Since the nightclub concealed an underground casino, authorities had trouble discerning if his death was connected to the club or the illegal activities underneath. Now that Mr. Santos has been identified, we're hopeful the police can find new leads—"

Eeeeeee!

We spun around.

The teakettle screeched on the stove, trumpeting his readiness, and no one in the kitchen to respond.

The front door hung ajar—swinging as rapid footsteps faded down the hall.

Chapter One

I stood—jaw hanging, eyes wide at the open door.

Sinjin sprang into action.

"Hey!"

The next thing I knew, the guys were tearing off. Sinjin, Cash, and then Baris shot past me. They raced out the door, giving chase.

I didn't follow. Turning back to the television, I fixed on the woman in the box, trying to make sense of what she was saying.

The body of Mercer Santos? What does this mean?

"—have not been able to track down next of kin. Authorities are asking anyone with information regarding Mr. Santos to please come forward."

It's just a name, I thought. *It's not even an uncommon one. There must be a million Santoses in the States. Why wouldn't there be more than two Mercers?*

Then why did he run? another voice asked.

My mind didn't supply an answer.

If that Mercer isn't connected to mine, why isn't mine here with me now, explaining the simple misunderstanding? But if the two are connected, what does that mean?

The real Mercer Santos has been dead for four years and the man I love is... who?

I burst into Gianna's room.

She was sitting up in bed, eating breakfast and watching a movie. She raised a brow at my entrance.

"Something wrong?" she asked.

"What did the ledger say?"

"What?"

"What did it say?!" I snatched up her waffles and flung them across the room.

"I was eating that."

I planted my arms on either side of her, probing the amusement in her eyes. "Tell me everything you know about Mercer right now."

"Ahh. I see the news finally ran the story." Gianna settled into the pillows, grinning away. "You should keep watching. My failsafe packed a lot of juicy details. Just wait till they run the headlines on Judge Lee. Hint: He trades shorter sentences for bigger boats. A crapload of people are going to file for appeals after that goes live—"

"Are you enjoying this?" I was shaking. "Mercer—or whoever the fuck he is! He just beat it out of here while a body with his name flashed on the screen. What is going on, Gianna? If you know something, why aren't you telling me?"

Fire lit her brown pools. "Why do I have to? They're your great loves. Mercer is the man you chose over me again and again. He's the one you want me to trust with the ledger and my future. Why do you need to hear from me who he is?" She leaned forward till our noses bonked. "Don't you know?"

My nails dug half-moons into my palm. It was everything in me not to punch my best friend dead in the face. "You're smug as shit right now because you know I don't know. What do you want me to say, Gianna? Tell me what it will take to end these games."

She held my gaze steadily. "You know what to say."

"I wasn't wrong about him. He loves me," I stated. "There's an explanation for this."

"Then, ask him for it." She peered over my shoulder. "If you can catch him."

"Gianna—"

"Say it."

I ground my teeth hard. For the briefest, barest flash, hatred for Gianna Cross turned my stomach. It was gone as quickly as it came, doused by acceptance it wasn't her I hated. It was her being right.

"I should've listened to you." The words burned coming out. "I don't know everything I should know about these men. I trusted too blindly and too soon.

"I'm sorry."

Nodding, Gianna's face softened. "You weren't the only stubborn bitch. I didn't trust any of them—least of all *Mercer*. But I took things a step too far. This ah-ha moment isn't as satisfying when you're about to cry."

Tears spilled out. I dropped on the mattress, face sinking in my hands. *Pull yourself together. You had weeks and months to cry about the little you knew about Mercer and just as long to do something about it. Now it's time to know.*

"Tell me what the ledger says about Mercer, Gianna." Wiping my face, I looked her in the eye. "No more games."

She was quiet for a beat.

I waited for the demands. She'd tell me if I unchained her. Or let her go and I'd hear the story from her taxi cab to the airport.

None came.

"Mercer Lucas Santos was twenty-eight years old. Born on April third right here in the city. He attended Cinco University and graduated years before us. He and a friend from college invented some kind of security program in their dorm room. A more secure way of storing data. It took off, but his partner became the face of the business. Mercer worked background in the tech department."

I frowned. *Security program? Data storing?*

This story didn't track with the one my Mercer told me of Alaric and his dropping out to pursue carnal pleasures.

Was everything he told me a lie?

"As people riding a sudden influx of cash tend to do, Mercer used his money to indulge his whims—including almost weekly dates with escorts, and spending every night till closing in the strip clubs. He died chasing down one vice too many. Buying a night with a man named Montecito using money he shouldn't have."

She grabbed my hand. "That's what the ledger said about Mercer Santos. The *real* Mercer Santos. Who the fuck that guy is that you've been screwing for months...? There's nothing in the ledger about him. There's nothing *anywhere* about him."

"We haven't been screwing."

I can't say why that was the first thing out of my mouth, but it was all my brain supplied for me.

"What's he said about himself?" she asked.

I replied, as if on autopilot. "He dropped out of Cinco to become an escort and started working in a strip club. He wasn't clear on if Alaric was his real name or a stage name. Either way, it became the name on everyone's speed dial."

A thought occurred to me. "Part of that story must be true. Saint, Killian, and Brutal met him while he was on a date. They tried drugging him and got more than they bargained for."

I slipped my hand out from under her. Other things were occurring to me as well. "Why didn't you tell me that he wasn't who he said he was? Were you hoping the imposter would slit my throat in my sleep or something? I've told him my entire history and I didn't even know his name. This is beyond teaching me a lesson. You risked me, you, *and Dad*. Why?"

"I didn't tell you because he asked me not to."

"Excuse me?"

Gianna took my hand again. "I wasn't waiting for him to hurt you, Addy. He had that option for months and didn't take the countless opportunities you gave him. That was a pretty good hint that killing you and the Merchants wasn't what he was after. I figured he wanted exactly what they all wanted: the ledger.

"When I tested them at the Fairfield, I half expected Mercer to grab that gun and finally reveal his true intentions. But he just stood there like the rest, letting his chance go by. I figured by then I didn't know what he wanted and why should I find out? He was your problem, not mine."

"Real nice, Gianna."

"How many hints did I need to give you, Addy? I practically took out a billboard on Vinton Street, saying that dude was shady. Did you do anything about it?"

"I asked him why he wanted the ledger and what it said about him," I admitted. "He refused to say and even went so far as to tell me he'd rip his page from the ledger before he'd let me see it."

Gianna's brows drew together. "So, he is in the ledger? Interesting. There's a handful of people in there that I couldn't identify. Their names and naughty activities are in the book, but when I researched them, nothing came up. No photos. No address. No phone number. No social media. Nothing. The fake Mercer could be one of them."

"How many are a handful?" I asked.

"Thirty."

Great. The man I love could be one of thirty dangerous strangers who erased himself for reasons that cannot be good.

"What kind of naughty activities are we talking about?"

"Wetwork, selling secrets, trafficking. Businesses where you don't give your real name."

I shook my head. "And you kept that from me because he asked you to? I'm supposed to believe that?"

She looked away. "Mercer came into my room the night you guys brought me here. He said he knew by now that I learned he stole the real Mercer Santos's identity. He swore there was more to the story than I understood, but if it all came out, the person who would be hurt most was you."

"I would be hurt most?"

"Yes," she said. "I asked if he killed Mercer Santos and if he was in the ledger. He wouldn't give me anything except to point out that if he was willing to kill everyone in his way, we were alone and I was conveniently chained to the bed."

I shivered. That was a chilling and accurate fact to point out.

"He didn't even ask me where I hid it, Addy. He just said to let him tell you the truth on his own. I told him to be quick about it, leaving out my little failsafe."

"He wasn't quick enough."

"I don't know what to do with this," I said honestly. "How can he pretend all of this is about me? Mercer Santos was killed four years before we knew each other existed. And if he wanted to tell me the truth himself, why did he run out the door?"

"Couldn't tell you," she replied. "But if the escort thing is real, I'd start there with finding out who this guy really is."

My gaze drifted up to the ceiling and the bedroom on the other side of the plaster, soundproofing, and wood. I tucked a card away in my room. A card I couldn't possibly use.

"None of this makes any sense," I whispered.

"Because you don't know how to feel."

I nodded, tears welling. "Do I have a right to be mad at him? I wasn't Miss Honesty when we met. He didn't hide that he had secrets," I said. "At the very least, I thought I knew him. Now... I don't know."

"Still believe that he loves you?"

I was quiet for a long time. So long footfalls broke our silence.

"Adeline? Where is she?!"

"I'm in here," I called. "I didn't take off too."

Sinjin stormed into the room. Blue hair stuck up in an odd formation and my first thought was horns.

"What does she know about this?" he demanded.

"*She* has a name," Gianna replied.

"*She* has five seconds."

"She doesn't know anything," I broke in. "I'm guessing you didn't catch up to him."

Sinjin grabbed my wrist and towed me out. He slammed the door on Gianna.

"The cab was speeding around the street by the time we got out there." Sinjin carded his hands through his hair, thoroughly messing it up, and somehow still looking perfect. "What did she tell you?"

"The real Mercer Santos has been dead for four years. The one you've been living with took his identity for reasons unknown. He asked Gianna to keep his secret, claiming he'd tell the truth himself. He didn't tell us quick enough to beat that broadcast."

Sinjin eyed me. "What's wrong with you? Why are you so calm?"

"I'm not calm, Saint." I sidestepped him, making for the stairs. "I'm the farthest thing from calm."

MERCER

"Buddy, want to tell me where we're going—?"

"Just drive!" I yanked out a wad of cash and threw it at him. "Go wherever the hell you want. Don't stop until I tell you."

The cabbie gaped at the pile of hundreds on his lap. "Yes, sir."

I twisted in the seat, peeking Killian skidding onto the sidewalk and searching the street for me.

Shit. Shit, shit, shit!

This was not good. Channel Eight broke the story. It would be on every station and their website by nightfall.

I was lucky as fuck they were distracted and there was nothing between me and the door.

What would Cross tell Adeline about me now that the mask was gone? What were the guys thinking of the last few years we've worked together? How would I explain the news and running off in the middle of it?

All of those were good questions.

I straightened in my seat as we lost Killian and Sinjin around the corner.

But they're not the most important ones.

Leaning back, I crossed my ankle over my leg and fished something out of my pocket. The contact lens case balanced on my thigh.

Years of work, I thought. *So close.*

I popped out the contact lens. Then the other. My naked eyes blinked in the first real look at the world in years.

Once it's known Mercer Santos is dead, it won't be long before—

My phone rang.

"Shit."

Chapter Two

A deline
I paced up and down my room, flicking the card in my hands.

By no stretch of the imagination was it a good idea to call Thiago Pais. He attacked Gianna. Hung her off a balcony. Witnessed me kill his girlfriend and received a crack on the head as a parting gift.

Was he holed up with the fake ledger he rescued from the bushes, killing himself to decode its secrets?

If I call this man, I'll be announcing he has something I want. The absolute worst thing I can do when he wants a trade.

Thiago knows Mercer/Alaric/Whoever-he-is. Mercer refused to attend the tournament matches because Thiago would peg him as a Merchant.

There could be more to it than that. If the Merchant persona was the fake all along, maybe Alaric is the real one. Mercer said they knew each other pretty well—chatted each other up at every party they attended. He could tell me who he is in that world Mercer kept me out of.

But why would he? a voice reminded. *He's got no incentive to do that for free.*

A man like him doesn't help an old lady across the road out of good intentions. That lady must have some use to him.

Jaw tight, I returned the card to the drawer.

I wouldn't be another sucker caught up in Thiago Pais's web. He revealed his true self to me. I wouldn't land in his pocket to discover Mercer's.

I moved to the window, casting an eye over my endless city. Somewhere in the thousands was the man I loved.

"You said you did all of this to keep me," I whispered. "Prove it."

MERCER

I stepped out of the shower, steam billowing out ahead of me. I wrapped the towel around my neck and padded into the living room. Black furniture with chrome frames—and their fine layer of dust—awaited me.

Toweling off, I reached for the remote and clicked a button. Sliding doors broke apart, revealing their eighty-five-inch secret behind. I flicked to the news and turned the television on low.

My towel dropped beside the remote on the couch. Bare as the coffee table, I surveyed my apartment.

It'd been too long since I'd been here. Everything was covered in dust. A musty, closed-in smell hung in the air. I popped the lid on the trash can and the smell rushed out in full force.

The person I hired to clean while I was away apparently kicked back and enjoyed half their egg and pickle sub before taking off on a long vacation on my dime.

They would have to be dealt with after my current situation was taken care of.

I moved into the kitchen, searching the pantry for coffee, found it on the wrong shelf, and pulled out the pot.

It had been even longer since I had French roast. Alaric didn't drink coffee. Stained teeth and coffee breath weren't an aphrodisiac. It's the little things that catapult you to the best, and when I step into a role, only the best is acceptable.

I crossed the room as the brew bubbled, standing before my floor-to-ceiling windows, naked as the day I was born.

It didn't matter this high in the sky. I gazed down at my city.

Busy Leighbridge traffic. Rushing dots doubling as people. Buildings that didn't stretch as high as the twenty-third floor. I saw it all, but no one saw me.

No one knew me.

I slid a look to my phone, anticipating another call. Not that there was more to say. The identity of the real Mercer Santos hitting the news cycle was a problem I knew could happen. I'd been ready to run for four years, and then... Adeline.

She was a complication I hadn't foreseen.

The truth was, I should've left two seconds after our home above the sandwich shop blew up. Got in my car and disappeared. The Cross versus Redgrave War was bound to have casualties, and with Cross possessing the ledger, there was nothing to stop her making Mercer Santos one of them.

Except I thought I could stop her. A lapse in judgment I wouldn't have made before Adeline.

A niggle of irritation worked its way in.

There were many paths I should've taken that were ignored or rationalized away because of Adeline. I deserved the calls. I deserved the harsh words on the other end of it. I broke the first rule—the only rule in my line of work.

I got too close. I let the mark make me her mark, and got caught standing over a stove making tea like a house-trained husband.

My phone went off.

Sighing, I let it go to voicemail in favor of pouring my long-awaited cup of coffee. I needed it for round three of this conversation. And afterward, I'd need another for what I must do next.

Adeline Redgrave.

The lights were on. The spell is lifted. There is still a job to be done.

Time to get rid of the problem.

ADELINE

"I know you looked him up."

The four of us sat around a table of untouched sausage, veggies, and garlic knots. I stuck my fork in my food a few times. It didn't make it all the way to my mouth.

"Everything about his life and where he came from," I continued. "Are you saying his fake life held up to your scrutiny, Killian?"

"Impeccably," he said. Speared sausage hung on the fork tapping his plate. "I found death certificates for Mercer's supposed parents. His accounts had pics of him from childhood to cheesing with coeds before a Cinco University backdrop. I watched him in action playing Alaric and he received the coy smiles, not-so-subtle flirting, and constant touching from more than a few people he knew intimately. On their own they could be faked, but all together, I had no reason to believe he was anything other than what he claimed to be."

Saint made no show of trying to eat his food. He had scooped it back into the pan and sat clutching his beer in a death grip.

"Plus," Cash went on. "We'd give him a target and he came back with the information every time. It's been four years, Adeline. If he gave us reason to suspect him, we'd have gotten rid of him a long time ago."

"Which he knew," I whispered. "That's why he refused to come clean to me. The truth is poison."

"We don't know what the truth is. All we know is we've been working with an unnamed stranger for four years who infiltrated the Merchants for reasons unknown."

"The ledger," I said. "That's everyone's reason. He must've changed his mind about getting it by any means after falling for me."

"Doesn't track." Saint's voice was a low growl. "Like you said, we were all after the ledger. We made no secret of it. Why hide yourself and not your motives? Doesn't make sense unless he's after something else and he needed to be a Merchant to get it."

"What could that something be?"

Silence was my reply.

"Think about it," I said. "Was there ever a job that went unexpectedly wrong, or target that proved more formidable than they should be? Mercer—for lack of another name—came through every time you asked something of him. I don't know why he worked so hard to become a Merchant, but it wasn't to sabotage the gang."

"You can't know that," Killian gritted. "You want to think well of the man who became our partner and your boyfriend, but that man did not exist. He played the long game for years. I'd like to hear from his mouth what that game is."

"I would too," I said. "Every good lie is anchored in the truth. Real photos of him. Real clients. Real results. Somewhere in the lie, something is true. We use that to find him."

"Fuck him," Saint announced. "If he was interested in giving up the truth, his ass wouldn't have hightailed it out the door. We're not tracking him down while Cross kicks back in the next room, holding on to how we get back into her fortress to get the ledger. The ledger the whole fucking city knows she has."

He slammed his beer on the table. "The ledger has always and will always be the priority. Whatever Fake Mercer was after, he didn't get that. Far as I'm concerned, we were done with him by the time the cab turned the corner."

I pressed my lips together. I understood where Saint was coming from. He was angry and betrayed, but with the identity of his father's killer finally within reach, he refused to spare the attention.

I won't force him to. The ledger is our focus.

But I am far from done with Fake Mercer Santos.

He is no less mine than when he shot out that door. He whispered sweet assurances in my ear. Told me he loved me and painted a future where we could be together—no holding back. I wasn't letting that go any quicker than I was letting him go.

"Right now, no one can get into Gianna's apartment but her," I said. "Leah killed all the people with access to it, and then she died with a garrote around her throat. Once Thiago was out, there was no getting back inside for him. But—"

"But there's nothing stopping him from camping out around the building with a hundred Kings ready to move when Gianna comes back for it," Killian finished.

"Yes. That."

Baris slipped his hand under mine, dropping a kiss on my knuckles. He hadn't said a word since Mercer took off. Doesn't mean there wasn't plenty going on in that head of his.

"I wouldn't be so quick to think there's no one with access to her apartment," Killian said. "All apartment management has a legal right to enter as long as they give notice. The Fairfield is no different. Sure, one lone corrupt employee won't find it easy to sneak around. But going through official methods, I could see the manager logging in to the system and using their override access to get onto her floor. Especially if there's a gun to her head."

"I thought you said there was no way to break into the Fairfield."

"There's no way to sneak in undetected, Adeline. There's always a way to get in. Enough firepower and people with keys who value their lives. You'll get in."

I inclined my head. "True. The Kings can always storm the place. But would Thiago Pais make such a move? He couldn't keep it quiet. Every panic button would be set off. Leighbridge police would have the place surrounded in minutes. Onlookers would be on the scene just as quickly with their camera phones. Even if all that could be swept away by the cops in his pocket, everyone would know he has the ledger. The strongest defense a Kieran has is their anonymity. That's why I'm currently protecting my duplicitous best friend by chaining her in the spare room."

"Heard that," Gianna called.

Brutal squeezed my hand. "Pais won't wait."

"He won't," Killian agreed. "We may not know how or who or when, but one thing is certain. Pais will make a move for the ledger, or the person he believes can translate it for him."

"I'll get the ledger," I said. "Trust me. She will tell me how to get it out of the Fairfield, and we'll put an end to all of this. I've seen the future."

Visions of mossy eyes and a wicked smile floated through my mind.

"I'll do whatever it takes to make it happen."

After forcing myself to scrounge down half of my dinner, I brought a tray into Gianna's room.

"Yum." She set down her book. "Chicken and apple?"

"Andouille."

"Even better."

I placed her tray on her lap and climbed in next to her. She swallowed a bite and hummed.

"You know, I think you're enjoying your captivity a bit too much. It's hardly a punishment."

She laughed. "Am I being punished or protected? If you're going for the former, you shouldn't fill me up with your cooking."

"Fair point."

Gianna sobered. "You and I both know what's waiting for me when I step outside the door. You can't keep me in here forever, Addy. They'll always believe I have the ledger, just like people are still searching for a Kieran Foley who has been dead for years. Eventually, I'll have to start my life with that target on my back."

"Which I'm sure you're ready to do once you pick up the ledger and find a new place to rule from behind the safety of your castle walls."

"You always did know me too well." She gave me a look over her fork. "I'm supposed to give up the one thing that everyone is trying to kill me for? That's subsequently the single thing that can save me from the mob? Might as well tie me to a pole in the square and broadcast the bloodbath."

I watched her eat for a while.

"Want to know why I didn't dump you after all the shit you pulled?"

Gianna replied without skipping a beat. "Because you're stuck with me like a conjoined twin."

"Besides that," I said. "You're a reminder, Gianna, of the cost of being too trusting. You're a lesson our fathers didn't learn in time."

Her mocking grin faded.

"The ledger ruined three men who were closer than brothers. Cost two their lives and the other everything that mattered to him. We swore we wouldn't make their mistake, and you fell at the first fucking opportunity."

She looked away, jaw clenched tight.

"The ledger brought us down too. It killed the trust between us—the one thing I could rely on through everything.

"There's still a part of me that loves you. That young girl who clutched your hand on the way home from school, terrified her mother was waiting around the corner, while you swore you'd never let her take me. She can't let go yet, because then the ledger truly will have destroyed every good thing in her life.

"Whatever prompted this cry for help, I'm willing to stand by you through it because I believe we still have a friendship left to save. One without trust that's teetering on the edge, but still something." I turned her chin to face me. "If you don't, tell me now. Admit you don't give a shit about what I want, Gianna. Tell me you'll always expect me to choose between you and my guys. After Dad, Kaylee, Bellona, and Baris—it's not as difficult a choice as it was."

Slowly, she leaned back, pulling out of my grip.

"It was never about you, A. I'm still the little girl holding your hand, willing to protect you where everyone else failed—even if I was bound to fail too. I've never let anyone fuck with you. I wasn't about to start now."

"You didn't take that ledger for me, Gianna."

"I took it from them!" she cried. "I didn't trust the Merchants. I didn't know them. The war has always been between me and them. You were in the middle." She tossed her head. "You say I'm a lesson in trust? Well, have you learned it, Addy? One of your precious guys abandoned you at the first chance.

"Imagine if you found the ledger that day in La Roche's safe and handed it right to him. I might've walked into that sandwich shop and found your corpse bleeding on the floor. You were blind to the men you were falling in love with."

The dagger twisted in my heart.

"I admit I went too far but—"

"There it is," I said. "*But*. You keep doing that. Every almost apology comes with a 'but' and ends with why you were justified in doing the shit you put me through. This isn't about Saint, Killian, Baris, or even Mercer. This is about you and me, and the fact you're about to lose me for good. We won't get very far from here without trust, Gianna."

I made for the door.

"You should start thinking about how you'll earn it back."

I shut her in, turned, and walked into Saint.

He leaned against the wall. Clearly he'd been standing there for a while.

He tracked my approach as I leaned to kiss him.

"You're not letting her suck you in her web of bullshit anymore. That's something at least."

"You all were convinced that I was taken in by her," I said, keeping my voice low. "Gianna had me by the nose, and I was crushed under too much sentiment to fight back. But I ask you, love, which one of us is chained up in a dumpy loft in Leighbridge working her way up to forgiveness. I always get what I want in the end. When are you going to learn that?"

He cracked a grin. "Want a few orgasms too? 'Cause I can make that happen."

"I would," I said, nose in the air. "I'd like that very much."

Saint wrapped my legs around his waist, carrying me to his room. "After we're done, you'll tell me exactly how you'll get that woman to give up the name of the man who killed my father within twenty-four hours before I take over." He gave me the same cheeky kiss. "You'll find I get what I want too."

"ADELINE."

A sweet, smoky voice wrapped up my dreams, carrying them away.

"Adeline."

Mercer materialized—unfolding like a curtain drawing up on a one-man show.

Legs shapely and powerful in pants that managed to hug him just right without being too tight. Strong, confident hands just beginning to explore my body. A well-built chest housing the heart that soothed me as I rested on top of him. Full smirking lips. Glinting green eyes. Sweeping black hair.

It was a sin how gorgeous this man was.

"Adeline."

My skin shouldn't prickle for him. Even in my dreams.

"Adeline, wake up."

I peeled my eyes open. A figure stood over me.

Reacting instantly, I struck—punch swinging for his face.

He caught my wrist one-handed. "Whoa. No need for that."

The curtain came up, and it wasn't on green eyes, crow-black hair, and a mischievous smirk.

"Who are you?" I blurted.

"That's a long story," replied Fake Mercer. "Come with me, and I'll tell you."

I blinked, trying to make sense of what was happening. My skin wasn't prickling for him. It was for the blast of cold air hitting me courtesy of the covers flung off my body.

Saint lay under the mound, sleeping soundly. Too soundly. I had to creep around like a mouse to avoid waking him when I snuck out of our room. Mercer calling me and tossing blankets should have woken him.

"What did you do to him?" I hissed.

He held up his little black case.

"You drugged him?!"

"He'll wake up in a few hours. They all will." He held out a hand. "Are you coming?"

Frowning, I inched away. "Who are you?" And I didn't mean his name.

Gone were the forest eyes and waves of black. Hair closer in shade to mine hung over dark eyes, observing me as I slid out of bed, putting distance between us.

Even his voice was different. Deeper. Lower. Fuller. It was nothing like the light flirtiness of the guy I'd come to know.

"Was anything about you real?"

"If you want to find out, come with me. I'll tell you how we got here."

I moved as he moved, maintaining our space. "Why do I need to come with you? You can tell me right here, next to my drugged boyfriend, and then you can explain it to him when he wakes up."

Sighing, he stuffed his hands in his pockets and strolled right past me—ignoring me shooting out of the way.

"My conversation with St. John and the rest won't go nearly as smoothly. I can trust you to at least hear me out before coming for my throat." He paused in the doorway. "I felt you were owed an explanation, Adeline. One that would reach you ahead of the poisoning they'll do against me. Guys like us don't take betrayal lightly. But then, you were always the better Merchant."

I breathed hard—my shaking visible in my nakedness.

"If you want that explanation, we do this my way. Otherwise, the next time I go through that door, I won't come back."

"That's excellent emotional manipulation, No-Name, but I don't know you. I have no idea what you want or what could possibly justify killing a man, stealing his identity, and lying to my face for months. I'm supposed to skip off with you and end up in another psycho's basement?"

"You're supposed to believe that I came back for a reason."

"What reason would that be?"

"I haven't questioned my ownership."

I bit hard on my lip. Of all the things to say, why did he have to say that?

"Fine," I heard myself say.

He stood, his back to the door as I changed into jeans, a shirt, and pulled on a sweater and shoes. I berated myself the whole time.

You can't trust him. He could be taking you anywhere. He drugged Saint and everyone in the loft. What explanation could he give that would make all of this alright?

Through all of that, my voice of reason had one thing to say.

You deserve to know the truth.

"Where are we going?" I asked, trailing him out into the hallway.

"Where all this started."

I fell quiet—for two seconds.

"Is this what you really look like? Hair? Eyes?"

"Yes."

"And the *real* Mercer Santos? Did he have green eyes and black hair? Did you change to look like him?"

"Mercer Santos looked nothing like me. Not to brag, but very few people could be so handsome."

I stopped dead on the stoop. That was spot-on something the man I loved would say. But that man did not exist.

Is this more of that act?

Mercer's car idled on the curb. He opened the passenger door and stood aside, pointedly waiting for me to climb in.

"Do you believe you could take me somewhere or show me something that will make this all okay?" I asked. "I really hope the answer is yes. You better make this right, or I will beat the shit out of you. Pop those color-shifting eyes out of your head."

He grinned. "Duly noted. After you."

Stiffly, I climbed off the stoop and into the car.

I was out of threats and questions.

Mercer took off, molding into early morning three a.m. traffic.

He didn't speak on the drive. He didn't look at me, make a move toward the radio, or do much of anything but check his mirrors and signal lane changes.

He said he loved me. Was that real?

Do I want my explanation to come with an honest answer to that question?

What would be worse? Mercer faking feelings for me to keep his cover? Or he truly cared for me and was happy to lie to my face till the end of time?

"You're staring."

I jumped. It'd take a while to get used to the new voice coming through his lips.

"Of course I am."

"You can take comfort that your imaginings aren't as bad as the truth."

"If that was the case, you'd have told me," I replied. "You point-blank refused to because you'd lose me. I'm a killer and we're in a dangerous street gang hunting down the criminal's version of the holy grail. If you thought the truth was worse than that, then what I'm imagining doesn't come close."

"But you're here."

I switched to staring out the window. It hurt less.

Mercer got on the expressway, driving toward an exit that was becoming familiar.

"Harlow," I stated. "What business could the two of us have there?"

"I told you. We're going back to where we started. It's the only way you'll understand this."

"Why does it matter to you if I understand?"

"We've been through this before, Adeline. If you have something to ask me, ask—"

"Do you love me?" I cried, whipping around. "Was everything that happened between us an act too?"

"Yes," he replied. "And no."

I stilled. My heart shot in my throat. "Yes to what?"

"Yes to loving you. No to everything being an act."

My jaw worked for a full thirty seconds. He responded so easily. Like it was a simple fact of life and didn't need to be questioned.

"Then, there's just one question left. If Gianna's failsafe hadn't triggered, would you have told me the truth?"

Mercer didn't take his eyes off the road. "I can't answer that question yet. Give me a chance, Adeline. It will make sense soon."

"I should hope so." I settled in my seat. "You know the consequences if it doesn't."

Faint chuckles filled the car.

Through the window, the scenery changed. Curving stretches of highway melted away to be replaced by brownstones and brick buildings close together and stacked on each other in a street of brown Lego pieces.

We drove past a pizza shop I knew well and I figured out where we were going.

Mercer drove to the end of club street. Turning into an alley, we parked between a closed bakery and jewelers. He rounded the car to open my door for me.

"Opium." He held a hand out.

"Back to the scene of the crime. How original."

I ignored the hand and stepped out. Across the street, the boarded-up, abandoned building that used to be the hottest club in the city greeted me.

Mercer touched the small of my back as we crossed. He was determined to touch me. I was determined not to feel anything when he did.

He slipped his fingers under my hem, drawing small circles above my tailbone. Goose bumps rippled over my flesh.

How's that working out?

He dropped his hand just as I moved to make him.

"In here."

Mercer twisted the knob, the door swung in with its warning and danger signs plastered uselessly on the front.

I didn't move.

"This is a crime scene again," Mercer said. "It's late, but it's still better people don't clock us hanging around." He jerked his head. "Come on. The cops had the electricity turned back on. There's nothing to be afraid of."

"I feel many things toward you, No-Name. Fear is not one of them."

I brushed past him and that amused smile. I took a few steps into the dark, then a light shone over me. Mercer went ahead carrying his phone flashlight. I tried following till it winked out.

Light flooded the club.

"Mercer Santos became quite a regular of The Pleasure Center."

His voice reached me from somewhere I couldn't see. I ventured farther inside.

Opium was not what it once was. Debris littered the floor—proving many took advantage of the open door and unused space before us. Newspapers, crushed cans, old glow sticks, and broken glass crunched under my feet.

The couches were ripped and spilling their stuffing. A few of the strobe lights fell from the ceiling. They dotted the floor from the platform to a lone door tucked away at the back—no doubt leading to the club beneath the club.

"Lots of people were regulars of The Pleasure Center," I said. "What was the importance of this one?"

Mercer crossed to the VIP area, claiming a booth.

"What was his importance to you?"

He gestured for me to sit.

I did so, sliding in opposite him. Our eyes met over the cracked, graffitied table.

"The first thing you need to know," he said, "that will put all of this into perspective, is that Mercer Santos was Kieran."

I reeled back. "Excuse me?"

"He wasn't *the* Kieran, as you know. He was *a* Kieran. He had the ledger."

"He— You— Explain," I stated.

"Mercer and his business partner created a program that securely stored data. Four years ago, their business was taking off. They were getting more high-profile clients knocking on their door, and an offer even came from Global Consolidated. The company offered to buy their IP and retire them as very rich men."

I put up a hand. "What does this have to do with anything?"

"I'm getting to that," he said, voice calm. "Trust me."

"No."

"Then, listen to me," he amended. "Without interruption."

Teeth grinding, I gestured for him to go on.

"His partner had no desire to sell their work. He saw the potential in their business and wanted to take it all the way—have their skyscraper in the Cinco skyline. Mercer wanted to sell up, move out of the tech room, and live in one of those skyscrapers. It became a point of contention for them, and things were not looking good for their future.

"Then, one day a woman hired them to upgrade her home systems. Her husband routinely brought his work home and he handled sensitive information. She thought it a nice treat for him to come home to."

"Why do I have a bad feeling about where this is going?"

Mercer inclined his head. "It turned out there was an entirely different reason why her husband forbade her from touching his computer. Mercer found a file detailing several odd transactions. A payment here. A favor there. Names of important people.

"He put together fairly quickly that the man was a blackmailer, and with his free rein in their system, he searched for the source."

"He found the ledger." It wasn't a question.

"Tucked away in a safe behind a painting," he said. "Mercer didn't know what he had. The opportunity was there, so he grabbed the book, stashed it with his supplies, and walked out the door like it was nothing."

"What an idiot. The wife knew his name and company. She had his freaking number. The theft would be traced back to him immediately."

"Mercer Santos was proof intellectual genius does not translate into common sense. The husband came after him the moment he found out, of course, but Mercer threatened to tell the man's wife *everything* he found on his computer. The long string of escorts he blackmailed pimps into letting him sleep with for free being one of them."

"My goodness," I breathed, stomach twisting. "How could anyone question that I need to take the ledger out of play? Look what disgusting beasts it makes out of people. Did the husband back down?"

"He did. His wife would get everything in a divorce, so he backed down quick. But from there, Mercer did not wise up."

I nodded. "Gianna said he had a weakness for strip clubs and escorts."

"Weakness does not cover it, Adeline. Sex addiction comes closer. Every other night he bought time with the escorts he once couldn't afford, and the other nights, he threw hundreds at his true obsession—Montecito."

"His little black book gave him all the money he needed."

"And then some," he said. "Maybe if he knew in the beginning that he had the ledger, he would have gone about things differently. As it was, he contacted almost everyone in the book demanding grand sums of money. He took precautions, of course. Sent secure emails that couldn't be traced. Set up dead drops. The whole deal. But when someone taps you for ten grand and then a kid shows up in your club, dropping money he shouldn't have, you put things together."

I leaned back in the ripped seat, taking it in. "My dad said he traced someone he thought could be Kieran to this club four years ago. It's because

Santos came on the scene—making too much noise." I fixed on him. "Where did you come in?"

"I was one of the people to receive his email, Adeline." A smile stretched across his lips. "Unfortunately for him."

I shivered. "You went after him."

"I did not." Mercer shifted, draping his ankle over his knee. "I replied that he would rethink this current course of action, or he would die in the extremely graphic method I detailed. Attached to the email was the encryption I used to hack his security, his IP address, name, and home address. I did not hear from him again."

"Okay, then why are you sitting here now bearing his name?"

"Because Santos did not learn from his experience with me. Montecito was still so far out of his reach, and he couldn't stand it."

"Who is Montecito?"

"He was one of the highest-paid escorts back then. He didn't have a pimp or manager, so he set his own prices, chose his clients, and participated in the auction when he felt like it."

My brows came together. "Was Montecito... you?"

He laughed. "No, Adeline. Although what sweet irony that would've been if Mercer wound up blackmailing me and then running into the arms of his obsession—also me. I am not Montecito, but I did meet him once. Nice guy."

"So, what did Mercer do that led to this?"

"Eventually, he got deep enough into our world that he learned of Kieran, and realized that he had the ledger. When he went after the biggest fish in the book, he used the name Kieran to demand ten million dollars."

My jaw dropped. "Ten million dollars?" I cried. "That's not blackmail money. That's move-out-of-town-because-they're-going-to-send-a-hit-man-after-you money."

He spread out his hands. "Thus, I was hired."

"Hired?" I repeated. "You're— Are you a hit man?"

Eerily black orbs followed me as I stood, backing away.

"I prefer the term infiltrator," he said evenly. "My job isn't to kill, per se. It's to retrieve—information, items, secrets. Every now and then, it's necessary to take a life in the process, but I only do so if it's necessary."

He got to his feet. "Where are you going, Adeline? This is the same job I performed for the Merchants, and it didn't bother you then. Don't be a hypocrite."

I bristled—though that stopped me in my tracks. *He doesn't talk to me like this. He doesn't use this flat tone like nothing matters—this conversation included.*

"I'm not backing away because you're an infiltrator. I'm backing away because someone hired you. Who are you working for, No-Name?"

"It doesn't work to skip chapters." He motioned to the seat. "Please, sit."

I folded my arms, feet planted.

"Your stubbornness is one of the things I love about you."

Love.

The word threw me—physically knocked me off-balance. I recovered quickly.

"I'm finding it very irritating in you," I said.

"Please," he repeated.

I sat.

"As I was saying." He came around and sat next to me, closing me in. "I was hired to get the ledger back. Some time had passed, but it didn't take long to figure out it was the same guy who tried it on with me."

I was rigid—stiff-backed, arms crossed, and hair standing on end at his nearness.

"The address and IP had changed, but eventually, I tracked him to this club and Montecito."

"I don't need the build-up. Just say that you killed him and took the ledger."

"I can't," he replied. "If that happened, you and I wouldn't be here right now."

Understanding dawned. "You didn't get the ledger."

"No." Mercer slipped his hand into mine.

I tossed him off in surprise, scooting away.

That got no reaction. Mercer let his hand stay where I dropped it. "That night, Santos paid fifty grand at the auction for a night with Montecito. I was in the club—close but not too close, waiting until he was alone. After the auction, he went into the alley to wait for his date, and I took my chance.

"I killed him, disfigured the body, and stole his wallet. Witnesses later found John Doe."

The news went in, stirred no emotion, and went out. It wasn't a surprise this handsome near stranger was Mercer Santos's killer. I didn't think he claimed his identity by chance.

"What went wrong?" I asked. "Why did you end up taking his name instead of the ledger?"

"I was too late," he replied. "His new address was in his wallet, but the key wasn't. I went there anyway, planning to break in and take what I came for. I found the place ransacked and the floorboards in the bedroom pried open. The ledger was gone."

"What? Someone went after it on the same night, snatching it within minutes of you? How does that happen twice?"

"Easily in my case. No one had to listen in on phone calls. Santos got too loud, Adeline. He took too much, too fast, and inspired rage over fear. I imagine there were dozens of hit men after him by the time a smart man figured out the way into a person's confidence, is through his vices."

I shot up straight. "Holy shit! Montecito!"

He smiled at me—a mix of pleased and impressed. "Yep. Before our final meeting in that alley, Mercer met up with his date. I don't know what happened between them, but at some point, Montecito was able to pick his pocket, get his key, and give it to the man who really bought his services for the night."

"Richard La Roche," I whispered.

"Damn." He was full-blown grinning now. "You put that together much quicker than I did. You really are a formidable woman."

"Flattery will get you nowhere. The truth might," I said. "Keep going. When did you figure out Montecito got the jump on you?"

"The witnesses found the body an hour later. If Montecito went to meet him in the alley like they arranged—"

"—he would've been the first one to stumble over Santos," I finished. "Good point, but it's still possible Montecito did find him and decided to beat it out of there instead of getting caught up in a police investigation."

"Very true, and I was set to ask him about it, but he disappeared." Mercer snapped his fingers. "Poof. Gone. Even with my skills, I couldn't track Montecito—real name Caleb Lopez—down."

"Pretty damning evidence. So, ever the gentleman thief, La Roche hired Montecito to do a simple lift and drop the ledger in his hands. I'm surprised he didn't keep it for himself."

"Not everyone is sucked in by the temptation of the ledger. Some of us see it exactly for what it is."

"What's that?"

"A death sentence."

I fell quiet. It was hard to argue with him. Almost every former owner of the ledger is dead.

"I realized that day in the club when we faced Lorenzo Bianchi where the ledger went all those years ago," Mercer said. "I had many suspects—La Roche being one of them—but I couldn't be certain. Over the years, I've broken into each suspect's place to have a look around. In La Roche's home, I found his forged pieces on display and stacks of money in the safe in his office. Nothing else."

"You didn't know about the vault behind the painting."

"I did not."

"So, that's why you became a Merchant? So you could keep searching for the ledger with Killian's research, Saint's instinct, and Baris's muscle behind you."

"I have all those things, darling." He slipped into pet names and cheeky grins so easily, it took me aback. "I didn't need them for that."

"Then, why?"

Mercer got up. "To answer that, we have to go to the next stop on the field trip."

"Next stop? What needs to be told somewhere else that you can't tell me here?"

"I need you to see, Adeline. Believe that this all has a point."

I studied him.

I did believe there was a purpose to this that couldn't be killing me and disposing of my body. If he wanted to do that, we were in an abandoned building with no one else around. Talk about a clear shot.

"Alright. I'll go."

He gave me his back.

"If you tell me your real name."

"Jasper," he replied without slowing. "Jasper Croix."

MERC— JASPER DROVE into a parking garage and killed the engine in a designated spot. I caught a sign on the way in.

Palais Estates.

"Is this where you live?"

"Yes," he said.

My mind flashed to the crappy motel and defiant mice we shared a room with.

"I'm guessing you've been dipping out over the last few weeks, reclining on your settee and knocking back beers in between pretending to be homeless and in the shit with us."

"Before last night, I hadn't been back here in over a year. You can't maintain a second life if you continue returning to the old one."

"Ah. More of Mercer/Jasper's shadow tips," I bit out. "I'm so happy you drugged my boyfriends and dragged me out of bed for a prolonged explanation sprinkled with life lessons."

Jasper kissed my cheek, making me squawk.

"You keep snapping at me to deflect the fact you're madder at yourself than you are at me. I lied to you. Hid things from you. But you did the same to me." He cocked a brow. "Frustrating, isn't it? Righteous fury is bitter going down when it's tinged with hypocrisy."

"I'm wondering now why I refused when Gianna told me to kill you."

He barked a laugh.

"No, *Jasper*," I said. "I have no trouble being angry with you. I laid it all out on the table. Everything. I was honest with you, and you told me you loved me. The woman you love shouldn't call you by a dead man's name!"

He punched the dash. "I said I couldn't tell you everything!" Exasperation broke through the calm mask he'd been wearing all night. "I was honest too."

"You were honest on your terms—which isn't honesty at all. It's more walls. It's barriers and rules and tricks to make me believe we were in a different relationship than we were. No, I don't have any room to judge the man you were before you found me in that bathroom, but I do have every right to feel betrayed at falling in love with a man who wasn't real!"

Jasper white-knuckled the steering wheel. His anger was a palpable thing, spreading through the car, and leaving no trace in those dark eyes.

"Do you want me to take you back?"

"No." I unlocked my seat belt. "I deserve the whole story, Croix, and I will get it. Afterward, I'll decide what happens between you and me."

"Is there still a you and me?"

I paused opening the door.

"Have I been freed?"

My heart thumped hard and painful against my rib cage. Even now, I sensed him beneath my skin. The ghost of his lips. Playful fingers flicking my nipples. Warm breath in my ear. His hand holding mine over the gulf between us.

"It's too soon to ask me that question."

"I will ask again when this is over," he said. "You're correct. Whatever your answer is will decide what happens next."

Mercer got out and opened my door again, reaching his hand in for me to take. I curled over his palm, allowing him to lead me out of the parking garage and into the bottom-floor elevator.

We stood side by side—not touching apart from the linked hands.

I had endless questions for Jasper Croix. They remained inside. He was taking me to his home. Peeling back those walls and barriers. I would wait to see how far his honesty would go.

The elevator dinged on the thirteenth floor. Jasper motioned for me to go ahead.

"Last door on the right."

We passed through a silent hallway. Snapshots of the lives on the other side weren't given away. I couldn't hear so much as a television.

I forgot about them and tried to picture myself on the other side. Me in the kitchen baking with a purple-haired kid. Saint in the living room teaching a little blond boy something he likely shouldn't know. Killian bouncing from the television to the laptop. Baris with his arms around me—quick to clean up a spill or wipe a floury cheek.

Was Jasper there?

The film reel broke apart—bubbling and burning, fading to white. The new name enough to set the fantasy aflame.

How can I picture a life with him? I didn't know him.

"Adeline."

I started. Coming to, I found myself planted in front of a random door and Croix down the hall, standing in the entrance to his apartment.

"Something wrong?"

Everything's wrong.

"No," I replied. I picked up my feet, stepping over the threshold.

A strangled noise escaped my throat. Whoever Jasper Croix was in his previous life, a poor man wasn't one of them. The chrome chairs were leather. The paintings priceless. The marble black and gold, and a minimalist kitchen that still screamed expensive.

"Not everything I told you was a lie." Mercer draped his coat over a bar chair. I didn't move past the welcome mat, opting to watch him go into the kitchen and pour a drink. He held up a bottle of wine.

"No, thank you," I said. "What wasn't a lie?"

"Alaric is a real persona. The people that know him do believe he's a Cinco University dropout that drops his pants for bills."

"You are an escort."

"I am many things." Mercer walked out with his glass of wine, took my hand, and brought me inside. "Many names. Many people. And always who I need to be in any situation."

I was first to let go. Sitting in his armchair, I tucked my tingling hand under my thigh.

"Why was Alaric who you needed to be? Why was Mercer Santos?"

"I told you this too."

Mercer sat back, filling his chair. This was different too. The Mercer I knew would melt into a seat like a boneless feline. This man dominated it.

Legs spread, upright, and arms straight on either side of him. He appeared ready to command a thousand gangs. Sink the city under his role as true king. He said he didn't need the Merchants to make up for made-up shortcomings. Looking at him then, it was difficult not to believe he was capable of anything.

"Infiltrating, or retrieval. It's infinitely easier when the target invites you into their home. Despite those spy movies of men rappelling down the ceiling and attaching a chewing gum bomb to a safe, the real work is nothing like that. It's analyzing the different methods for acquiring what you need, and choosing the straightest, simplest path to it. Becoming an escort was one such path.

"As I stood in Mercer Santos's trashed apartment empty-handed, another path presented itself to me."

"Take his place."

"Yes." He stopped for a sip. "And now we return to the backstory. Mercer Santos had no family, no friends, and a souring relationship with his business partner. He didn't know what he had at first, but at some point, he wised up and took precautions to hide himself and his true identity. He erased the work records connecting him with the man he thought was Kieran. He moved to an apartment with better security and erased his digital profile. He began the work needed to become someone else. Then, he died."

Was murdered, I mentally corrected.

"Losing the ledger presented me with a problem. My employer paid for a dead body and the book."

"Who was your employer?"

"It's a short list of men in this city who can be blackmailed for ten million dollars."

I thought about it. "Richard La Roche is out. That leaves Mateo Evans, CEO of Evans Building and Co. Lincoln Wood, founder of Bamber Pharmaceuticals. David Prescott, Carlos Gray, Joseph Lombard—"

Jasper dipped his chin.

"Wait. Joseph Lombard?" I cried. "You're not serious."

"Consider what you know about him."

"He..." That day outside the clinic came back to me. "He's a smuggler. Uses his clinics and fronts for his second business. And he cheats kind old nuns."

He nodded. "If Sinjin and Cash were able to find that out, it's not a stretch another Kieran did too and put it in the ledger."

"Joseph Lombard hired you to kill Mercer Santos and bring him the ledger." My eyes narrowed. "And you didn't deliver."

"Adeline—"

"You've been working for that bastard the whole time, haven't you?" I don't know when I jumped to my feet, but I was up and bearing down on him.

"Adeline—"

"Haven't you?!"

"Just listen," he snapped.

"It's a yes-or-no question."

"Nothing is a yes-or-no question. There's always a deeper reason. Do you want to hear it or not?"

"I don't want to hear another fucking thing until you tell me right now if you've been reporting our every move to Lombard. Does he know about me and my father?" My nails pierced the leather gripping his chair. "Does he know Gianna has the ledger?"

"I'm certain he knows now after Brutal used his newfound voice to shout it from Trapp Tower. If he found out before then, it wasn't from me." He leaned in, peering into my eyes. "I didn't tell him a word about you, your father, or Gianna Cross. I swear."

Glittering, black pools reflected me. "Do you believe me?"

My arms shook, struggling to hold me up. The same for my legs, my neck, my heart. Do I believe him?

Can I afford to?

"Why not?" I rasped. "I assume you stepped into Mercer's ready-made identity to get the ledger for him. Why didn't you tell Lombard how close you were?"

Mercer's lips peeled back from his teeth. "Joseph Lombard is a vile, loathsome cockroach, and that he's been forced to wait four long years for the ledger is a pleasure greater than sex."

Deep, pungent hatred blew me back a step. A lot of things can be faked. Emotion like this wasn't one of them.

"Not every employee wants their boss to succeed, Adeline."

"Four years," I said. "You're not where you want to be, are you?"

"I wasn't." The words were forced out of him. "For the first year, I fantasized about killing Sinjin in his sleep twice as much as he dreamed about killing me. But time passed, the Merchants grew on me, and then... you came."

I crouched down, resting my chin on his knee. There was another emotion that couldn't be faked, and it finally accomplished what shaky limbs were on the verge of doing.

I buried my face between his legs, breathing slow. "I'm listening."

Jasper stroked my hair. "Lombard made it clear he wanted that ledger, and I wouldn't get full payment until he did. I had limited options, Adeline. There'd be no way to track the new Kieran until he made a move. Blackmailed the wrong person or let something slip through his security. If he was smart, it could be years before either of those things happened.

"That's what I was looking at—years," he said. "So, I did the best thing I could think of, and stepped into the old Kieran's place. I moved into his apartment, got into his computers, answered his phone, and emailed a resignation letter his partner didn't question. I *became* him because the only people who knew he was dead were me and Lombard. His enemies thought he was still alive, and one of them would have plenty to boast about."

I raised my head. "You thought La Roche might contact him. Throw a 'haha, bitch. I've got the ledger now' his way."

"Exactly."

"But that message didn't come."

"No message came. Days turned to weeks, and I didn't have a trace of Montecito or the man who hired him," he said. "I used my time well. There were emails on his computer. Texts on his phone. I used them to track down the men and women he blackmailed as Kieran. Alaric was on a date with an employee that worked for one of them when he keeled over on the bathroom floor."

"You ran into the Merchants," I finished.

He sipped his wine. "I had the same idea as you. Attach myself to a gang and use their resources to get me closer to the ledger. Took a few years, but it worked."

"Did it? Gianna told me about your late-night visit. You didn't ask her where she hid the ledger. All you had to say was don't tell me Mercer Santos is dead."

Jasper twirled the strands around his finger, tugging gently. "Cross was bound to tell you where the ledger is sooner rather than later. I didn't need to interrogate her when you'd do a better job. The failsafe caught me off guard."

I pulled his hand away. "Let's not dance around the question, Jasper. What were you going to do if you got your hands on the ledger? You already have damning knowledge about Lombard. Smuggler. Fraud. Killer. You didn't use it to break ties, so I assume you had another idea in mind."

"I do, and it's simple. Use the ledger to lure Lombard away from his guards and kill him. An outcome I doubt the Merchants would object to."

"They wouldn't," I agreed. "Which is why it makes no sense that you didn't tell them all of this years ago. They would've understood. Backed you up. Saint, Killian, and Baris were under the weight of the ledger. Who could understand better than them?"

His brows crept to his hairline. "They would have understood? Do you honestly believe that? The night they busted into that hotel room, if I said I was a professional liar, chameleon, and killer under contract by one of the most dangerous men in the city, and I'd like to use their resources for my own purposes, they'd have said *sure, come aboard.*

"What was your first reaction when I told you I was hired, Adeline? *Have I been spying on you? What does Lombard know?*" He shook his head. "It's like the serial cheater and the new boyfriend. In the back of their minds, they'd always wonder where my true allegiances lie. Except in Sinjin's case, he wouldn't waste time wondering. He'd get rid of anything he wasn't sure about."

"Jasper, I admit opening with that information wouldn't have gotten you far, but things have changed and you said so yourself. You four became true partners," I said. "We met and fell for each other. Have you kept yourself from feeling anything real for so long, you don't know true love and trust when it's right in front of you?

"Saint, Killian, and Baris opened up about their lives. In Baris's case, you know how difficult that was. These last few weeks— Hell, these last few days, there wasn't a truth you could tell that either of us would judge you for.

We would have understood. We would have helped you get out from under Lombard's thumb. But now...

"Where we are now isn't because of Saint's volatility or my risk of dumping you. You just don't give us enough credit. Plain and simple."

Jasper traced my cheekbone, collecting a tear. "I give you all the credit in the world, Adeline Redgrave. I've seen you with Cross these last few weeks. How could I doubt your capacity for forgiveness?"

"Then why?" I whispered.

"There isn't an easier way for me to say this." He touched his forehead to mine. "So, I'll just say it. Mercer Santos does not exist."

"I know he—"

"No, Adeline." His voice was hard. "He doesn't exist. The man who drank Sangiovese on the couch while watching television. Who laughed and joked and flirted with everyone that moves. Who breezed through life never taking anything seriously. He does not exist.

"I can't stand red wine."

My gaze drifted to the glass of white.

"Television for any reason other than watching the news or keeping up with popular topics of conversation is a waste of time. Laughing, joking, and flirting are a means to an end. I do not breeze through life. I slip quietly around it—never letting it touch me.

"You want the real reason I refused to tell you? Why I would have ripped that page out of the ledger and still wish I could now?" His fingers dug in the back of my neck. "Because you fell in love with Mercer. He made you smile. Held you while you cried. Pulled you back from tipping over the edge. It's *him* you want, and as long as I was him, I had you."

Closing my eyes, I wrapped my arms around his waist.

"Tell me, Adeline. Can you love Jasper Croix?"

I raised my head, drawing a line over his chin and lips, rubbing my nose on his. "That was still you. Holding me. Making me laugh. There aren't two men, Jasper. There's just you."

"No." Finality rang gong-like through the word. "The real me is nothing like that man, apart from one respect. I love you too."

Jasper pressed a soft kiss to my lips.

"There will be two questions to answer when this is over: Does Jasper have a future with you?"

I waited. He didn't say more.

"What's the second?"

Mercer stood up, bringing me with him. "I will tell you that in"—he glanced at the clock—"three hours. We have one more stop to make."

I sighed. "Jasper—"

"Don't give up on me yet." He smiled slightly. "This is the most important fact you need to know about me. It puts everything into perspective."

I've come this far.

"Okay."

He dropped my hands. "It's five in the morning. If you're hungry or still tired, feel free to take anything from the kitchen and use my bed. I'll be up."

I took him up on that for need of space.

Jasper settled in the armchair with his glass of wine, peering out the windows while I heated a warm glass of milk and carried a PowerBar to his room. It wasn't a surprise his bedroom was as impersonal as the rest of the apartment.

A floating bed claimed most of the space. Black silk sheets welcomed me as I slipped inside. On both sides of the mattress, matching bedside tables held a book, remote, and a peace lily. That was it. I looked inside and found the drawers bare. A television hung on the opposite wall that was shared by the dresser. The room had nothing else to say for it.

I recalled *Mercer's* room in our old home.

Massage oil and toys in the drawers. Paintings and photographs on the walls. Personality in everything you saw.

There was nothing here to point to the kind of man Jasper Croix was.

Isn't that what he's trying to tell me? Choosing to be with him means starting over.

The man I love is gone.

There is only Jasper.

Chapter Three

"**A**deline."

I woke at his gentle shake. Stretching, I felt the kinks and coils in my body pop.

"I didn't mean to fall asleep," I said. "Just wanted some time to think."

"That comes later. There's one more place we need to go."

I caught his arm as he moved away. "After this, will you come back with me? Talk to the guys yourself."

His back was to me. "I'll bring you back. Tell them what I told you and see if they're as understanding as you believe."

"It's better coming from you, Jasper. You four were together long before I came along. You owe them an explanation, and the fight that comes with it."

"I think you overestimate our brotherhood. We're just four guys working toward the same goal. The only relationship that would've survived past the ledger is between the actual brothers: Sinjin and Cash. The rest of us are expendable."

"I don't believe that and neither do you."

"Come on." He tugged free. "We'll be late."

I gave up. For now.

Jasper waited outside while I brushed my teeth and shoved on my shoes. In the elevator, his second question crossed my mind.

What could he be about to show me that's bigger than the revelations he's revealed this morning? Bigger than the question of if I can start over with a complete stranger?

"My food," I began. "Did Mercer have a different favorite meal too?"

"I prefer lighter meals," he said slowly. "Simple, fresh ingredients. And I'm a vegetarian."

My mouth fell open. "What? Are you serious? Why didn't—?"

I clocked his grin. "You're messing with me," I cried, whacking his arm. "And you say Jasper doesn't joke."

"Jasper gets perverse pleasure from making your jaw drop. Is that the same thing?"

"Ugh. That's just a man thing, love. You're not happy unless you're driving us to buy a fake passport, board a passing cruise ship, and never come back."

He laughed.

"You say we have to start over." The doors opened on the garage. "Let's do that. What's your favorite color?"

"Black."

"Favorite music?"

"I don't listen to music."

"Everyone listens to music. Spill it, Croix. It's the Spice Girls, isn't it?"

"Do you want me to say yes so you don't feel bad about them being yours?"

I cracked a lopsided smile. It struck me how well I knew the fake him. Mercer would've said something like "Dammit, you got me. How did you know?"

Would I get to the place where I'd know everything he said before he said it?

"Caught me," I replied, getting inside the car. "What is yours?"

"If I have to pick one, I'd say I'm partial to Dire Straits."

I bobbed my head. "Answer accepted. Why drink red wine if you don't like it? Your covers can't be that involved."

"They are." He shifted the gear, pulling out of the spot. "Red wine is popular among seventy percent of adults. Alaric, and then Mercer, sought to be liked by everyone he met. People like mimics—if you can excuse another Mercer/Jasper shadow tip. They gravitate toward copies of themselves. Those who listen to, like, and think the same as they do."

"That's another way of saying we hang out with people who have common interests. Nothing earth-shattering about that."

"It's more than that. There is no one anyone knows better than themselves. To get a mark to trust you. To invite you into their home and fall asleep on the pillow next to you, they must feel they know you just as well. If my mark likes a good red, so do I. If they bemoan the millennial generation, I get on the gripe train with them. There is no Jasper Croix. Only the mirror my mark sees themselves in."

"Makes for an effective infiltrator," I said.

"Yes."

I rested my hand on his. "And a lonely man."

We made the rest of the drive in silence.

Jasper's apartment was in Leighbridge. Wherever he was taking me, it didn't require hopping on the expressway. We drove through the neighborhoods of Cinco's wealthiest borough—passing pristine parks, high-end shopping plazas, and sports cars pushing the speed limit.

I pressed my head against the window, trying not to imagine what waited at the end of the explanation tour, and failing.

What could be worse than telling me I don't know a thing about him? Discovering he's Kieran Foley's long-lost son? Finding out he's Angelo's long-lost son? Can there just not be any long-lost sons?

"We're here."

I picked my head up, gazing around us. *Here* was another stretch of homes as nice as the ones we've seen.

White, power-washed sidewalks wrapped around wrought-iron fences of different sizes and styles. Rare for our city was the patches of lawn on the other side. They added bright green life to the identical three-story sandstone buildings.

"Why are we here?"

"I'll show you." Jasper freed my seat belt and met me on the sidewalk. He stuck out his elbow, obviously intending for me to put my hand through.

I hesitated.

I hadn't answered the question yet. It was probably better I didn't respond to the hand-holding, kisses, and jaunts down the street like we were the couple we were just beginning to be.

I waited too long, and Jasper dropped his arm.

"I had some things in common with Montecito." He set off, leaving me to fall in step with him. "I also set my prices, chose the clients I'd take on, and worked alone. My name spread by referral."

I frowned. *Where is this going?*

"When Lombard first contacted me, I turned him down."

"You did?"

"Yes. I knew about the ledger. For a time, I put my skills toward acquiring it for myself." Jasper ran his finger along the fence—the casual picture of a man with his hand in his pocket and not a care in his head. "I did my digging and discovered how many people have died or lost everything for that book. Before you told us, I figured out the ledger had been changing hands, and previous owners died as the price. I had to ask myself if it was worth it.

"Did I need a little black book of secrets when there is nothing, *nothing*, that anyone can hide from me? If I was inclined, I had enough on my clients to sink the city. Was the ledger worth the target I'd put on my back?"

"Shadows don't like the light turned on them," I said.

"Naturally." Jasper veered in front of me and leaned on a tree. I stopped beside him. "This makes me rare, but my answer was no. The ledger wasn't worth the trouble it could cause me for many reasons. When Lombard made his offer, I turned him down. I wanted no part in the search for the ledger. He called again offering double the price, and I still said no."

"What changed?" I asked. "How did he turn that no into a yes?"

"The usual way. Found my pressure point, and dug in without mercy."

Shrieks broke the quiet morning.

I turned as a woman and two children came out of their home. The kids took off running like balls of energy freed from captivity. One of them, a little girl, saw us and waved.

I waved back. "What pressure?" I asked, turning back. "Did he find out something about you? Did you discover the hard way that you're in the ledger too?"

Jasper didn't seem to have heard me. Gaze fixed over my shoulder, he sidestepped me, moving to the gate.

"Jasper?"

"I'm not in the ledger, Adeline."

The girl broke away from her brother. She raced to us, tawny curls bouncing. "Hi!"

"Hi, sweetie," I said. She couldn't be more than five years old. "Pretty dress."

"Thank you."

She reached her tiny hand through the gate, and Jasper took it.

"Jasper, what are—?"

He bent over the metal and she planted a loud, wet smooch on his cheek. Giggling, she tore off to catch her brother as the woman looked on, watching the entire exchange without reaction.

I went rigid. *Oh, no...*

"I'm not in the ledger," he repeated. "My daughter is."

My mind. My breath. My everything stopped.

"Six years ago, I was good, one of the best, but not as wise as I should have been. I was working as Alaric, building my name and contacts, embedding myself within the Cinco elite. At the time, I was regularly seeing a senator's wife."

His words were barely penetrating. All I saw was that little girl.

"Her husband split his time between Cinco and D.C. Sometimes, he was gone for months and she turned to me for companionship. She bought out weeks of my time, Adeline. My hourly rate didn't slow her down. A year in, her husband went away, and she offered me a hundred grand to move in and live with her the month he'd be gone.

"I turned her down. Partly because it's difficult to do my kind of work when a roommate clocks how often you go in and out at odd hours. But the bigger reason was I sensed there was something not quite right—"

"She's your daughter," I sliced in, voice barely a rasp. "That little girl is your child."

Jasper laid a hand on my arm. "She is."

"How old is she?"

"Five."

"What—?" The question lodged in my throat.

Jasper has a child? A beautiful girl living happily in Leighbridge who clearly knew him, while I knew nothing.

Jasper mistook my silence as a cue to go on. "She wasn't pleased at my turning her down and the argument got nasty. I threatened to drop her as a client, then she pulled back. Breaking down, she sobbed that she was sorry. She was just lonely and couldn't stand being in that house by herself for another minute. She said she'd ask someone else to stay with her and the matter was dropped."

My grip tightened on the fence. *Why does he think I want this backstory?! Just tell me the truth.*

But I said nothing.

"Things went back to normal, so I continued to see her. Access to a senator's home was too good to give up. It was three months later she told me she was pregnant." Jasper followed my line of sight. "The look in her eyes," he said. "She presented that pregnancy test with such triumph, she didn't have to say it. *I own you now* was written all over her face."

"Why do you blame that on inexperience?"

"Because I did everything right. Never drank from a glass that had been out of my sight. Didn't fall asleep in another's presence. Turned down requests to go bare—no matter how much extra they offered. I did everything... but make sure the clients weren't poking holes in the condoms when my back was turned."

"Goodness," I breathed, eyes closing. "Who would do something like that? How obsessed was she with you?"

"Dangerously obsessed, Adeline. She babbled on about us finally being together, me leaving the profession, and the life we'd have once her husband was *gone.*"

My head snapped up. "Are you saying she wanted you both to murder her senator husband and run off together with your love child?"

"That is exactly what I am saying."

I looked from him to his daughter. "But then... what did you do? That woman isn't her, is she?"

"No. Elise Hughes is currently living in a treatment facility for various mental illnesses. Her husband checked her in shortly after she gave birth," he said. "It was the solution we settled on."

"You went to her husband?"

"He was the only one who could declare her mentally unfit. Mr. Hughes and I came up with a plan. I'd convince Elise to wait. Tell her to put on a show for everyone that she and her husband were expecting a child and couldn't be happier. Tragedy would strike and the baby would be stillborn. Stricken with grief, her husband 'commits suicide' and then we'd move away with our daughter."

"She agreed," I said.

Jasper nodded. "My daughter was born in their home, delivered by a single midwife tied under contracts and nondisclosure agreements. Three days after Rosie's death hit the media, Elise poisoned his drink like we agreed, and Hughes turned the plan on her. She was suffering postpartum depression after the loss of her daughter and needed treatment. My kid was handed over to me and that was the end of it. Or I thought it was."

I blew out a breath. "A story like that has ledger material written all over it. The truth got out, didn't it? Kieran, or a Kieran, found out."

"I can't say for certain who spoke. Maybe the midwife. Maybe Hughes sharing too much with a friend after a few drinks. Maybe Elise herself, talking to all those psychiatrists over the years. Either way, someone unearthed that Baby Hughes wasn't dead after all. Then came the natural question, why would the senator and his wife get rid of the perfectly healthy baby girl they were so excited for?"

"But it's you," I said. "Even five years ago, if you knew how to hide yourself, then you could hide a baby."

"I covered my tracks. I arranged a private adoption through discreet channels. I forged her birth certificate so it wouldn't read that she was coincidentally born the same day as the Hughes baby. But like I said, I wasn't as wise as I am now."

"What did you miss?"

"The midwife they hired. It turned out something she does for every birth is print the baby's feet to frame and gift to the mother. She did the same for Elise. Months later when Kieran or his agent did their digging, they found the print Elise tucked away in her room at the facility, and it was all they needed to track her down."

"Footprints are as unique as fingerprints," I said. "Just like that, Elise, the senator, and Rosie are in the ledger."

"Just like that."

"But I don't understand how that led to you under Lombard's thumb. How did he connect you to Rosie? He'd have no reason to go to Elise Hughes asking about you?"

"After turning him down twice, he used his considerable resources to track me down. He wanted the best and he would have it. I was photographed right here on this sidewalk with Rosie." He made a noise in his throat. "I'm told the resemblance says it all."

It was true. If you looked hard enough at little Rosie, you saw her father in her curls, her wide smile, and the inky uniqueness of those eyes.

"Jasper," I began carefully. "I'm not judging you. I can't imagine how difficult it was to be separated from your child, but you must have known how dangerous it was to have any contact with her. Especially in your line of work."

He looked away, muscle ticing in his jaw. "Of course, I did," he forced. "I left her to live in peace, until I got a call from Senator Hughes. Kieran tried to blackmail him with the discovery of Rosalie. He refused to pay.

"Actually, he laughed at the person on the phone and said there was no scandal in letting the child be raised by a safe, loving family while he looked after his ill wife. If anything, it'd likely get him sympathy in the press. He told Kieran to do his worst and hung up the phone. The next number he dialed was mine. Hughes gave me a heads-up that Kieran knew about Rosie, and he had no intention of lifting a finger to protect a child that wasn't his. She was my problem."

"Of course. You came back into her life to make sure she was safe." And then it was me reaching out, lacing our fingers together. "For fuck's sake, you really found the right strings to pluck with the daughter of Oscar Redgrave."

He chuckled darkly. "I wish this was another manipulation. Even at my most creative, I couldn't come up with a story like this." Jasper squeezed my fingers, dropping a kiss on my palm. "I had no choice but to introduce myself to Rosie's adoptive parents. Tell them who I was and why they had to take extra precautions. Including call me if anything suspicious happened. Sure enough, shortly after Hughes got the call, the Bakers noticed a strange car parked outside their house in the evening.

"To be safe, they rang me, and I looked into him. It turned out the guy was a hired thug. I *questioned* him and he spilled that he was paid to kidnap the Bakers' daughter."

"Kidnap Rosie? But she was a baby then," I cried. "What kind of soulless, piece of shit would send someone after an infant?"

"A soulless piece of shit accurately describes the Kieran who came before Mercer Santos. I told you he blackmailed pimps into letting him have the pick of the escorts. Well, that was on his list of minor crimes. He did much worse during his reign as Kieran—including trying to get a senator in his pocket by proving he was serious, and having his secret daughter kidnapped.

"I killed the first man he sent. He died with the name Kieran on his lips. The guy couldn't tell me the true name of the person he worked for."

"Which left Kieran free to send someone else."

"And he did," Jasper said. "I caught the second man trying to break into their house a week later. The Bakers were terrified. I warned them off calling the police since we couldn't know who was on Kieran's payroll. Instead, they asked me to stay close, knowing they could trust me with her life.

"After a couple of months, the attempts stopped. Santos had stolen the ledger by then. Once he called me, I realized I was dealing with someone new. Green. Stupid.

"This new Kieran didn't have the balls to attack Rosie. I refused to get me, or her, caught in the sights of another one, so I let him slink back into the shadows and be done with it. Though I still visited frequently—checking on her and making sure their home was secure. Then one day, I led Lombard's man right to her."

"Oh, Jasper." I folded him in my arms, burying my nose in his soft, sweet-smelling neck. "It wasn't your fault. You were protecting your daughter."

"It is my fault, Adeline." He rested his cheek on my crown, holding me just as tight. "It's my fault for thinking I could be free of the ledger. No one in this godforsaken city is. Through a thousand people and a thousand more threads, we all find ourselves on Kieran's hook one way or another. The ledger has to be taken out of play—for good. That's the truest thing you ever said."

"Lombard threatened your daughter to make you work for him."

"If it was just that, I would've killed him and been done with it," Jasper said. "Lombard bought out this entire block. He created a false trail of documents citing negligence in Ronald Baker's company. He hired former students to come forward and say they were sexually harassed by their professor, Sarai Baker. One call and my daughter's family would be homeless, broke, jobless, and investigated. He wasn't going to touch her. Lombard planned to blow up her entire life. I accepted the job."

I turned my neck, watching little Rosie play. "Does she know you're her biological father?"

"Not in those terms," he admitted. "The Bakers told her I'm someone important in her life. That if there was ever trouble, she should trust me and I would protect her. That I always visit with gifts is enough to make her happy to see me."

I smiled, though it wasn't happy thoughts on my mind. "I'm surprised Lombard has been patient all this time."

"He hasn't been. More than once he's tried giving me deadlines. 'Find the ledger in a week, or I make that call.' Threats of that nature."

"How have you put him off?"

"By reminding him I can blow up his life too. Cinco City loves a bad man," he said, "as much as they love tearing him down. I've dug up every bit of incriminating evidence there is on his smuggling operation. If anything happened to Rosie—if she fell down and scraped her knee—the truth would go wide. Mutually assured destruction."

"Still, he can't have made these years easy for you."

I felt his head shake against me. "He hasn't. Lombard demanded weekly progress reports. Names of the potential Kierans that I've investigated and crossed off the list. I've been chained to that fucker, and therefore the Merchants, all this time."

"So, you did need them."

"The three of them were as highly motivated to find Kieran and the ledger as I was. Unlike the rest, they weren't driven by bloodlust, wealth, or easy sex. I could trust they wouldn't put a knife in my back once they got their hands on it."

His jacket crumpled in my fist. "The knife in the back is for Lombard."

Jasper released me. Waving goodbye to Rosie, he led me back to the car.

"I can't get to him alone, and I have tried. Joseph Lombard is another resident of the Fairfield. No one knows better than me how impossible it is to break in unawares."

"What about his routes?" I asked as we climbed in. "Ambushing his car. Or paying one of his security to drive to an arranged location."

"Lombard drives himself where he needs to go, with his guard riding shotgun, and he doesn't do it through the back streets. An assault would have to be done out in the open. I don't work like that. Too many things can go wrong. Too many variables to account for. I can't risk it with Rosie on the line. No," he said, striking the wheel. "The best plan is to get him exactly what he wants. Lombard wouldn't want anyone to know he's Kieran, so obviously, he'll leave the army of bodyguards behind for the exchange. When he shows up, my daughter's page will have been ripped out, and the last threat will die on a warehouse floor."

Jasper Croix trapped my gaze. "You asked me why I didn't tell the guys, and then you, about Santos, Lombard, and Rosalie. If anyone could understand what I'm going through, it's you four."

"We do," I said. "I do."

"Do you?" Dusky eyes blazed. "You understand that in a choice between my daughter and everyone else, it's not a choice at all."

"I..." The sentence trailed off.

"You know Saint, Killian, and Baris better than anyone. You tell me, as much as they might sympathize, could they trust a man whose loyalties they knew were divided between the Merchants and their own child? If it came down to it, wouldn't they know what I would do?"

I didn't want to. My muscles screamed at me. My lips pressed hard together. Unbidden, my head moved up and down, nodding.

"Would they let me work and live down the hall with Lombard's grip on my throat?"

Eyes filling, I shook my head.

No.

"Oscar Redgrave's daughter knows what a man will do to protect his child from the ledger, and now she knows what the stranger who's been lying to her for months has to protect. So now it's time to ask the second question, Adeline." Jasper brushed his lips over my forehead, rippling shivers down my spine. "Do you want Jasper Croix to return to that cramped loft with you, Saint, Killian, Baris... and Gianna Cross?"

I closed my eyes, spilling wetness down my cheeks. I parted my lips and told him what was genuinely the truest thing I ever said.

"No," I whispered. "I don't."

JASPER AND I MADE THE drive back in silence.

Or near silence.

My phone ringing shattered the quiet every five minutes. The guys were up and going crazy calling me.

I looked down at Killian's number flashing for the sixth time. Taking a breath, I swiped *end*.

My time with Jasper wasn't over.

"I'm sorry," I said. "I want to trust you. I want that more than anything, but you and I are starting at zero. It can't come that easily."

"I understand, Adeline."

"For what it's worth." I rubbed his thigh. "I don't believe you would hurt us. Even if Lombard demanded it, you'd find a way to protect us both."

"I would try."

"And I wouldn't ask you to put me before your daughter," I replied. "The guys might not want you in the Merchants after this— I can't say for sure. Your relationships are separate from me. I'm leaving you four to work it out amongst yourselves. Either way, your daughter's page will be ripped out of the ledger. And if we get to Lombard first, he's dead."

Jasper shifted into the other lane, saying nothing.

"The answer to your first question is yes, by the way. I can—I *do* still want you."

He jerked the wheel, nearly veering into oncoming traffic. "What?"

Laughing, I shrugged. "I wanted the truth and you gave it to me. You can't think I'd fault you for being a liar and a killer." I waved a hand over myself. "Hello. I'm both and likely better at it than you."

Smashing that shadow act to bits, he gaped at me. "You're not serious."

"Course I'm serious, you doof. A Mercer by any other name, is still mine."

"But you said— You said you don't trust me."

"I don't. Not even a little bit. I don't trust you to come back to the loft. I for fuck sure don't trust you around Gianna. Confusing, isn't it?" I scoffed. "It is for me too. But what do you want from me? I can't flip a switch and make my feelings go away. Gianna did say you guys were my weakness."

"Then, where do we go from here?"

"I'm going to tell the guys what you told me."

"Cross," he said.

I squeezed his thigh amid the blaring horns. "You all have waited long enough. Rosalie too long. I will get the ledger—whether it's in the Fairfield or hidden somewhere else. Gianna will tell me tonight.

"Just don't do anything drastic," I said. "I'll call you later with news."

"But me. Jasper," he pressed. "After everything I've told you, you still want to be with me?"

"Jasper, I've been sitting here trying to think of what I'd do differently if it was my daughter at risk. If I'm honest, I would have done much worse. I'd have done just about anything."

Mercer pulled up to the curb. He killed the engine and cupped my cheek. "I killed Mercer Santos that night believing I was putting an end to the threat against Rosie. I wanted this to be over. You don't know how badly."

"You were afraid we'd turn on you, then you'd have four more obstacles between you and the ledger."

"I'm not convinced that still won't happen."

"Let me talk to the guys," I repeated. "I'll calm them down. The five of us were meant to do this together. Wipe the Hunts' slate clean, end the Alexanders, avenge the death of Paul Bellisario, and protect Rosalie. This is what we do.

"We're Merchants."

I kissed him—a light peck on the lips that thrilled and terrified me in equal measure.

This man wasn't my Mercer. I barely knew this man at all. It felt like cheating.

I drew away and his hand slipped around my neck, pulling me back.

His lips crashed on mine in a shower of sparks. Demanding entrance, he bit my lip. A gasp and I surrendered to his order.

By all the deities and saints, Jasper Croix may have changed everything about him to become Mercer, but he didn't change this.

He nipped, teased, and played with my tongue—undoing me strand by strand. Molecule by molecule.

I moaned into the kiss, running my hands all over him.

Hair, cheeks, chest, legs, and cock. I pressed my heel to his hardening ridge, stroking it to life.

"You won't come in your pants again, will you?"

He bit my lip.

"Ow," I cried, giggling.

"You should know, Jasper is more punishing than Mercer."

"Oooh. I guess I better be scared."

"Terrified."

His grin faded. "They won't want you near me," he said.

He didn't have to say who *they* were.

"Not while we're figuring this shit out. If they don't write me off straight up. Promise me you won't let that stop you." He stroked my cheek. "Come and see me. Even if you have to sneak away."

My heart thumped. "I can't lie to them. We're doing this honesty thing. I can't backslide now."

"Then, tell them the truth about where you're going, but come to me." He kissed me soft and sweet. "Promise."

Come to him? Strain the three relationships that aren't completely fucked up to save the one that is? How can I do that?

"I promise."

What did I tell you? Love is weakness.

MERCER DROPPED ME OFF at Anderton Park. For a while, I walked aimlessly, turning over everything that happened that morning.

Did I trust him?

How could I? I didn't know him.

Did I understand why he did what he did?

How could I not? If I'm honest with myself, I made the same choices.

I didn't tell the guys who I was when they stumbled on me during a hit, just as they stumbled on him. I kept my true motives a secret fearing they'd kill me. Then, after they fell for me, I kept my secrets so I could keep them.

Yes, Jasper Croix and Adeline Redgrave were two sides of a devious coin. My guys loved and forgave me after the truth came out. To turn my back on Jasper now would make me a hypocrite as accused.

But...

When it came time to make my choice between the Merchants and the people I loved, I refused to choose. Jasper has made it clear he won't have any such dilemma.

I respected that. A father who put his daughter above everything wasn't a man I could fault. But there came the harsh reality. The only way to be sure I don't end up on the wrong side of that decision is to cut him from my life. Without malice or anger, Jasper and I break up so he can focus on the woman who truly needs him.

There was an issue with that route too. We were both after the ledger and Gianna Cross was tucked away in our loft. We couldn't break paths when we were driving down the same one.

It felt like hours later I finally looked up and found myself on a random street in Leighbridge. I lit on a café across the intersection, Buttermilk. My stomach trumpeted its hunger. The milk and PowerBar were a long time ago.

Armed with their strongest coffee and two maple donuts, I called the guys.

"Adeline! Where are you?" Killian asked. "Are you okay?"

"I'm fine. Are you okay? I'm betting Mercer's little cocktail did a number on you guys."

"Mercer. He did this?"

The low hiss shook me.

"He invited me out to explain how we got here. The three of you, we should meet somewhere and talk."

"He can fucking bring you back here. The *five* of us have a lot to talk about."

"He's not with me. I'm at a café—"

"Which café?"

"Buttermilk in Leighbridge—"

"We'll be there in twenty minutes."

Killian hung up.

Setting my phone down, I went to work demolishing my comfort food. This was going to be a long conversation.

JASPER

I turned the corner, leaving Adeline and the park behind. As if their watchers had me in sight, my cell rang.

"Hello?"

"Is it done?"

"It's done," I replied. "I gave Adeline the story you told me to say. Word for word."

"She believes Lombard is your employer?"

"She has no reason not to." The taste of her lips lingered on mine. "I also revealed my daughter's location—a move I better not regret."

"Surely you're not afraid Adeline Redgrave or the Merchants will harm her? There's nothing more ineffective than a killer with a code."

"What next?"

"You know what next."

"It all hangs on if they let me back in."

"I hired you because getting in where you're not wanted is your specialty. Get it done."

Click.

"I will," I said to no one. "Believe me, the Merchants will not get rid of me that easily."

Chapter Four

A*deline*

"That's loyalty for you, Bunny. Leave your man drugged and drooling in his pillow while you gallivant around the city with a traitor."

Sinjin paced the length of the alley. Outside and he still gave the impression of a caged animal.

"That's a bit harsh," I muttered. "I wasn't gallivanting. I was finding out the truth for all of us."

"What is the truth?" Killian asked.

Brutal stood in front of me—saying everything with his silence.

"His real name is Jasper Croix. I know why he impersonated Mercer Santos and hid the secret all these years."

I told them the entire story. From Elise Hughes sexually assaulting him, to his daughter, and ending with Lombard keeping them both in his hold until the ledger is delivered.

The men traded unreadable looks.

"What?" I asked. "What is it?"

"Merc— Croix," Killian corrected, "told us he wanted the ledger because it detailed indiscretions he made in his past as Alaric. He pledged to tear the pages out to finally wipe the slate clean."

"I guess in a way that was true."

"Every good lie is partially the truth," Saint said.

This is why we're soul mates.

"He believed telling you guys about Lombard and that he plans to use the ledger to draw him out, would cause trust issues between you. How do you trust a man when someone else is yanking his chain?"

"He was right," Saint barked.

"I can see that." I snagged Sinjin's hand, pulling him to me. "But can you see he had no choice? In the last four years, you guys have become partners. Brothers. Now that we know about Lombard, we can help Jasper end this threat. Then, the chain is gone."

"It's not that simple," Killian said. "The entire city knows the real Mercer Santos is dead. Lombard knows he's been outed, and whatever plan Croix convinced him to wait on has just fallen apart. He may have told him to get back in with us by whatever means necessary. His *daughter*"—Killian threw up air quotes—"was the perfect emotional tactic against you."

I stiffened. "It wasn't a con, Killian. I saw her for myself. She ran up and kissed him like he was her favorite person in the world. The child actor he hired in the last twelve hours couldn't pull off an act so well."

Stony faces looked back at me.

"I'm telling you she was the spitting image of him."

"We see what we want to see," Killian said, golden eyes hard. "You want to believe him, Adeline. Falling in love with a sociopathic fraud who never cared about you is too hard to accept."

I closed the distance between us. "Now I'm the gullible one? Who dangled off my every word, toy boy?"

He growled, lips peeling back from his teeth. "I did. I swallowed every sweet lie from those lips. Forgive me if I'm not interested in round two."

"Will you just hear him out?"

"No."

"See Rosalie for yourself. Jasper and her together—one look and you won't deny they're related."

"No."

"Saint?" I spun on him. "Please. I don't trust him either. It'll be a long time before I do. But the five of us"—I laced my fingers together—"we fit. We're a bunch of misfit toys that only work when we're together. I know you feel it too."

He cocked a brow. "I don't feel anything close to that. I barely liked Mercer, and I like Jasper even less. He can fuck off to wherever he came from. One day soon, I'll kill Lombard for my own reasons. Croix's problem will be handled and the matter settled. We'll call that good enough."

"I'm not buying it. I saw your face when Mercer's name flashed on the screen. Then I saw it again when you chased him outside and he got away. You guys aren't as unaffected as you want me to believe. Just talk to him."

"No."

"No," said Killian.

"No," Brutal added.

"The Merchants are done with Jasper Croix," Saint said. He hoisted me over his shoulder, ignoring my protests. "Besides, you have bigger things to worry about. Time is running out on getting me that name, Bunny. You don't want me to take over."

The four of us trotted out of the alley, me slung like a sack. We passed a guy heading the opposite way. His brows crept up at the sight of me. He shook his head, amused as he fished out his phone.

I'm not a captive. We've moved past that part of our relationship, though you wouldn't know it.

"Can we drop the threats, Saint? Gianna will tell me. I know she will." I jabbed his back. "And you, Killian, Baris, and Jasper will make things right. I always get what I want."

I hoped it sounded as menacing to his ears as it did to mine.

"Always."

The guys tossed me in the back of their stolen car. We sped back to the loft, arguing the entire way.

"If he proves that Rosie is his, will you believe him?"

"I'll believe he spawned," Saint said. "How does that get him a place in our gang?"

"He was trying to protect her from Lombard."

"So he says," Killian replied.

"Would any of you have done differently? Killian?"

"I was protecting my family," Killian said. "I didn't use a dead man's name to do it."

I flung myself back in the seat. "I'm not here to be his spokesperson. I told Jasper he has to settle things between you guys himself. But you should know I'm not ready to give up on him."

"The fuck you aren't," Saint dropped.

"I'm not. Jasper was willing to risk coming back and telling me the truth—"

"Did he tell you the whole truth?" Killian broke in. "Know his parents' names or where he was born? How about *when* he was born? Where did he go to school? How many aliases does he have? How did he get into his business so young? Do you know the answer to any of those questions? Do you?" he challenged when I didn't answer.

"That's what I thought. He didn't tell you the truth, Adeline. He told you just enough to doubt your doubts. Take it from a con man. The things we don't say can be just as effective manipulation as the things we do."

"There is still a lot I don't know about him," I admitted. "I didn't expect his entire life story in a single morning. But I am willing to give him more mornings to give me the rest. At least until he proves he's not worth hearing them."

"He proved it," Saint said, "when he watched every reasonable opportunity to open his fucking mouth go running out the door—exactly how he did. We're done." Angry eyes trapped mine in the mirror. "Stay away from him."

I folded my arms, considering my words carefully. Killian once compared my blue-haired love to a feral cat. The personalities weren't far off.

Coming at him head-on would leave you bleeding. You had to back down and let him come to you in the way most women had to trick their stubborn men into thinking an idea was theirs. In the way I had to sneak into his affections.

"I could stay away from him, but he's not likely to stay away from us. He needs that ledger to lay a trap for Lombard, Saint. It's his daughter we're talking about. The next time he sneaks in and drugs us, it'll be to find out where the ledger is from Gianna."

"There won't be a next time."

"You're right," I returned. "Because I'm not interested in sticking furniture against the door, bolting the windows, and sweeping for bugs first thing before I brush my teeth. We have enough to worry about without adding Jasper Croix and Rosie Baker to the list. If I keep him close, I'll know where he is, what he's doing, and more importantly, what he's going to do next."

Sinjin turned on Liberty Street. Fifteen minutes and we'd be at the loft.

He slowed his breakneck speed for traffic. "You're giving a good sell, Bunny, but it's not working. He's out. We're done with him."

It's not working yet. It will.

The man who used to be Mercer didn't hide that his secrets could break us. He was certain they would. I promised that day in the Perezes' building that I would prove him wrong. I'd show him I could love him through any sin he committed.

And I could. As long as those sins were in the past. If the lying, hiding, and scheming were over, I was willing to see if we could make something of the feelings I still had for him. Even if my alter ego was yelling as loud as Saint.

When would I learn my lesson?

You can't trust anyone. Especially someone who tells you not to.

"What?" Sinjin turned to me—despite the fact that he was driving. "No comeback? No argument? I know you haven't given in that—" Sinjin flicked over my shoulder.

Twisting around, he yanked the wheel and sent us flying into the doors.

I crashed hard on Brutal. "Saint!"

He punched the ignition, speeding through traffic and honking horns.

Crash!

I struggled to right myself. Craning my neck, I saw the car that was in front of us stopped and a figure slumped against the wheel. Their lights out from the rear-end collision.

The car that smashed into them was crammed with people. They poured out of their ruined vehicle and aimed their guns.

"Down!"

Brutal and I pitched forward. The back window exploded, showering us in glass.

"Who are those people?!" I screamed. "Who the fuck did you steal this car from, Saint?!"

"The eighty-year-old woman who lives in 3B!" Saint zoomed in and out of lanes, knocking Brutal and me around like bowling pins. "I saw the hood ornament when they tried to ram us. They're Kings." A slam on the brakes smashed my head on the stick shift. "And there are two more on our tail."

Eyes watering, Brutal helped me up. I peered through the gaping hole. A Jeep and an Escalade mowed down traffic. They were gaining.

"Kings? But— But how? How did they find us so fast?" I asked. "Did they follow you from the loft?"

"No, if they knew about the loft, they'd have taken us there," Killian said. "And they'd have gotten want we know they want: Cross."

My blood ran cold. "Thiago got tired of playing with that book of scribbles. He wants the woman who can translate it."

"Get out of the way!" Saint bellowed.

"The express," Killian ordered.

"It's ten blocks away. We won't make it."

I twisted again and looked straight into the eyes of one of the deceased Lane's men. He pointed to me, shouting something to the driver.

He rammed our bumper.

"Turn up the flames of hell on Leah Tyler." Brutal tucked me under his arm as the next hit popped us off our back wheels. I peeked the Jeep coming alongside us.

The barrel slid through the opening window, pointed at Sinjin.

"Saint!"

Bang! Bang!

A loud noise burst our ears.

The car suddenly jerked.

"Shit!" Sinjin roared as we lost speed.

The Jeep pulled ahead of us. Brake lights filled my vision.

They were stopping us cold this time.

"Hold on."

Saint veered off the road. We plowed straight for a looming green cross.

"Ahhh!"

Mrs. Odette's car crashed through the pharmacy—glass, metal, furniture, and pills went flying.

I sat there in a daze, debris covering my lap and hair, staring at the pharmacist gaping at me.

"What did you do?!" she bellowed.

The squeal of tires sounded behind me. "Get the girl!"

That woke me up.

"Get the *woman*, asshole!" I scrabbled for my seat belt.

Baris ripped it out and grabbed me. He threw his shoulder at the crumpled door, forcing it open as the Kings converged on the pharmacy.

"There's nowhere to run, Redgrave," someone called. "Our boss has something to discuss with you."

Baris and I tipped out onto the shattered glass. He put a finger to his mouth and pointed to the red exit sign in the back. We had to get out quickly before they surrounded the place.

Cash dropped down next to us. "Go," he hissed. "I'll cover you."

I grabbed the handle when Baris tried to pull me away. "You're not covering anything. We're outnumbered, Cash. We're all getting out of here now."

"I'll be right behind you." He brushed his finger on my chin. His touch was gone in a breath. "Go!"

Brutal pried my hand off. We army-crawled toward the exit.

"Come out, bitch!"

The Kings opened fire.

"Sinjin." Cash tossed his brother a gun.

The two fired from cover of the totaled car, keeping the Kings from entering the building.

I squeezed under a tipped-over stand, moving fast for the exit. The sooner I was out, the sooner my guys could stop covering and be with me.

We reached the back door. Baris climbed over, stood beside the frame, and threw it open.

A man rushed in.

Brutal moved in from behind and snatched his arm. He broke it over his leg.

The gun clattered to the floor over his screams. I grabbed it in time for his dead body to flop on the spot.

We bolted out the door and into the alley. A narrow space, it split our choices into the top of the street or the chain-link fence separating the buildings. Men crashed over the bags and crates stacked around the dumpster. Our decision was made for us.

I fired blindly behind, keeping them pinned, and trailing Baris to the fence.

"Adeline!"

I dropped my gun. Saint and Cash poured out, taking over.

Heart in my throat, I seized Baris's shoulder and stepped into his laced fingers. He vaulted me over the fence.

"Redgrave!" someone shouted. "Go around. She's getting away."

I fell to the concrete. Ignoring the shot of pain through my arm, I faced Baris, reaching through the bars for him.

"Come on."

He broke away. "Run."

"What? Bar— No!"

"Go!" Brutal took off after Sinjin and Cash to meet the horde of Kings.

A scream burst out of me.

This is not happening! After everything we've been through, I'm not losing my guys in a dirty pharmacy alley, taken out by an enemy not fit to lick our shoes.

Think, Redgrave. Think.

Spinning around, I landed on the small parking lot between the pharmacy and its neighbor.

I ran toward it and climbed the fence, going back to the death sentence I just escaped.

Two cars loitered in the lot. A simple four-door Camry and the Ford towering beside it.

I scanned the ground. "Come on. Come on, come on, come—"

There.

A rock tucked in a mess of weeds growing by the fence. I picked it up, hefted it over my shoulder, and sent it sailing through the truck's window.

Throwing it open, I brushed the glass off the seat and climbed in.

A scream echoed over the gunfire.

I'm coming, I thought, yanking down the visors. *Don't you dare fucking die.*

I pawed inside the glove box. My hand bumped the spare key and knocked it out. I dove for the passenger floor.

Boom!

The windshield blew out.

"Where do you think you're going, Redgrave?" It was a voice becoming familiar to me. "You must be special."

I closed over the keys.

"Thiago doesn't usually put this much effort into snagging a bitch." His voice was getting closer. "But then, most bitches aren't friends of Gianna Cross. Get out of the car. You won't like it if I come in there and get you my-self."

I inserted the key in the ignition. Carefully, I peered over the hood, landing on my new friend and the two men flanking him, advancing on the car—guns in hand.

"Get out of the car! Thiago said to bring you in alive, but he didn't say you had to go in with all the parts you came with. Get—"

I twisted the key. Throwing the car in gear, I peeled out of the parking space.

"Hey!"

The bangers ran out of the way—one not fast enough. My car thumped over his body, popping me out of my seat.

I squealed onto the sidewalk and whipped the car around. The Kings shooting up the alleyway didn't see me coming.

I mowed them down—feeling the screams and crunch of bone as if beneath my own boots.

A body rolled over my hood. Half alive, the man groaned on my dash.

"Come on!" I shrieked to the guys. "Get in."

They didn't need to be told twice. Cash, Brutal, and Saint piled inside.

Saint held my neck, crashing his lips on mine. "You are so fucking sexy right now."

"Love, this is not the time."

"It's always the time."

Shaking my head, I grabbed a fistful of the last living King's hair and lift-ed him. His eyes rolled in his head.

"Tell your boss he and I will be speaking very soon. There's no need to rush the date. And if he tries again, I'll cut off his main source of income and shove it down his throat."

I pushed him out. Peeling off, he landed smack on his buddies' corpses. I couldn't tell if he was still alive to deliver the message, but it was fine if he wasn't. Like I said, Thiago and I would be meeting up real soon. I've always preferred delivering my threats in person.

Amid gaping onlookers, camera phones, two collisions blocking the street, and a shouting pharmacist, I tore off.

"HOW THE FUCK DID THEY find us so fast?"

The door slammed into the adjoining wall, rattling the building. I trudged to the couch and pitched forward, dropping facedown on the cushions.

I was bone tired. We ditched the stolen car a few blocks from the pharmacy and went on foot for an hour—cutting through alleys, sticking to side streets, circling back on ourselves to be sure we lost any tails. Finally, we lifted hats and sunglasses, and slipped into a taxi. He dropped us a half an hour walk from the loft, and we made the twisty journey back, paranoia stretching thirty minutes into an hour and thirty coming back.

I was sure of two things. One, if anyone was following us, we lost them, and two, I had a blister the size of Texas on my right toe. Seriously, they were putting that thing in the Guinness Book of World Records.

"They were ready," Killian said. "Two cars, ten men for an armed assault. Someone made us and called the Kings down on our heads."

"Mercer," Saint hissed.

"No." My voice was muffled by the cushion. "It wasn't him."

"Bunny, I'm getting real fucking sick—"

"It's not him." I turned to meet those blazing eyes. "We're all hot, tired, and angry, but you're St. John Bellisario. You're always thinking five moves ahead and reading every player at the table. Tell me, Saint, could Jasper truly be behind this?"

Saint ground his teeth. I could practically hear his jaw cracking from across the room.

"No," he forced. "Croix knows where we sleep. If he wanted to send Thiago after us, he could've skipped the massacre on First Street."

I nodded. "Exactly. Plus, Jasper dropped me off in the park and then I wandered for miles till I ended up at the Buttermilk. The wrong person must've seen us and called Thiago. The Kings have people outside of Harlow too.

"I'm betting they tried ambushing us on the street because they didn't know what was waiting at the end of our trip. We could've met up with the rest of the gang and four targets becomes over a dozen. If they knew we were going straight to Gianna Cross, they would've played this much smarter.

"It was impulsive," I said clearly. "These are not the acts of a man with an informant. Thiago is scrambling to get to Gianna before anyone else does."

Brutal lifted my feet and placed them in his lap. I winced as he carefully peeled my shoes and socks off my aching feet.

I was wrong. The blister was beating Russia out for size, not Texas.

Brutal got up, I assumed to get the first aid kit.

"We have to move her," Killian said. "We have to move period. We can't afford another one of Croix's late-night visits, knocking us out when we have the entire city hunting us."

I couldn't argue with that. Jasper made it clear he wasn't letting me go so easily. Drugging my boyfriends every time we met wouldn't do so well for our chances of getting out of this mess, or my chances of not getting dumped.

My eyes swung back and forth following Saint's pacing. *Is that truly on the table? Is there no way the guys can get past this? Am I risking my relationship with three men for the love of one?*

"Where do we go?" I asked, pushing my thoughts down. "Brutal never got the money he was owed for winning the tournament. Something tells me the Kings aren't paying up anytime soon. We're barely affording this place."

"The cabin," Baris spoke up. He returned with the kit and set to work taking care of me. I stroked the nape of his neck, loving my equally ruthless and gentle man. "If Pais has everyone on the streets looking for us, we get off the streets."

"Might be a good idea, Sin," Killian said. "For a few days at least while Adeline works on getting her to hand over the ledger."

"She doesn't have a few days. Cross has until"—Saint made a show of looking at his watch—"eight o'clock to give me that book or the name within it. Once I know who had my father tortured and killed, I won't be stashing away in the woods." He slammed his fist on the coffee table. "Nothing will stop me killing him. If Pais wants to get in the way, let him. I'll take care of two problems at once."

He jerked a chin at us. "You and Brutal take them both to the cabin. It's Cross who Pais wants and he knows Adeline can draw her out. Take them both out of play and—"

"Don't finish that sentence, Saint," I snapped. "Using me could draw Gianna out, and using the Merchants would draw *me* out. Pais, Lane's men, and half the Kings saw us together at the tournament matches. They've pegged me as your banger girl. We are all on the wanted list. The last thing we're doing is splitting up."

"Fine by me." Sinjin popped a kiss on my lips. "I'd like my Bunny there while I take my final revenge." His finger glided down the valley of my breasts. "You hold him down while I carve his chest open."

"Looking forward to it," I whispered against his mouth.

"But first," he said, drawing slightly away from my kiss. "Get me that name."

"I will. I know what will help, but it means going back out there."

"Not alone," Killian said. "I'll go with you."

"I'm going to Edie." Sinjin rescued his jacket. "She'll know a place we can stay while we ride this out."

"She must have seen your face on the news by now," I said. "What does she think of all of this?"

"What do you mean? She knows it's bullshit." He winked. "Her sweet St. John would never do those things."

I heaved a sigh. "Her sweet St. John isn't going alone either. They sent ten men after us and it wasn't enough. Thiago won't underestimate the number next time."

"Brutal, you coming or not?" he asked.

Baris rested my bandaged feet on the chair arm, kissed me, and blew out the door with Saint. Killian took his place.

"Where are we going?"

"To get the one person who may get through to her."

KILLIAN AND I WALKED a fair distance down the road to the Leighbridge Botanical Gardens. Admittance was free. The indoor gardens were cool, and the path broke off here and there to little sweetheart benches tucked between the trees.

A sea of roses of such a breathtaking soft pink surrounded me. Beads of moisture clung to their leaves, bathing my finger as I stroked them. As far as hiding places went, this was my favorite by far.

"—fifteen minutes," Cash said. "Leave the keys in the ignition."

He clicked off.

"How did Lucky take it?" I burrowed into his side as he leaned back on the bench. "No complaints about us calling him in the middle of the day and demanding his car?"

"None that he was foolish enough to say out loud."

"I've been thinking," I said. "Thiago's got a hit out on us. What if one of the men decides to collect?"

Cash shook his head. "While I always factor in the potential stupidity of an opponent, I can't attribute that to Thiago Pais. He's smart. Crafty. The man was caught running his own scheme on King turf and managed to work out a deal with Angelo that made them both rich. Now he's running the entire gang.

"Today's attack was impulsive, but it almost worked. Pais knows what he's doing. He's not letting anyone get to you that he doesn't trust implicitly. You're closer to the ledger than he is. Pais has to stop you before you turn it on him."

A thought crossed my mind. "We could," I said. "Even if Pais isn't in it, we'd have enough to build an operation bigger than the Kings will ever be. We'd grind them under our heels."

"How do we know he's not in it? Cross hasn't been forthcoming."

"Trust me, if there was something in that ledger that would destroy Thiago Pais, she wouldn't be sitting on it. He hung her off a balcony. Gianna doesn't forgive and forget."

"Does that apply to you?" Killian tipped my chin up. "I know you want to believe you can fix what happened between you, Adeline. That only happens when both parties are willing. We shouldn't be out here, tracking down something that would get her to spill the truth. If she really wanted to make things right between you, she would've told you everything two seconds after her apology."

I cupped his cheek. "It's not me she doesn't want to talk to. It's you," I said bluntly. "And Saint. And Brutal. And... Mercer. As much as I hate to say it, Jasper Croix confirmed every fear she had about you guys. She's gone from trying to show me up, to trying to protect me from men I can't trust. I once said there's no worse crime a parent can commit than being right when you're determined to prove them wrong. That goes twice with smug-ass sisters.

"You thought she was stubborn before? That Gianna was a pushover compared to Gianna protecting me. Doesn't help I lost all the legs I was standing on when Jasper ran out the door. She's not going to hear that I can trust you guys with the ledger, but she may listen to someone we both trust."

"Your dad."

"Yes," I said. "Dad has this way with her—though Gianna likes to pretend they're not close. He could always reach her in a place I couldn't go. Where they mourned losing their family, Soren."

He turned his attention to a sprig of lavender trying to tickle his forehead. "Can't hurt."

I watched him for a bit, tracing the firm line of his jaw, then my lips took up the task. Why not? This wasn't a look-but-don't-touch kind of situation. Killian Hunt was mine. I'd touch him whenever and wherever I wanted.

A late-night drugging, the rush to find me, and then a pharmacy showdown got in the way of his usual morning routine. Stubble prickled my soft skin, raising goose bumps on my flesh.

I ran my hand down his shirt, then slipped under it. Killian rippled beneath me—hard, tight, and warm. No matter how long we'd been together, a sense of danger still climbed my spine at touching this man who once coldly dismissed me as a waste of time and space.

My phone buzzed.

"Leave it," Killian growled. "You're busy."

I giggled. "These bushes aren't giving us that much cover. What if someone sees us?"

"There's barely anyone here."

"Ah. So I can take my time with you till my heart's content."

"Of course." Killian rubbed my nipple through the fabric, hardening it to attention. "I'll tease you as long as you tease me."

"Well played, Hunt," I whispered. My hand traveled lower. "Very well played."

Our noses bumped—dancing with each other as our lips came close but not close enough.

"That patch of grass over there looks good."

"Killian!" I couldn't contain my laughter. Cash reached under my shirt and popped my bra. "We'll be thrown out of here. They'll probably call the police, so that's us arrested."

Killian palmed my breast. My breath caught as he lifted my shirt up and took me in his mouth.

"The Kings will probably get to us in our cell. We'll die behind bars and our hopes for the city will go with us."

His tongue rolled over my nipple and then it disappeared like a happy slut between his teeth. My panties were soaked in seconds.

"All because we couldn't behave ourselves," I breathed, eyes falling shut. "Fucked in a public botanical garden. There you guys go again, proving I've got more firsts for you to notch in your belts."

Killian put my hand on his belt. My cell buzzed again.

"Speaking of."

Despite what I said, the gardens concealed us in their world. Vines, stems, and growing flowers hid us from sight of people coming around the corners. They wouldn't know we were there until they were on top of us—as long as I didn't get too enthusiastic.

I stroked his length, moaning simply for the feel of him, hard and wanting in my hands.

Penises weren't the most attractive of appendages, but I swear, Killian's was hot as hell. That wasn't just the love talking. He was both thick and long—filled me to my limit and then kept going. My fingers slid around him, easy over soft flesh tinged pink like these flowers.

No wonder I like them so much.

Killian stopped his torture, raising his head to meet me. Our lips touched.

My phone rang.

I nearly fell off the seat.

"Turn it off, Adeline." Killian drug me back and attached to my neck.

"Doing just that." I fished it out of my pocket.

The screen flashed *Jasper*.

"Croix?"

It was too late to stop Killian from seeing, and why that was my first panicked thought, I had no clue. Jasper was not my dirty little secret. Though the look Killian gave me as the fire doused said otherwise.

"What does he have to call you about, Adeline?"

"I don't know. It's not a surprise he knows my number. I've been dating him as long as I've been dating you."

"It's not that he knows yours." He jabbed the screen. "You've got his programmed and named."

"I fell asleep at his place, Cash. He must've put his number in then." The call ended. "You know, I'm really not appreciating being treated like some traitor. You've known Jasper for longer than I have, and you didn't see what he was. Stop taking it out on me."

"I'm not pissed that I was taken for a fool. I'm pissed that you don't care that we were!"

Yeah, the mood was definitely gone.

I shoved off the bench and straightened my clothes. The happy sluts were stuffed in their bra to get their kicks another time.

"How can you say I don't care? I thought someone flattened me with a steamroller when I saw that broadcast. It was one of the worst days of my life. And you know I've had fucking plenty of those. This isn't any easier for me than it is for all of you."

"Then why does he think he can call you up whenever he wants?"

My phone rang again. We didn't have to look to know who it was.

"Why don't I find out, Killian?"

I answered the call. "Jasper."

"Adeline, are you alright?" That new, deep voice flowed out the speakers. This time not laced with calm. "Where are you?"

"I'm fine. Why?"

"Why? Your shoot-out on Liberty Street is all over the news. The videos are too grainy to make out your face, but I'd know you anywhere. Cops are out looking for the auburn-haired woman who mowed down seven people in the street."

"I didn't mow down seven people," I protested. "I mowed down seven Kings. Huge difference. Ugh." I threw myself down. "I can't believe the news got hold of it so fast. At this rate, they'll send the national guard in to round up the Merchants. We don't have time for this heat."

Killian's eyes were hard on me. He was listening to every word.

"Where are you? The loft isn't safe. Stay at my place."

"I can't." My heart panged for that being my automatic response. "I said the same to my dad. I'm not getting warm and cozy in a hideaway while the guys are out here cleaning up my mess."

"This isn't your mess."

"Leah Tyler told Pais all about my connection with Gianna. Our stupid fight led to him chasing us down in the streets."

"Adeline, if Pais didn't find out from her, he would've learned it at the match along with half of Cinco. Brutal announced the woman you were cuffed to was Kieran. If they're not looking for her, then they're looking for the woman she ran off with."

"But you weren't there that night."

"I wasn't and I heard about it anyway. Don't you understand? Adeline Redgrave is no longer the mild-mannered chef from Rockchapel. Everyone who matters in this city is looking for you."

The hairs on my neck prickled. I twisted in my seat, scanning our eerily silent hiding place in a new light.

I swallowed hard. "You make a valid point."

"Stay here," he repeated. "All four of you. No one knows about this place. You'll be safe. I'll stay somewhere else."

"Where?"

"I've got money and more changes of identity than pairs of shoes. I'll be fine. No one wants the man they think is Mercer Santos as much as they want Adeline Redgrave."

Killian plucked the phone from me. "We do," he hissed. "We're not moving in with you, Croix, but believe we'll meet up real soon. Stop calling my girlfriend."

Clear as if he was speaking in my ear, Croix replied, "She's my girlfriend too, and I'll stop when she tells me to stop—which she won't. She loves me."

Heat suffused my cheeks.

"She wants me. She won't give me up any sooner than I'll give her up. You're not dealing with Mercer Santos anymore, Hunt. I'll always respect what we built these last four years. Allies or enemies, it's up to you. But Adeline is mine."

Killian hung up the phone and flung it into the bushes.

"Killian!"

"We'll get you another one."

I shot up to go look for it. Killian caught me around the waist, carrying me off.

The loud, colorful tirade I gifted him down the path and out into the parking lot drew looks.

"—possessive, manhandling Neanderthal! Animated sack of testosterone with a face painted on front! 1950s husband with a 1950s haircut!"

"That's just below the belt," Killian said mildly. He idled on the sidewalk, waiting for our ride. "First rule of fighting: never say something you can't take back."

"Ugh!" I scared a family walking past us. "What is with you, Killian? My eyes are wide open. I see Jasper Croix for what he is. If I'm willing to let him prove that man is worth my time, why can't you? Do you realize everything Jasper did to you, I did too? You were willing to hear me out before making up your mind. Why can't you do the same for him?"

"Completely different situation."

"How?"

"You suck my dick."

Fuming, my jaw worked for a full ten seconds. "You're going to be waiting a long time for that."

He laughed.

I didn't know what was more insulting. That Killian thought he could police my relationship with Jasper. Or that the guys never took my threats of celibacy seriously.

I took a deep breath, held it, and let it out slow. All this hanging upside down was making me dizzy. We needed to find another way to settle issues.

"Killian, I need my phone," I said in an even tone. "My dad wants his address kept private. Should I remind you of Tara Duncan? He's texting me the place to meet him."

Killian didn't move.

"Come on." I poked his butt. "Do we really want to explain to Saint that we didn't do everything we could to find his father's killer because Jasper is as possessive as you?"

"Jasper," he scoffed. "You call him that like it's nothing, Adeline. Like he wasn't Mercer for four damn years. You believe it's the same situation, but you didn't wait nearly half a decade to tell us the truth, and then didn't. The truth had to be revealed for him. If you had pulled the same shit, I promise I'd be just as angry."

I rubbed his back. "I know this isn't easy for any of us. Whatever happens with Croix, I promise I won't lie to you. I'm done with that."

Killian said nothing. He put me on my feet and returned inside. He came back out fifteen minutes later with my phone. I checked it and found the earlier buzzing was texts from Jasper, asking me if I was alright or needed help.

I would like that minimalist penthouse in the sky since you're offering. But it won't happen while Gianna, Killian, Saint, and Baris are between us. At least I hope they are the only ones between us.

Lucky soon arrived with our ride. We left him calling a taxi on the sidewalk and headed into Waterford to meet my dad in a bar not far from the first home I grew up in.

I leaned over the booth to kiss his cheek. "Daddy, do I have to be worried about you? Our issues with Waterford Retirement's staff aside, at least I didn't show up and find out you were hanging at the bar."

"I've had a few beers. I'm practically drinking water."

I gave him the stink eye. "You're not supposed to have any alcohol while on your meds." I rested my head on his shoulder. "You're going to live a long life, Oscar Redgrave. Bounce your grandchildren on your knee. Visit all the places I'm going to take you. Can't do that if you croak over a few light beers."

"Yeah, yeah," he muttered. "Nag me worse than a wife." All the same, Dad pushed the beer away. "Happy now, brown eyes?"

"Yes."

"Good." He kissed my crown. "Who's this guy?"

Killian stood a respectful distance away—waiting.

"This is my boyfriend, Killian Hunt. His parents own the circus I was telling you about. They're looking after little Kaylee."

"Nice to meet you, sir." Killian approached, holding out his hand. "Adeline has told us a lot about you. From a grifter to a fixer, I'm impressed by your work."

"Are you?" Dad rose. "I wish I could say the same. You and your Merchant boys are all over the news. Least I knew enough not to get caught."

"Daddy," I cried.

A smirk stretched across Killian's face. "What can I say? Your daughters wreaked havoc on us. Gianna probably could've used a few more spankings growing up."

My jaw dropped. No one spoke to my father that way. A cop once called him "boy" during a traffic stop and Dad knocked him out. He threw the man in our trunk, dropped me at school, and to this day I still don't know what became of him.

Dad burst out laughing. "Wreaking havoc is what my girls do. Adeline used to throw her dirty diapers at me when I put her in time-out."

"Dad!"

"Full of fire those two," he mused. "Anyone who makes a wrong move gets burned. Unfortunately, the same sometimes applies to themselves." Dad reclaimed his seat, drawing my steaming self to his side. "I've heard what they're saying on the streets. Gianna Cross has the ledger. When I told Alexander to end the war between you, this isn't what I had in mind."

"What?" *Dad knows what happened at the match too?*

"When did you have that conversation?"

"Around the fiftieth call to Gianna that went unanswered. He took away her biggest weapon, but also her most effective shield. I assume you're here because it's finally time for me to intervene."

"Yes," I said. "I tried to get her to talk to you. She knows the talk she has coming will blow away the lies she told herself to justify her actions. Either way, it's long past time you two spoke."

"Why is that?" Dad reached for his beer out of habit and I slid it away. "So I can convince her to tell you where the ledger is? You know I won't do that. If she tells me where it is, I'll burn it myself."

"I know where the ledger is."

"You do?"

I nodded. "I can't get to it right now, but it's sitting pretty until I can. What I really want from Gianna is for her to tell me the name of the man who sent those monsters after a priest and his little boy. That's a conversation Gianna and I will have on our own. You, Dad."

I hugged him tight. "I just want you to do what you do. You always had the words to put our ragtag family back together. We need that, Daddy. If we go on like this for much longer, we won't find our way back."

Dad gave me a long, assessing look.

"All right. Let's go."

Half an hour later, Killian parked Lucky's car down the block from the loft.

I ducked my head against his arm, avoiding eye contact with the people brushing past us.

"What's this I hear about Mercer Santos turning up dead?" Dad asked under his breath. "That name sounds familiar."

"Goodness, Dad. Do you know everything?"

"Yes."

I sighed. "Look, Mercer is a long story. I'll fill you in tonight. Stay for dinner."

"Only if you make that applesauce barbecue chicken thing with the steak fries and corn on the cob."

"Really? I'm getting grilled, but you get to pick the menu."

"That's how it works."

I laughed. "I'll make the heart-healthy version of that meal. Take it or leave it."

"You've never put a thing in front of me that wasn't delicious. I'll take it."

I hugged my dad tight. There he went again—making me feel like everything would be okay when there was no good reason to.

"How did you do it?" Killian spoke up. Our building came into sight. "Keep your identity and the truth about Kieran secret for decades. All the clients you came into contact with, it's your name that should be known in the streets."

"It might have been, but there was a reason we structured the Lords how we did. Kieran was the name. The face. The voice. Clients spoke to him and fell under that charm he always had about him. No one could help but like

Kieran Foley. Even our worst, orneriest foster parents gave him second helpings of the scraps. Once he had them under sway, I'd show up and be dismissed as the help.

"The most powerful man in the room is not the king, Hunt. He's the silent figure in the shadows. The one passed over as a non-threat until the knife is between your ribs." Dad climbed the steps with me. "Too bad for us, Kieran turned out to be both."

Killian had no more questions after that.

We went up to our loft and pushed inside. Dad threw his hand out, knocking me back.

"Dad?"

"Outside. Now," he barked.

"What's wrong?"

"Look."

Dad pointed to the floor, and the tiny droplets of blood.

Throat closing, I followed their trail to Gianna's door.

"Gianna!" I ducked under his arm, racing to her room.

"Adeline, wait!"

I tripped over my feet, stumbling onto her bed. Her empty bed.

Gianna was gone.

"Who knew she was here?" Dad demanded. "How long has she been on her own? They might not have gone far."

I gazed at the bloody shackles on the carpet. "There is no they, Dad." My thundering heart slowed. "Gianna wasn't taken."

"How do you know?"

I got up, revealing the letter I landed on. "I doubt they would have given her time to leave a note."

Killian picked up the chains. "She broke out of this?" Disbelief colored his tone though he was holding the proof for himself. "How?"

"Painfully."

"Then, your father is right. She can't have gotten far, especially on a hurt foot."

I unfolded the note.

"I'll find her. A woman limping down the street will be hard to miss."

I barely heard him or his fading footsteps.

Addy,

This is super fucking lame, doing this in a letter instead of to your face, but I'm hoping since it won't come with a but or justification, you'll still accept it.

I'm sorry.

Sitting in this room for the last week gave me time to think. Not about warming up to the Merchants like you hoped, but I have been thinking about something they said. You had everything while all I had was you.

I didn't handle the idea of losing you well. That was my problem, not yours. I should have gotten my head out of my ass and noticed that this is what you do. You create families out of the unlikeliest of people. Then you protect them with everything you have.

Even now, little sister, you're protecting me, and I can't let you do that anymore. If Thiago wants me, I'm more than happy to entertain him.

I will kill him.

After, I'll make sure all of Cinco knows the ledger is out of their reach. Coming after you will get them nothing.

I know this can't make up for what I've put you through, but I hope this is a start toward earning it back:

Nicolas Katz.

If this is the last thing I say to you, then it needs to be this.

Do not underestimate him.

-Gianna.

I read the last word, looking up at Dad.

"Nicolas Katz?" Dad repeated. "Why would she put him in her letter?"

A bucket of ice water tipped on my head, trapping me to the spot.

"Because it's him, Dad." I could barely recognize my own voice. "Katz sent those men to Our Lady of the Sacred Heart Cathedral. He had Saint's father killed."

"The former mayor of Cinco."

"Former mayor," I rasped. "Now governor."

The look in his eyes was one I'd never seen before.

"Gianna did not do you a favor, my girl." He slipped the letter from numb fingers. "You will wish you never heard that name. For the rest of your life, you'll wish you never heard that name."

Chapter Five

I closed and locked us in the room.

"What do you mean, Dad? You said you had no idea who hired those men."

"I didn't." His expression was grave. "But now that I know it was Katz, everything makes sense."

"Everything makes sense? It makes sense that our former mayor, now governor had a priest tortured and killed, and left his son orphaned? How does that make sense?"

"Sit."

I propped on the edge of the mattress, reaching for Dad's hands as he reached for mine.

"I told you as our business grew, it became necessary for me to set rules for the jobs we would and wouldn't take."

"Yes, I remember."

"What I didn't tell you was Katz was the reason those rules had to be made," he said. "Our first job for him was the staged shooting. It garnered the voter sympathy he needed to turn the election his way. I should have known then. It's a steely, ruthlessly ambitious man willing to be shot to advance his career.

"I should have seen it," he hissed, "but as I told you, I was a foolish, arrogant man back then."

"What happened?"

"What happened is I'm good at what I do, baby girl. I made Nicolas Katz mayor of this city, and once he had what he wanted, he kept coming back for more. For his reelection, he hired us to bury his opponent. When he ventured into real estate, again he called us to smooth his way. Pressure reluctant owners to sell. Buy off inspectors.

"The first look into the man he was came on September twelfth, the year before you were born. Katz called Kieran in the middle of the night and told him to send his cleanup man to the Imperial Majesty Hotel. The cleanup man was me.

"I walked into quite a party. Drugs, booze, sex toys everywhere, and on the bed, a half-naked escort lying dead."

"He killed them?" I cried.

"He said no. They were doing lines of coke. She suddenly fell over and started convulsing. Katz claimed it happened so fast there was nothing he could've done to save her."

My lips twisted. "Certainly no time to call an ambulance. So, why let this ruin his reputation, his career, and his family? He had to look out for himself now."

Dad inclined his head. "He was crying and pleading. Said nothing like this would ever happen again. He just needed help to make this go away, and he'd pay anything.

"The next time it happened, he didn't bother with the act."

"The next time? Are you saying he wound up in a hotel room with another dead escort?"

"No. He'd gotten more discrete about his affairs by that time. Acquired a property out in Elmshire Woods, drew up nondisclosure agreements, and took his dates there when he was on *business trips*.

"The second dead body he called us to get rid of was of his deputy. Katz had gotten smarter about hiding his affairs, but not about who he trusted to arrange them. His deputy decided to try his hand at blackmailing. He cornered Katz in his office one night, demanded half a million to keep quiet, or the whole city would know how much of the city fund had gone to paying off the mothers of his illegitimate children.

"Katz refused to pay. The fight got nasty—physical. Webber attacked him and Katz claimed he had no choice but to shoot him."

"Did you believe him?"

Dad's gaze drifted out the window. "There were signs of a struggle. The office was a wreck. Katz had a bloody lip and torn clothes. It's possible it happened exactly how he said, but—"

"He wasn't weeping and wailing this time," I finished. "He was too cold for a man who just killed someone."

"Cold. Matter of fact. He looked at Webber's body like it was dog piddle on the carpet. 'Take care of it,' he said, and then he left."

"What did you do, Dad?" I asked, squeezing his hand. I didn't want it to sound like I was judging him. My father was a different person before I was born.

"I did what he paid us to do, and that night the ledger was born."

"That night?"

Dad flashed a mirthless smile. "Your old man wasn't that far gone. I sensed something was off about him. That night, I removed the body, set his office to rights, and buried Webber. What Katz didn't know is I photographed the entire scene. After, I made Webber's final resting place Katz's property in the woods. I put him in the hole they dug for his hot tub."

"Genius."

"Thank you, brown eyes. It was one of my smarter moves. Afterward, I went to Kieran and Soren, told them the truth about our latest job, and said we had to protect ourselves in case a man like Katz ever decided we needed to be cleaned up. We'd start by not getting into bed with men like Katz from then on. The Lords didn't hide bodies. We didn't carry out hits on witnesses, or destroy the lives of innocent people.

"Kieran and Soren agreed, then Kieran took my proof, said we'd record everything from now on, and Katz became our first entry."

"Is Webber's body still there?"

"I couldn't say. There have been many Kierans over the years, Adeline. It's more than likely one of them used the details in that book to blackmail Katz on his rise to the top. All it would've taken was one of them hinting at the body on his property, and he'd have torn the grounds up."

"Could they have been that stupid?"

"There's only one way to know."

I sank onto the pillows. For as many years as Kierans have used the ledger to their advantage, it was just as possible fools used it to lose its advantage as well. Photos of a body were well and good, but digging up Webber ten feet from his love shack would have been impossible to explain away. We were about to go up against one of the most powerful men in Cinco—no matter his name, I knew Saint would not be stopped—and we had no teeth.

"Did you have any dealings with Katz after that?"

He nodded. "Katz made us his go-to fixers. He dropped the charm and politician's smile entirely. We got jobs to kill mistresses who decided an NDA wasn't going to stop them. Once his son got older and turned out to be just like his father, Katz called us in to make two of his pregnant girlfriends go away. I'm not counting Bellona Alexander. Marshall called personally and ordered her killed and disposed of."

"You mean Young Katz got three separate girls pregnant in high school and ran to Daddy to take care of it? What the hell is wrong with this family?"

"Fathers tend to mold their children into versions of themselves." He cuffed my chin. "For better or worse."

"I'm the best version of you, Dad. For all my diaper flinging, I've brought light and joy to your life."

Dad laughed. "Won't hear me say otherwise."

We smiled, relishing the brief moment of levity.

Dad's grin wiped clean. It could only last for a moment.

"We took those jobs, Adeline, because if we didn't—"

"—Katz would've called someone else to kill those women. Someone without a conscience," I finished. "I know, Dad. *Kieran* wasn't always the monster that's feared in the streets. And that's when he was you."

"For all the good me and my rules did," he scoffed. "We fielded one more request from Katz before we decided the kingmakers would become kings. Katz was running for secretary of state at the time—his stepping stone to becoming governor. One day, Katz had a thought. Public sympathy worked so well for getting him elected mayor, why wouldn't it work again?

"There would be another attack, but he wouldn't be the victim."

"Who?" I asked. "Who did he want you to attack?"

"Marian Katz. Nicolas hired us to brutally rape and murder his wife in their home."

My mouth opened. Nothing came out.

"I didn't take the call," Dad continued, "but Kieran told me he had quite the plan worked out. We were to slip in during the guard change and catch Marian in her room getting ready for bed. We'd brutalize her, leave her for dead, and then the news would get shots of him running out the house covered in her blood, screaming for help.

"He'd put on a brave, if broken, face for the cameras in the weeks of coverage, and after he was elected, become a strong force for justice and cleaning up the streets of Cinco City. Ten years prior, and he was laying the groundwork toward becoming governor."

I held up a hand, shaking my head. "I'm sorry, hold on. Katz hired you to *rape and murder* his wife of forty years. Mother of his children." Saying it out loud didn't help either. "But— but you didn't. Marian Katz is still alive."

"She is." He made a harsh noise. "It's hard to believe among the decades of death and destruction that book has brought, but the ledger saved her life. We were already thinking about getting out of the business and building something to leave to you girls. When we got that call, it sealed our decision.

"Kieran told Katz in no uncertain terms that if Marian Katz didn't live a long and healthy life, every single job we'd done for him would see the light of day. The fake shooting, shady real estate deals, and that very conversation. His career climbing would end ascending the top bunk in his prison cell."

My head moved up and down as it came together. "Kieran threatened him," I said. "The man that I'm now understanding he is wouldn't let that slide. He didn't have to either. The wife he so callously wanted to get rid of is worth millions. He had more than enough to start the hunt for the man on the other end of the phone. It eventually led him to that church."

Dad got up, moving to the window. "I'd broken from Kieran by then. I had no way of knowing if enemies new or old were tracking him down. All I know is one succeeded. I wonder now if we can lay his death at Katz's feet too."

"Katz could have killed Kieran," I admitted. "You never did find out who it was. But we know he didn't get his hands on the ledger. He would've ripped his pages out, and Gianna would not know enough to give me that warning."

"A warning you won't heed."

"It's not about me, Dad." I went to his side in time to spot Killian coming up the front stairs. Gianna was not with him. "It's about Saint. Nothing will stop him. Nothing would stop me if it was you."

"There's nothing I can say to convince you this isn't your fight, is there?"

Smiling, I shook my head.

"Then, tell me what to do." Dad tucked my arm under his. "If I'm honest, I've wanted to wipe that self-satisfied smile off his face for decades."

The loft door opened. Killian called for me.

"You'll get your chance soon, Dad," I said.

"We're killing the governor."

MERCER

People reduced to moving headlights and lit rooms blanketed the city. It was a sight people shelled out thousands to see before they fell asleep.

I wasn't born in Cinco. Life dropped and then trapped me here as it does to so many people in countless places where they wake up and wonder what happened.

I didn't feel the connection that shone in Adeline's eyes. She loved this city despite the life she's had living here. The mother who destroyed her childhood. The father who held her to the whetstone till she was sharpened into the deadliest of weapons. The war she inherited on her first day in the world. Still, if you cut her open, her veins bled light pollution, traffic congestion, and five boroughs more different than the last.

I didn't feel such things for Cinco City. Most days it was just another collection of buildings, streets, and potential employers or targets.

Most days.

Other days, I gazed from the window down at people too far to see, going about lives I knew nothing about, and their nondescript movement about my world was the closest connection I felt to other people.

They were all blank dots. Their stories to be filled in by my imagining.

The moving figures through the curtains in the apartment across from me were a sweet, well-meaning couple trying to raise a son to be a contributing member of society. They'd fail, but no one could say they didn't try.

I flicked down.

Those particular pair of headlights belonged to a single father driving to pick his daughter up from the babysitter. After they'd buy takeout on the wrong side of healthy and eat it on the couch while watching a movie. A normal, everyday scene I'm told, but one I've never been a part of.

Grinning, I palmed my phone.

Adeline plays this game in the hallways of random apartment buildings, imagining a slice of life on the other side.

She and I had this in common. Not just this. We had a fair amount of things in common which still surprised me.

I told Adeline once that people were easy. Discovering their code, deciphering it, unlocking their secrets. No one was as complicated as they liked to believe.

All my life, I've understood everyone, and related to no one.

Until Adeline.

It's no wonder I chose her to love.

Love.

Such a strange concept. It was basically favoritism on steroids.

Out of hundreds of thousands of billions of people, places, and things, you must choose one above the rest. One place to make your home. One job to do until you die. One woman to build a life with.

Rosie's home was the place I had made mine. Protecting her was the job I'd do until I died. Adeline Redgrave was the woman who'd share our lives.

Whether anyone fucking liked it or not.

I had made my choice. According to every movie, song, and book about love, that meant I fought to have her by any means necessary.

"Hmm. Mhh."

"Quiet," I said, looking at my phone. Willing it to ring hadn't worked, but then, all those movies, songs, and books indicated I was in the doghouse. This is the part where I groveled, gave her presents, and locked her in my room for constant make-up sex. The last I was on board with.

I pulled up her name and hit dial. She answered on the second ring.

"Jasper."

"Adeline." I moved from the window, padding into the living room. "I didn't think you'd answer."

"Then, why did you call?" Amusement laced her quip. My cock twitched to attention.

It had been doing that since our first day in the fire station when she told us to name the offense that would get her killed and out of our lives forever. It was the first time in years my cock responded without my permission. I should've known then she'd be trouble.

"On the off chance Killian hadn't stolen your phone, I held out hope to hear your voice."

"Don't try your sweet talk on me. I'm immune now."

Shouting bled through her side of the phone, followed by a crash.

"Everything alright over there?"

"Killian and Saint are having a discussion." I heard a door shut and there was quiet on her end.

"Hmm. Mhh. Mhh."

But not on mine.

I walked past the man hanging from the ceiling, giving him a spin on the way past.

"Mhhh!"

"Something I can do for you?" she asked.

"You can get on your knees for me. Part those full, plump lips and swallow every inch of this swelling cock."

Adeline choked. "Ja— Jasper!"

"What?" Now amusement laced my tone. "You asked."

My mind supplied the picture for me. Adeline sinking in the plush carpet. Slender fingers pulling my belt through the loops and me slipping the bra straps off her shoulder, one and then the other.

Adeline had the perfect breasts—and I had done enough study to give an expert opinion. They weren't so big you lost a nose burying your head in them. Neither were they too small they slipped out grabbing a handful.

She pushed those shapely little lovelies together for me—that impish glint in her eyes as she licked her lips, eager to be painted with my cum.

"This is going to take some getting used to." Her voice brought me out of the daydream.

A dream is all it was. Unlike my Merchant counterparts, I was the only one who hadn't partaken in the sinful buffet that was Adeline Redgrave other than a couple fumblings. Not that I didn't have the opportunity to multiple times. It was just, as stupid as it may seem, I haven't had sex with a single person as myself since I was nineteen years old. I'm all for costumes in the bedroom, but for my first time with Adeline, I didn't want to wear Mercer's.

"Mercer liked to hide behind ten layers of flirtation, winks, and not-so-accidental brushes," she said. "You being direct is new for me."

"You wanted to know the real me."

"Am I getting to know the real you? Cash helpfully pointed out I don't know anything about your parents, where you're from, or how you got into this business."

I reclined on the couch. Nudging my tools aside, I propped my feet on the coffee table. "I've told you many times, Redgrave. If there's something you want to know, ask."

She sighed. "Fair enough. But I'm not sure now is the time to have this conversation."

I sat up straight. "Come over to my place tomorrow. I'll pick you up a few blocks from the loft."

"You're desperate to get me alone, aren't you, Croix?"

"You have no idea," I growled.

She groaned. "Damn, this new voice of yours is lethal. One sentence and I'm wet. Why did you give Mercer a different one?"

"I dealt with one client becoming an obsessed stalker. Didn't need them all hooked."

"Oooh. He's cocky too," she replied, laughing.

I was hard as a rock now. All it took was her saying "cock."

"You give me reason to be. Are you really wet?"

"Mm-hmm." I pictured her forcing it through bitten lips. "Can't help thinking about that voice in my ear while I claim my final Merchant as my own."

"Show me."

"Show you?"

"That wet pussy, and what you want me to do with it."

"Jasper," she hissed. "I'm not sexting you right now."

"How about in an hour?"

Adeline giggled, kicking my pulse into overdrive. It amazed me Jasper could do that as well as my alter ego.

"How about I tell you when we're ready for sexting?" she offered. "You haven't even taken me on a real date. I'm a girl who likes to be wooed."

"Good thing I've got a present for you."

Raising my phone, I snapped a picture of my entertainment for the evening. I sent it to Adeline over her questions about the present.

"Who is this?"

"His name is Marlon Thibodeaux. He's a business partner and friend of Thiago Pais."

"Is he now." The flirty tone was gone. "What have you and Thiago's friend been talking about?"

"Marlon hasn't been saying much," I replied, meeting the man's eyes.

Sweat dropped off his brow and stuck to his eyelashes. He looked to be crying, but that part hadn't come yet.

"He will tell me every home, second home, summer home, penthouse, and yacht that Thiago owns. Pais will not come after you again."

"From the lack of blood, it looks like you're asking nicely."

Marlon stood on top of a stool—hands bound, gagged, and rope around his neck. Much like my conversation with Raul Perez minus the fricasseed legs.

"I'm an artist, Adeline. I never do the same thing twice. No, I've come up with something special for Marlon here," I said. "I've spent the last couple hours going through his computer, safe, and records. It turns out our friend here has been very naughty.

"He's been embezzling from Pais's club, running a side drug business, and—" I hesitated, knowing Adeline wouldn't take this well. "He aided Corbin in his sex-trafficking racket. There is a record of payments in his accounts, totaling three hundred grand for 'special items.'"

"I see."

"Considering this information." I stood before Marlon. "I am giving him two options. If he refuses to tell me what I need to know, I'll kill him, leave evidence pointing to Pais as the killer, and release everything I've dug up. His kids will discover on the six o'clock news that their father is a child-selling, pedophile-supplying drug dealer."

Marlon's sobs leaked through the gag.

"Or he gives up the information, I frame Pais for his murder, and the cops don't discover what I found during their investigation. He dies either way, but at least if he goes with option two, people will come to his funeral."

"I must say, you give the best gifts."

"Good enough for me to make you dinner tomorrow night?"

"Now it's dinner?" she teased.

"Dinner, conversation, etcetera. I'm an incredible cook."

"I—"

A bang broke through the speaker. "Bunny? Who are you talking to?"

"Jasper," she said without hesitation.

"Hang up."

"Are you ready to listen to me?"

"Are you ready for that ass to be spanked raw?" Sinjin returned.

"Yes."

"Hang up the phone."

"I have to go, Jasper. Believe it or not, Thiago Pais is not the worst thing we're dealing with."

I chose a knife from my collection. "What happened?"

"Gianna took— Hey!" Sounds of a scuffle. "Saint!"

The line went dead.

Shaking my head, I tossed my cell on Marlon's couch.

"So," I began, "which option are we going with?"

ADELINE

"Saint!"

Sinjin hung up and tossed my phone somewhere over his shoulder. He was wholly unrepentant, blocking me from getting to it.

"Those glares turn lesser men into cinders, Bunny. That's why you traded up for me," he said. "You were about to tell Croix that Gianna gave up Katz's name. For all we know, that's who he's really working for."

"I was not," I cried. "I was going to say Gianna *took off*. End of sentence. I wouldn't talk to anyone about you and Katz before we've figured out what to do. We're talking about killing the freaking governor."

"We're not talking about it." Saint put his fist through the wall. "We're doing it! Now! Let's go!"

"We can't." Killian stormed in. "We can't go after a guy like Katz without a plan, Sinjin. The governor's mansion is locked down tight. There are cameras and guards on every exit or entrance—"

"Let them try to stop me." A wild, insane rage in his eyes brought me back to the night of Raiden Spencer. "They'll have as much luck as you."

Saint charged him. I was suddenly in his path.

I wrapped my legs around his waist, holding him snarling to my chest.

"Saint, you said you wanted us to do this together. I hold him down. You cut out his heart." His heaving chest pushed me away. I kissed his blue strands. "If we go off half-cocked, we'll be in prison by the end of the night. You didn't wait twenty years to watch Nicolas Katz conceal his smirk during the press conference while he thanks the Cinco police for their swift action arresting the fugitive Merchant leader who attacked him unprovoked.

"We don't just want him dead, baby. We'll make sure no one goes to his funeral." I spoke Jasper's words without thinking. "All of Cinco will know exactly who Nicolas Katz is and what he's done." I raised his head and pressed a kiss to unsmiling lips. "What better revenge than him dying knowing the secrets he killed your father to keep are trending on every news app?"

Sinjin was silent for a long time.

"Alright, Bunny. You have my attention. I'll try things your way," he said to me and Killian. "Katz doesn't live past the end of this month. Understood?"

"Understood and agreed with," I replied.

Sinjin put me on my feet. "Pack your stuff. Edie's arranged a place for us to stay. We leave in twenty minutes."

There was no good reason to argue with him. Too many people were after us. We had to change locations and stay ahead of this fight before it ambushed us in the street.

I packed up my things with half a mind on the task. The other half was on Nicolas Katz.

I didn't have to scout his place to know security would be tight. His position aside, a man who'd done the things he has would have reason to be paranoid. His systems would be the best on the market. His guards well-paid and put through vigorous checks. Not to mention the manhunt there'd be for his killer.

The police were already looking for Sinjin, the Slasher, and his associates. They'd get their asses in gear for Sinjin, the governor's assassin.

Wonder if Katz has men looking for Gianna Cross and the ledger? He must be. He knows what it says about him, especially if Kierans have been blackmailing him with the information for years.

Years, I thought.

That's how long he's had to create contingencies for his contingencies. Destroy evidence trails. Kill people who know too much. Dig up the buried bodies.

This man must get a hundred threats before breakfast. Coming at him with a "we know what you did" won't get us far.

But once you know what a man wants, you're halfway to owning him.

Katz wants the ledger. The plan Jasper has for Lombard might work just as well on him. Lure him free of his tower using the ledger and lay the trap.

The only problem is I don't have the ledger.

I flicked to my phone, resting innocently on the pillow.

The first thing Gianna will do is assess the problems in her way. She'll need to get into the Fairfield and get out again, skipping over the capture and imprisonment by Pais's men.

That'll mean a sniper's nest. Somewhere she can observe the situation from afar. Once she had what she needed, maybe she would call me. Killing Thiago Pais was the perfect Christmas gift, but nothing had changed. Now more than ever I needed the ledger to put things right.

Decades ago, three men created a book that changed the course of Cinco City's future. From here on, I take the wheel.

Picking up the phone, I emailed Gianna. I had no way of knowing if she was checking the account, or if she'd respond, but I typed out my message. I said Dad missed her and hoped to see her soon. I told her we were leaving the loft, so if something happened, call and I would tell her where to find me. I asked after her foot, told her she didn't have to go after Pais alone, and finished asking for more information on Nicolas Katz.

My finger hovered over send. I couldn't describe the state we were in now.

She apologized. She made an effort to earn my trust back, and still is—going after Pais and ending the manhunt for me. I couldn't answer yet if it was enough to put us right. I didn't have any answers.

I just wanted to talk to her.

"Adeline."

I jumped.

Brutal reached around me and zipped my bag. "Time to go."

"I'm ready."

I hit send.

There was another car waiting for us by the curb. No need to ask if this one was stolen or gifted from one of the men. I wasn't asking much of anything. My mind was preoccupied.

Do not underestimate him.

For Gianna to say that, carried weight. Not that I didn't believe my father and his warnings about the man. It had been years since he went up against Nicolas Katz, whereas Gianna went against him today and clearly ran into a wall she thought too big to scale.

Baris kissed my cheek, bringing me out of my reverie.

I hadn't noticed we stopped.

"Where are we?"

A cute rowhouse with flower boxes in the windows looked back at me. A leftover Christmas wreath hung on the door, and little gnome statues lined the steps—waving, winking, or smiling at people passing by.

"Edie's sister rents this place during the winter," Saint said. "She's between tenants and Edie convinced her to let us stay."

"As long as it has a kitchen and a bed, that's all I need." I stuck my head through the seats. Saint was still to the kisses I dropped on his jaw. "Why don't I make your favorite tonight? Glazed pork chops with roasted potatoes."

"I won't stop you."

Together, the four of us gathered our things and went inside.

A musty smell hit us in the face. Too long shut up without fresh air, the lingering scents of cat urine and mothballs had time to collect into a powerful combination. I went around opening the windows.

A clean, old-fashioned living room complete with fireplace, floral-patterned sofas, and china dolls judging me from their spot on the mantle. Then into the modest, linoleum kitchen before going upstairs to check out the three bedrooms and bathroom.

"Small but perfect," I said to Saint as he came in behind me. "Thank Edie for me."

He grunted something.

"I'm going to order groceries. Dinner will be ready in a couple of hours."

Saint stretched out on the floral sheets, resting his head among the dolls sharing his pillow. I left him as he pulled his knife, flipping it on his palm.

I couldn't imagine what was going on in his head, though I knew it couldn't be far off from Nicolas Katz. For years he's searched for the man who killed his father only to find out the death that destroyed his life hadn't touched Katz at all. He sailed through the last twenty years collecting riches, respect, and elections. He wasn't a suspect in this crime or any other.

No one was going to stop him. Until us.

I walked in on Killian in the kitchen.

He made himself at home fast. Laptop in front of him and papers spread out on the table. He was back to work while his bags littered the living room carpet.

"How bad is it?" I asked.

I browsed GreenEats for my grocery delivery. I wouldn't be roaming the streets anytime soon.

"Can't say for certain," he replied. "I've got Diego on hacking the security system. I'll scope out the governor's mansion, though my gut says we shouldn't bother."

"What do you mean?"

"Trying to take him at the mansion will be difficult. His children are all grown and out of the house, so we wouldn't have to worry about them, but even with just the governor and his wife living there, the place will be locked down tight. We're better off grabbing him at another location. En route probably. Armed guards are one thing. Armed guards, security systems, and triggered alarms are another."

"What about his love cabin in Elmshire Woods? I doubt he has cameras and fifty guards tracking his every move up there."

"We'd have to know in advance when he'd be there. And that's assuming he still uses that place," Killian reminded. "Your dad's been out of the game for years."

"My dad is the game," I replied, receiving a snort. "But you have a point. Seems to me we need someone to get close to Katz and—"

"No."

"I didn't even finish the sentence, Cash."

"We're not calling in Croix."

"Right now, Jasper is torturing one of Pais's crew to find out where the man is and stop him for good. He hasn't walked away from us completely."

"He's not doing that for us. He's doing it for you."

"Everything you guys do is for me." That got a louder snort. "Your wants and needs are aligned. Why not work together?"

Killian rose from the table and trapped me against the counter, arms locking me in on both sides. "Croix says he's working for Lombard. Maybe he is, maybe he isn't. Either way, he's not working for *us*. I'm not doing a job with a man who has divided loyalties."

"Jasper wants the ledger," I said. "Katz does not have the ledger. What would he gain by sabotaging us? It wouldn't get him any closer to Gianna or the book. All I'm saying is we have a man who can't keep it in his pants, and a former escort who knows everything that goes on in this city. I don't think we can afford to leave Jasper out of this, Cash. We'll need to tap all the skills we have to get close to Governor Katz."

"We don't need him."

"Well, we need someone." I hooked my fingers behind his neck. "Are you dusting off your grifter side, toy boy? I'd love to see you in action again."

"Would you?" He lifted me onto the counter, grinding his growing erection in my middle. "What is it about me lying through my teeth that turns you on?"

"Who knows? It's something I'll work out in therapy one day," I breezed.

Killian tangled in my hair. He bent my head back, licking a stripe up my throat that chased out a sigh.

"I can tell you right now. You love yourself a lying, scheming, deadly bastard. They go down harder."

"Speaking of going down." His chuckle tickled my skin. "Are we picking up where we left off?"

"Remind me."

"I believe your hand was somewhere around here." I guided him under my bra. "And mine was... here?" I smacked his ass.

"Close." The sound of his zipper going down teased my ears. "Pretty sure you were here."

He wrapped me around him. Killian's nose skimmed my chin, traveling up to my forehead where he left a kiss.

My phone chimed, signaling my grocery order was on the way.

Killian shoved it off the counter and into the trash. He swallowed my protest.

Muscles wound as he slipped through my waistband. I couldn't help it. Just being in the same room with Killian Hunt made me tight with anticipation. A band squeezed my chest. My fists balled. My pulse raced. Every part of my body held still for Cash to take and set me free.

He matched my pace. Slowly probing to my languid strokes, then picking up speed as my tugs grew urgent and jerky—losing control as he spurred me on.

Killian nudged my legs wider. I moaned as a third finger joined the party, spreading me past full.

Another chime from the trash bin—a text this time.

It barely penetrated the fog descending on me. I'd been coiled and ready since our interrupted tryst in the gardens. Nothing was distracting me from Killian.

He thrust in my hand and nudged his own deeper. This is what it was to be perfectly in tune. I felt his heart pounding before I laid my head on his chest, listening to the effect I had on him.

Thump, thump, thud, thud, thump.

No one could get his heart racing but me. I darkened his eyes to molten pools of black. I prickled sweat on his brow and shattered his cool mask to pieces. The real question wasn't why I was drawn to them. It was how did cold, hard Cash fall before the harmless chef.

He angled his finger, striking that spot dead-on.

I nearly fell off the counter. "Holy shit! Stop playing with me, Killian."

You haven't known true evil until you beheld this smirk. "You got a problem? Do something about it."

"I fucking swear, I both want to kill you and be with you for the rest of my life, every minute of every day. It makes for a very confusing existence."

Killian pecked my lips. "I just want to be with you."

His husky voice curled inside me, drawing heat on my skin. I positioned Killian at my entrance, stroking beads of precum to the tip. "This is the kind of thing I'm talking about. Don't be sweet when I'm mad at you."

"Don't be mad at me"—he pushed in with one smooth thrust—"when I'm fucking you."

Trapping his gaze, I tugged his hand up my chest, pulling the hem over my breasts, and placing his fingers on my lips. Killian stiffened. A low hiss escaped his throat as my mouth covered him to the knuckles, sucking every drop of me clean.

"You understand what this means, don't you?"

I giggled. "Gentle, tender lovemaking?"

"Fuck no."

Killian's thrust knocked my head on the cabinet. I ducked under, bending in half, heels digging on the outdated countertop.

Cash slipped free of my mouth. He painted an "x" on my eyelids.

"Look." He grasped the back of my neck, tilting me up. "You're going to watch."

My body contracted, squeezing down on him, and me seeing the result.

Cash treated me to the unobstructed view of his cock plunging in and out of my hungry pussy. I said his was more attractive than average. Well, right then it was the most gorgeous thing I'd ever seen. Hard and glistening with my need for him.

I came on the spot—jerking and screaming myself hoarse. I flopped half in the sink.

"Damn," I breathed. "We're really good at this. Why do we ever leave the bedroom? Or kitchen."

"Lessons to teach." He tugged me up by the shirt, indulging a sloppy kiss. "Cities to rule."

The waste bin sang a tune.

"That's our food," I giggled, skipping away from grabbing fingers. "Don't you want to eat sometime tonight?"

"What else do I need to eat but your pussy?"

Heaven's sake, I'm marrying this man.

Killian did not let me get dressed and leave easily. He peeled my clothes off as I put them on, and bent me over the table when I tried to make a run for it, squealing as I was lifted and carried back. Finally, I went out and rescued our food from the stoop. The delivery guy had long since left.

Killian took his laptop into the living room. The television spoke on low, adding background noise to my prepping, cutting, and seasoning.

My brown sugar pork chops were simmering on low when my phone went off again.

Jasper Croix flashed on the screen.

I peeked in the living room. Killian was preoccupied. Nothing short of stripping down would get his attention—yes, I've done that many times to drag that man away from his computer and return his focus on me where I liked it.

"Hello?"

"Why are you whispering?"

"Why do you think? I'm about to put my sweet and spicy peace pork chops in the oven. They never fail to defuse a tense situation, but this is tenser than most. Better we don't add fuel to the fire."

"We," he repeated. "I like you saying we."

"It's too soon for flirting, Jasper."

"It wasn't too soon earlier."

"You should expect me to be very inconsistent while my feelings for you flip-flop like a sun-drenched trout on the beach."

He laughed. "You're nothing if not honest, Redgrave."

"It's a new personality trait. Still finding my balance between unapologetically blunt and cagey."

"Are you at the loft?"

"No, we left today. The pharmacy shoot-out is streaming on the cell of everyone I pass by. But we have bigger things to worry about than Thiago Pais."

Jasper's voice changed. "I wouldn't be so certain of that."

I paused opening the oven. "You got something from Thibodeaux."

"I got *nothing* from Thibodeaux, Adeline, which is worse. He feared Pais's wrath from beyond the grave more than he did the truth about him coming out."

"Thiago Pais slices people up and leaves them to bleed out in the cold. You said he had children. I assume he rather they curse their father than receive Pais's punishment in his place."

"I assume so too," he replied. "Doesn't look good for the present I wanted to give you. The opposite, I'm calling with a warning. Marlon died laughing through his tears. He said the ledger would be Pais's in a matter of days, and I should get to work kissing his ass. I'll want to be on his good side."

"A matter of days? But Gianna's gone. He doesn't know where she is, neither does he know where to find me. What has his cronies so sure he's about to win?"

"Be careful. Pais is a rare type of criminal. Charming, likable, and sometimes even kind. Thiago isn't controlled by ego. He has a steady hold over his bloodlust that you don't see in most leaders. Angelo, Lorenzo, or Corbin would've snatched you at the tournament matches and left your tortured screams on Cross's voicemail to get that ledger.

"Pais was patient. He waited for Leah Tyler to build trust, get close, and then slipped away at her call. If the match hadn't ended early, you'd still be frantically searching for the ledger while Pais grinned across the aisle, the picture of innocence. He's the only devil I've met that doesn't want people to know it. He has too much fun hiding behind his mask."

"Ugh." I shivered. "I don't know what's worse—the monster masquerading as the gentleman, or the beast finally taking the mask off. Either way, we'll be careful."

"I offer again for you to stay with me. No one will get to you here."

"That's not possible right now, Jasper."

"The longer you're away from me, the easier it gets to say no. I'm not letting you go, Adeline. I'll tear through every layer I've built. I'll place you on a throne of my broken lives and worship you till I finally crumble into nothing. I'll reduce your body into quivering orgasms, round your belly with my babies, and prove love truly is the most destructive force on this planet. But what I will not do is make it easy for you to let me go."

"I—" The words faded on my tongue. What was there to say in response to that? The most eloquent speaker on earth would stand dumbfounded.

"You are mine, Adeline Redgrave. There's nothing either of us can do about it now. So, what time should I pick you up for dinner tomorrow?"

"I... can do seven o'clock," I rasped.

"Seven it is. I love you."

His confession ended the call and released his hold. I fell on the dining table, breathing hard.

Why did I say yes?

We were about to undertake the deadliest hit of our lives. Saint was in a dangerous headspace, and simply walking outside could force a choice between death on the sidewalk or capture by the Kings.

I had no doubt the story between Adeline Redgrave and Jasper Croix would be an epic one. We just weren't ready for it yet.

Which is what I have to tell him. My thumb inched up my screen. *Call him.*

I set the phone on the table. Sinking low in my seat, I shut my eyes.

I couldn't call him. I hadn't been away from Jasper long enough to say no.

"Adeline." I opened to Saint leaning on the doorframe. "Is that my dinner burning on the stove?"

"Shit!"

I rushed to turn off the heat. My peace pork chops were charred rounds of meat in the frying pan.

"Sorry," I said. "Dinner's going to be another half an hour."

"Tell me what to do. I'll help." Sinjin rescued the last package of chops from the fridge.

"You will?"

Sinjin cocked a brow. "Do I detect a tone of surprise? Acting like I'm not a modern gentleman."

"I've never seen you so much as boil an egg in the months we've been living together."

"That's your fault."

"How?"

"Every time I think about coming down and helping you cook, I get distracted by your ass. See? Your fault."

I rolled my eyes, inwardly pleased he sounded like his old self. "What am I supposed to think now? You're helping because my ass is losing its effect?"

"I'm helping so I get some food in me sometime this decade. I'll resume playing with that ass upstairs."

"Seems fair." I snagged a kiss while his good mood was going. "I'll do the prep, you do the cooking. This time I'm lazing around and ogling you."

Saint and I kept up a light banter while we worked. I wanted to broach the topic of Nicolas Katz, tell him what I've been thinking could get us closer to him.

I kept it to myself for the time being. Soon we'd be sitting down to discuss the man who had brought us all to this moment. When you think about it, if Nicolas Katz hadn't sent those men into Saint's church, he wouldn't have ended up in Merriman Circus hunting for loose change, but truly looking for a family.

Kieran affected the Hunts through different circumstances, though I had to ask myself if Killian grew up and made the same choice to form the Merchants to pay the blackmail money, would he have the same reaction as Saint when he found a witness hiding in a bathroom? Owing to how open he was about getting rid of me in the beginning, the answer is no.

Katz cast a long shadow over countless lives. Maybe as long as Kieran's, and no one could deny the damage.

No, we couldn't avoid the conversation about Governor Katz. Even so, I'd give Sinjin an hour to cook, joke, and swat my bottom every time I turned around.

I hip-checked him to the side, bending to stick the potatoes in the oven. "What's for dessert?"

"You have a choice between caramel shortbread pie and Oreo cheesecake?"

"The choice is yours, Bunny. I'll be eating it off you."

"Caramel, please. The cheesecake will be cold."

Saint caught me on the way to the fridge. He pressed my back to him, tucking my head under his chin. "Say it."

"Say what?"

"You've been holding yourself back from saying something for half the day. Go on."

I relaxed in his arms. "Stop pretending like you read my mind."

"Who's pretending?"

"I was thinking," I began, choosing my words. "It's been decades since Nicolas Katz became the first entry in the ledger. I doubt the Kierans that came after were able to resist blackmailing the mayor and now governor of the city. Still, it hasn't slowed him down. If anything, they've probably prepared him for all we could throw at him. This isn't going to be easy."

"Never thought it would be."

My finger traced small circles on his skin. "You're not going to do what you're thinking, are you? Going off and killing him yourself."

"Why would I be thinking that?"

"I know you, Saint. Doing this together was the plan when we thought we were looking for another Angelo or Pais. Someone very few people would miss. A death the police would secretly dub the trash taking out itself, and put zero to no effort into finding his killer. We weren't expecting a governor of the United States, and now you're imagining me in a real cage—locked up with no chance of parole.

"Don't do it, Saint. Don't give me one last night of cooking together and kinky sex only to leave me sleeping in bed while you slip out into the dark. I know this revenge is yours, not mine. I know taking him out will be next to impossible. I know all of that," I said. "But I also know you promised me and Sole a future. Nicolas Katz stole your life and family once. Do not let him do it again."

"You give a hell of a speech, Bunny."

I turned to him. "Tell me I didn't need to say it."

Sinjin lifted his gaze, looking somewhere over my shoulder. "What if I agree with you? Katz will not get another chance to destroy my family. That's why I have to do this alone."

"Wouldn't work," I murmured.

"Why is that?"

"Because I'd hunt you down. I'd level the city coming after you. I'd become Katz's second shadow, following him around waiting for you to show up. Not only would this sacrificial lamb routine not work, but it would seriously piss me off."

Saint chuckled. "I better stick around, then."

"Yes, you better."

That night, after he enjoyed his dessert in bed, I cuffed Saint to the metal frame just in case.

His laugh shook his chest as I shut off the light and snuggled on top of him. "Good night."

"Night."

THE NEXT MORNING, I woke alone in bed. The cuffs lay neatly on the pillow.

Mocking me.

"Saint?" I shot up. "Saint! When I get my hands on you, I'll—"

"—give me the blow job of my life?" The door swung open, revealing Saint holding a breakfast tray. "That's what you were going to say, right?"

I eased onto the pillows, eyeing the apparition suspiciously. "Yes," I said slowly. "That's what I was going to say. What have you got there?"

"Breakfast. We're heading out early today to scope out the governor's mansion. Killian passed on your wisdom that his fuck shack will have less security. We'll check it out too, but it's unlikely to be our target since we don't know when he'll be there."

"There's also the capitol building."

My love and I reclined in bed, chatting our assassination plot over eggs, toast, and jam.

"It sounds like suicide, but hear me out," I said. "At his mansion, Katz can install the best security money can buy and stuff the place full of bodyguards. In the capitol, he's got the state-funded security cameras and a million people going about their business, they won't notice a young woman in another pantsuit sneaking into his office."

"Getting in won't be the problem. Getting you out after I've gutted him may prove to be difficult."

"Getting *us* out," I corrected.

"Isn't that what I said?" he replied, light and breezy.

"I mentioned this to Killian—"

"No," he sliced in. "We don't need Croix dropping his pants around the city to dig up information on Katz. We carried out jobs before him. We'll do it now that he's gone."

"Fine, I'm not going to push it. But if it turns out the capitol and the mansion are out, we'll need to find when he's making his next trip into the woods."

"If you do get into his office, it'll be to bug his phone. Croix left his bugs behind when he fled like a smacked horse's ass." Saint nodded. "Yeah, I like it. We'll scope out the capitol today too."

"Alright. There's just one thing." I popped a slice of toast in his mouth. "I have to be back in time for my dinner with Jasper tonight."

The toast fell to the plate—my distraction foiled.

"Bunny, are you trying to see how far you can push me before you're the one handcuffed to this bed?"

"No, I'm trying to figure out if there's anything left to the feelings I still have for him. I wish I could turn it off as easily as you believe it should be." I grasped his jaw. "It's not that simple, Saint. As much as I love you, is as much as I loved Mercer."

"Mercer never existed."

"Don't you think I've told myself that a hundred times! I know he's a different man who's done nothing but lie to me since the day we met, but there isn't a switch that I turn off and months of loving him just goes a-away." My throat clogged with emotion. "He may give me a reason to go looking for that switch. Until then, he's a man who has committed the same sins as me and is asking for the same chance to make it right."

"How is this different from Cross?" he flung.

"It's completely different. I knew whatever happened between me and Gianna, eventually she'd wake up and remember what's important. With Jasper Croix, I can't see how this will end. I just can't help feeling I'll regret it if I don't find out."

Sinjin picked his toast back up. "Okay."

"Okay?"

"Yep. I get it. You need closure before you dump him for good."

"That's not exactly what I said," I muttered.

"Go ahead, Adeline. See for yourself he's a blank personality in an Armani suit. He has nothing to offer you than a lifetime trying to feel the emotions he deadened years ago. Jasper Croix will drive you away all on his own."

Seemed better to leave it there, so I did.

We finished our breakfast, then dressed and went down to meet the guys.

I had them hang back, idling in the car while I reported what I found to Killian through the phone. The Cinco underground was after me, but *everyone* was after them. At least if the governor recognized me, he wouldn't send his men to chase me down and shoot up a city block.

The capitol building was easy. The first floor was open to all who passed through the metal detectors. No areas were roped off. Instead, cameras did their sweep and I counted five guards patrolling the top floor.

I didn't come this far to go home playing guessing games.

I climbed the stairs, searching for the executive office building. They wouldn't let me in to find out where, still, the governor's space would be in there.

On the third floor, I spotted the frosted glass bearing my sign and the two guards next to its door. I strolled past without a glance, typing on my phone.

Killian started the car when I came into view. I slid in and we took off just like that.

"What are we looking at?"

"Heavy on the guards, but this is Cinco," I said. "Anyone who thinks this is the land of rainbows and bunnies has never been here."

"Cameras?"

"Full three-sixty sweep. No gaps in the coverage."

"Where's his office?" Saint asked.

"Third floor. There are two guards watching the entrance. Easy enough to take out, but the rest would be on us long before we got to the governor. I still say our best play is the clueless new intern bumbling around on her first day, and asking the lady-loving Katz to show her the way."

"We'll see," Cash said. "I still need word from Diego."

Our next stop was the governor's mansion.

We did one sweep around the place—careful not to drive too slowly or make it obvious I was snapping pictures as we went by.

Nicolas Katz's home was on the outskirts of the city where you could have three-story homes and a yard to put them on. Any farther and we hit woods.

The place was a colonial-style home with pillars, and white columns holding up the third-floor balcony. The mansion was ancient. The beefy men and cameras hanging over every entrance were not.

"Last is the cabin," I said. "Chances it's as well-monitored as this?"

"Can't say," Killian admitted. "Probability leans toward him not wanting cameras recording his activities up there. He's no stranger to blackmail, so why dangle the temptation in front of his guards?"

I bobbed my head. "Webber should have taught him that lesson."

"Cameras outside," Sinjin said. "Checking who is trying to get on his property who shouldn't be there. Possibly none on the inside."

"We won't know until we check," I said. "I see now why Mercer being invited right through the door made this part so much easier."

"There are other ways to recon," Cash replied. "Give me a few days to dig up blueprints and research his team for weak links. I have a profile on Katz, but it's surface. I started it when you told us he paid your father to become mayor. He can help me fill in the rest of the details."

"We're not waiting around while you chart his astrological sign, and if he prefers whips or chains," Saint snapped.

"Yes, we are." Cash was cool in the face of his brother's shifting moods as always. "Without a complete profile, we're going in blind. Risk your girlfriend's life, not mine. Oh shit—we have the same one."

"Everyone's so sweet worrying about me." I draped Baris's arm around my shoulder. "We all know I'm most likely going to be the one saving your asses by the end of this."

"We are notoriously helpless," Saint said, making me laugh. "Play with your profile, Kill. We take him at the end of the month—complete or not."

The end of the month.

That gave us sixteen days exactly. And we spent one day admitting we didn't know enough to make a plan.

But we will. All that matters is that St. John doesn't run off and do this alone. If we stand a chance, it's only by doing this together.

We parked on the side of the street leading to Elmshire Woods and pulled up the coordinates my dad gave me.

"There's definitely a cabin there." I honed tighter on the satellite picture. "It's not as deep in the woods as I was expecting. Down a private road, but there's a public trail a mile and a half away." I looked to Brutal. "We could be a hiking couple who got lost if we run into any guards."

"If they're experienced, they'll ask for your names and ID before giving you directions back," Cash said.

"We need guys we're not using for the hit to do the lost routine," Sinjin added. "Put Lucky and Petey on it. Tell 'em we want the whole area mapped in the next three days."

I checked the time. It was almost five. I needed to get back and start getting ready.

"Are we keeping you from your date, Bunny?"

Cash's and Brutal's heads snapped up.

"Date?" Cash asked. "What date?"

"Jasper is making me dinner. He says it's my chance to fill in the rest of those blanks—discuss everything else I don't know about him."

"You're not going out with him alone."

"Why? Because he forgot to murder me the last time he had me completely at his mercy, and tonight he might remember he has the option?"

"Because we don't trust him," Baris said simply.

"I get that, but you should know, he hasn't stopped being a Merchant. Jasper questioned one of Pais's men last night. No details, but he's planning something. A move Pais thinks will have the ledger in his hands in a matter of days."

The guys shared a look.

"Chances he found out where Cross ran off to?" Sinjin asked.

"None." There wasn't a doubt in my mind. "Gianna is a sniper. With the exception of me, no one sees her until it's too late."

"Then, it's you. Pais is planning something to draw you out."

Grudgingly, I nodded. I came to the same conclusion. "I don't know what that could be. He's researched me. He knows where I worked and went to school. A deep enough dive, he'll find out my dad's name, but it's not like he's easy to track down, and Pais would deeply regret it if he did. I'm told the only other weaknesses I have are you." I kissed Brutal's cheek. "That's why I'm keeping you close by."

"That's why you should be close by," Cash said. "Instead of fucking around town with Croix. Someone saw you last time."

"I'll be careful." I climbed inside the car. "Don't stalk me," I warned Cash.

"If you don't see me, I wasn't there."

I could not tell if he was joking.

It was three not pleased men who drove me back to the doll-and-flower rowhouse and hovered as I chose an outfit, dressed, slipped on my shoes, and stuck their dinner in the oven.

Cash sat in the kitchen, writing in a new binder. The expert he was at multitasking, he planned a hit on the governor and bore a hole in the back of my head at the same time.

"Does this really bother you?" My potato and sausage bake browned golden in the oven. "Is Jasper going to come between us?"

"Would you dump him if I said yes?"

"Would you say yes to make me dump him?"

"Come here."

I perched on the table, resting my feet between his legs, and letting out a soft noise as they received a massage.

"What you felt for Mercer, I know you can't just turn it off," he said. "Eat his dinners. Go for his rides. If he is truly done playing the part, the real Croix is all that's left, and you don't love him. Eventually, you'll end it with him on your own, and you won't resent us for it after."

I pulled away, returning to the oven.

I wasn't mad at him. Honestly, I couldn't fault him for believing this thing with Jasper would fizzle all on its own. Already I was seeing the difference between the man I fell in love with and the one I was starting to know. And the first man didn't have lies and deception in his strike column.

My phone beeped seconds after my oven timer.

It was time to leave and meet Jasper.

"Dinner's ready." I swooped in for a kiss. "I love you."

"Where are you meeting him? I'll drive you."

"No, it's okay. It's not far."

I left the kitchen and was intercepted by Brutal and Sinjin in the living room. Saying bye to them slowed me going out the door. It was minutes to seven when I hit the stoop and made for the end of the street.

There was a basketball court two streets down. Jasper's car was parked beside the entrance. The door opened as I came into view.

My breath caught.

Six feet of hard, ropy muscle poured into a suit as light-stealing as the darkening sky. He slicked his hair back, and the unobstructed sight of those new eyes bowled me over.

"Evening." Jasper placed a single orange rose on my palm. "You're beautiful."

I didn't know what to wear for dinner at his place. What toed the line of elegant without screaming toss me on the floor? In the end I went with a fit and flare dress that tied on the shoulder with cute blue bows. I went simple with the shoes and chose matching blue boots.

I buried my nose in the flower. "Thank you."

"Change of plan." Jasper rested his hand on the small of my back, burning a print in the fabric. "We're not going back to my apartment."

"We're not?"

"No. I figured while I have you to myself, I'll do this properly."

"'Dinner and a movie' properly? I'm not sure how safe it is for us to be out. You're still a sketch on the Cinco PD station wall, and I've got Pais and an irate pharmacist after me."

Jasper opened my side, leaning on the door and motioning me in. "Neither will get to you tonight. Trust me."

"There's that word."

"Obey me?"

I swatted his arm. "Going the wrong way."

"Bet me, then," he said, chuckling. "If I don't drop you off in this spot whole and blissfully postcoital, you choose where we go on our next date."

Closing the distance, a smile played on my lips. "I'm seeing how this bet is win-win for you, but what do I get out of it?"

"Did you miss the part where I said blissfully postcoital?"

I nipped his bottom lip. "If this night ends with us running through the streets or me knowing less than absolutely everything about you, you come with me to see the guys. Talk it out. Apologize."

Jasper's eyes were unreadable black pools. "I have nothing to apologize for. I did what I had to do to protect my daughter, and I didn't harm a single one of them doing it."

"Those are my terms."

"Alright. Whatever you want, Adeline."

He says the right things, but still I can't guess what he's thinking.

I climbed in the car and let him close it after me. A heavenly smell hit my nose. Riding in the back seat were two large, fluffy blankets and a picnic basket.

"Wow, Jasper. What did you make?"

"Fresh bread, smoked duck and vegetable rolls, tomato ricotta tart, caprese salad, and warm nut brownies."

"Sounds delicious. Are you worried about serving your dishes up to my refined palate?" I teased.

"I will more than satisfy you, Adeline Redgrave."

I bit my lip, hiding a smile. This man played the seduction game at expert level. I had to be on guard or I would be dropped off missing my underwear and smelling like his cedarwood Creed cologne.

Would that be so bad? a traitorous voice supplied.

See? It's already starting.

"How should we do this?" I spoke up. "I don't want tonight to be an interrogation. I want us to get to know each other in a real way."

"We'll just talk, Adeline. We don't have to put more pressure on it."

"Okay." I flicked to the back. "When did you learn to cook?"

"I lived in Paris for a year, tracking down an embezzler that bankrupted a small company and left fifty families with nothing. The cops weren't close to finding him or recovering the money. The former CEO was getting raked by the media. His wife left him and took their kids. No one believed he wasn't in on the theft. They assumed he was biding his time before he hopped on a plane to Belize.

"He got ahold of my name, hired me to recover the money, and deliver the punishment he felt fifty ruined lives deserved."

"It took you a year to find him?"

"It took me a month to find him. Sixteenth arrondissement—living in the richest neighborhood in the city. I trained under a chef. Arranged for his personal cook to receive a better job offer, got hired for the opening, and used my access to discover where he hid the money. After it was returned and he was dead, I stayed on for another eight months, cooking and living in the apartment he used for his mistress."

Jasper turned on Holly Street. The quiet neighborhood fell away, and shops and restaurants filled the window. By my guess, we were going to a park. Jasper had plenty to choose from in Cinco.

"Did your job take you out of the country often?"

"No. Mexico a few times. Once to Costa Rica."

I hummed. "So you figured, while you're in Paris you might as well enjoy it. Lucky for me. I can't wait to try what's in that basket."

Did I sound normal? I was going for normal and shooting *trying too hard* on the bull's eye.

My skin prickled to a million ants marching beneath the surface. I kept shifting in my seat, changing from looking at him, to looking out the window, to turning to him because it was strange to not face your date.

I didn't know where to put my hands, which part of his story to question, or if I should ask him more about work when I wanted to know about him. But if I didn't let the conversation flow naturally, I wasn't exactly keeping the pressure off.

I was jacked up on first-date nerves for a man I'd been dating for months. It was strange and there was pressure.

A lot of freaking pressure.

"Adeline—"

"I know what you're going to say," I broke in. "Just ask what I want to ask. But this isn't easy, Jasper. It feels like you woke from a coma with amnesia, and I'm sitting at your bedside with pictures and stories, trying to convince you I fit into your life."

"I would've thought it the other way around." He pressed his lips to the back of my hand. "It'd help us both if we stopped looking at it like I have to fit into a Mercer-shaped hole. May help even more if you thought of it in a different way."

"Like how?"

"We get to fall in love with each other again."

"Mercer used to do that," I whispered. "Say exactly what I needed to hear."

"He got his people skills from me."

I snorted. Clapping my hand over my mouth, my giggles leaked out. I'd say something for Jasper Croix. He made me laugh.

"Okay, here goes. Regular first-date conversation. Tell me about your family."

"Don't have a clue who they are. I was brought into Sinai General Hospital in Illinois when I was a few days old. I was surrendered without questioning. I couldn't tell you if the guy who handed me over was my father or someone who found me behind a bus station.

"The woman who ran the orphanage grew fond of me. She sabotaged attempts to adopt me."

"She what?"

He shrugged. "Sometimes the truth is stranger than lies. Her favoring of me grew obvious. I got away with more. She bought me expensive presents on my birthday. Snuck me cake and extra helpings. Once I was old enough, I connected her behavior to how odd it was none of my adoption interviews amounted to anything."

My jaw worked for a minute. "Were you... angry with her?"

"No, if you can believe it. She never abused or hurt me. Actually, Nina was so desperate for me to love her as a mother, she treated me like a prince. It's hard to be resentful of someone who wants to make you happy."

"Do you keep in touch with her?"

"She died when I was sixteen."

"Oh," I said softly. "And by then, all the couples who wanted a sweet, little baby dried up."

"They did."

"So, Rosie and us. Were we your first real family?"

"You could say that," he replied. "Nina left me everything she had. I used the money to move out here and pay for tuition."

"Why Cinco City of all places? We don't come off well in the news reports."

He cracked a grin. "It's the kind of place someone can get lost in."

"Start over."

"Exactly." Jasper took his eyes off the road. "What about you? Jealousy was coming off you in waves when I said I trained as a chef in Paris."

"It did not," I cried, semi-convincingly.

"You want to see more of this world, Adeline. Why do you stay in Cinco?"

"Cinco City is two personalities. Cherry blossom festivals in Mercy Park. The candy apple street fair down Main. Wandering through Old Leighbridge. Enough gangs and crime families to rival New York. Highest overdose deaths in the country. The entire city is a chessboard manipulated by shadow kings.

"Cinco is me, Jasper. The best and worst version of itself all at once. It's the only place a person like me belongs."

"Eh, I don't know. I could see you lying naked on my chaise in our Paris apartment, playing with yourself while I feed you homemade pissaladière."

"Is that what you see?"

"As clear as if I already had you out of those blue bows and boots."

I laughed. "As appealing as that sounds, Paris isn't my dream. I've had this idea about Bora Bora or Bali ever since I learned about them. Warm, green, and sandy. Everything Cinco denies me."

"Making love to you on white-sand beaches? It is now my life mission to make that happen."

"Are there any fantasies of yours where I'm clothed?"

"Not one."

I leaned back in my seat. "Good. I'd hate to think I had less of an effect on Jasper than I did Mercer."

We fell into an easy conversation, talking about the places we'd visit, and the nonsexual things we'd do there.

We talked for so long, it was thirty minutes before I noticed we passed half a dozen parks and were currently merging off the express toward Elmshire Woods.

"Um, Jasper. I thought we were having a picnic."

"We are."

"In the woods?"

"Yes."

I blinked at him. "Are you worried about me being seen? We could find a secluded spot. Jefferson Park has this little hill behind the trees. It's perfect."

Jasper shot me an amused look. "Trust me. Obey me. Whatever we're going with, this place is better than anything Jefferson Park has for us."

We continued driving for another twenty minutes. Jasper slowed when we reached the sign for Copperhead Trail.

There's no way he could've known I was looking at this trail on a map only hours before, charting its closeness to Governor Katz's mansion.

"Is it far?" I asked. Jasper came around to help me out.

"No, it's a reasonable walk." He reached in to get the food and blankets. I held the basket for him, hesitating for only a second at his outstretched arm.

I linked mine through, setting off with Jasper into the dark.

"Can I ask about the people who have hired you? Or do you work by client confidentiality?"

"My reputation is built on discretion." He grinned at me. "Can you keep a secret?"

"I'm known to be good at that."

"I've worked with a lot of the major players in Cinco. My rates are high. Mainly, only the Leighbridge elite can afford me."

"Ever do a job for Leonidas O'Hare?"

"Three," he replied. "The man has spent half his inherited wealth cleaning up his daughter's scandals before they hit the tabloids."

"You mean there's more than what's already floating around the internet about Hazel?"

"Much more. Much worse."

"Wealth is wasted on the rich," I mused. "I'd be a good rich person."

"You intend to use wealth and status to become a dictator."

"A benign dictator dangerous only to my enemies. Don't leave that part out."

"Of course. Excuse me."

Laughing, I nudged him. "What about Andrew Hudson, owner of Organics?"

"Did a job for him. Nice guy actually. His wife had a doll when she was young," he said. "It was a gift from her mother that she lost during a move.

Discontinued years ago, and he asked me to track it down at any cost to give it to her in time for their anniversary. I was invited. She bawled her eyes out."

The trail was lit by nothing but moonlight. We strolled among the trees, chasing critters into their dens.

"That's so sweet."

"It's not all staged suicides and safe-cracking. I offer my services through different personas and in different ways. Andrew Hudson knows Calvin Sanders—owner of a nonprofit who likes to find things in his spare time."

"Not going to lie to you, I'm relieved Hudson is one of the good guys. I live in his stores. Did you know he hires chefs and nutritionists to craft his *Organics Frozen Food* line? Before I started working for Salvatore, I dreamed of getting that job. Great hours, better pay, and headquarters smack in the middle of Leighbridge where I planned to do the most damage."

"He's one of the few. Calvin's phone doesn't ring as much as Jasper's."

"Milo Wilson?"

"Yes. Jasper job."

"Edward Harris?"

"Alaric client."

"Helena Reddy?"

"Jasper job."

I eyed him in the dark. "Nicolas Katz."

"No."

"No?"

"You sound surprised."

"Katz used my dad for every job he could think of back in the day. I can't help but think our governor has hired more people to get him to the top."

I felt his shoulders lift. "I'm sure he has, but he was just a city politician then. Now he's a governor and real estate mogul. Somewhere on the way, he'd have put fixers, retrievers, and hit men on the permanent payroll. No need to hire out."

"True."

He pointed. "It's just up ahead. The trail breaks off and goes on another quarter of a mile till it opens up on our spot."

"Trail breaks off? Jasper, you're pointing at a bush. The trail doesn't break. We get *off the trail* and wander through the dense woods."

The outline of his smirk shone in the moonlight. "What's the matter, Redgrave? Scared of being alone out here with me?"

"I kill things I'm scared of, Croix." I pointedly stepped over the bush. "May want to keep that in mind."

"Duly noted."

We kept up the teasing, flirty banter over the raised roots and trodden earth. Glowing eyes gazed down from the trees, lit by our flashlights. I moved slowly—cautious about scaring them away. Owls still creeped me out, but I had respect for the beautiful, deadly creatures. They defended their home with the ruthlessness I'd use to defend mine.

My gaze drifted over my shoulder to Katz's unseen cabin.

"Something wrong?"

I shook myself. "Yes, I'm about to chew through your arm to get to that food. The smell is tormenting me."

"Not much farther. Actually, I'm surprised you haven't heard it."

"Heard it? Heard what?"

His voice tickled my ear. "Listen."

I fell silent, listening close to—

"What's that?"

A low, steady hum filled the forest, growing in sound and insistence as we approach. Jasper guided me over one last bush. We broke through the trees and he went on without me, leaving me gaping at the sight.

The waterfall spilled into the small pool—babbling to make itself heard. The mound of rock seemed to stretch for the sky, dreams of being a mountain, and weeping for reaching only sixteen feet high.

This small tucked-away spot needed to be no bigger, nor could it be more gorgeous. Yet Jasper made it so. Tiny, sea glass fairy lights dotted the waterline, casting a soft glow over the clearing.

He laid out the picnic—setting the plates, lighting citronella candles, and popping a bottle of champagne. Jasper came for me carrying a glass.

"Jasper," I breathed. "How did you find this?"

"It's a well-kept secret. It was purposely left off the maps. They say it's good luck for any couple that finds it on their own. The stars lead them where they needed to be. Together."

He held my hand, helping me onto the blanket.

"Did you find this place with someone else?"

"Saying yes won't be good for me, will it?"

"Completely torpedo your chances of getting laid."

"In that case, absolutely not. First time here."

"Then, who put these lights here?" I asked, brow raised.

"Shit. You caught me."

"Jasper."

His rich, smooth laugh rolled over the rippling water. "I looked up places to take you where we could be alone and this spot came up. I spent all day tramping through these woods looking for it." Jasper reclined by my side, unveiling his creations one by one. "Hope the blessing still works on us."

Okay, now I was jealous that he spent a year in Paris learning to make this. Just a look at the smoked duck spring rolls had me salivating. The translucent rice paper was bursting with color—red peppers, vibrant carrots, crunchy cucumbers, and fragrant, expertly cooked duck.

"You never know." I swallowed champagne to stop myself from talking. All of this was too amazing. I didn't know a single person who could be here and not wish for forever with the man who made it reality.

"Open." Jasper placed a nibble of tomato ricotta tart on my tongue.

I moaned, each chew bursting with flavor. "Incredible. I will take a little bit of everything, please."

We talked while he served my plate and we got down to eating our picnic meal. Jasper was right about not putting pressure on the conversation. We spoke like normal couples did on a date and he answered with ease. Already the picture of Jasper Croix was clearing in my head.

His first day into the world, his family cut ties with him. After, he was placed with a woman who refused to let him form ties with anyone else. Using all manner of lies or tricks to keep him within reach. Jasper claimed that had no negative effect on him, but how could it not?

I believed that Nina didn't physically abuse him, but she impacted him in other ways. If a child is raised witnessing a person use deceit to get what they want—in this case what they desired was a living, breathing person—and never sees the consequences for those actions. Does anyone look further when a bunch of money is dumped on their young lap and they grow up to do Jasper's line of work?

No one taught him lying, stealing, or cheating was wrong. In my case, those traits were actively encouraged. Dad applauded me when my big eyes and chubby cheeks swindled some random out of their pocket change while he made off with their wallet. Daddy's little grifter.

"You're like me," I whispered.

He blinked, sentence trailing off. "What do you mean?"

"Two sides. Two Jaspers. The person you were raised to be. And the person you were forced to become to survive. If anything, we should be soul mates, but our real selves... they don't know how to love."

Jasper reflected my humorless smile. He stretched out next to me. "No, they don't. I think I loved Nina." He said it like this was the first time he considered the notion. "I was fond of her. She saw that I was taken care of. Although, it's different from what I felt the first time I saw Rosie. Everything shifted. I redefined all I thought about life and love and anchored it on her. If nothing and no one else shifted the world in that way, could I say I loved them?"

He met my eyes steadily. "You do."

"You did."

"Mercer."

Heart squeezing, I nodded. "I loved him. He shifted my world."

"And I don't."

"Argh." I sat up, pushing the plates away from me. "I don't know. If a person changes everything you loved about them, how can you not change too?"

"You can't love me the way I am now." Jasper didn't sound mad. The opposite, his tone said he'd been waiting for this.

"I didn't say that. You're handsome, you're smart, and you make me laugh. I understand you better than anyone probably ever will. But it's not the creature you're trying to reach. She doesn't love you, Jasper. She can't. It's Adeline who lost the man she wanted. It's she who is trying to love you and this"—I flung my arms out—"isn't helping."

"What? The picnic? The waterfall?"

"Yes."

"Why? What's wrong with it?"

"It's another part to play. This time the perfect date. We were supposed to find this place together, Jasper. You made all this food—and it's delicious—but we could have cooked it me and you. The messy, dirty-bowls-in-sink, oil-splashing-on-the-stove part. The tripping-over-roots, getting-lost-in-the-woods part. Those are the moments where you fall for someone. Those are real."

I swept my hand out. "This is a fairy tale."

"You stopped believing in those when you were ten."

My skin tightened. "I never believed in them."

Jasper bobbed his head, looking out over the water. "You're right."

"Am I?"

"Yes. You're right, and this is wrong." He got to his feet. "Come on."

"Come on where?" I asked, brows narrowing on his outstretched hand.

"I picked out the perfect date for the perfect girl to play the part of perfect boyfriend." Jasper stripped off his tie. "I haven't dated anyone as myself in years. Letting someone see the messy parts? I've forgotten how."

"Why are you stripping?"

His shirt, then his belt fell on my lap.

"We're going swimming."

"Um, I don't think we are," I said quickly. "The water's freezing."

"Tough."

"Ja— Jasper!"

He flung me over his shoulder, marching off for the water.

"Put me down! Don't you dare!"

I went flying.

I hit the pool screaming, water rushing inside to fill my lungs. Thrashing to the surface, I got my feet under me to Jasper laughing his head off.

My carefully chosen dress was soaked. Half the stream was in my boots. My hair plastered to my forehead. Jasper slipped on the stones, he was howling so hard.

"You are *dead*!"

He put his fingers to his mouth, fake chattering his teeth. "I'm so scared."

"Argh!" I jumped on him, shoving his head beneath the surface. Jasper grabbed me around the waist and flung himself back. We both went down.

We broke through—half laughing, half choking. Just like that, a too-perfect date became everything but.

"Don't drop me," I said.

"I won't."

"Don't."

"I just said I won't."

"You're a professional liar."

Chuckling, Jasper held me still on his shoulders, reaching for my hands.

I discarded my dress and boots long ago. Jasper suggested I lose the bra and panties if I felt so inclined. It earned him a smack on the backside, although I don't think it taught him a lesson.

"Are you sure about this?" I asked.

"You wanted to do it."

"Because you said you used to be a cheerleader. You can't drop something like that and it go unchallenged."

"Nina was a cheerleader. She signed me up against my will." Jasper held tight to me, holding me up as I climbed onto his shoulders. "Thankfully, the flexibility came in handy."

I bonked him on the head.

"I wasn't talking about sex work. Damn, girl. You've got a dirty mind."

I giggled. "You were talking about sex work, and yes I do."

"All right, now straighten. Lock your knees."

"Are you sure you got me?" I was more than a little nervous. If I was going to be this high in the air, I preferred a ladder, or a building, under me. Dangling off the slippery shoulders of my date wasn't how I thought this night would go.

My mouth gets me in so much trouble.

"I won't drop you, Adeline." He trailed a finger along my ankle, erupting heat through my chilled flesh. "You can trust me."

In that moment, I did.

Straightening, I locked my knees, shrieking delight as I adopted my pose.

"Ready to get down?" he asked. "You'll have to go with me on this one. Don't be scared. Back straight. Keep your knees locked."

"Knees locked and loaded."

He snorted. "You're so cute."

The comment turned the fire on in my cheeks. I should be used to directness. Saint certainly never held back his sexual desires and the ways he wanted me to fulfill them. Still, it was different with Jasper. He didn't just tell me that he wanted me, he said why.

"Ready?"

"Ready."

Jasper slipped my feet off his shoulders and tossed me in the air. I clamped on a scream as the forest blurred.

I came down, feet planted, and slapped on his palm. He raised me higher—holding all of me one-handed.

I couldn't see the man's smirk, but I felt it.

And it's deserved.

"Wow." I wobbled a bit, and he moved with me, helping me steady out. "Did you learn this cheerleading?"

"This is one of the advanced moves." Jasper lifted me high overhead. "If I was going to do it, I had to be the best."

"Amazing."

Slowly, he lowered me down. Inch by inch, I disappeared in the water.

"You are full of surprises, Jasper Croix."

"In a good way, I hope."

I smiled, wrapping myself around him for warmth. "Definitely a good way."

He brushed my hair back. "I want to be real with you, Adeline. It's different with you and me. You say there's two of me, like there's two of you, but that's not true. You built one persona to survive. I created dozens.

"Even as a child, I was everything Nina wanted me to be to hang on to the closest person I had to a mother. I never had to figure out who Jasper Croix is. Now you're asking me to be him. I don't know who he is."

Jasper's coal eyes split open. Suddenly, I could see everything. His uncertainty. His fear. His need.

His love.

"He's empty."

Jasper blinked and it was gone. Nothing shone in his eyes but me.

"Go ahead, Adeline. See for yourself he's a blank personality in an Armani suit. He has nothing to offer you than a lifetime trying to feel the emotions he deadened years ago. Jasper Croix will drive you away all on his own."

I closed the distance, crushing my lips to his. Surprise stiffened him—for a second.

Jasper grasped my neck, holding me firm, strong, never letting go.

We went at each other like starving animals. Splashing, moaning, and fighting to get to the bank.

Jasper bit my lip, and my soft "oh" gave him entrance.

I finally understood the meaning of tongue-tied. It had nothing to do with nerves or stumbling over your words. It was wholly about kissing Jasper Croix. Now I just had to figure out how they came up with the term before he was born.

His tongue locked with mine. Teasing. Tormenting. Tickling.

Wetness pooled in my already soaked underwear. I broke away gasping.

"You aren't empty, Jasper. It's not an empty man who takes cheerleading lessons and smiles for the woman who loves him. An empty man doesn't sacrifice everything for his child. And he for fuck sure doesn't kiss like that. You don't have to worry, Jasper." I caught a droplet running down his nose. "I see who you are."

"Is this man someone you could love?"

I kissed him, smiling. "I'll let you know."

"We should go. You're shivering."

Jasper carried me the rest of the way. There was little point in dressing in my wet clothes. Instead, I let him dry me off with the picnic blanket and wrap me in the spare.

I studied him while he dried me. It was difficult to make sense of what I felt. The attraction was there in volumes. Just him touching me pebbled my nipples and broke goose bumps on my skin that had nothing to do with the cold.

He was just as easy to talk to as before. He made me laugh in a different way, but he still made me laugh. There was a lot to love about Jasper Croix, but was it enough?

My feelings for Mercer were pushed further and further aside the more I was confronted with the reality that he wasn't coming back. They were being placed in a spot where maybe I could one day accept I lost my love and move on. Until I got to that place, was it a good idea to date Jasper? To deal with the disapproval from Sinjin, Cash, and Brutal? To weather the pang every time I saw Mercer's face, but Jasper's eyes, hair, and voice came back?

I didn't believe love could be forced. Nor did I stomach leading someone on when the spark wasn't there.

You have to say goodbye. When he drops me off, I'll say I hope he patches things up with the guys, but he and I can't be more than friends.

"Why did you bring two blankets?" I asked, distracting myself from depressing thoughts.

"In case you decided to have your way with me. Didn't want the forest animals taking a peek."

I cracked a grin. "Oh, so he's modest?"

"Very." Jasper flicked up. "Hold still. You have a bug in your hair."

"What?" I did the opposite of holding still, flying up to smack at my strands.

"Don't do that." Gently, Jasper removed the critter and carried it to the water. "There you are, little guy. Back where you belong. Go find your family."

My heart thumped.

"Is this man someone you could love?"

Shit.

Chapter Six

I stared hard at Jasper during the trek through the trees and out on the trail. He carried me the whole way, refusing to let me put on my wet shoes or tramp through the dirt in my bare feet. The lights, basket, and food were left behind for him to retrieve after he left me in the car with the heat on.

A sweet gesture rewarded by my boring a hole through his skull, undeterred by the gloom.

That flash of *something* I felt when he rescued that bug couldn't have been real. It was a blip. A glitch. Brought on by watching too many Disney movies. I had an automatic reaction to gallantry.

It didn't mean I was catching feelings for the multi-talented chef who could flay a man with a smile on his face and lift me one-handed. That wasn't my type at all.

It's not.

It's *not*.

Shut up.

Jasper beeped the car, turning the light on the empty street.

"I'll be right back." Jasper set me on the passenger seat and tucked the blanket tighter around me. "Give me—"

I circled his wrists. "Can I try something?" I pushed Jasper back, got out, and threw open the back seat. I shoved him unceremoniously inside.

"What the fuck?" he cried. I tossed my bra on his chest. "Please proceed."

I laughed. I intended to proceed. We were settling this right now. If I was gearing up to do this again, after the battering love had already given me, I was finding out tonight.

Climbing inside, I perched on the running board, gliding my hand up his thigh. Even his legs were powerful. Two sculpted hunks of granite wrapped in a suit and given the breath of life by Zeus himself.

I stopped my exploration at his belt, drawing the zipper down.

Jasper hissed as he sprung free. Mine was just as strangled.

I said it was a rare man who didn't have an unsightly penis. Jasper joined their ranks.

Smooth, tan shaft. Cut helmet. I could feel him sliding down my throat and filling me with salty sweetness. My tongue darted out for a taste, licking the tip.

"Are you sure about this?" Jasper asked.

"I've never been more sure about anything."

"Want to bring that pussy up here so I can return the favor?"

My lower belly tightened. I wanted to do that. Very much so, I'd like to give his tongue freedom to plunder my folds to its content. But doing so would defeat the purpose.

"Sixty-nine is distracting," I lied. "I like to focus on the task at hand. Afterward, I'll have your full attention."

"Fine with me."

I palmed him, swallowing till my lips touched knuckle.

You can tell a lot about a man by how they react to a blow job. Do they shower you with praise like you dropped a million dollars on their lap? Do they demand or wait for it to be offered? Do they grab your head, pushing you down? Do they pull your head back and fuck your mouth like a nail needing hammering?

I had eclectic taste in the bedroom. Or dungeon. Or theater. Or car.

I was up for pretty much anything, be it spanking, chains, and if I was feeling really adventurous, public sex. But I did not, in any circumstance, appreciate when guys fisted my hair and pounded my mouth. It instantly brought me back to my first experience with blow jobs, and refusing to give them. They all pulled my hair. They forced my mouth open and threatened terrible things if I bit down.

Some things should be talked about first. You ask before you pull out the video camera and ball gag. You talk about it before your boyfriend pops his ex out of the closet, saying gear up for a threesome.

This was one of those things for me, and I didn't care if it seemed harsh. I dumped more than one boyfriend for jolting me out of a pleasurable experience and dumping me into my nightmares. A few of them doing it even after I blatantly said not to. They got their asses kicked on the way out the door.

What kind of man are you, Jasper Croix?

I ran my hands over his chest, drawing his shirt up. His body was a masterpiece of hard mounds and soft russet hairs—tickling my palms.

I swallowed him whole, moaning as I bobbed.

"Holy fuck. You are the most beautiful thing I've ever seen." Jasper tangled in my hair. Spreading his fingers, he fanned my water-darkened strands around me, letting them fall gently on us.

That was new.

His fingers continued down, finding my breast smooshed on the seat and tweaking my nipples.

That was new too.

"Is this distracting you from the task at hand?" Where did men get this gift of making things sound sinister and sexy at the same time?

Each tug sent shock waves rebounding through my core and made my pussy scream at me, why wasn't this man serving her right now? Yes, I was distracted!

Jasper sat up. Continuing his torture, he pressed his fingertip to the top bump of my spine, slowly gliding down. "I wonder if you can really fuck someone so hard you break their back. Please don't take this the wrong way when I say, I'm going to do my damn best to break yours."

I gulped on him, knees clamping together. I ached to touch myself.

Or have him touch me. Jasper was better. He was much better.

Crap on a stick. If I thought this was going to help crush my burgeoning feelings, it was not going how I expected.

"Fuck yes, that's amazing," he growled. "I know all the reasons why I refused to touch you as Mercer, but I am cursing every fucking decision I made in my life that led to me not taking you the second I saw you."

Can you come from words alone? Because Jasper was seriously testing that myth.

And then he grabbed my hair.

Holding firm, he drew my head up and his dick slipped out with a "pop."

I clutched his shoulders as Jasper tipped my head back, kissing my throat. "I love you," he whispered against my chin. "But if I go another second without being inside that pussy, every single one of my personas will lose their fucking minds. If you have objections, please voice them now."

Shit.

Shit, shit, and shit.

I was in trouble.

"No objections," I rasped.

Jasper flipped me onto the seat. I was still blinking at this turn of events while the door was slammed shut and his clothes joined my bra on the floor.

Jasper peeled my panties down with such reverence, I thought he'd steal and frame them. We both knew how long we've been waiting for this to happen. To hear he'd been holding back until he could do this as himself was another nail in the coffin.

He snaked around my waist, and I found myself upright and on his lap.

If I was doing this, I wasn't going to be a bystander, and hell yes, I was doing this.

"Dammit, Jasper. You couldn't make this easy for me." I kissed him—nose, mouth, cheeks, eyes. Everywhere.

He chuckled. "What am I not making easy?"

"My life is a shambles and a half." I positioned him at my entrance. My hand was shaking I wanted him so badly. "I'm about to undertake a suicide mission. Every criminal in Cinco is hunting me and Gianna. I'm falling out with the three guys I love with every corner of my soul for the one who ran through the wall like the Kool-Aid man, rather than stay and tell me the truth."

He laughed. "Kool-Aid man. I like that."

"That is so not the proper reaction right now."

"You're not going to get another emotion other than blissed out and droolingly ecstatic w-while you're doing that."

I sunk onto his lap, greedily devouring every inch of him.

Jasper hooked around my thighs, angling me up and going deeper still.

Yes, I was in trouble.

"Are we going for the tender and sweet first-time shit?" he asked.

"Fuck no!"

"Thank God."

Jasper started pumping like there was a time limit on when I'd change my mind. I clutched the driver and passenger seat, meeting him thrust for thrust.

He fucked me through the seats and against the dashboard. Jasper pressed my face against the mirror, pounding me as my gasps fogged the glass and he etched "Jasper's Owner" in the condensation.

The man was an everlasting battery. I was hoarse. Hair a mess. Two nails broken and a bump on my head from an orgasm that smacked my skull on the dashboard. He wasn't slowing down for a second.

Jasper rutted between my legs—reducing me to a gibbering idiot as he hit that spot over and over again with wild precision.

I was hanging off him like a monkey. Arms hooked around his shoulders. You couldn't slip a grain of sand between us.

"Ah," I cried. "Why are you doing this to me?"

"'Cause you begged." *Thrust.* "Me." *Thrust.* "To." *Thrust.*

He knew what the hell I was talking about and his double answer did not help.

"I beg for a lot of things when the shit's getting fucked out of me— Holy fuuuuuck." I grabbed the seat pouch and tore it half off.

I came so hard, I cracked my back. Literally, the bones popped and shifted in there, nearly giving Jasper his wish to break the damn thing for good. He came seconds later, spilling inside me.

We flopped in a heap on the back seat. Sweaty, sticky, and breathing like we ran a marathon and screwed the whole way.

I did believe you could have love without sexual chemistry. Plenty of people walked down the aisle as virgins. But if I was going to factor mine and Jasper's into our equation. That category got an A-plus star.

Jasper nestled between my breasts, listening to my heart hammering out of control.

"I lied to you."

The silent confession stilled the fingers stroking his hair.

"About what?"

"I said I wouldn't make it easy for you to say no. I will, Adeline." He pressed a kiss on my collarbone. "If this is too much. If it's ruining what you have between Sinjin, Killian, and Baris. If it's distracting you while you need to focus on getting through this war alive, then say so. I'll let you go. Drop you off tonight and I won't come back. My world's shifted again, and it only makes sense if you're happy. Even if you're not with me."

I traced his lips as he spoke, feeling him form the most selfless words ever given to me.

I had made up my mind a couple of hours ago to walk away from him. Retreat, find closure, accept the love affair between Mercer and Adeline was over.

Here he was, giving me that out. Saying it was okay.

"Promise me something."

"Anything," he said.

"Never make it easy for me."

JASPER

I dropped Adeline in front of the rowhouse. She argued about it, saying the guys would be pissed that I knew where they were staying, but I simply drove around the block, refusing to stop the car until she gave it up. It was three in the morning and this was Cinco City. Only someone desperate to die by mugging walked the streets this late.

"It's cute you're worried." She smooched my cheek. "Like there's anything out here more dangerous than me."

"There isn't," I replied. I turned and captured a real kiss—sinking in her heady scent of freshly baked cookies and jasmine shampoo. I could bottle that smell and jack off to it alone. Thankfully, I had memories of the real thing to get me through going to bed without her that night. "That's why they roam in packs."

"You'll have to make it up to me."

"Why?"

"Because I lost the bet." Her impish wink had me ready for round two. Actually, five. "You know I hate to lose."

"I'm happy to make that bet with you as many times as you like. The terms were I leave you high and thoroughly fucked every night, right?"

"Yeah, or you and the guys talk about your feelings." She giggled. "I'm seeing now I need to change these terms up."

"Don't. You want me highly motivated to win."

"Good night."

"Night."

I watched Adeline go inside. The lights flicked on upstairs as she shut the door, proving they waited up. I mentally noted the house number.

I was fortunate Adeline gave in to me dropping her off at the door.

"I'm about to undertake a suicide mission."

What mission would that be, gorgeous?

It couldn't be Thiago Pais, because she let out another slip on the phone that he wasn't the worst thing they were dealing with.

Something was up. Something she wasn't talking about. I had to ask myself if that's why Adeline suddenly had an interest in my former clients. Were they going after someone and she wanted intel she knew the guys wouldn't ask me for directly?

Stupid.

If that was the case and they were going after someone in a job Adeline openly called suicide, why would they put her at risk and refuse to get every scrap of information I could give them? Adeline was bigger than our egos.

St. John Bellisario was a lot of things. A strategic thinker used to be chief among them.

Unless he thinks I'm double-dealing. The thought slipped in and stuck. *Openly asking me about who I might really be working for would tip their hand and seal their coffins.*

Touché, St. John.

For a brief, almost fatal moment, I underestimated him. Your reputation holds.

I started the car, pulling away from the curb.

It's no matter now. I knew where they were staying. Whatever they were planning, I'd find out soon enough.

Breathing deep, I inhaled cookies and jasmine. Even sooner, I'd have Adeline leaving that scent in my bed. On my couch. In the shower. Hers was a promise I had no intention of breaking.

ADELINE

"What did Diego say?"

I stretched out on the couch, my head on Saint's lap and feet on Baris's. Saint was unashamedly undressing me. Redoing my buttons got my hands tied with a doll dress and put over my head.

It had been four days since my date with Jasper. Four days, and he was still soaked in my skin like the midnight dip that left me pruney. And he wouldn't let me forget it.

Jasper was not one of those guys who slept with you on the first date and ghosted. He texted me as I curled up next to Saint that night, and every day since. Between the calls, we were in a pretty serious sexting situation that got my pulse racing every time my phone went off. Even if it was the DoorDash guy texting he was outside.

"Has to be the cabin," Cash replied from the armchair. "There's complete coverage of every inch of the capitol. They can track you from the parking garage to the coffee cart. They'll see if you washed your hands after using the bathroom."

"Can we disable the system?"

"We can. The security system isn't that expensive or sophisticated. It's easily hacked, but where they were wise was to install an automatic call to emergency services if it goes offline. With heavy security in the building and the police station in front of the capitol, the response time is sixty seconds or less. Hard to pull off a kidnapping of a high-ranking official in a minute."

I nodded. That was too tight a window. "We can't take him there."

Saint had my top off and was tracing the outline of my bra. He wanted me to beg for it as punishment for trying to keep these babies covered.

"Our best chance is the cabin," Killian continued. "The security system is impressive, but it's nothing like the capitol's. Plus, no cameras in the house."

Saint flicked my bra on and off—freeing my eager nipple and then smothering her hopes with fabric.

"You're just being mean now," I told him.

"Don't know what you're talking about, Bunny."

Shaking my head, I turned to Killian. "I knew the perv wouldn't want video of his sex games."

"The place is deserted when he's not there. The only thing keeping an eye are the cameras."

"Which we can take out."

He nodded.

"Then, that's where we do it. We kill him at the cabin," I said. "We have the where. Now for the when." I looked up at Saint. "What do you think?"

"We'll do it the next time he goes out there. Too much of a risk for one of us to get close. Send Diego or one of them to do a lift. Clone his phone."

"Might not be possible with those guards on him," Killian said.

"Don't hide from them. Get in Katz's face, crowing about it being an honor to meet him and can they take a photo together. Slip a hand in his pocket while he's cheesing."

"My dad said he would help," I offered. "He's still the best fixer this city has ever seen. If anyone can find out when Katz is entertaining his next booty call at the love shack, it's him."

Sinjin's phone went off. "It's Edie," he said.

"Hello. Ed— Wait, slow down. They're what?" Saint shot up, popping me off his lap. "No, get out. Get out now!"

"Saint?"

"I'm coming."

Sinjin shoved off, snatching his coat off the rack. He didn't hear our shouts, or didn't pay attention to them.

I fell over myself doing up my buttons, racing to follow him. I got enough from his side of the conversation to know something was wrong with Edie.

Sinjin was running down the street when I stumbled onto the stoop. He jumped in the car and peeled off.

"Saint!" He sped off in a squeal that set my teeth on edge.

I ran inside. "Killian, where are you—"

"Here." He thundered down the stairs, phone to his ear. "I'm calling a taxi. Put some shoes on."

I glanced down at my bare feet. I chased after him without them.

I was dressed and armed by the time the taxi arrived ten minutes later. I didn't know what we were walking into. Neither Edie nor Sinjin were answering their phones.

"Our Lady of the Sacred Heart Cathedral," we shouted at the poor guy. He sped with the urgency our tone demanded.

Edie's sister's home wasn't far from the church. I assumed it was chosen for that reason. We turned the corner leading up to the hill in fifteen minutes. The entrance was blocked by cars.

"Who are all these people?" I asked. "The church is usually empty around this time while Edie is prepping for the children to come for recess."

"Adeline, stay in the car," Killian ordered.

Cash and Brutal got out, slamming both doors in my face. Cash tossed a wad of money at the cabbie. "Drive. Get her far from here."

"Don't you—!"

"Yes, sir."

He hit the gas, slinging a U-turn and speeding back the way we came.

"Stop the car!"

"Sorry, ma'am. I'll bring you back where I picked you—"

I shot through the seats, clamping my hand around his throat, and bugging his eyes in the rearview mirror. "Stop the fucking car," I hissed.

"Ok-k-kay." He slammed on the brakes.

I tumbled out, sprinting up the sidewalk, and imagined throttling my boyfriends the whole way. Until I saw what Killian did.

Skidding to a stop, I fell against a blue Porsche rocking a gleaming crown hood ornament.

The Kings.

"Then, it's you. Pais is planning something to draw you out."

It worked. I was out.

That's why Killian tried to send me back. The men who rode in these six cars must be here for me.

"Edie," I whispered. "What have they done?"

The question propelled me forward. I couldn't sit safely in the dollhouse while Saint and the only woman he loved other than me were in danger.

Shouts reached my ears as I bounded up the hill. I closed on the door handle.

Crash!

Lurching back, I fell off the steps and collapsed on the gravel. The office chair struck the spot where I'd been standing, chair legs snapping under a shower of stained glass.

I clambered to my feet and hurried around the back. Slowly, I cracked the door, peering inside. It was a sight worse than I imagined.

A King tore a tapestry off the wall, flinging it in the direction of his friend who kicked at the altar, tipping it over.

The church was a ruin. The pews were overturned. Trash bins upended and its contents scattered through the nave. Two Kings had hold of the priceless candelabras, using them to batter portraits decades older than them off the wall.

Saint struggled with a King by the confessional—a look I'd never seen on his face. He roared, his pain a living, breathing thing that seized the man before Saint clamped his hands on his head, smashing it into the stone wall again and again.

On the other side, Cash and Brutal fought off no less than nine men. Cash charged the men wreaking destruction, and Brutal took down the Kings charging him.

Or it seemed that's what they tried to do till they were outnumbered.

Their backs were closing on the wall. Each man Brutal knocked out was trampled by the next one rushing to take his place. And amid the chaos, Sister Edie knelt on the platform before the hanging cross—rosary tight in her grip, tears soaking her cheeks as her lips moved.

Maybe there was a shred of decency left in these men that they skirted the invisible barrier surrounding her, keeping their hands off an innocent nun praying to her lord.

But then they weren't here for her.

I moved to my guys.

And they weren't pulling their guns.

It was me they wanted—Gianna Cross's best friend. They'd take advantage of their four bargaining chips when I appeared. Drawing their weapons on the outnumbered Merchants to drop me on my knees and put my hands behind my back, letting them take me without a fight.

Then so be it. They want me, they can have me.

I hurried down the hill, did what I had to do, and raced back.

Sweat beaded my hairline. Three times up and down the hill, and charged with adrenaline, I couldn't suck in a breath long enough to hold it. I burst inside.

"Stop!" I bellowed. "That's enough."

"Look at this." One of the men tossed the candelabra away. He bore down on me, narrowly missing being taken out by the debris from the priest's office thrown off the second floor. "You've finally decided to join us, Redgrave."

"I have," I bit out. "I'm here, so—"

"Adeline!"

Cash and Brutal rushed the line holding them back. More men piled on, jumping Saint and dragging him over with the rest. Their guns were out now.

"I said stop! You want me, let's go." I looked at Edie, stooped and broken under the true heart of Cinco. "You're disgusting. Look at what you've done to get your hands on a book that will kill you. Do you hear me? The ledger will destroy the Kings like it has done to everyone who dares to own it. Take a good look at this place. Know exactly what you'll answer for when the ledger sends you on an early trip to hell."

"Shut this bitch up."

Kings came down the stairs. They grabbed my arms and shoulders, dragging me toward the door. I broke free and punched one across the face. They leaped on me and wrestled me down.

Forced on my knees, I focused on their leader and said, "Let Sister Edie and the Merchants go, or you don't make it back to your boss with me."

He kicked aside the pile of tapestries bearing down. "Look around you, sweetheart. There's thirty of us and five of you."

I tossed my head back laughing. "It's cute you think that matters. Believe me, *sweetheart*, I can go willingly, or I don't go at all. The choice is yours."

He trailed a finger down my cheek. "Hard choice. I might like you putting up a fight—"

I chomped down on the tip. He howled, screams breaking the sound barrier.

"Get off! Get her off!"

His thug tore at me—grabbing my neck, pulling my hair. I bit harder and metallic blood filled my mouth.

"Crazy bitch!" My new friend punched me once. Twice.

"Adeline!" Cash shouted.

I let go, spitting blood and skin at his feet.

"Want to choose correctly this time?"

His slap spun my head around.

"Fine. We'll let your precious Merchants live. Go on, men," he ordered. "Clear out!"

The bastard parade led their procession out the front door. Cash, Brutal, and Sinjin were left bound, but alive, at the feet of the confessional. Edie hadn't moved from her spot, though without their noise her words became clear. She prayed for the souls of the men who attacked her, and for the life of the boy she loved.

The bleeding King curled his lip at her.

"Don't even think about it." My voice chilled even me.

"There's no need. You're going to stand up, walk out of here, and get in the car without a fight. Or I dangle your mutilated corpse in Trapp Square and see if Cross shows her fucking face to cut you down."

"I suspect the authorities would've gotten to me long before then," I returned. "Hello. Body in Trapp Square? What will that do to tourism?"

Clear through the church, Saint's laugh rang out. "I swear, I'm marrying that woman."

"But I get your clumsy point." I shook their hands off me, getting to my feet. "You keep up your end, I keep up mine. I go without a fight."

"Beck, you sure about this?"

Beck put up his hands, one covered in blood. "We have an agreement. Walk her out, guys."

Their guns trained on my head by way of escort. I cast the Merchants one more glance as I stepped out the door. Thiago Pais was the one I shouldn't have underestimated.

He will learn the same of me. Let them bring me to him. The first beating I owed him was interrupted by his bitch ass fleeing out the door.

I stepped out into the tauntingly bright morning. A minute ago I was curled up with three of my guys and dreaming about the fourth. Jasper warned us Pais was planning something that wouldn't fail. Thiago Pais picked through my life. He picked through the Merchants' lives.

Why hadn't my idiotic self remembered there were more people I cared about other than Gianna and Dad?

"One last thing."

I turned as Beck flicked the lighter. He set fire to the mound of tapestries.

"No!"

The brutes grabbed me, yanking me off my feet.

"Let's go!" Beck slammed the door shut.

I broke free and ran at Beck as he ran at me. I ducked his hands, reached for the door, and a white blur shot past my vision.

Our Lady of the Sacred Heart shone stark on the side of the van rammed into the building. It trapped the door behind four thousand pounds, keeping me out, and them in.

"Beck," I screamed.

"Take her."

Our deal was off. I put up a fight.

I thrashed and bucked in their grip. Kicked one in the face. Wrestled the other for his gun. Three more Kings were forced to join in and subdue me. They carried me by the arms and legs, marching me down the hill as smoke billowed from the shattered windows.

"You're going to regret this, Beck! All of you! You'll never find the ledger!"

Beck seized my hair, sticking his face in mine. "I wouldn't be surprised if Cross abandoned you to us. If the bitch has any sense, she'll let you die and rid the world of one more cunt."

I spit in his eye. "Watch your language. This is sacred ground, and I'll be the one judging you for your sins."

"Argh!" He drew his gun. A King knocked his hand, sending the shot wide.

"The fuck is wrong with you, Beck? Pais wants her alive."

"Put her in the truck!"

The procession stopped short of the line of cars.

"What? What the hell?"

"Oops," I sang. "Did I forget to mention something?"

I shot out the tires of every single one of their cars. It left my gun a useless block of metal on the church steps, but I knew there wasn't a chance of killing them all before they got to me, the guys, or Edie. The true goal was to not get anywhere near Thiago "Slasher" Pais.

The string of filth Beck pelted me with definitely wasn't suitable for hallowed ground.

"Lock her in the truck," he ordered. "One of you, steal a car. Go!"

I was flung none too gently in the back of a gray Dodge. I plastered myself to the window, panic rising as high as the smoke from the steeple.

Someone would see it. They would call for help. Please!

The Kings swarmed the streets. A pack of them made for the Catholic school and the cars idling in the lot. My chest tightened thinking of one of them breaking in and demanding the keys directly.

How is no one seeing this? Call for help!

"Roddy?" Beck circled my truck, keeping a close eye on me. "Roddy?! Where's my car—"

Beck jerked. He dropped out of sight and hit the ground with an audible thud.

The truck rocked, then a face appeared in my window.

"Jasper?"

"I leave you guys alone for a minute and look at the trouble you get into."

"Hey!"

His gun came up, shooting the King running at us with barely a glance.

"Back up."

I scooted back. Jasper broke the window and opened the door. I fell into his arms.

"You weren't the cavalry I was wishing for, but I'll take it." I kissed him all over, squeezing him so tight, it was a wonder he could breathe. "We have to hurry. The guys are trapped in the church."

We took off up the hill. The Kings too busy searching for their getaway, they hadn't noticed two of their men were dead and I was out of the car. We had to free Edie and the guys before they did.

Stone benches blocked the front entrance, stacked one on top of the other. They rattled as my guys rammed the door, but didn't move.

"Saint! Killian," I called. "Baris, I'm here!"

"Adeline, take that side."

I gripped the foot of the bench. "One, two, three." We lifted.

My muscles strained under the effort. Tearing, ripping, screaming in pain, tears of frustration leaked from my eyes as we moved it slow—wretchedly slow out of the way.

Blood scored my palms, painting the second bench red.

"One, two, three," Jasper counted.

Again, we lifted as the flames rose higher, consuming all in its stone oven, and roaring over the shouts of its victims.

The second bench joined the first, and the Merchants' ramming gave way, forcing the final one over the steps.

Killian, Saint, and Baris tumbled out with a rush of smoke. Coughing and hacking, I pulled Saint onto my lap.

"Saint, are you—"

"Edie." He gripped my thigh, trying to use me to get up. "She's still... in there."

"Where?" Jasper asked.

"The altar," Killian rasped. "Couldn't get to her... Too much smoke."

"Edie!" Saint shot up. A coughing fit knocked him sideways. He fell onto the column and kept going. Jasper ran past him.

I screamed as the smoke swallowed him.

Saint's second attempt to follow was his last. He fell over the bench.

He didn't get up.

"Hey! Look! Beck's dead," someone shouted. "She's out."

"We have to get out of here." I gathered Sinjin in my arms. His head lolled against my stomach. "Hurry and take him."

"You get out of here, Adeline. It's you they want," Killian said. "Run. Go!"

Kings ran up the hill, joined by more when they ended their car search and saw what was happening. None of us were going anywhere.

"I'm sorry," I said. "I love you."

"Don't fucking do that," Killian snapped. "Don't say goodbye." He grasped me under the shoulders. "Run behind the church. Run, Adeline!"

I spun, holding him tight. I buried in his shoulder, peering into the fiery, black maw that still had a hold of Jasper and Edie. "I'm not going anywhere." Closing on his hilt, I drew his gun from the holster. "Stay behind me."

Cash reached for me and grabbed air.

I raced down the steps, planting myself before the charging Kings. I wasn't leaving my men to die, and I would not go with the Kings.

Coughing sounded behind me. "Brutal, take her," Jasper wheezed. "She's unconscious."

I shot the first one leading the pack. He dropped and took out two men rolling down the hill.

They aimed their guns. A bullet struck the ground between my feet.

Noise halted my finger on the trigger.

Is that...?

The fire truck whipped around the corner, squealing to a stop at the line of cars blocking the way in. Riding their bumper were two police cars.

The Kings scattered. Some ran for the edge of the property where a high, dangerous jump would land them in the passage between the grounds and neighboring building. Others fired on the responders.

I was picked up from behind. "Let's move," Killian shouted.

We tore for that high jump—our decision made. Brutal carried Sister Edie. Jasper slung Saint's arm over his shoulder, aiding him stumbling over the grounds, and Killian had me.

I shot every King I saw standing, screaming my rage as we disappeared into the trees.

JASPER

"They're all suffering from smoke inhalation. Mr. Bell and his mother the worst of the four."

Adeline held my hand in a death grip. I lost sensation in my fingers ten minutes ago, but I didn't pull away.

"We're monitoring them both," Maggie said. "We'll know more after a few tests."

"Will they be okay?" Adeline asked.

"I'll call you if there is any change in their condition," she replied, using that doctor method of avoiding giving hope.

"Thank you, Maggie," I said. "I'll take care of the costs for the tests and your discretion."

"Anything for you, Alaric." Maggie squeezed my arm. "They'll only be attended to by nurses I trust."

Adeline zeroed in on that hand. Couldn't blame her since the use of Alaric told her exactly how we knew each other.

She left us in our little corner of the hospital, tucked away in the wrong wing on the third floor where three wanted felons and a nun would receive their treatment, and be gone before the cops got wind. Cinco truly was a criminal's paradise.

I made to return to their room. Adeline stopped me.

"How did you know, Jasper?" she asked.

I knew where this was going. Pretended I didn't. "How did I know...?"

"That we needed help. Have you been keeping track of us?"

"Yes," I said easily. "I have. Keeping track of you to be specific."

She drew me over to the window. Floor to ceiling, it was a straight drop below to the army of dumpsters the view afforded us.

"Why were you specifically keeping track of me? Not to sound ungrateful. You came when I needed you, and you saved Edie. But it's hard enough convincing the guys to salvage what's left of the Merchants when you're skulking around in the shadows."

"I never skulk," I replied, "and are you trying to convince them to let me back in? Why?"

"Why?" She gave me a look like I asked why she didn't marry Thiago Pais and spend her days sleeping with a knife under her pillow. "Because we're us. The five of us. That's how it works."

I fixed out the window. "What if I'm done with the banger life? There were fewer sex auctions, child trafficking, nightclub shoot-outs, and burning buildings when I worked as a straight retriever. What if all I want from my time as a Merchant is you?"

"What if that's bullshit?" she returned without skipping a beat. "Those guys in there are your brothers. You risked your life running into that church because— because if Saint did, he wouldn't have made it out. You saved their lives. If the last four years didn't mean anything, we wouldn't be here now. Why won't you just talk to them?"

Because I'm still lying. To them, and to you. The difference is you want to believe me. And the guys are looking for a sign.

"I'll talk to them. We'll see how interested they are in what I have to say." I cocked my head. "But does this mean our bet is over? Because I vote to continue ending our dates with vigorous car sex. Your footprints look good on my roof."

"Don't distract me." She leaned into me anyway, propping her chin on my chest. "Why were you watching us?"

"I had no choice with those hints you were dropping. Comments about a suicide mission, and a problem worse than Thiago Pais."

Her lips pressed in a thin line. "I was wrong about that last one. Pais almost had me, Jasper. He had a plan to draw me out, and it worked. Like a fucking charm, it worked. I was one preschool teacher's car away from being held down while he carved his initials in my face."

I hugged her. "I'd never let that happen."

"He didn't buy that I was just a Merchant's girl." Her breath tickled through the part in my shirt. "He dug up information on all of us. If he knows about St. John and his connection to the church, then he knows about the Hunts and Merriman Circus. They're in danger too."

"Killian will have thought of that. He'll make sure they go to ground."

"They can't do that forever. The circus is their livelihood. The purpose is to attract as many people to it. They shouldn't have to worry about the next group of guests entering the fairgrounds packing guns and brass knuckles!"

Holding her closer, I stroked Adeline's hair. I felt her worry. Understood it. Shared it on a small level. A level too small to induce her panic.

I didn't do panic. My entire life since I was nineteen has been charting the obstacles, and deciding if I was going over, around, or blowing the damn thing up. Panicking did not help complete any of those tasks.

Thiago Pais would not hurt the Hunts. He'd destroy no more of Sinjin's legacy, or harm another hair on Sister Edith's head. He would never touch my Adeline.

"Finding Pais is my new obstacle," I told her. "I've never failed on a job before, Adeline. Never."

"Where do we start?"

We.

"There's a person I need to find. Someone who likely won't be as tight-lipped as Marlon Thibodeaux, but it's a long shot," I admitted. "They may have changed their name or moved out of the city."

"Do whatever you have to do. Gianna is going after Pais, but clearly he's not waiting around to die. He's a distraction we don't need right now. A deadly one."

"What is going on?" I made her look me in the eyes. "Are you in trouble?"

"It's not about me. That's why it's not for me to say." She rose on tiptoe and kissed me. "Talk to the guys. Fix this. The longer this goes on, the bigger this becomes."

"Like four years long?"

She gave me a look. "Yes, like that. You can go into retirement after I get my city, but you have to be around for the car sex and late-night swims to happen. That's less complicated when the men in the house aren't trying to kill each other."

"Wait here."

Cash and Brutal looked up as I came inside.

Sister Edith and Saint were in the room across the hall attached to more monitors, and in Edie's case, breathing through a tube.

The two were sitting on the edge of their beds, speaking through their oxygen masks. Cash tugged his down.

"You've been watching us."

We didn't call him the brain of the Merchants for nothing. The man put two and ten together and found three offshore accounts, two mistresses, and a propensity for Asian porn. He didn't miss a thing.

"Have I? Maybe Adeline called me. She was trussed up in the back of a van and on her way to Thiago Pais. Where were you two?"

They stiffened.

"Stop reading ill intent into my saving our girlfriend's life. Just struggle your way to a thank-you."

Killian sat back, the expression on his face changing. "Adeline's right. You are different. Certainly more of a bastard." He scoffed. "The irony is Sinjin would've liked the real you."

"That guy loves me." I sat in the armchair, crossing my ankle over my knee. "So do the rest of you. That's why everyone's feelings are hurt that I *lied* to you." I waved my hands. "Pretty rich coming from the three of you." I motioned to Baris.

"This guy's the suicidal son of a billionaire. Kept that tidbit to yourself and had us chase you up a roof. Hunt's secrets prevented us from figuring out Richard La Roche was Kieran till it was too late. Let's not forget he tricked us into believing Adeline robbed us blind and ran out on us.

"And does anyone know if a single thing St. John says is the truth? He told me five times not to take a shower because there was a dead man in my bathtub. Three of those fucking times he wasn't kidding."

I twirled my finger. "We don't do the truth, gentlemen. We're a bunch of fucked-up psychopaths that wandered into the same bar and ended up going home together. The morning after lasted a bit long, but we all knew what this was."

"You finished?" Killian's smoker's rasp made him sound twice as menacing. "We don't give a fuck about your secrets, Croix. No one asked you to sit cross-legged on the carpet, spilling your life story while we braided your hair. You could've called yourself Miss Muppet if it tickled your balls. The only thing that mattered is loyalty."

"And yours is to Lombard," Baris said.

Killian shrugged. "Not much more to say than that."

"I'm not loyal to Lombard."

"But you are to that kid of yours," he said. "You'd slit our throats and run the ledger to Lombard like a dog with a Frisbee if he threatened Rosalie Eden Baker of Crest Lane, Leighbridge."

"Keep my daughter out of your fucking files, Cash!"

"Ahh. There's that fatherly protectiveness." He smirked. "Proves my point, doesn't it? While Lombard has you on a leash, you're a threat to us. To Adeline. I'll say this once: Stop following us.

"You get one pass for saving Adeline. But if you come near us again, we handle you like we handle every threat to our business."

I let the death threat go in one ear and out the other. "The four of us have worked together for too long. Sinjin swore to skin me three times before I had my breakfast. If you're trying to make me tremble in my loafers, it's not working."

Brutal busted the oxygen tank coming for me. He smashed his fist on my jaw. Recovery time was zero.

He hauled me up and tossed me across the room. I hit the window hard enough to crack it and fell on the food tray. We both hit the floor with a resounding crash.

I was sure this wasn't what Adeline had in mind when she encouraged this open exchange of communication.

I pushed myself up, face calm. "Touché, Baris." I spat out a mouthful of blood. "You never were one to bluff. Alright, so Brutal kicks the shit out of me the next time you catch me hanging around. You planning to do that in front of Adeline?" A bloody smirk stretched from dimple to dimple. "Because our girlfriend's made it clear she's going to continue fucking me."

The stress on "our girlfriend" had the desired effect of ticcing the muscles in their jaws.

"Stay away from Adeline," Killian barked.

"Nope."

Brutal advanced on me.

"Not the face this time. That's the money, Alexander."

A hand on the shoulder stayed him.

"I'm sure you're a reasonable man, Jackson... Cunt, was it?"

I chuckled. "Close enough."

"If you love Adeline even a fraction of what we do, you know you're putting her in danger too. Lombard—if that's who you really work for—isn't an enemy to have. Cross's games have already threatened her life. Don't make her a chess piece on another board."

The idea that I would cracked my jaw. "She's safe with me."

"She's safe with *us*." Killian moved to the side. "Get out of here."

I didn't need another invitation.

Adeline waited in the hallway, arms crossed and leaning on the wall beneath a bland watercolor of flowers. She didn't raise a brow at my busted lip.

"Decided not to intervene, I see."

A smile tugged at her lips. "You don't need me to fight your battles. You guys have to work this out among yourselves."

"Brutal tried to throw me out a window. They threatened my life if I come near you again."

The smile remained. "You're not going to let that stop you, are you, baby?"

Dear Lord, this woman's going to be the death of me. Literally.

"Not a chance."

"It's a process," she continued. "No one expects to solve all their problems in the first therapy session. Though, you'll probably see more progress if Lombard was dead."

"I stick pins in his doll every night, Redgrave. So far nothing."

"He's another target like the rest, Jasper. You haven't failed before. You won't fail now."

"I have no intention of failing. The end of this is coming," I said, thinking of the true person I worked for. "It hinges on one thing: the ledger. Right now, we have the same endgame. The Merchants don't see it, but I can't betray them while our interests are aligned."

"Is that what this is about?" She stroked my arm. "Are you looking for Thiago Pais for me, or for your interests?"

"Silly question. They're one and the same." I kissed her. "I'll call you when I know something."

I left Adeline standing beneath those flowers.

When I was out of sight, I fished out my phone. This time, I was the one to call.

ADELINE

"How does this help with your recovery?"

I stretched out on the sheets, stark naked barring a pair of diamond earrings.

"You gotta get your blood pumping after smoke inhalation. Helps you recover faster from the carbon dioxide poisoning."

"You made up everything you just said."

Sinjin winked over the sketching pad. "Prove it."

Sinjin was released from the hospital the day before. After three days, Doctor Maggie cleared him to go home. Sister Edie was still in the hospital. She was conscious, though due to her age and a cough that wasn't going away, Maggie insisted on monitoring her for a lung infection. Her actual sister had flown into town to look after her. Which meant, after she was discharged, Edie and her sister were moving in here.

Our bags were partially packed and waiting at the foot of the bed. Time to move again.

"Where will we stay?"

"Chin up, Bunny." Saint kicked back in a rocking chair, his long legs forming a bridge to the kitty-patterned ottoman.

He looked fine. He said he was fine. But he hadn't uttered a word about the destruction of his father's church and almost losing Edie. Unless you counted the long string of inventive tortures for Pais that he came up with on a half-hourly basis. Shoving his dick in a bucket of snapping crabs was particularly creative.

"We're moving out to the cabin," he said. "Any day now, your old man's coming back with a date. We'll be ready to move."

"Okay. Cool with me. We'll stop for food first. We can't live off canned peaches and packaged rice."

"Push the girls together for me."

"This isn't sounding like a tasteful, artistic sketch."

"Is that what I said it was? I lied."

I couldn't stop a giggle. He was undoubtedly masking his feelings, but I knew my Saint. When he wanted to talk to me, he would talk. Not a minute sooner.

"Sinjin, what's the plan?" Cash strode into the bedroom. "Looks like the work is done."

"We were working," I protested. "Sinjin and I reviewed the sketch of the cabin's floor plan. Is Lucky sure this is accurate?"

"Oscar said to leave approaching Katz to him, so I put guys on Mercer's former job. Katz's architect registered the cabin's floor plans with city hall. Lucky took pictures. I sketched them to scale." Cash flipped back to the cabin plans. "Our points of entry are either this back door or this window into the basement."

"We argued about that before Saint stripped me," I said. "How can we pick a point of entrance while the cabin is deserted? We'd have to wait for Katz to be there to see where he stations his guards, and where he spends his time. What if that's a sex basement and we bust in on him chasing Mindy around in a dog collar?"

"There's an element of conjecture here, Redgrave. We don't know how often he goes out there. We can't waste an opportunity on recon, even if we should." He slid a look to his brother.

"Wait as long as you want, Kill. He's dead in a week if I have to burst in on him and Mindy myself."

"Then, I vote we come in through the back door," I said. "It's away from the kitchen and the living room. Both places I'd hang out if I was a bored guard occupying myself while my boss banged his way through every eligible woman in Cinco."

"Back door," Sinjin agreed. "All the guys on this one. Diego will short the power, then we take out the men in the back. Three, three, three, four," he rattled off, pointing out where he wanted the guys. "The four of us go in. Brutal takes out the guards. Kill, remove his date and impress upon her the short lifespan granted to people who can't keep their mouth shut. Bunny and I will take care of the rest. See?" He flipped back to my sketch. "I never stopped working."

"Why do you want me to kill him with you?" I asked.

"I very much enjoy watching you kill people, Bunny. Edie says I must find peace in happiness. Watching you torture the man who took my father will make me transcendently happy, and therefore, I will find peace. No one can say I didn't listen during Sunday school."

There was a lot to unpack in those statements. I wasn't touching it with a ten-foot pole. I wanted to be by his side either way. I loved Saint more than life, but the night he lost his father unhinged something deep inside him—forever transforming St. John into Sinjin.

This final standoff with Katz could heal him. Or it could change him into someone else entirely.

"I'm getting cold lying under the fan."

"I know," they said at the same time.

"Is someone going to get in this bed and warm me up?"

"If you insist." Killian jumped on top of me. He draped my ankles around his ears, bending me in half.

"Fuck off," Sinjin said. "I haven't had my fix in three days. Brush with death over here. Adeline's been saving a dirty, creative, thorough marathon sex experience for me."

"Have I?" My laugh broke off in a moan. Killian wasn't wasting any time, working two fingers inside me.

"Yes, and I'm ready to collect. Cash. Out."

"Why does anyone have to leave? I can do a dirty, creative thorough marathon sex experience for two." I held my breath. This was the first I put forth the idea of a threesome. It crossed my mind once or twice, but I put the thought away knowing they would *break me*. Some mornings Baris had to carry me to the shower. I was still twitching from chain orgasms. Two, or even three at once, would cause my brain to short-circuit.

Killian grinned at Saint. "Pay up."

Pay up?

"Hold on. What's happening?"

"I bet you'd bring up a threesome within the next two months. He said you were still hiding from your freaky side and would need five."

"Hiding from my freaky side? Saint, I do things with you that I've never seen in porn. What am I hiding from?" I propped myself up, still on the receiving end of Killian's fingering. "I haven't suggested it before because I'm fairly certain both of you at once would kill me. Dead. Buried. Six feet under. Smile frozen on my face.

"I'm suggesting it now since Saint is fresh from the hospital and operating at half capacity. I figure that ups my chances of survival."

"I'm never at half capacity," Saint said. "Want to withdraw the offer? 'Cause if I get in that bed, I'm coming to kill."

Holy shit. This is really happening. Dare I call for Brutal? Fortune rarely smiles on me. I shouldn't test her patience.

"I—"

My phone rang.

"Ugh!" See? I told you that wench was two-faced.

"Ignore it," I said, but Killian was getting up.

He fixed on the phone sitting on the nightstand. "It's Croix. Why is he calling you? I thought you were done with him."

"No, you didn't. I never said I was done with him."

"He's stalking you."

"*You* stalked me."

"I had good reason."

"He's trying to find Thiago Pais for us."

"He's finding Thiago Pais for him," Killian corrected. "Cross is after the same man. Croix is after Cross. They're bound to run into each other."

"Even if that's true, we still need to know where he is."

"We'll find him on our own."

"When? While we have all our men and resources focused on Katz?" I spun on Sinjin—sexy time was over. "Saint, can you help me out here? He saved you and Edie. You can't feel the same way you did about him."

"Jasper Croix cannot be a Merchant and work for Lombard. I'd say the same thing if it was that guy, so don't make that face." *That guy* being his brother. "All the same, Pais almost got his hands on you three times. He's upping his game, and if I have any feelings, it's that the next time he'll make sure he doesn't fail. If Croix has information, we need to know it. Answer the phone."

The phone in question had stopped ringing. At least one boyfriend wouldn't fight me when I called him back.

I slid off the sheets and got dressed. Killian went out and returned with Brutal. Bruises covered his knuckles courtesy of Jasper's face. I hit redial under their watchful eyes.

"Adeline."

"Hey, Jasper. Everything okay?"

"You busy tonight?"

I checked the clock. "I start dinner in about twenty minutes. Otherwise, no."

"They can feed themselves. I found her."

"Who her?"

"Her name's Sloane Wright." There was a whooshing sound on his end like he was driving with the windows down. "She did change it, but I dug up the official documents. Tracked down where she works. She's the one person who may be able to tell us where Pais is."

"If that's true, why is Pais letting her walk around free to be found by you?"

"Pais doesn't *let* her do anything. There is no love lost between these two."

"Then, why would she know where he is?"

"Love, can I answer these questions on the way? I'm outside the house. Come down."

"You are?" I moved to the window. Sure enough, Jasper was pulling up to the sidewalk and shutting off the engine. "Is there a time clock on this?"

"Do you want Pais out there breathing for another night?"

I balled my fists. "While Sister Edie is doing it through a tube. No, thank you."

"Dress for a party." He ended the call.

I told Sinjin, Killian, and Brutal what was going on while I dressed. Restocking my party clothes wasn't high on my list after the explosion. Options were limited.

"Why does he need you there?" Sinjin asked. "If he's got something, give it up and we'll check it ourselves."

I tossed a black skater dress aside and pulled a green, strapless number from my suitcase. "In the time I've come to know the fake Mercer and the real Jasper, I've noticed he plans everything to the last detail. Leaving nothing to chance. If he asks me to be there to get information from this Sloane, then I need to be there. Guys, we agreed Pais is a distraction we can't afford right now. All of Cinco is after me, but the rest don't have the Kings at their disposal."

"Wear a belt," Sinjin said. "Take the garrote."

"Good idea."

Sinjin grabbed my hand on the way out the door, pulling me up short. "Be careful of Croix. Something is off about him. If you find out what that is tonight, don't hesitate to kill him."

"I'm not killing anyone. Well, I might kill someone, but it won't be Jasper. I know it's hard for you guys to understand, but I trust him." As I said it, I knew it was true. "Whatever he wants, it's not to hurt us."

"Adeline." Sinjin wasn't calling me Bunny. He was serious. "Everything about him is designed to hurt you. He fashioned his looks, speech, manner, and personality to win over everyone in his path. Once he gets what he wants from them, they're left as he is inside. Empty. You think you're dancing with him. You haven't noticed the music's off and he's already gone home."

"What the fuck does that mean?" I snapped. "Why are you all questioning my judgment now? I'm the only one in this room who has put in the effort to find out who Jasper Croix is. So don't tell me like your standing back and judging gave you special insight."

"Why is he following you around? Why has he made finding Pais his personal mission when he should be tracking down the ledger that'll free his daughter from Lombard's hold? He's waited four fucking years, hasn't he? You'd think he'd be desperate to get rid of that cloud over her. So desperate, when Gianna 'Kieran' Cross was right down the hall, he should've spun her the same sob story and made even the smallest attempt to get the ledger."

"Croix isn't acting like a man doing whatever he has to do to protect his daughter. And if he's not in this for her, what does he want?"

Sinjin let go of my hand. "Think about that while you're on your date, Bunny. Hope it doesn't spoil the evening."

I slammed out of the house.

Jasper was standing on the sidewalk, holding the door open for me. If he noticed the thunderclouds brewing on my face, he made no mention of it.

I distracted myself with an email to Gianna, relaying the Kings' attack, the fire, and our progress planning the Katz assassination. I emailed her almost every day since we left the loft. A few times I asked for dirt on Katz. Once I asked if the ledger said anything about a Jasper Croix. Not a single reply came back.

"Where are we going?" I asked after too long a silence.

"Club in North Quay."

"Who is this person? Who is she to Pais?"

"Ex-fiancée."

The straight answer loosened the tension in my shoulders.

"I can see why there would be no love lost between exes," I mused. "Why do you think she'll know where he is?"

"Sloane is hiding from him. That's harder to do when you don't know where to avoid. Plus, she's gotten as close to him as you can get to a person. Pais is almost as good as me at hiding his real self. She'll have seen it. Sloane can help us end this fight for good."

"How did you know about her?"

"You know this," he said, giving me a strange look. "Pais and I have traveled in the same circles for years. Met more than once at the parties of mutual friends."

Of course I knew. Saint's earworm had burrowed in, stirring me to question everything.

"He didn't hide it when he got engaged six years ago. He did hide it when they broke up. Suddenly, he stopped bringing her to parties, and when we met up for a shared job four weeks later, I noticed his ring wasn't in his wallet."

"Shared job?"

"The ladies wanted the top two escorts in the city as their dates."

My mind ground to a halt. "You've slept with Thiago Pais?"

"Do you want the answer to that?"

"No," I said quickly. "I do not. Can't even tell you why that came out of my mouth."

He chuckled. "Good. But I'll tell you anyway because you're drifting to the worst. That job was for show. They were sisters. Nana and Pop-Pop were threatening to cut them out of the will because they were thirty, unmarried, and childless. That was until they showed up at Christmas dinner with two gorgeous fiancés. In the end, only Freya said what the hell and took him to bed. Mine wouldn't even shake my hand without gloves and a sanitizer bath afterward. Hiring escorts was not her plan A."

I smothered a laugh. "Oh no, I'm picturing her pinched lips whenever you kissed her cheek and played the part."

"Adeline, I wished she pinched her lips. I leaned in to fake whisper sweet nothings and she reacted like I knifed her under the table. Woman dumped a bowl of scalding soup on my lap. I waddled for half the night."

I howled, falling on the dashboard.

"I'm glad my trauma amuses you."

"It does. It really, really does," I wheezed. "I'm tapping you for more funny Alaric stories."

"That's your last one."

"Ah." I pushed out my bottom lip. "Even if I want to listen while we're soaking in the bath at your place tonight?"

"I'll tell you everything you want to know."

I cracked up, and that questioning voice faded.

The club in North Quay turned out to be Honeybees.

"I've been here before with Gianna," I told him.

Jasper parked the car in a lot down the street. We set off holding hands—him caressing the soft skin between my thumb and forefinger, and shooting bolts of electricity through my veins.

It was highly distracting and definitely the reason I tripped twice walking in my heels.

"They had this cute honeycomb light-up dance floor and the signature drinks were dusted with pollen."

"Hasn't changed since you've been. I checked to be sure she's working tonight."

"What makes you think she'll talk to you? You know Pais, but did you know her?"

"Wouldn't you drop everything and listen if someone showed up offering to get revenge on your ex?"

"If it's the one who slept with my mom, I'll buy his ass a steak dinner and offer to fund expenses."

"I think I need to hear your stories," he said.

I burrowed under his arm. Jasper smelled like pine needles and petrichor—the earth after it rained. I was flashing back to us in his car, wet from the rain-fed waterfall and molded together like broken pieces soldered back together.

"If we're getting into the soul-baring, it's going to be a long night."

"Fine with me," he said. "I've got nowhere to be."

"Why has he made finding Pais his personal mission when he should be tracking down the ledger that'll free his daughter from Lombard's hold?"

I'd find out. I'd discover everything there was to know about Jasper Croix.

Whatever Saint, Killian, and Baris thought, there was one thing I knew about Jasper for certain. A fact he left on my lips, burned into my skin, and said with every look.

Jasper wanted me.

A want so consuming it charged the air with heat. To have me he would give me everything like Saint, Killian, and Baris before him. The boys didn't have to worry about my judgment.

I pulled Jasper down for a kiss.

There wasn't a man on this planet who could fool me.

JASPER

The guard lifted the rope, letting me pass on sight.

Honeybees was packed. People jostled us on all sides, heading to the bar, making for the themed dance floor, or standing around pretending to talk while secretly hoping someone sidled up and grinded on them. I got the look from a few women, and two men, as we pushed into the middle of the dancing. Probably why Adeline held me tighter. Saint was correct about one thing. She was a possessive little bunny.

"Are we dancing?" she shouted. "I thought we were looking for Sloane."

"Why can't we do both?" I spun her around, snapping her laughing to my chest. Adeline's body was an amusement park I was staying in after closing, riding the dips and rises of her curves till my heart exploded.

I gripped her hips, molding her to me as I moved.

"Ohh," she said in my ear. "He can dance too."

"I'm a man of infinite talents. All I hope to demonstrate to you tonight."

"Won't hear a no from me." She twisted. My hands pressed against her, Adeline slid down my body, her breasts cupped in my grip. The journey back returned me to her thighs, and then between them. "I was planning on break-ing a few sexual barriers tonight."

I licked the shell of her ear, feeling her shudder. "Those barriers won't ex-ist after tonight."

I didn't recognize the song playing. Honestly, they could've been spinning "Happy Birthday" and I'd have said I didn't know the tune. My senses were honed on a single point in the universe around which we all revolved.

There were people out there who didn't know it. Farmers in Malaysia and food stall owners in Perth. The news may come as a surprise at first, but given time they'd realize what I had come to accept. The world hinged on Adeline Redgrave.

We descended into our own haze. Grinding, wining, spinning, and bumping, our rib cages weren't given room to expand, let alone space given for our bodies to unglue.

My cock was rock hard and poised to blow. Back to me, Adeline covered her hand and its activities in my pants with a crafty dance. Smooth, slow strokes taunted in opposition to the pounding beat.

She was undoing the last ties to my sanity thread by thread. I was about to come in my pants like a pimply teenager—again.

From somewhere deep inside of me, in a well of strength I didn't know existed, I forced myself to look at my watch. We were supposed to meet Sloane five minutes ago.

"Adeline, we have... to go."

"Am I holding you up?" She swirled her finger around the tip, collecting my precum. She grinned as she licked it clean. "Oops. Let's get going, then."

She walked off.

All right. At this point, she understands I cannot be held responsible for my actions.

I picked her up, locked us in the women's bathroom, and fucked her in a stall. The line of people judging us when we came out was seven people long.

"How late are we now?" she asked, ignoring the stares.

"Very. We'll have to wait till eleven thirty."

"What happens at eleven thirty? This is so mysterious."

I hope you're still grinning like that when it's time.

I led Adeline upstairs to wait by the VIP entrance. If I danced with her a second longer, we wouldn't make it to see Sloane tonight.

Pressing her against the wall, my arm framed her above while the other played with her hair.

"Did the guys give you shit for coming out with me?"

"Yes." She played with my belt buckle—a harmless act that revved me up to go. "You're lucky I beat Baris out the door. What were you guys like before I came along? Did you always disagree like this?"

"We got along well enough. Baris and Sinjin fought at least once a week when he made a mess of something. Sinjin and Killian argued almost every damn day. They're closer than brothers, but they could not be less alike. And Sinjin threatened to cut off my smart mouth every time I opened it. Are you seeing the common denominator here?"

Her laugh cut my chest open and carved her initials inside. "Again I ask, why did you live together when you had the money to get your own places? Buy out an apartment floor and live as neighbors if you had to."

I shrugged. "Chasing the ledger is an all-day, everyday fight, love. You saw it for yourself. You and Cross were separated by minutes. One phone call snatched it out of your reach—and La Roche's. It was easier to stay close. Keep an eye on each other. Despite the difficulties every person on earth would have living with Sinjin, there was a mutual respect there. It kept everyone alive."

"I love living with Saint."

"He hung you from the ceiling, starved you, and put you in a cage."

"Point made." She left my belt, traveling up my buttons. "So, when the fight to own the ledger is over, where will you live? What will you do?"

I anticipated this question, though she hadn't really asked it. She was dancing around, expecting me to take the hint and say it first.

"Once I'm free of Lombard and the ledger, there's no need for me to remain a Merchant. Even less for me to be a grown man with roommates."

She nodded, expression giving nothing away. "You'll be free, Jasper. You should do what you want with that freedom."

"What I want isn't to steal for rich bags, or pretend to be their boyfriends and wind up with a lap full of soup for the trouble."

Adeline looked away. I held her chin between two fingers, bringing her back.

"I want to steal for myself, and be one woman's boyfriend. I want to live in a home with my family, and watch you grow big with my kid. Another girl," I said. "I'm partial to daughters."

Her lips trembled, tears dotting her lashes. "That's an excellent use of your freedom, Jasper Croix."

I brushed my lips over hers. "What will you do with yours?"

"You'll find out."

The curtains parted. A stout man shaved on top and five rings on his right hand beckoned us over. "Alaric?"

"That's me."

He ticked a box on his clipboard. "Andrena's ready for you. No phones. No cameras. No recording devices of any kind. Understood?"

"Understood."

He swept out a hand, pulling back the curtain. "Enjoy yourselves."

"We will."

ADELINE

"Andrena's ready for you. No phones. No cameras. No recording devices of any kind. Understood?"

"Understood."

No recording devices of any kind? What kind of conversation is this?

"Jasper, what are we doing?"

He winked. "Obey me."

"I did not approve that alternative."

I got a laugh in response.

The two of us strode down a hallway covered in glitter gold hexagon wall decals. The club leaned into the honeycomb theme hard.

Three doors lined each side of the hall. The thumping bass made it impossible to hear what was happening behind them. My mind supplied the possibilities in its place.

Jasper stepped into the room on the far end. I followed him inside, blinking as my eyes adjusted.

The entire space was bathed in golden neon light. A black velvet sofa encircled the room, and we had to step off the platform and down into it. In the middle of the action was a pole.

"Is there an explanation forthcoming?"

"Did I forget to mention Sloane works as a stripper?"

I looked around, sweeping the honeycomb shelves, each sporting a different kind of beer or bottled alcohol. Glasses and a bucket of ice were placed beside us.

"Help yourself." Jasper plopped on the couch. "It's all complimentary."

"I didn't know this place had private strip rooms," I said.

"Hundreds of people didn't know The Pleasure Center existed beneath Opium. The crafty businessmen and women of Cinco find a way. Come on." He patted the seat. "We'll make out like fumbly juniors under the bleachers until she's ready."

I poured us two glasses of white wine and settled in to do just that.

The heady, adrenaline-pumping thrill of getting each other off in the club was incredible. Just me and Jasper together was its own kind of amazing. The music muted. The bumping crowd gone. The societal standards holding me back vanished.

We kissed slow and deep. Jasper returned my hand to his buttons.

I teased him, unbuttoning one, skipping down the other, returning, and making like I'd keep going. We flirted about going to his place, but it was set in stone now. I wanted to explore all there was of this new man.

Jasper was right. Of all the difficulties that news report brought, there was one gift.

We got to fall in love again.

Oh, hell. I smiled to myself. *Love has turned me into a sappy mess.*

Def Leppard poured out the speakers, springing us apart. The lights dimmed even lower, plunging us in the sexy atmosphere. What made it sexy? The smoke piped in from the ceiling, cool washing over us.

Sloane slinked inside. Dressed in a gold sequined bikini, platform heels, and a heavy veil. She grabbed the pole and got to business. I jerked back as her heels swung inches from my nose.

"Are you sure she's Sloane?" I whispered to Jasper.

"Positive." He pointed to her ass—currently being shaken in his face.

A bottle of spilled ink traveled up her back and transformed into a flock of ravens. A cool idea for a tattoo, and distinctive.

Sloane climbed on top of me and ground on my lap. I'd never been this close to a pair of boobs that weren't my own. Seriously, Jocelyn didn't even breastfeed.

Sloane ripped off her bra.

"Jasper, whenever you're ready," I snapped.

He snorted in his glass of wine. "Sorry, I had to see how long you'd let it go on before you said something."

A voice came from beneath the veil. "Is something wrong?"

"Sloane, do you remember me?" She scrambled off at the sound of her name. "We're here because we need to talk to you."

"Who are you? How did you find me? Chris?" Sloane climbed on the platform, banging on the door. "Chris!"

Jasper put up his hands. "There's no need for that. We're not here to hurt you. It's me. Alaric."

"Who?!"

"We met a few years ago at the Benton-Williams Charity Ball. I was a... colleague of Thiago Pais."

Sloane stopped her banging. I couldn't see the look on her face, but I felt it.

"Get out."

"We need your help to kill him."

Sloane froze. I froze.

I wasn't expecting Jasper to drop a sentence like that in the middle of the conversation and return to sipping his wine.

"What did you say?"

"Thiago is threatening my girlfriend. He's attacked her twice. We don't feel safe going outside anymore. We need your help, Sloane. Believe me, if I wasn't desperate, I wouldn't be here."

She turned in my direction. "Did you date Thiago too?"

"I—"

"Yes," Jasper cut in. "They dated for a few months. Addy ended it to be with me. We haven't had a day of peace since."

"Oh, I'm so sorry." Sloane stepped down. She held me with both hands, soothing my confused self with waves of comfort. "Thiago is a monster."

"He is," I agreed. "He set fire to the home of someone close to me. Just to draw me out. She's in the hospital, fighting for her life."

Sloane gasped.

I glanced at Jasper, silently asking if that was the right thing to say. I didn't know how much honesty we were going for.

He nodded imperceptibly. "It'd help if we could find him. Pais moved out of his place three weeks ago. But the attacks haven't stopped."

"I don't know where he could be. I haven't had anything to do with him for years." Sloane rescued her bra and put it back on.

"What about old apartments or properties he owned when you were together?"

"We lived in a hotel suite back then. It was owned by the Kings. Thiago didn't pay a cent. If he bought other property back then, Thiago didn't tell me about it."

Jasper leaned forward. "But you got away from him, Sloane. How? Did you pay him off? Did you blackmail him? What do we do to make him stop? Because my last option is killing him," he growled. "He will not touch her again."

"It wasn't easy," she said.

"What happened between you two?" I asked. "Did he drive you crazy with that smarmy gentleman routine while underneath he was a controlling sadist? Then when you couldn't take it anymore, he punished you for daring to leave?"

Sloane shook her head, veil swishing. "You took the words out of my mouth. Thiago was a master manipulator. For years he had me fooled, then I began to see the real him. We worked as escorts in the beginning. When we got engaged, we both agreed to quit. His club was making more than enough to support us. We could move on from employees to management."

"Thiago had other ideas."

"He never stopped," she said. "When I caught him, he banged on about not having a choice, and they were dates Angelo forced him to take as a part of a deal. Eventually, I got tired of his lies and cheating, and I turned to someone else."

Oh no, I thought. *Why is Sloane still wearing that veil?*

"Ethan," she continued. "It started as revenge fucks and turned into something else. Being with Ethan helped me see everything that was wrong with Thiago and our relationship. One night I got out of his bed and asked myself why the hell was I going home to a man I stopped loving a long time ago."

Sloane grabbed the hem of the veil. She tugged it off, revealing a lovely, unblemished face. Big, robin's egg eyes swam with tears. They dripped onto her heart-shaped lips.

"So, I didn't. I called Thiago and told him it was over. I was leaving him. He didn't take it well."

"What did he do?"

"Harassed me, Ethan, and Ethan's family," she said. "Ethan picked me up at work one night. I came out and found Thiago beating him in the alley. He put him in the hospital with three broken ribs and a concussion. After that, I quit, we moved to North Quay, and I changed my name. If I had the money, I would've left Cinco completely."

"Are you and Ethan still together?"

A soft smile broke out on her lips. "Yes. We got married last June."

"A happy ending," I said, smiling back. "But how? What made him finally give up?"

"Not money. Thiago has plenty. And not by trying to kill him, even though there were days I wanted to plunge a knife in his chest and find out if there was a heart to stab. No, in the end, only one thing forced him to back off and let me go."

"What's that?" Jasper asked.

Sloane got up and walked out of the room. We sat there throwing big eyes at each other, wondering what to do next. She returned as we were getting up.

"Go to this address." Sloane placed Honeybees' business card on my palm. "Actually, just mention this address to him. Thiago will never bother you again."

"Thank you."

Jasper and I held our tongues till we were out of the club.

"Looks like this address is outside of Harlow," I said. "It's late, but we should check it out. Get a hint of what we're dealing with."

"We can't."

"Can't? Why not?"

Jasper picked up the pace. "Because I'll be fucking you in the shower in the next twenty minutes."

Well, that settled that.

"WHY DIDN'T I KNOW MY men were so artistically inclined?"

"Am I your man now?" He blew on the skin just above my knee. "Signifies another step in our relationship."

"What does body art signify?"

"Ownership."

I flicked his nose, leaving a spot of red behind.

If you asked me how I started the night planning to kill the governor, and ended up lying on a pile of blankets in Jasper's living room, listening to the blues while he fed me strawberries and covered me in paint, I wouldn't have an answer for you.

I wouldn't be able to verbalize much in any way. All I could say was being there with him—watching Cinco through the window and feeling the paint dry and tighten my skin. It's the closest I ever felt to him.

"Your turn," I said.

"The mommy–son fetish you experienced your first time out. I've gotten that three times."

"No," I cried. "Were you the mommy or the son?"

"Cheeky."

I giggled.

"Hey, no moving, love. Or this is going to look like shit."

"What are you drawing?"

"You."

It was perfectly fine Jasper would only allow me a peripheral peek. I had a full view of him.

Jasper was stretched out on our makeshift bed like the depiction of Adam receiving the touch of life in the Sistine Chapel. Young, strong, gloriously naked.

"Damn," I breathed.

I ran my fingers down his stomach, leaving my red paint on his sculpted abs.

The first time we had sex in the car was a frantic rush of limbs and attraction. My mind blocked off the memory for my own protection. Going near it sent me into an orgasmic coma. But that was different. Tonight we explored each other body and soul.

The spot under his ear that made him suck in a breath. What it did to my toes when he kissed my spine. Every new find was a gift I locked away.

I hadn't admitted it to him. I barely admitted it to myself.

I was falling in love with him.

"Your turn," he said.

"There was this guy junior year of college. He asked me out and then tried to trick me by having his twin brother show up at my door."

He snorted. "You're kidding?"

"I wish. They both thought it was hilarious and didn't know why I refused to date either one of them."

"How'd you know?"

"Twin Two had a tiny mole under his collarbone. Daddy taught me not to miss a thing. Once again, my unconventional childhood education saved me."

"How am I the escort, but you have the most interesting dating stories?"

"I attract weirdos like gunk in a drain strainer."

Jasper chuckled. "What does that say about your current boyfriends?"

"Says I finally got it right."

"Oooh, she's smooth."

Laughing, I relaxed on my pillow, letting the music and good mood wash over me. "How much do you mind a red penis?"

"Paint me all the colors of the wind, baby."

"Childhood ruined," I got out, my sides in stitches.

I was well on my way to covering him in paint when my phone rang.

"I've got it." Jasper reached behind and picked it off the table. *Cash* flashed on the screen.

"Put it on speaker," I asked, "and no arguing."

He acted zipping his lip and tossing away the key. Jasper hit *accept*.

"Adeline."

"Hey, baby. What's up?"

"What's up?" He repeated the greeting like I slipped into another language. "Where are you? What happened with Pais?"

"We spoke to his ex. She dumped him and managed to survive the breakup without unscheduled surgery. Jasper brought me to talk to her."

"What'd she say?" That question came from Sinjin.

"She gave us an address. Apparently, all we have to do is mention it and he'll back off."

"Where is it?"

"A house in outer Harlow. I looked it up. Seems pretty normal."

"Let me get this straight," Cash said. "Croix rushes you out in the middle of the night to speak to a woman he dug up just in time, who happened to have the magic words to make Pais back off. And it's all yours for nothing at all."

"What are you implying, Killian?" Jasper spoke up.

"Did I imply? Let me say it straight out. You knew Pais's weakness. I'm guessing for years. The show you put on for Adeline tonight was nothing but a con. Separate her from us. Ingratiate yourself by being helpful and solving a problem for her. Now you're balls deep whispering how much you love her."

"Correction: I was balls deep. Past tense. I will be balls deep. Future tense." Jasper's grin dripped wickedness like I'd never seen. "Currently, I'm feasting on this perfect body before we hit round five."

I heaved a sigh. "So much for not arguing."

"You're a con man, Croix. And not a very good one."

"Good enough to fool you for four years."

"Guys, please," I broke in. "Can we not do this? Whether Jasper is trying to con me or not, all I care about is if Sloane's address works. We can't work with Pais breathing down our necks like this. We get him out of the way, and Gianna will take care of the rest. You and I can focus on what's important."

Cash grunted. "Where are you? I'll pick you up."

"In the morning," I said gently. "We're going to check out this address first."

"Give it to me. We'll meet you there."

I didn't see a reason why not. If anything, it'd be good to get the four of them in the same place again and talking. Regardless of their first conversation/fight at the hospital, I wasn't giving up hope that they could work this out.

"Love you." We hung up.

I gave Jasper a look. "Another aspect of your personality I've learned. You're a fire starter."

"Nah. I just don't take as much crap as Mercer did. That guy was out to make everyone like him."

Tracing my name on his chest, I asked, "And this guy?"

"Is out to make you love him."

He always says the right thing.

"Why do you care so much about me? All of this—tracking down Sloane. Going after Pais. It's not as important as freeing yourself and Rosie from Lombard's grip."

Jasper was silent while he painted a design on my knee. "Want the truth?"

"Always. Unless I'm asking how's my cooking, or if you like my new food pun T-shirt. I will only take I love it in those cases."

"Rosie is safe as long as I don't have the ledger, Adeline. It's the minute I get my hands on it that the end is decided between me and Lombard. He'll have me killed," Jasper said flatly. "He'll have no choice. I'd have held the ledger, had time to read its secrets, and then I'll know his. That he's the new Kieran.

"If I can't take him out during the exchange, I'll have to run with Rosie. Hide, plan, and plot until I get my chance to finish him for good." Jasper rose, peering down at me. "There's your answer, Adeline. I want more time. With you. Like this. I want more nights my daughter sleeps safe in her home without a worry in her head. Maybe that sounds like another carefully crafted response from a con man—"

"No, Jasper," I whispered. "I believe you. I don't know why but... I know with me is where you want to be."

"That's a good place to start."

Chapter Seven

I twirled in the front of the mirror, admiring Jasper's creations.

I was all of the elements. Earth, water, air, and fire.

Crashing waves rushing up my legs. Flames sprouted from my palms. He covered me from neck to toes, and if there were smudges, they were from us fooling around before the paint was dry.

Jasper stirred beneath the sheets.

He was a light sleeper. He clocked me getting out of bed an hour ago to turn on a pot of coffee and have a good snoop.

"Check under the floor panel in the closet," his side of the bed muttered. "That's where I keep the fake passports and ten thousand in cash."

"Good tip, baby."

I strolled naked around his apartment, sipping my coffee and smiling whenever I caught my reflection.

Jasper's place was the same above and beneath the surface. Weapons, money, and tools were the secrets stashed under couch pillows and in false bottoms. None of it said personal. If his face wasn't in the pictures, you couldn't tell a thing about the person who lived here.

"Where are the baby photos?" I jumped on top of him and was snatched out of the air. Jasper flipped me over, trapping me beneath him.

"Whose?" he asked. "Mine or Rosie's?"

"Both."

"Don't have any of myself, but Rosie—" Jasper pounded the dresser. A false side popped open. "These are hers."

I snuggled next to him, flipping through the small photo album. A squalling baby grew through the years—from her sleeping in a bassinet to playing on a jungle gym with the little boy I saw before.

"Can I ask a question that you don't have to answer?"

"Yes," he said.

"Do you ever wish things were different? That you were raising her."

"I do. Some days." Jasper closed the book. "But I made the best out of our situation. It's enough for me that she knows who her father is. I didn't get the option."

He got out of bed, taking me with him. We showered, dressed, ate a light breakfast, and were out the door in time to catch Saint's call asking us where we were.

"We're getting in the car now. Where are you?"

"Outside the house."

"You are?" I checked the time. "We said eight o'clock."

"Came early in case Croix told the actors to come at seven forty-five."

I shook my head. Of course.

"Did he?"

"I see why that woman sent you here, Bunny, and you're not going to like it."

"What does that mean? Who lives there?"

"I'll save the news to see the look on your face."

He hung up.

I love this man. I love this man. I love this man. The reminder helped reduce Sinjin-related frustration.

Jasper drove us out of the city. We took the long way to outer Harlow, avoiding the city centers and the Old West wanted posters nailed to every door.

Jasper parked behind Sinjin, Killian, and Baris. We were two houses down from 148. I noted the house-shaped mailbox and pink shutters on the window from the satellite photos.

Sinjin rolled down the window at my knock. "Should you be out right now?" I leaned in for my kiss. "You need to be at home resting."

"Home is now a pile of wood in nature's toilet."

"Lovely way to describe our cabin in Elmshire."

"Plus, I lost my nurse. If you want me in bed, you'll have to give me a reason to stay."

"Hmm. Message sent and received." I opened his door. "Are we going? What's the deal with this place?"

It was Baris who got out. He brushed past his former brother and laced our fingers. Together we walked toward the house—by that I mean the three of us. Jasper matched us step for step, walking by my side.

"Lorenzo Bianchi," Baris said. "Remember he told you what he did to get Pais to give up his bid for leadership."

"Bianchi?" I searched my memory. "Uh, yeah. He said he tracked Pais's illegitimate..." I trailed off.

"Yes, Adeline."

We stopped before the house. Three pairs of boots walked up the porch. An adult pair, and two with fire engines and yellow daisies.

"His kids," I said. "Sloane and then Enzo forced Pais to surrender by threatening his kids."

"It's an effective motivator." A dark undercurrent laced Jasper's words.

"What do you want to do?" Baris asked.

"It's up to me?"

He inclined his head.

I knew why. I went down this road with Jasper. It was my decision to see it to the end.

I stared at those daisy rain boots. "Pais is too strong to be left unchecked. He has hundreds of men at his disposal, and he's willing to cannon fodder every last one at us if it gets him the ledger. We're not going to touch his kids," I said, "but he doesn't have to know that."

I snapped a picture of the house.

"Let's go before we're caught lurking."

Brutal steered me toward their car. I broke free and ran up to Jasper.

"Nobody punched anyone," I said against his lips. "That's progress."

He finished the task and kissed me. "I'll see you Friday night."

"Will you?" I teased.

"I'll be outside your place at eight o'clock. Friday night and whatever night I choose to show up at your door." He backed toward his car, shooting me a wink. "I won't make it easy."

That night, I lay on the couch with Baris, staring into the fire.

The cabin was just as small and oppressively quiet as we left it. But it was safe, it was warm, and it was five miles away from Governor Katz.

The name drew my eye to the card. Using children as blackmail was a low I prayed I'd never reach. With monsters like Pais, their twisted deeds corrupt. They poison people until they become them, or they commit worse acts to stop them.

Leah Tyler. Desmond Lane.

Adeline Redgrave.

I couldn't let this man rampage through our lives unchecked. Saint has waited decades to avenge his father to now fear losing his surrogate mother. Killian sacrificed everything to protect his family who lived in fear of the next hit coming.

We couldn't fight a war on two sides.

The ledger would be safe with Gianna until it was time for us to face off once again—hopefully on better terms. She would find Pais and kill him.

In the meantime, our focus was Katz. A mistake here would get us killed or life in prison.

It had to be Katz. I had to make this call.

The phone rang once. Twice. Three times. I considered what I'd say in the voicemail.

"Who is this?"

"Thiago," I said. "It's Adeline."

"Adeline Redgrave." I heard music and conversation from his end. Was this guy throwing dinner parties while we were holed up in the middle of nowhere? "This is a surprise. I was just thinking about you. I'm glad you called, love."

My skin crawled. A cute pet name from Jasper was a derogatory slur coming out of his mouth.

"I'm not your love, Pais. I called because you're done. The attacks on the Merchants stop as of four days ago."

"They stop when Gianna Cross puts the ledger in my hands."

"You must not have heard me. Maybe this will open your ears." I sent him the picture I took of the house.

"What will open my ears? Don't leave a statement like that hanging. I... will..."

"Seems I have your attention now."

A pregnant silence beat my eardrum.

"So many thoughts are going through your head. 'How did she find them?' 'What is she going to do?' 'Why, oh why, was I such a coldhearted bastard I sent my thugs to burn down a church and terrorize an innocent woman?' 'How will Redgrave make my children pay for that?'"

"If you touch them—!"

"Ah ah," I sliced into the tirade. "I'm speaking now. The answer is nothing, Pais. I won't touch a hair on their cute little heads. You see, I haven't reached your level of reprehensible yet. To do so would take an extraordinary feat of science where I'm transformed into a cockroach. Until then, your children won't be harmed by me.

"No, they'll be harmed by you," I hissed. "I'll expose you for the man that you are. Daddy is a bad person who cuts up people and leaves them to die. He burns nuns alive. Throws women off balconies. Abuses and controls everyone who has the misfortune of meeting him. You have a daughter, right? Think this information will have an effect on her psyche?"

"You're not going near my children."

"Let's say you do get to them before me. How deep into uninhabited jungle would you be relocating them to? The internet spreads wide, bitch. If you and the Kings don't fade into vapor, the world finds out what truly lives behind that smile."

The smug, charming tone vanished. "You've made a very big mistake tonight, Redgrave."

"Yawn. Skip the empty threats and agree to the terms. Thiago Pais forgets about the ledger, Gianna Cross, and Adeline Redgrave. In exchange, your children grow up in blissful ignorance."

"I do not accept," he forced through clenched teeth.

"You—"

"Adeline? Hello?"

I shot up, startling Baris awake.

"Baby, is that you? Help—"

There was a scuffle. Someone screamed. A door slammed. Music and conversation filled my ear again.

"I assume we understand each other," Pais said. "I'll text you with further instructions."

Click.

"Adeline, what is it?" Baris tugged the phone from my stiff grip. "What happened?"

"Jocelyn," I rasped. "Pais has Jocelyn."

"—TRAP!"

Their arguing filtered out the screen door. Cash, Saint, and Brutal went back and forth for half the night, without my input.

Sunlight peeked through the trees, casting scattered pockets of light over our slice of forest. A bird hopped among the grass and drank dew from fallen leaves. She was a pretty little thing boasting black, white, and yellow feathers.

"If she can do it, so can you."

Of course I'd think of that now. When I was young, not long after Dad found me, I'd watch birds flit through the trees with envy. They flew away from danger—high in the clouds where nothing and no one could touch them.

"Why hadn't I been born a bird?" I asked.

Dad pulled me aside right there on the sidewalk, crouching to look in my eyes. "Birds have it hardest of all, brown eyes. Their homes are destroyed. Their eggs stolen. They are hunted, killed, and caged. Their wings are clipped and they're put on display to live a short life as objects of fascination. You shouldn't look at these creatures and wish you were them. You should see how she fights to survive. To be free. And believe if she can do it, so can you."

"You always know what to say, Dad."

"—kill him."

Sinjin slammed onto the porch. "Are you sure Pais has her?" His broad chest blocked my sight of the bird. "What the hell's he been doing all this time? Kicking back on the bearskin rug while she screams in the closet?"

"It's her," I said. "I know her voice."

"Whatever you're thinking of doing, you're not."

"You don't know what I'm thinking, Saint."

"You're thinking of saving her from Pais." Killian gripped my hips, drawing me to his chest. "He won't let you walk out of there, Adeline. Pais will get exactly what he wants."

"I don't know what he wants." My voice was light—conversational. "He hasn't given me instructions yet."

"Bunny, you're not risking your life for that woman. I should've killed her months ago. Let Pais rid the world of another disease-ridden carrier and be done with it."

"I'd put it more tactfully," Cash said, "but my response is the same. It's not like he has your father. You owe Jocelyn Daniels nothing. If anything, she might finally get what she deserves."

I broke out of his hold. "I don't expect either one of you to understand. That's why I'm not asking you to do this with me. It wouldn't be fair to you. Your focus has to be on Katz."

"What the fuck are you talking about?" Sinjin returned.

"I'm handling the Pais problem on my own from here on."

"The hell you are," Cash said.

"I am. I couldn't ask you to drop everything to rescue my mother. We're too close to taking down Katz and running out of time to do it."

"No," they said in unison.

I smiled. I was filled with an odd mood. I couldn't describe it, but as I glanced at the bird, hopping from leaf to leaf, surviving on the little life had to offer and it being more than enough—I knew what I had to do.

"Yes," I said gently. "Pais doesn't want me dead. I'm bait to draw out Gianna. A catch who is actively trying to kill him, so he's sure to regret that move. It'll be okay. I know what I'm doing."

Sinjin threw Cash a look. "You're hearing me, right? I said no. No came out of my mouth multiple times."

"I heard it," Cash agreed.

"Oh, good. I was worried for a second." Sinjin tipped my chin up. "You even think about risking your life for Jocelyn Daniels, I'll kill her myself."

I took his hand, holding it between us. "This isn't your decision to make."

"This isn't your fight alone," Cash said. "Pais signed his death warrant when he attacked you in that apartment. He signed it just by taking over the Kings. We'll kill him, Adeline. Together. On our terms. In our trap. When that text comes, tell that fucker we'll see him soon enough."

I stroked the stubbly gold hairs on his jaw. Traces of red paint matched the color staining his lips.

"Thiago Pais is a sadist. He will torture her while I stand back, delaying a meeting we were always meant to have. It won't accomplish what we want, Killian. If he finds out I don't care what happens to Jocelyn, he'll dump her on the docks and find new leverage. Maybe it'll be my dad, maybe it'll be yours."

The muscles in his neck bulged.

"I can take care of myself, guys. I've been doing it long before you put me in a cage and decided I was helpless."

"Don't give me that shit," Sinjin said. "I could drop you in the middle of the desert with a pack of gum and a capful of water. You'd come back riding a hyena with a necklace made of fox skulls. I know you can handle Pais. He knows it too." Saint's eyes were hard. "This is a trap. Once you're in, you're not getting out."

I threw up my hands. "All right, I hear you. I don't want to fight about this anymore."

I went inside, found Brutal standing over the stove, and shoved myself between. He let me be as I buried my face in his chest, breathing him in.

My phone buzzed.

Leaning back, I looked into his eyes, and something passed between us. He nodded.

"I love you."

"Love you," he said.

"What are you making?" I hopped on the counter, placing my phone facedown beside me.

"Spiced chicken wraps. Same ones you made a few weeks ago." He looked down at his pan of sizzling meat. "It's supposed to be the same."

"Smells delicious, ku'uipo. Can't wait to try it." I slid a glance outside. Killian and Saint talked in low tones on the porch. "Have you ever thought about finding her? Your sister's daughter."

If the question surprised him, he gave no sign. Baris added the ginger, garlic, and seasonings. The smell hit the back of my throat. My mouth watered.

"No."

"Why not?"

"She isn't one of us. She was born free."

"You're not one of them, Baris. I hope you know that. You were always your mother's son."

He brushed his lips on my forehead.

"I am my mother's daughter."

"No."

"Yes," I whispered. "I can't deny I'm what she made me. In the same way I'm what Oscar Redgrave made of me.

"Since I've met you, Killian, Saint, and Jasper, I've changed. My rage, pain, and bloodlust split me in two. I was Adeline—small, simple, and defenseless. And something else that couldn't be touched, and couldn't be stopped.

"It's only when I fell for you that both sides of me came to know love. Sacrifice. Forgiveness. Family," I said. "It's bringing me back together again. I'm becoming something... new. I can't say for certain what, but I know what I'm meant to do. I have to listen, Baris. I can't return to how I was."

"I understand."

"Do you?"

"You have to go up to the roof, Adeline."

I threaded my hand through his. "I'll come down for you."

THAT NIGHT, I SAT BEFORE the fire, reading Pais's message for the fifth time.

Pais: Come to 411 Dunston St. tomorrow. Noon. Apartment 501. I'm certain you recognize the address. I'm also certain you know to come alone. We're done with these games. Any chance of receiving mercy vanished with your last call. Bring the ledger or your mother dies.

411 Dunston St. was Fairfield Palace. Pais clearly was done messing around. He was tired of fishing too. He wanted the ledger now. Or tomorrow night to be exact.

Then, that's what he'll get.

I dialed Jasper.

"Hello?"

"Jasper, are you busy? I need you to pick me up."

"I'll be there in an hour."

An hour later, I kissed Saint's and Cash's sleeping cheeks, and said good-bye to Brutal. He didn't ask me where I was going. He didn't have to.

Jasper parked well away from the cabin. I found his headlights following a fifteen-minute trek through the trees. He opened the door for me.

"What's going on?" he asked. "I have no doubt my skills in the bedroom would lure you back early, but you sounded odd on the phone."

"Thiago has Jocelyn."

Jasper lowered his hand reaching for the ignition. "What does he want?"

"The ledger, Jasper. Screw using me as bait. I bring him the book tomorrow night, or he kills my mother."

"What are you going to do?" He started the car, leaving the cabin and my boys behind. "Isn't the ledger locked away in the Fairfield? That's if Cross hasn't found a way to remove it by now. And I don't see why she wouldn't have. She's the only one who can get up to her floor, and the Fairfield prides itself on privacy. The parking garages are guarded and shielded."

"It's possible she got in to remove the book. I know a few places she would hide it if she's going the 'separate the cookie from the jar' route. But knowing her, she'll want it close by. Either way, I don't have time to check every spot, and then track her down if it turns out they're not there." A thought occurred to me. "Unless…"

"What?" Jasper prompted when I didn't finish speaking. "Unless what?"

I shook my head. "Nothing. I'll check the Fairfield anyway. There's no reason not to while I'm in the area," I said bitterly. "Listen, I'm going to need your help with this. Will you—?"

"Yes."

The automatic response twinged that part of me trying, and failing, not to fall for him.

"If you want help, why are we speeding off in the middle of the night?" he asked. "You don't want the guys in on this?"

I looked away. "We're having fundamental differences on how to approach the situation. Saint sees no reason for me to risk my life for my mother. Cash refuses to do anything on Pais's terms."

"Because this is an obvious death trap. Once he has the ledger, he'll have no reason to keep you or your mother alive."

"I haven't mentioned the part about him moving into the Fairfield. I'll be going in alone."

"I see why you had fundamental differences."

"You're not going to tell me I can't do this?"

"Would it stop you if I did?"

"No."

"Then, no. But I will ask, why are you risking your life for her?" Jasper met my eyes in spite of driving. "Would she do the same for you?"

The question drove a nail through my chest. "Probably not," I rasped. "But I have to do this, Jasper. Jocelyn Daniels made me who I am. She split me in two, and I understand now that I can't be put back together without finding closure with her. If she dies like this, I'll never get my chance, Jasper. I know what she's made of me in life. I'm afraid to find out what I'll become if I don't lift a finger to stop her death."

"I can't say I understand, but if we're the same"—he laced his fingers with mine—"then a bitch like Thiago Pais is nothing against us. Tell me what to do."

"We'll need to make a few stops," I said. "Pais wants a ledger, I'll give him one."

JASPER BROUGHT ME DIRECTLY in front of Fairfield's entrance. It didn't matter if Pais had people watching the place. He was expecting me.

Still, I looked around. If anyone was paying particular attention to me, I couldn't tell. It was another day in Leighbridge.

High-heeled nannies pushed little kids in strollers down the sidewalk, and pretended they couldn't hear their screams to get out while they talked on the phone. A sign for the fifteenth annual orchestra charity fundraiser hung on the old-timey lampposts. The flag pole trumpeted our allegiance to state, country, and Fairfield. I continued the journey up, seeking out the balconies that could be Pais's, and looking for the one I knew to be Gianna's.

Time to go.

I checked my phone as I passed through the revolving door. A bag dangled from my fingers.

Eighteen messages. Seventeen from Cash and Sinjin. One from Brutal telling me he loved me. I messaged them all back that I loved them too.

I would've called, but then that would be allowing the idea that these would be my last words. They wouldn't be. I had no intention of dying today.

Stewart's eyes widened at my approach. He remembered me.

"Hello."

"Good morning," he said. His eyes flicked to the guards within shouting reach. "How can I help you?"

"Relax. My boyfriends aren't behind you. Sorry about that, by the way. They can be a little protective."

"A bit?" he mumbled, then jerked like he couldn't believe he said that out loud. "Excuse me, ma'am, I didn't mean—"

"Don't apologize, my friend. I like a bit of snark." I placed the gift bag on the counter. "Now that all's forgiven, I was hoping you could do something for me."

"Yes?"

"I'm on the guest list for apartment 501. It's my friend's birthday and..." I gave Stewart the whole rehearsed spiel. "So, when we're ready. I'll call and you can bring the present up. Cool?"

Stewart pushed the wrapping aside, taking a peek. "I don't see why not. Tell Mr. de Silva happy birthday from all of us."

"I'll be sure to do that."

Stewart let me through. I lost my smile in the elevator, tensing as it brought me closer.

The last time I'd seen my mother was when she and her latest boyfriend mugged me, stole my car, and left me on the street. Now we'd meet again in circumstances like this.

The doors opened, pushing me out into a plain, simple hallway. I stared at the door on the end without making a move toward it.

What would Dad say about my coming to rescue her?

My father couldn't speak Jocelyn Daniels's name. He hadn't set eyes on her since she found out he was in the retirement home and stormed the place, shouting that he was her husband and she had a right to see him. A lie that got her in.

I don't know what they spoke about that day. Dad refused to talk about it, but Jocelyn restricted herself to jumping me when I came outside, never setting foot in the place again.

But that was just it. Jocelyn wasn't a topic my father and I broached. A fact I didn't change with Thiago's phone call.

He didn't know I was here. I couldn't imagine what he'd say about what I was doing—the risk I was taking.

I knocked on the door.

"Come in."

But it was too late now.

Pais's apartment was night and day to Gianna's. Both were spacious, luxurious, and adopted the same layout. That's where the similarities stopped.

Thiago opted for dark, understated furniture shadowed by pops of color. A red vase on his gray coffee table. A blue accent wall among white. A green tailored suit wrapped around the smiling man reclined in a black ball chair on the platform leading to the balcony.

A throne.

What was it about calling yourself a King that made a man think he was one?

"Adeline."

"Thiago."

Three other men shared the room. Two sat on the couch, and one leaned against the kitchen bar, sipping a beer. They didn't get a greeting.

Pais slowly looked me up and down. "Is the ledger tucked away in your purse? Smaller than I thought."

"Let's not talk about pesky ledgers right now." I snapped my fingers at the men taking up the couch. "Up, gentlemen. It's rude to be seated and leave a lady standing."

They gave me matching crazy looks.

Chuckling, Pais waved them away. "Sit."

I did, crossing my legs at the ankles. "First, where is my mother?"

Pais swiveled his chair. He pointed at double doors that led to the master suite in Gianna's apartment. I assumed it was the same for him.

"Good. Here's how it's going to work. An associate of mine is standing by with the ledger. Once my mother is safely out the door in a taxi, they will send it up. Simple."

"I see." He was grinning wider than ever. That lopsided smile revealed both rows of his perfect, professionally whitened teeth. This time, they had no effect on me.

I can honestly say I'd never seen an uglier man.

"And how do I know they're going to send along the ledger? It could be another book of gibberish or your eighth-grade diary?"

I said nothing. Standing up, I crossed to him, stepping up to the platform. I reached into my purse and three guns aimed at my head.

Ignoring them, I handed Pais my phone. "There's a sample. Zoom in and read the text. Check out the newspaper next to it. Today's date. I have the ledger right here, right now. You get everything you want. You just have to let my mother walk out the door."

Pais dropped both feet on the floor. He bent over my screen, squinting at the text.

I moved behind him.

The blackout curtains were drawn to give the wannabe king his air of villainous mystery.

I pulled them back, then opened the sliding door for good measure, stepping out onto the balcony.

"See? I have what you want." I peered five stories below to the clear shot of the street. "This is where I'm going to stand to watch her get in a car and drive away from here. When it's done, you get your ledger."

"Fair exchange. Well thought out. Bases covered." Pais put his arm around me, leading me back inside. "I have no reason to not agree to your terms."

"So, agree."

"I would. There's just one issue."

I stiffened—disgust crawled beneath the skin he touched. "What issue?"

Pais withdrew a small, black plastic item from his pocket.

"Use your words, Pais. What is the—?"

He pressed it.

A scream punched through the silence, startling me off my feet. I fell onto the ball chair. It spun and dumped me out.

"St-stop," cried a voice I'd know anywhere. "Please, stop."

Thiago pressed the button again.

A choked-off cry leaked under the door. I heard the thud of a body hitting the floor.

"Stop it!" I screamed.

"Shock collar," Pais said. He shook the remote. "Great for bitches of all sizes. Of course, I modified it to pack a real punch."

"You piece of shit!"

"Yes, that's one of the things I called you when you tried bringing my kids into this. Along with jumped-up cunt. Merchant cock–sucking bitch. Stupid little slut playing at being one of the big boys." He sauntered off the platform, smirking down at me. He clicked the button.

"I was quite angry, you see. I tracked your mother in some underground whorehouse only the day before. I was making plans to contact you and set up an exchange." Click. "But then you called me."

Click. Click. Click.

"Stop it," I roared over my mother's screams.

"I'm afraid we won't be doing things your way today, Adeline. So, these are my terms." He hauled me up by the hair, throwing me at the couch. "You have the ledger here in two minutes, or I tape down the *on* button and we discover what gives out first: her voice or her heart?"

Slowly, I straightened, glare setting him alight where he stood.

Not yet, fucker. You'll be paying your coin to pass the burning gates of hell soon enough.

"Do all male escorts need toys and tricks to exaggerate their manhood, or is it just you?"

"I'm not an escort, Redgrave." He got in my face. "I'm king of the Kings. Ruler of this city."

"Right, so it is just you."

He jammed the button.

"Stop it with the temper tantrum! You want the fucking ledger. I'll give it to you."

I dialed down to the front desk.

"Hello. Thank you for calling Fairfield Palace. This is Stewart speaking. How may I help you?"

"It's party time." My papery voice fought to inject cheer. "You can send the present up."

"Right away, ma'am."

Pais shoved me down when I made to stand. "Wesley," he barked. "Go. If they've got anything other than my ledger in their hands, shoot them."

The guy abandoned his beer and went out to intercept my package. Pais watched the front door. I watched his. Jocelyn was on the other side, and my plan to get her out had failed.

What happens now?

The guard returned. In his hand, he held a blue gift bag.

"Got it, boss." He tossed the wrapping on the floor, holding up a beat-up, leather-bound book.

The look on Pais's face as he took it made me think I should excuse myself from the room. He was about to jizz on the pages.

"You got what you wanted." I rose, planting myself behind him. "Let her go."

Pais flipped through the pages. "Ooh. Milo Wilson, very naughty. What do we have on Chase Legend?"

"Did you hear me?" I raised my voice. "Let her go! She's no use to you now."

"I wouldn't say that." The book closed with a snap. "Jocelyn seems to be a pretty useful leash around your neck. I wonder if a little tugging will get me four for the price of one?"

"It won't. You can't own the Merchants any more than you'll own me. Better men than you have tried. Hint: they're dead now."

Shaking his head, Thiago faced me. "You just can't shut that ignorant little mouth. You're not in control here, Adeline."

"Oh, but you are. You finally have your little book, and get to flaunt it like the biggest penis in the locker room. Pathetic."

He snarled.

"When will you all understand the ledger is a curse? It's the serial cheater spinning his tales of love and change. It hasn't changed, Pais. It'll hurt you like it's hurt everyone who's come before."

"I'll take my chances."

"I'll take my exit! Let us out of here now, or the Merchants will plague you for the rest of your short life. We're two for three in killing your leaders and up millions in the revenue we've cost you. You don't want us for an enemy any longer."

"Let my mommy go, or I'll sic my big, bad boyfriends on you." Pais tossed his head back laughing. "You don't get it. I have *this*." He shook the book at me. "You think you've won something because you killed Angelo and Enzo? Does it look like I'm mourning them? And the money? The ledger might as well be the bank account passwords for the rich of Cinco. But you know what, you held up your end, so I'll hold up mine. You want her so badly."

Pais cupped his mouth. "Jocelyn? Jocelyn, join us, love."

The bedroom door opened. A figure draped in blue stepped out of the room.

I almost didn't recognize her.

Jocelyn wore a form-fitted, blue Herrera dress that swept her ankles. Her auburn hair had been dyed black and streaked with waves of dark red. Her throat was smooth, pale, and devoid of a shock collar. She didn't have a mark on her.

Haggard, dark eyes disappeared behind expertly applied makeup. Glittery brown lipstick adorned a mouth usually twisted when she saw me.

She smiled. "Hey, Maddy girl."

My jaw locked. She knew I hated to be called Maddy. The nickname that would've been mine if she wasn't high as a kite while filling out the info for my birth certificate.

"How cute are you? Coming to my rescue." Her heels click-clacked on the hardwood as she came closer, closer, closer to me. "But as you can see, Mommy is doing just fine."

She went to pat my head. I reeled back, stumbling toward the balcony.

"More than fine actually." Pais took her outstretched hand. He placed a tender kiss on her knuckles. "Thiago is taking care of me now."

"A new apartment. New clothes. More money, and the upper-class clients a beautiful woman like you deserves. All things she would've had if her ungrateful bitch of a daughter hadn't abandoned her to the streets." He grinned. "Her words, not mine."

"And that's putting it nicely," Jocelyn spat.

There's that curled lip I knew so well.

"Bent over backward for the piece-of-shit father who abandoned her, but her own mother who sacrificed, starved, and sold herself to put food in her mouth is treated like garbage."

A white-hot band constricted my throat, searing through my flesh. It pained me to breathe. It hurt to even think of speaking.

Jocelyn scoffed, giving me her back. "Do what you want with her, baby. It's past time she learned a lesson."

Thiago held out his hands. "You heard the lady. You're owed a lesson."

His words came from far away. All I could do was stare at my mother, sitting and accepting a beer from Wesley as though she was a spectator to a scene that had nothing to do with her.

She sold you, Adeline. For clothes, jewelry, digs, and richer johns.
She sold you again.

"So, this is what's going to happen." Thiago moved out of the corner of my eye, coming closer. "You work for me now. You're a mouthy bitch. I'll have to break that out of you before you're put to work, but a rare beauty like yourself, you'll bring in enough that one day you'll get back in my good graces.

"St. John Bellisario will have to die. Former leaders don't take well to demotions. Killian 'Cash' Hunt could be useful to me. Baris 'Brutal' Alexander is already considered one of the Kings. He will be the champion to beat in next year's tournament. Cash and Brutal should easily fall in line under the hope I'll retire you one day and let you go back to them. After you've made back the money you've cost me—with interest."

I barely heard him. "You'd let him do this," I whispered, "to your own daughter."

Jocelyn spat at my feet. "It's better than you deserve."

"Don't look so heartbroken." Pais blocked my view. "It's well known I take care of my people. The first couple months, I teach you myself." He stroked my cheek. "You may even come to enjoy it."

"No."

"Excuse me?"

"I said no." I backed out of reach. "You outlined a horrific little fantasy, but none of it is going to happen."

"Oh no?" Amusement etched into the wrinkles around his eyes. "You're not getting out of this apartment that way." He pointed to the front door suddenly blocked by the guards. "So your choices are either that exit"—Pais motioned to the balcony—"or working for me."

"I'll go with neither."

"Defiant to the last."

"Stupid to the last," I said. "You're feeling pretty full of yourself. Unfortunate you haven't noticed that isn't the real ledger."

The grin melted off his lips. "What are you talking about? Yes, it is."

"No. That's an old journal I bought in an antique shop yesterday. My boyfriend and I spent half the night filling it with interesting details he's learned over the course of his work. At one point, we ran out of stuff and made it up."

Pais gaped at the worthless bundle of leather and paper.

I pulled a face. "I say boyfriend. It's still new. I'm trying to sort out my feelings for him, and the amazing sex isn't helping me be sensible about it—But you don't care about that. You care about the fact that you're standing in front of an open balcony."

Pais tore his eyes away. "An open balcony?"

I raised a fist.

Bang!

Thiago blew off his feet. He crashed over the coffee table and tipped it on top of him. The book thudded at Jocelyn's heel.

"Boss!"

Wesley ran to him and was taken out.

I held up another fist and ran for the dropped gun. Grabbing the piece, I vaulted over the couch, ducking behind cover as they opened fire.

Jocelyn screamed and ran for the kitchen.

"Bitch!" one of the guards roared. "What did you do?!"

"How many times," I snapped. "I do not appreciate being called a bitch."

I shot up—firing a shot that winged him, then the second that put him down for good.

The final man shoved Jocelyn out of the way. He ducked behind the kitchen island.

"Whoring was too good for you!"

I crab-walked out from behind the couch. Throwing up one more signal, I rolled out of the way.

Gunfire rained down on the apartment to the tune of my mother's screams. I skirted the wall, coming up on the right side of the island. Jocelyn saw me before he did.

"Look out!"

He snapped around.

Bang!

Jocelyn gaped wide-eyed at the blood and brain matter covering her new dress. She twisted to me and gazed up the barrel of the gun.

"Adeline," she croaked. "What are you doing?"

"Stand up."

"Ade—"

"Stand. Up."

She rose on shaky knees. "You don't need that. I don't have a weapon."

"You are a weapon." My voice was dull. Flat. "Your very existence brings destruction to those around you. Look what happened to Pais when he made a deal with you. His final mistake."

"Addy, baby. Calm down."

"Addy now, is it? Not going to call me Maddy girl?"

Jocelyn moved as I did, maintaining our distance. The hail of gunfire ceased, leaving the screams of tenants sure to be calling the police.

"Adeline! Put that down!"

Sweat beaded on her upper lip. Her eyes darted between me and the gun. The panic in them didn't move me.

I followed her into the living room. "I knew. I knew after he hung up the phone what you'd done. How convenient that Pais dug you out of your hell-hole just in time. But he didn't, did he? You came to him. Heard on the street the Kings were looking for me, and you served your own daughter up without a thought."

"That's not true. He found me. I didn't have a choice, Adeline. You didn't see where I was living. What I had to do to survive."

"You're always the victim, Jocelyn, and I'm the one who has to sacrifice to save you. I realized that as I sat before the fire, contemplating whether I'd run in to do it again. You are never going to change."

She tossed her head. "I can change. I *want* to. But I didn't have anyone who was there for me. Who put me in a fancy nursing home, or cooked me gourmet meals every week? I didn't have anyone paying my way, so I did what I had to do!"

Jocelyn swiped at the gun. I darted out of reach as the real Jocelyn Daniels reared her head.

"Where we are is because of you, Adeline. You tossed me aside and now you're whining and crying because I grabbed the first hand up I've been given in decades. Thiago was going to change my life." She shouted for the man bleeding on the carpet. "You've ruined everything."

"No one is whining or crying here. My eyes are clear."

Jocelyn's shins hit the platform. "Get that out of my fucking face now. You're not going to shoot your own mother."

"I understand why you think so. I've let every chance to stop you go. From the nights you were passed out on the floor, needle in your arm, and I stood over you with a knife—telling myself one thrust and the pain would stop. To the countless times you've tortured me since. It's not familial loyalty that's shown you mercy all these years, Jocelyn. It's fear."

Inside, the creature reared. Her wings fanned out—flapping in the flames of a dying fire.

"Through your callous cruelty, you made me into something cold, dangerous, unforgiving, just, and driven to right wrongs. But if I took that final step and killed you, I didn't know what I'd become. If I'd turn into something I couldn't control." My lip curled. "If I'd become like you.

"Now I see that's not possible. I'm knitting myself back together again, Mom. Adeline's heart. Her fire. I've found my way back, and one thing is very clear to me." My voice changed. "It's time for you to go."

Maybe she saw something in my eyes. Paling, she raised her arms. "Adeline, wait. Just listen to yourself. You're not making any sense."

"You will be a plague on me for my entire life. You'll haunt my children. Cast your shadow over a happy life because you've deluded yourself into believing I denied you one." I clicked my tongue. "No more. I'm ending the chapter on the Jocelyn and Adeline story."

"Stop! What are you doing? Stay away from me!"

I picked up the fake ledger. Closing the distance, I tossed it at her.

"Here. Take it," I said. "Some fool will believe it's the real thing and pay anything you ask for it. There's your hand up, Jocelyn. You can buy yourself a whole new life—far away from mine." My eyes hardened. "And I mean the other side of the planet. If I ever see you again— look at me."

Jocelyn dragged her gaze from the book.

"If I ever see or hear from you again. If you come at me in the street or plot another fake kidnapping, I will kill you, Jocelyn. And I can say with certainty, there won't be any whining or crying afterward. It'd be no more than you deserve."

I turned my back on her. "Goodbye, Jocelyn."

"W-wait. Adeline, stop. I said stop!"

A hard blow smashed the back of my head.

Jocelyn leaped on me, throwing us both to the ground.

"You'll kill me?! How dare you speak to me like that, you worthless, ungrateful—"

Twisting, I punched her across the face, throwing her off me.

Jocelyn flew back and returned swinging. Her nails raked down my cheek. Pain exploded in my face.

Grabbing her arm, I wrenched it up her back.

We grappled over the bodies.

"What more do you want?" I screamed.

"You don't get to walk away from me!" We crashed onto the platform. "You're mine!" Jocelyn pinned my wrists. Bulging eyes filled my vision. "I say when I'm done with you."

A loud, harsh laugh tore my throat. "Now we get to the truth. You never wanted Dad's money or mine. What you need is someone to make feel lower than you. Well, you're gonna have to find someone else. Last chance—"

I got my feet between us and kicked her off. She fell onto Pais's body.

"—take the book and go."

Jocelyn rose as I did. Her makeup wasn't so perfect, and crimson stained her blue dress—seemingly dripping from her matching locks.

My true mother had broken through the façade. Her hatred shone inside and out.

"Argh!" Jocelyn flew at me.

We tripped out onto the balcony. She shoved me against the rail, fighting my arms down.

"What are you going to do, *Mom*? Kill me? If you can't have me, no one can?"

My taunts enraged her. She fisted my hair, trying to bash my head on the rail.

"Of course not!" I buried my fist in her stomach. "We both know you don't care that much."

"You don't care. You left me!"

"You let them rape me!" I grabbed her shoulders. Forcing her back, I bent over the rail.

"That's when you lost me," I cried. "It's over, Jocelyn. Take your damn money and die alone."

"No!" She pummeled my arms, face, chest—everything in reach.

"Then, just die."

Raising my hand, I made a fist.

Jocelyn grabbed me around the waist. I didn't have a chance to react.

She threw me over.

I swung in an arc, world spinning, and struck the railing. The impact rattled my bones, and the single hand clutching the metal jarred free.

Bang!

I plummeted five stories below.

Chapter Eight

I t didn't occur to me to scream.

My heart ricocheted up my chest. Wind circled me, cradling my body, and then letting me go. I was surrendered to my fate.

I hit the pool with a resounding smack.

"Adeline? Adeline!"

Blurry figures surrounded the edge. I tried to speak to them as darkness crept in, swallowing me whole.

JASPER

"Where the fuck were you?"

"I couldn't get through the door," I snapped. "You know that."

"That excuse letting you off the hook, Croix? Make you feel good about yourself while you were fishing her out of a pool. 'It wasn't my fault. The rent-a-cops were too big for me.'"

I snatched the kit from the cabinet and slammed into my room. If I stayed out there a second longer, I'd punch Sinjin in the face. Then, he'd punch me back. Weapons would get pulled. Blood would be spilled. And then he'd say something else to kick the whole thing off again.

Adeline lifted her head from Brutal's chest as I came in. Her soft smile cooled my rage in an instant.

"Thanks, but I'm okay." She gestured to her scratches. "It looks worse than it is."

"Put your head back where it was and hold still."

Smiling, she did what she was told. Baris squeezed her tight.

My apartment was always quiet, I didn't wander around talking to my-self. Even so, the silence as the four of us hovered around her—back in the same space again—heightened my honed fight or flight. The truce couldn't hold. Saint was already testing its limits.

Everything stopped when I saw that person tip off the balcony. The rent-a-cops were not too big for me. I plowed through them rushing the gates to get to her.

The lifeguard rescued her by the time I broke free with security in tow. A crowd formed around her, pointing up at the balcony, talking about the noises that sounded like gunshots, and dialing the police one after the other.

It took every favor and contact in my own little black book to get Adeline to the right hospital, and have the cops sent to the wrong one. In the midst of it, she woke twice to say two things. "It was done," and "call Baris, Saint, and Killian."

I couldn't deny her request. Now it was time to understand her statement.

"What happened up there, Adeline?"

"It was a trap." She closed her eyes as I dabbed her cuts. "Jocelyn made a deal with Pais. Me in exchange for the pay increase and new lifestyle that came with working for him."

Killian and I shared a hate-filled glare. It was automatic. Done like so many times before. We flicked to her just as quickly.

"I knew what she had done. Part of me hoped differently, so it didn't have to end the way it did, but it's over now. Pais and Jocelyn are dead."

"We know that much." The mattress dipped. Saint moved her onto him. "*Murders in the Fairfield*. It's already hit the news."

"Gianna killed them. I knew she'd be there for me."

"I'd have been there for you," Saint returned. "If you hadn't run off in the middle of the night with this fucker. If Pais had chosen a south-facing apartment, you'd be lawn decoration right now."

"I didn't anticipate Jocelyn throwing me off a balcony for handing her thousands of dollars. Definitely not the standard reaction."

"What happened?" Killian pressed.

She sighed. "I've been emailing Gianna almost every day since she left. After that call with Pais, I told her what was going on and passed on the address when it came through. I wasn't getting in there with a weapon and would obviously be outnumbered. I needed backup. I needed her... to hold my hand one more time. She came through."

"You couldn't have known she was there," I said.

"I did know. I saw when we arrived that there was a small purple wind measure tied to the flag pole. Purple. That's Gianna."

"Is there a reason you couldn't let us in on this?" Killian asked.

She gave him a look. "I believe I tried to talk to you and Saint. How did that go?"

"Don't give me that bullshit."

"That bullshit is all I have for you." Adeline reached behind her, taking Baris's hand. "I wasn't asking your permission. This was between me and my mother."

"Enough," I sliced in, heading off an argument. "It's done. She's alive. Pais is dead. That's a happy outcome all around."

"I love you, Killian," she murmured, burrowing into Sinjin. "Please understand."

I saw his muscle ticcing from across the room. He didn't want to—neither of them wanted to. Their anger was breaking.

"This had to be done," Saint forced out, "and it had to be done by you. She's hurt you many times. But she won't do so again."

Killian nodded. "You're alive. That's what matters." He kissed her forehead—tenderness I'd only witness him give the youngest members of the Hunt clan. Adeline has changed all of us. She said facing Pais and Jocelyn was her fight—and it was—but I don't think she comprehended what would become of us if we lost her. The men who existed before Adeline were jagged pieces of glass. Open flames. The men we'd become if we didn't have her to anchor us.

I didn't know a comparison as deadly.

"Are we done here?" Killian scooped her up. "We're going back to the cabin."

"Wait. I want to stay—for tonight at least. There's one more thing I have to do."

"What?"

"Nothing that requires leaving this bed, so everyone can loosen those shoulders."

My shoulders had stiffened. Adeline saying "There's something I have to do" was the equivalent of a bomb-maker saying "Wait here. I have to blow some shit up."

She wrapped herself in my covers like it's where she belonged.

She does.

"Use this time to talk, gentlemen. Get everything off your chest. Love you," she called.

We were dismissed.

ADELINE

Jasper closed the door behind them.

I stretched my aching body across the bed, snagging my phone off the nightstand. I pulled up my email.

Adeline: You don't get to pretend you're not getting these messages anymore. Call me. We need to talk.

I tucked my phone under my pillow and buried my nose in it, breathing in Jasper's smell. Maybe that was part of the reason I asked to spend the night. I wanted to be in one place with all of my guys. It was the least I could ask for after the woman who gave me life tried to end it.

I gazed unseeingly in the dark.

I wonder if I should have known what truly seethed behind her malice. I wonder if Jocelyn understood it herself.

Life had beaten her, and she threw me to the wolves rather than fight back. Then she lost me too. Misery and self-loathing rotted her to the core, and it wasn't escape she was looking for. It was someone to blame. Jocelyn couldn't stand that mirror being held up to her.

I hope you find peace wherever you are, Jocelyn. Because I finally have.

The pillow buzzed beneath my cheek.

"Hello."

"Adeline, are you okay?" Gianna rushed out.

"I'm fine. A bit cut up, and hitting that pool might as well have been smacking on the concrete, but I'll survive."

"I'm so sorry. I couldn't get a clear shot with you both struggling and—"

"I know," I said gently. "It wasn't your fault."

"How are you doing with this? I killed her, Addy. She's dead."

"I thought I would feel more to be honest. Positive or negative. There's nothing," I admitted. "I stopped seeing that woman as my mother a long time ago."

"Hey."

"Yeah?"

"I'm still holding your hand."

My lips trembled—tears welling behind my eyes. I felt that.

"I know."

"Love you, A."

"Love you too, G."

We blubbered for only a little bit longer.

Gianna roughly cleared her throat. "Pais is dead. I don't know what this means for the Kings, but I'm hoping the coming power struggle will distract them from chasing after you."

"Or they'll ramp up efforts to find us so the next leader can use the ledger to consolidate power."

"Could go either way. The streets are dangerous right now. More than usual. Burning churches. Shoot-outs in the streets. It's a powder keg, Addy, and it's about to go off."

"I agree. Now that Pais is dead, it's time you came in from the cold. We have a better chance of fighting this together, Gianna. You can't tell me you disagree."

"I don't," she replied, an odd tone in her voice. "It's just—"

"Just what?"

"I didn't only take off to kill Pais. He's just one head on the twelve-headed beast. I left to put an end to this for good. I have a plan. One that you won't like, and that's why I have to do it alone."

"What plan?"

"Focus on Katz," she said. "He's been walking this planet for far too long. You won't get a medal for it, but you'd deserve one for finally putting an end to him. Now that we're talking, I'll tell you what the Kierans have collected on him. He—"

"Now that we're talking, you'll stop trying to distract me and spill what this plan of yours is."

Silence echoed on the other end.

I shoved up, gripping the sheets. "Look, the bottom line is this. Either we're partners, or we're not. We're sisters, or we are not. I've never hesitated to call you when I was marching into guaranteed maiming or death. I know you have my back. Do I have yours?"

She blew out a breath. "You're really good at emotional blackmail, aren't you?"

"Do I have your back?"

"Yes. Of course you do."

"Then, what is the plan?"

"You won't agree," Gianna warned. "You're going to try to talk me out of it, but this is how it has to be."

"I'm listening."

Gianna told me her plan.

"No." My hand sliced through the air. "Absolutely not. What's plan B?"

"I have to do this, Addy."

"No, you don't."

"Everyone knows Gianna Cross has the ledger, and they're quickly finding out Adeline Redgrave is her closest friend. Next, it'll be Oscar who can't walk down the street without looking over his shoulder."

"He's used to it."

"I didn't do this to put my family in danger. We weren't supposed to be here, Addy, and I know it's my fault we are. I don't blame anyone other than myself. But that still leaves it my mess to clean up. The hunt for Gianna Cross and the ledger stops, if there is no ledger or Gianna Cross."

"G," I said slowly. "I hear what you're saying, and I hear the regret and shame underneath it. You think you have to do this to make it right between us, but this is *not* the sacrifice I want. Come home. To me. To Dad. Let's do what we said we'd do. Clean this city up crying and screaming against its will."

"There'll be daily assassination attempts. A Kieran's hidden identity is what keeps them alive. It's when people find out that their throats get slit."

"If you can trust me, Gianna, I'll think of another way out of this. We both will."

My phone beeped with another message.

"All right," she said. "I won't make any moves till we figure out another way out of this. But I can't come back home."

"Why not?"

"Separate the key from the lock. The gangs getting their hands on you is bad. The gangs getting their hands on me is bad. The gangs getting their hands on me, you, and the ledger is our funeral. I don't have it with me anymore. I got it out of the Fairfield and stashed it." She scoffed. "Bet Pais thought he was smart getting an apartment in the building and breaking through most of the security. Lot of good it did him."

"Where is it?" I asked.

"Don't you know? It's the only place you and I felt safe."

I didn't ask for more. I knew.

"I'll leave it where it is. You're right. Separate the key from the lock." I settled onto the pillows. "In the meantime, I would like to hear everything you've got on Nicolas Katz."

She whistled. "We've gone up against some bastards, my friend, but he takes the cake. I tried leveraging him. Told him to put fifty grand in a backpack in Franklin Park and had one of my runners pick it up. He found a tracker, discarded it, and rushed off to the meeting point. Three guys followed him and beat him to death in an alley. There was a second tracker in the bag handle. The news is still saying it was a mugging gone wrong."

"Goodness. Was that your last run-in with him?"

"No. He's the freaking governor, Addy, and there are whispers he's preparing for a presidential campaign. You know what it would mean to own him."

I whistled too. "I'm afraid to think about the ledger giving the Cinco criminal underground power over the president. The people of this country would be running around in war paint and waving torches of burning underwear in a week."

"Katz isn't too interested in that outcome either. It's not that it doesn't have enough to crush him. It does," she said. "It's the plain and simple fact that he won't let it. He practically dared me to try again, Addy. Said a couple weeks of unsubstantiated rumors in the press is nothing compared to the hell he'd rain on me for the rest of my life.

"I'm not one to back down before a man, so I said bring it on and hung up the phone."

"Naturally," I replied.

"Next, I arranged a bank transfer. No runners or dead drops. The account couldn't be traced to me," she said. "My instructions were two million in three days, or I email Cinco PD the truth about what happened to Emmanuel Webber. Three days came and went."

"He didn't pay?"

"Not a cent."

"Did you send the email?"

"Complete with scans of the photographs. A dead body slumped over a desk with his nameplate on it. I told them where it was buried and everything."

"And?" I pressed.

"That was a month ago. You tell me what happened next."

"Nothing? You served a dead body on a platter and the cops didn't lift a fucking finger?"

"He wasn't even brought in for questioning. I don't know what happened to that email, Addy. I hired a guy to hack into the system and there's no trace of it."

I let out a mirthless laugh. "Of course the bastard's cocky. He owns the police too. So, let me get this straight. The most powerful man in the city has his own hit squad, millions of dollars, Cinco PD on the payroll, and also happens to be a raging psychopath devoid of a conscience. Have I got all of that?"

"I warned you not to underestimate him. I don't know how to come at this guy, Addy. A blackmailer has no power when the victim doesn't fear you spilling his secrets. Have you and the Merchants come up with a plan?"

"We have one that isn't fully fleshed out because we can't get close," I admitted. "He has a cabin out in the woods that he goes to when he's on 'business trips.' We'll take him there."

"The ledger mentioned his serial cheating in a later entry. I think that a Kieran was his actual mistress. She got close, slept with him, and put some of his kinks in the book. She wrote that she threatened to tell his wife if he didn't leave her. He laughed in her face and said they had an open marriage. The show they put on was for the papers."

"I'm not surprised. The man offered her up to be raped and beaten for a few more points in the polls. There is clearly no love there." Shaking my head, I glanced at the door. "I have to tell Saint all of this, but it won't change anything. He wants him dead by October."

"Tell me how to help."

"I will once I know the next step. We can't move forward without Dad." I glanced at my screen. "Who I just noticed has texted me. I've got to call him. Stay up, I'm hitting you back right after."

"Why should I sleep tonight?" I heard the television flick on. "Talk soon, babe."

I smiled. Yes, in spite of everything that happened—wounds opened and closed. I would be fine.

"Talk soon."

JASPER

Killian leaned on the window. Baris circled the place, akin to the stalking beasts he was often compared to. Saint sat across from me—a grin on his lips and his knife free of its holster. He tossed it from palm to palm without looking. He didn't have to. The weapon somersaulted through the air and landed harmlessly hilt down. As though an obedient pet in love with its master.

"I've always wanted to learn how to do that," I mused. "You can learn a lot of skills on the streets. Professional knife throwing isn't one of them. Impressive, Sinjin."

He beamed. "Thank you. The trick is to practice in secret, so when you miss and bury it in the guy's throat, the witnesses all say it was a tragic accident."

I bobbed my head. "You are one twisted guy, St. John Bellisario."

"Two compliments in a row? Please, stop. I only have eyes for Bunny."

Chuckling, I said, "This is nice. The Merchants together again. I should pop champagne for the occasion."

"Adeline would like that," Killian said. "She's in there imagining we're working on our differences and hugging it out."

I held my hands out to him. "I will if you will."

Sinjin barked a laugh. "You're right, Killian. I do like this guy better than the other one."

The other one. As in the Mercer he lived and worked with for years.

"You've got this winning, pleasant quality about you. I have the same," Sinjin continued. "We currently have an opening for an infiltrator, and you've demonstrated your superior skills by infiltrating us."

Inwardly, my confusion mounted, though I gave nothing away. *What was he doing?*

"Jasper Croix, consider this your rehiring interview."

"What's the point of this?"

"Answer the questions." Brutal spoke from behind me. "If you've got nothing to hide—"

"—then you have nothing to worry about," Killian finished.

"Ah. I see what this is. I have Adeline under her adorably named 'dick-matism' and you have to question me yourself to check that I'm for real. Go for it," I stated. "I'm a Merchant. I'll always be a Merchant. It's past time we settled this."

"The whole story that you took Adeline on a city tour to tell. Tell us," Sinjin said. "All of it. From your mouth. Now."

"All right. Four years ago, I..."

I went through the whole thing from my first run-in with Mercer Santos, to Rosie and my circumstances leading to working for Lombard. The three of them listened without interruption.

"I had no choice," I finished. "I did what I had to do to protect my daughter. When we have the ledger, I'll set a trap for Lombard and end this once and for all."

Sinjin nodded along. "That it?"

"Yes."

"Nothing else you want to share?"

"Nothing else to share," I said, voice even. "That's the truth."

"That was a load of steaming dogshit, and I can only assume Adeline fell for it because you distracted her with a kid at the end."

I tensed. "What are you talking about? I told you everything."

He tossed his hair, blue locks swinging. "Not even close," he replied. "Killian. Baris. Should we proceed with the questioning part of the interview?"

"Let's." Killian dropped on the couch. "Why exactly couldn't you tell us you were under Lombard's thumb? You said a woman you loved was under the ledger's grip and you had to free her."

"She is. The woman I love is Rosie."

"And that was very well done," Killian said. "Embedding a kernel of truth in your lie, but we keep coming back to the question, why didn't you come out with it?"

"If you knew I was on Lombard's leash, none of you would've trusted me. I didn't see the point of living in suspicion. I had no intent to harm you."

"Sounds good," said Sinjin, "but you're lying. Killian was held up for ransom by a Kieran himself. He had a family to protect too."

"He's your brother," I snapped. "Forgive me for thinking I wouldn't get the same pass."

"You didn't trust us to give you a pass, because you know you didn't deserve one. If you were so desperate to get your daughter out from under his thumb, you wouldn't have sat on your ass for four fucking years. You had three brothers and an entire gang willing to storm Lombard Integrative Health and shoot the man at his desk."

Sinjin smirked. "You don't work for Lombard. How could you? He'd have killed and replaced you long before this. Rich bastards aren't known for their patience."

"You had your chance to get the ledger when we had Cross," Baris said. "You didn't take it."

"If you think I'm lying—"

"You are lying." Sinjin scented the air. "I smell it on you like the cologne left on my Bunny's skin after she comes home—her head filled with your fairy tales. Who do you work for, Croix? What do you want?"

Well, I can't answer that, can I? I'm being paid handsomely not to. Money that's going to buy me a new life with your Bunny.

I leaned back in my seat, considering my next move.

I did say the man was good. He saw through my cover—something people did not do. Though to be fair, I had made mistakes. Adeline Redgrave wasn't factored into the equation when I made my plans to infiltrate the Merchants. Her best friend getting hold of the ledger before I did wasn't ideal either. Anyone else and the outcome would've been much different.

Anyone else and I wouldn't be sitting in my own apartment getting dissected by the men I once called brothers.

But this is my story. The story we agreed on. They're not getting another.

"Do you want proof, Sin?" I tossed him my phone. "Check for yourself. It'll be the most received number. Lombard calls me every week, twice a week for an update.

"Go on," I pressed when he made no move to touch the phone. "Call Lombard and asks who works for him."

Gaze locked on mine, Sinjin hit call.

He put the phone to his ear. A faint voice spoke, said a few words, and Sinjin hung up.

"Well?" Killian asked.

Sinjin fixed steadily on me. "Lombard Integrative Health," he repeated. "How may I direct your call?"

"There you have it." I was a pro. You couldn't hear the triumph in my voice, but I was sure as hell feeling it. "There's no big secret. It's all exactly how I told you." I clapped. "So, interview over? Am I in?"

"I'll find out what's true, Croix." He got to his feet. "Don't call us. We'll call you."

The three filed off into the bedroom with Adeline.

I picked my phone up from where it dropped on the floor. Moving into the kitchen, I pulled some earphones out of the drawer and stepped into the guest bathroom.

Tapping into the mics, I leaned against the bathroom counter, listening.

"—sec, Daddy. Did you guys talk?" Adeline asked.

"We did," Killian replied.

Yes, I had microphones all over my apartment. I've lain in wait and ambushed dozens of people coming home after another normal day. You don't make the playbook and then fall for your own tricks. I made certain my place was empty before I stepped inside. If it also presented other uses, I'd do what I had to do. The guys were determined to plant seeds of doubt in Adeline. I'd have to undo the damage.

"Did you work it out?" she asked.

"Can't. That guy is lying through his bleached teeth," Sinjin said.

They're not bleached, dick.

"I'm intrigued to find out why. After we handle Katz, Croix will be grant-ed my divided attention."

I bolted up straight. *After we handle who?*

"The phrase is undivided attention, baby."

"The over-primped fucker isn't that important."

"Are you talking to Oscar?" Killian asked.

"Yeah. It's this weekend. Saturday. Katz will be at the cabin."

There was no denying it that time. Adeline said Katz. As in Nicolas Katz.

Why were they interested in the governor or his cabin?

"Time, guests, guards?" Killian asked.

I turned the volume to maximum, moving to the door as though being closer to the bedroom would help.

"You talk to him."

"No, we'll call back. We're not staying. Get dressed."

"I need to talk to him," Adeline said. "About today. Wha— No, Dad. I'm fine. Gianna is too. Have you seen the news?"

A noise filtered through the headphones. A persistent *tap, tap, tapping.*

"You don't have to stay the night. Pick me up in the morning, or I'll ask Jasper to drop me off."

"We have four days, Adeline."

"I know this is important. You have my dad's number to get the infor-mation. Tonight, I need to talk to him, and then I need to talk to Jasper. It's important."

"I'll pick you up," Sinjin said. "Eight o'clock."

There were kisses and murmured goodbyes. I shut off the phone before they were done.

I wouldn't listen in on Adeline's conversation with her father. I wouldn't listen in on her ever again after today. My aim wasn't to violate her privacy. I had to make sure Sinjin wasn't filling her with doubts, and that she had to stay to talk about something *important* didn't reassure me.

All of this. Everything. It was to be with Adeline.

But Nicolas Katz.

That was a problem.

ADELINE

I traced lines on his chest, gliding on the cooling sweat—his and mine.

It was wild how in tune with my body Jasper was. We'd been together only three times, and from the first, it felt like he knew what I needed before I did.

It was easy to say it was the result of his experience. Certainly easier for my conflicted heart to brush aside if it was just his sexual prowess. But deep down I knew, Jasper and I connected on a level I didn't know I could reach. Both sides of me were falling for both sides of him.

Our legs, arms, and bodies tangled beneath his sheets. It scared me how right it felt.

"*That guy is lying through his bleached teeth.*"

What is Saint seeing I'm not, or don't want to see?

"As much as I love a big sleepover." He kissed my crown. "I'm glad it's just you and me."

"Me too." I peeked up at him. "There's something I wanted to talk to you about."

"Anything. I'm listening."

"Thank you for coming with me. For staying up half the night giving up secrets that could get you killed and trusting that I had a way out."

"The balcony?"

I poked his side to him laughing. "Too soon to joke about your girlfriend plummeting to her near-death."

The hand stroking my thigh stilled. "Are you? My girlfriend."

"Well, that's what I wanted to say, Jasper. I can't explain it. I wish I could. I wish there was some rhyme, or reason, or rule book to falling for someone. All I know is you feel like someone I can rely on."

He grasped my chin, kissing me till my toes curled. "You can rely on me. No matter what happens or what's said. Even though I may not be able to tell you everything right away. I love you, Adeline."

"What can't you tell me?"

"Nothing," he said. "There's nothing you can't know, and when the time is right, you will. Like now. I have to tell you something."

"What?"

"There are hidden microphones in this room. I overheard you and the guys talking about Governor Katz."

"There are what?" I yanked the covers over me. "Are there cameras too?!"

"No," he cried. "I'm not some bush-lurking pervert."

"No, you're just an eavesdropper."

"Arguably much better in comparison."

I was steaming. "Jasper!"

"I'm sorry. I swear that was the first and last time I listen in on you. I only did it to hear what the guys were saying about me to you. I didn't expect to overhear you talking about Katz. *Why* were you talking about Katz? You don't want anything to do with a man like him, Adeline. And I'm saying this as someone who's met the worst pond-skimming scum the planet has to offer. Nicolas Katz puts them all to shame."

"I'm realizing that for myself. He's rich, powerful, and well-connected. Katz occupies the most powerful position in the state. And he happens to be a cold-blooded killer. I know he's not someone to mess with. The question is how do you know him?"

"The cabin you were talking about. Every once in a while, he organizes a party out there. The kind you don't bring your spouse to."

It took me a second to put it together. "And you know this because you were invited?"

He nodded.

"Orgy?"

"Pretty much. Katz brings in entertainment for the night, and he and a couple of his government buddies put our tax dollars to good use."

"But you said he's worse than the pond scum? It's more than the sex parties."

"Katz called Jasper's number not knowing he was also Alaric. He wanted me to find someone. A young boy around seven years old. I turned him down flat. I don't take jobs for kids, or tracking down regular people."

"Why not?" I asked. "The regular people, not the kids."

"One of the Kravets tried to hire me to find a murder witness in the witness protection program. There were also two abusive ex-husbands that wanted me to find wives that left them. I pick my clients, and fuckers like that won't be one of them.

"As for Katz, I told him no kids. He said the boy was his son. His mother ran off with him and he hadn't seen him since he was three years old. He just wanted to be in his life. Again, I said no and hung up on him.

"Katz took the request to a colleague with less scruples. He found the kid tucked away in some town in Wyoming. A few days after, a car jumped the curb and almost ran him down."

I clapped my hand over my mouth. "Are you telling me Katz tried to have his seven-year-old son killed?"

"That is exactly what I am telling you. It couldn't be connected to him, but I knew. I was to blame for not looking deeper into his request. I paid to have Parker and his mother moved to a safe place, but you don't forget something like that. People have hired me to do just about everything you can think of. But he was the first and only who ordered a hit on a child.

"What do you guys want with a man like that?" Jasper pushed himself up. "Is he threatening you?"

He sounded so enraged at the idea, it tugged the threads seeking to bind us together. I liked being someone he cared enough about to protect. For people like us, the list of those we gave our heart to was short.

I eased him back down. "No, Jasper. He doesn't know we're coming. Nicolas Katz is an old score we have to settle, and the most dangerous man after Gianna."

Saint did not want me to tell Jasper about Katz's role in Paul Bellisario's death. I had to respect his wishes.

"She's tried blackmailing him twice and lost a man doing it. Frankly, our state can do better than a murderer for a governor. That's the least we can ask for."

"This is a hit."

I nodded.

"Let me help— No, I'll rephrase. I have to help. Whatever you think you know about his security, you're wrong."

"We'll talk to Saint in the morning. Right now, we're circling back to you eavesdropping on me."

He held a finger up. "I believe I should get points for coming clean and telling you the truth at risk to my sex life."

"Do you?" I tried to be serious. The corners of my lips kept quirking up. "Why should I give you points?"

"Because—"

I squealed as I found myself on my back. Jasper's erection dug into my thigh.

"—I'm going to make it up to you."

"ARRANGE THEM ON THEIR sides in two circles. Going in the same direction." Jasper nipped little kisses on my neck, snaking his arms around my waist. "We'll cook it on low heat for an hour."

His deep, husky voice poured in my ear. "The apples have to be basted regularly."

I shuddered. "Oooh. Say baste again."

"Baste."

"Oh, shit. Now I'm pregnant."

He chuckled. "Did you really want me to teach you how to make tarte Tatin? Or did you just want to hear me say it?"

"Definitely both. Say more food with that voice."

"Chocolate."

"Yes."

"Tart." He popped the "t" and my nipples with them.

"More."

Jasper licked the shell of my ear. "Crème fraiche."

Moaning, I melted into his arms. "I've been learning to cook wrong my entire life."

"No." Jasper slipped my bra strap off my shoulder. A bra, thong, and an apron were all I had on. "You were just waiting for the right instructor."

Hera, help me. Everything with Jasper did feel right. Our relationship was different than how it was with Mercer. Though the feelings I had for the person I thought to be Mercer Santos were real, they never got the chance to mature. It was unripened fruit. A chick just beginning to poke his head out of the shell.

With Jasper, there was hurt, arguments, and frustration. There was cursing him out for spying on me, and then incredible make-up sex that made me forget what I was mad about. There was teasing him about bowls of hot soup, and sharing horrific dates. Swimming beneath the waterfall. Talking to him about Jocelyn. Listening to his stories about Nina.

This was real. It was ripe, and alive, and filling me to bursting.

And it scared the hell out of me.

I was falling hard and fast. As hard as I fell for Saint, Killian, and Baris. But it was different with them. We shared so many things in lots of ways, but Jasper is the one who closely mimicked my true self. All of her power, rage, lethalness, and deception. I'd know better than anyone how dangerous it is to fall in love with me.

"Got anything else to teach me?" I asked, wiggling my ass against his crotch.

But that wasn't going to stop me. I killed things that scared me, or I conquered them.

I tugged him by the collar, bringing him down for a searing kiss.

I had every intention of conquering Jasper Croix.

"I have a few lessons, but they won't be completed in twenty minutes."

Surprised, I checked the time. How was it already twenty minutes to eight? Sinjin was on his way, and I had the task of convincing him the Merchants had to get back together again for one last job.

Though I hoped it won't be the last.

The night before, I had something else to tell Jasper. I wanted him to know I wouldn't give up on us if the guys never accepted him back. The life he wanted with his daughter, living on his own terms. I saw myself in that future.

When the time came to say so, nothing came out. I wanted to be with him, and deep down, I wished he'd be with all of us. I wasn't ready to voice a different future, even though I'd accept it if it came.

"Why did we choose a breakfast that takes almost two hours to make?"

"Because you like the way I say tarte Tatin."

"Yeah, I do." I smacked his ass walking away. "Say it again."

"Tarrrte Taaatin," he drew out. "I'm going to hop in the shower."

I turned off the stove. If that wasn't a seduction for shower sex, I didn't know what was.

Jasper and I fooled around for too long in our steamy bath. I stumbled out in a towel to Sinjin pounding on the door.

"Sorry, baby. I'm almost ready."

"Bunny, if I ever get angry over you answering the door dripping wet in a towel. Shoot me."

"Will do." We kissed. "Come in, love. We have to talk."

"About," he asked, trailing me into the bedroom.

Jasper stood dressed before the vanity, sliding on his watch. I dropped my towel and slipped into my freshly laundered clothes.

"Katz."

Sinjin's face shuttered closed. "You told him."

"I overheard," Jasper corrected. "I was listening while you were talking about moving on Katz this Saturday. Afterward, I told Adeline the same thing I'm telling you. The Merchants need me on this job."

"Nope. Get your shit, Redgrave. I'm double-parked."

Redgrave? This was not good.

"Saint, I understand and respect how you feel about this. I swear I do, but Jasper's been inside the cabin. We underestimated the security system."

Small creases lined his smooth forehead. "How?"

"He has a Turvalene."

"Fuck." Saint slammed his fist on the wall. "Fuck!"

"What's a Turvalene?" I asked.

"It's a closed security system," Jasper replied. "It's not hooked up to a network, so it can't be hacked. Which is why Diego didn't know about it."

"How does it work? How do we get around it?"

"It's not that it's NSA-level protection or something. It just can't be disabled off-site. You have to shut off the security system, after you've broken in—which makes slipping in undetected rather difficult."

"Okay, then." I glanced at Sinjin's stiff back. "We need an infiltrator."

"Con-fucking-venient." Sinjin shook his head at Jasper, grin on his lips. He was a *tsk, tsk, tsk* away from rounding out his disapproval. "You just happened to overhear, and it just happens to be about a job we can't do without your talents. Next, you'll remember Katz already asked you to the cabin this weekend. The invite got lost in the junk mail."

Jasper grinned back. "Not quite. Katz is straight. I couldn't get myself an invitation to his private romps even if I wanted. I've only been to the party because his other guests had different tastes.

"It's not convenient, Saint. It's the facts. We've gone up against one Turvalene in the last four years, and I got us past it without setting off the alarm. If you've learned how to do it yourself, then thank me for the heads-up and we go on our way. If you haven't, let me in on the job."

"Why do you want in on this job? What do you get out of it?"

"Not having to burst in behind you and save your lives. Again."

Sinjin skipped over that. "Did Bunny tell you why we're going after him?"

"He wants Cross and the ledger. Truth be told, he should've been taken out years ago. There is nothing this man won't do. No one he's above hurting."

Sinjin clenched his jaw. He knew that very well.

"Which brings me to another thing you need to know about Katz. A man like him makes a new enemy before he sits down for his morning coffee. There have been other assassination attempts. He chooses his guards accordingly."

"What does that mean?" I asked.

"They're his personal hit squad, Adeline. As in, five of them are actual mercenaries and hit men he hired to work for him personally. I recognized them through my work."

"So, if a pack of Merchants break into his house, they'll take the order to kill us and bury our bodies in the woods without blinking."

"That is exactly what I'm saying."

Sinjin cocked his head. He wagged a finger between the two of us. "Did you both plan this script? I'm loving the way you're bouncing off each other. Bunny with the 'what will we do' and Croix coming in with the 'only I can save you.'" He clapped. "Well done."

"Jerk," I muttered. "This isn't a performance, my love. It's a question. Can you or any of the guys get us past a Turvalene?"

"No."

"What do you want to do about it?"

Sinjin eyed Jasper—face expressionless. "Tell us what to do."

"It'll take more than three days to learn. I have to rebuild the device I used to break the magnetic locks on the windows. My first was blown up. He keeps the access panel behind a false portrait in the upstairs bedroom. There's a code to open it. Then, a second code to get into the system. I can build the device, hand it over, and teach you how it's done. You'd have to wait for the next time he goes out to the cabin."

"No," Sinjin said immediately. "We're not waiting. You're in. You'll stay at the cabin."

"I'm good here."

"You're good where I can see you. At all times." He got in Jasper's face. "You have a problem with that?"

Smiling, he shrugged. "Nah. Just not interested in sleeping on a cabin floor. Let's stop off for an air mattress on the way—at the very least."

I blew out a breath as they took their rough, two horn-locked stags conversation out the door. All I wanted for Sinjin was the peace of knowing the man who killed his father had paid for his sins. I would've the help of Pais's ghost if he floated up from hell and offered it. But Jasper was better. The four of us living and working together again—that was how it should be.

Chapter Nine

"Are the guys ready?"

"They're waiting just out of sight of the cameras," Cash said. "Lucky says there are three guys on the outside, five on the inside."

"So many?" I asked.

"Katz, seven men, and five women entered the house. He's throwing another party."

I cursed.

"There was always a chance of this," Sinjin said. He hadn't slowed in sharpening his knife. "That's why we brought in the whole crew. Everyone will be tied up in the living room while we handle business."

"The guys are ready to move once we're in," Killian said.

"Good." Sinjin raised his voice. "Croix, you done?"

"I'm done."

Jasper came into the kitchen holding a hunk of metal and wires. "This will get us through the basement window."

Saturday night had come.

For the past three days, we'd gone over the plan backward and forward. I thought my biggest worry would be refereeing arguments between the guys. Surprisingly, there had been none. The weight of what we were doing hung too heavily.

No, my biggest worry was Gianna.

The silent spell was broken, and we talked or texted almost every day. The day before, the apartment she rented with a wig and false name was ransacked. She walked into the intruders crashing around in her bedroom. She turned tail and ran out of there. Now she was at my dad's.

"I thought I'd get a long talk bitching me out for losing my mind with the two of you," she said. "No, the long talk was listing the various bounties on my head, by which gangs, and how much. The address I was staying in is already out on the streets."

"How did they find you?"

"Kieran made another request. They must have traced the call."

"G, I thought you were staying low."

"I was," she said. "Until men showed up at Mom's facility dressed in police uniforms, asking if she was related to Gianna Cross. I had to move her immediately."

"They're coming at you faster than I thought they could. Our lives are being picked apart down to our favorite Saturday morning kids' show."

"Leonidas O'Hare is in the ledger. He's got money to buy the nuclear launch codes if he wants them. The birth records of one twenty-three-year-old woman weren't going to be a struggle."

"O'Hare? What's the ledger have on him?"

"A small Amazonian village wasn't allowing mining access to the caverns on their lands. He had the entire village slaughtered."

"Fucking hell, Gianna," I cried.

"I know. I wish that was the worst act committed in this book, but the Kierans before us truly unearthed the lowest of the low. And they all know my name."

"I'll be back in the city tomorrow," I had told her that morning. "Stay with Dad. You'll be safe."

I stuck a knife through my belt loop and handcuffs in my back pocket. The addition of so many people to the party meant the means to lock them up. Jasper would take out the security system. The men would take care of extras. Sinjin and I had Katz.

We were a silent group arming up. We had one shot at this. If Katz got out alive, he'd know the Merchants were after him, and another jaunt to the secluded cabin wasn't likely to happen again. He'd bury himself under more protection while the cops in his pocket redoubled efforts to track us down.

It had to be now. He had to die tonight.

"Let's go."

We filed out to the car.

Jasper drove us to the Copperhead Trail, parked in the lot, and we hiked from there. Anyone else looked like cartoony bandits dressed in all black and wearing black caps. That could not be said for my Merchants.

They marched through the trees—fabric clinging tight to their rippling backs, and metal weapons glinting in the scant light. Their air of power and menace struck the forest silent. The true predators had entered their turf. There was nothing to do but hide.

"Ten meters ahead," Killian called back. "Stay behind me. I'll tell you when we're clear."

I moved up behind Cash, stopping when he stopped.

Up ahead, the first camera hung in a tree approaching the property. Their sweeping scan made them easy to spot. Cash drew his gun, aimed, and fired the paintball dead on the lens.

"Next one, five meters ahead."

On we went, clearing our path one by one. Every now and then, we heard a rustle or cough of another Merchant's presence.

Killian's final target brought us to the edge of the property line. My first look at the cabin that wasn't through blueprints or photos, and it astounded.

The place was a mansion in its own right. A stone patio stretched out from the house, laying a path to the in-ground hot tub. A tiny oasis of piled rocks sheltered it. Perfect for semi-private hot tub sex.

Two floors of brick facades, wooden pillars, and a wraparound balcony screamed more luxury awaited inside. It was a beautiful cabin, but the two sights to see were the guards sweeping the property.

One stood beside the door—back erect and neck only moving to swivel his head this way and that, looking for threats. The other guard slowly looped around the cabin.

Killian passed me the paint gun. He screwed the silencer on his gun and lined the shot.

Guard number two disappeared around the side of the house.

He pulled the trigger. Guard number one dropped out of frame.

"Go."

I took off running. Ducking behind the rocks, I took out the last camera, and hurried to the dead guard's post.

Number Two didn't catch me out of the corner of his eye as he came back. He turned, facing me to step onto the patio, and our eyes met.

I dropped him with one bullet.

The Merchants emerged from the trees.

"Two minutes," Killian said. He and Brutal moved the bodies into the shadows. Sinjin and Jasper rounded the corner for the basement window.

I was slow to join either of them. Light seeped through the drapes on the first and second floor. Katz was in there, closing the curtains to whatever he was up to. Made it hard to tell where he was. Harder to pinpoint the guards inside.

"Adeline."

My footfalls were silent on the stone. I joined Killian and took his outstretched hand.

"Sweet, but it was my gun I wanted," he said, amused.

I passed it to him with my other hand and held tight to his. He kissed me.

"You and Croix are in first," he said. "Anything moves down there, shoot it. We're blind from here on."

Mercer held his device to the shin-high window poking from the ground. It was pitch black inside, which was its own good news. Katz didn't play his sex games in the basement like a certain gang and their girlfriend.

"Got it." Jasper beckoned me forward. "We're seven feet up," he whispered. "There's nothing under the window, so it's a straight drop down. I'll lower you."

"There was nothing the last time you were here. What if he's knocked up a drum set and stuck it in the empty space since?"

"We're screwed."

"You know, not everything you say in that sexy voice is what I want to hear."

"I'll lower you down slowly. Don't worry, love. This isn't the hard part."

Turning around, I lay flat on my stomach and stuck my feet through. Slowly, I inched inside till Jasper took over, easing me into the darkness inch by inch. I kicked out, checking for obstructions, and found none. I squeezed his hand, signaling to let me go.

Jasper released. I fell, landing on something soft. It tipped over.

I clamped my jaw, penning in a scream as I dropped through the dark and hit the floor hard. The thud resounded like a clanging bell.

"Adeline? Adeline, are you okay?" Jasper hissed.

"I'm fine." Squinting, my vision cleared on the leather ottoman that threw me off. "One second. Don't come down yet."

I moved it out of the way, then called for the boys to come down. It was all very black-ops super spy, but Jasper insisted we had to do it this way. The doors boasted keypads over locks. They couldn't be hacked and typing in the wrong code twice alerted the owner. Three times set the system off. The weakest point of entry was the windows—barring we got in without an armed guard on the other side waiting for us.

Our next barrier was weaving through the mansion without being seen by the thirteen guests and their guards, and shutting off the system. Then our men would flood in.

Baris was last to touch down.

The basement could better be described as a man cave. Dark walls that made the space gloomier. Dark furniture that blended in. I made out a pool table, bar, and a wine fridge as I headed for the stairs. The guys were right behind, and then in front of me.

Sinjin led the way upstairs.

According to the layout and Alaric's experience, the party would be focused in the living room. We could take the stairs up without being seen, but a stray wanderer in the hall posed a problem. We took into account everything we could plan for. Now it was down to luck.

Sinjin cracked the door open. "You're good."

"Eight minutes," Killian said.

Nodding, I slipped out of my pants and pushed my bunched-up dress down. The cuffs I stuffed in my jacket pocket and the knife in my boot.

If a straggler did see me tiptoeing through the hall, it'd be good to not make it obvious I'm an intruder.

Jasper took my hand. Together, the two of us stepped out into a dim hallway.

Cabins really leaned into the all-natural wood and rock décor. Everything I set eyes on was brown. Brown wall, light brown carpet, and brown picture frames of Nicolas Katz—walking us through his years of success.

Jasper pointed. The staircase was up ahead.

The murmur of voices reached us. Music played. It wasn't loud enough to cover the wolf whistles and sounds of flesh smacking flesh.

"Yeah!"

We hit the end of the hall where it branched off in two directions. One led to the noise, the other to the kitchen according to the layout.

I glanced around the corner, and landed on the guard standing in full view.

Back to us. Monitoring the party.

I gestured for the guys to come down. We were clear.

Sinjin went up, taking me and Jasper with him. Brutal and Cash claimed our spots on the bottom floor—ready to let in the wave of Merchants.

"It's that room on the far end," Jasper said softly. "The master."

Inside was pitch black. I closed the door behind us.

"The panel is in the bathroom closet. It'll take me fifteen minutes to get in and disable it."

"Only fifteen minutes." Light flooded the bedroom. "I need to upgrade my system."

A man reclined in an armchair before a pair of bookshelves. He dropped his hand from the light switch, folding it on crossed knees. A full head of thick, silvery hair matched the neatly trimmed beard clinging to strands of black. Blue eyes took us in like curious new creatures who had wandered in from the forest.

This was the first I laid eyes on Governor Katz in person. Newscasts, public addresses, and passing newspaper headlines were the only introduction we had. But while I was surprised to see him. Katz was not surprised to see me.

Behind him, six guards trained their guns on us.

"Hello, gentlemen, and lady. Thank you for being punctual. I was told to expect you around eight fifteen and"—he gestured to the clock—"here you are."

8:14 p.m.

Jasper moved behind me.

"Please, go on about how you were going to disable my system in fifteen minutes. What was supposed to come afterward?"

I didn't move. Didn't breathe.

Sinjin stood statue-still, gazing at Katz with an expression I'd never seen before.

"Come now, don't be shy." He smiled the same pleasant grin I'd seen from the podium. It lit up those classic good looks age had refined. "My guards are rounding up your men out in the forest. The party you thought was going on downstairs is really a roomful of my personal security. They'll be bringing your other friends up soon, so while we've got some time, tell me who hired you. Who—?"

"Sir. Please, sir!" Jasper shoved through us, knocking me aside. The guards shouted, twitching on the trigger as he fell to his knees. "Please, help me. I didn't want to be here. They made me!"

I gaped at him. Circling Jasper's wrists were a pair of handcuffs. I flew to my pocket.

Gone.

"What's this?" Katz barked. "Who are you?"

"They blackmailed me. Forced me to come here and disable your alarm system. Please, I have nothing to do with them. Arrest them, not me!"

The breath snatched from my lungs. If I thought I couldn't speak before. *What is happening? Why?*

"Don't move!" Katz halted Jasper's frantic crawling to get closer to him. "Bruno."

One of them pulled out his phone. "The leader has blue hair. There's a blond one. One's mixed, and the other's got black hair and green eyes. And Adeline Redgrave." He jerked his chin at me. "Her. This guy's not one of them."

"They're the Merchants," Jasper said, hands shaking in his binds. "They're here to rob you and they forced me to get them in. Please, Governor. Don't have me arrested. They threatened me. I didn't have a choice."

"Who are you?"

"Alaric Hale. I've been here before." The suggestion in his tone left no imagination under which circumstances.

"Have you?" Katz asked.

"The animal party. I was the leopard."

"Ah, yes. How could I forget? You fucked a gazelle in my kitchen."

A sentence I didn't expect to hear anyone say in my lifetime, and Katz dropped it with that bland smile on his face like he had to come to this mandatory meeting, but could we hurry it up so he could get on with his night?

"Why would you be chosen to help them break into my home?"

"I— I don't know!" he cried. "I can get past a Turvalene, but I don't break into houses anymore. I'm an escort." Jasper looked at us accusingly. "Somehow, they found out. He said he'd kill me if I didn't get them inside."

"Seems you've been put through quite an ordeal, Mr. Hale. Bruno, help him up."

Jasper thanked him profusely. He faced us across the divide.

"Weapons on the floor," Katz said. "Slowly."

I dropped the knife on the carpet. Sinjin didn't move.

"Weapons," Bruno barked, fixing his aim between Sinjin's eyes. "Now!"

It was me who finally patted him down, removing his knives one by one.

"Hands up. Step away."

I dragged Sinjin to the side.

It was amazing. Ninety-nine percent of the time, I didn't know what Saint was thinking. But right then, I read his mind like a broadcast trumpeting in my ear. Sinjin weighed his odds of making it across that room, and shoving his fist through Katz's chest. And that he was thinking it though he, and I, knew it was zero, made me move in front of him.

"What's this?" Katz cocked his head. "The supposed leader of the Merchants needs this little girl to protect him?"

"You need me to protect you," I corrected.

He laughed. "Is that so? Why? Have you come to kill me?"

"Is that a surprise? I'm betting a lot of people want to kill you. On Thanksgiving, your mom seriously considers plunging the knife in your chest instead."

Katz came back without a hitch. "True, but fortunately, she's dead." He closed the distance between us. He gestured and his guards swarmed around him, pulling zip ties from their pockets.

I sensed Sinjin coiling to strike. He put a hand on my waist.

"Together," I whispered.

He dropped his hand, and the chance passed.

We were wrestled to the ground. It took five men to bring Sinjin down and restrain him.

"Who sent you?" Katz demanded.

"No one sent us." Shouting echoed up the staircase. A crash shot my heart into my throat.

I fought to keep my voice even. "We're thieves and this is a mansion out in the middle of nowhere owned by Governor Nicolas 'Sex Addict' Katz. You do the math."

"I have, and it all adds up to a desperate attempt to save herself by grabbing on to me. I assumed she learned her lesson last time. I'll make sure this one sticks."

"Who is she?"

"Let's not play games."

The door flew open. Brutal and Cash were thrown inside. Brutal landed on my back, knocking the wind out of me.

"Adeline." Hands bound, he rolled off, and pressed his forehead to mine. Mine came away tacky with blood. A blow to the head must've downed my fighter. We were caught.

We were done.

"Um, sir?"

A hesitant voice dragged my eyes up.

"Shouldn't we call the police now?" Jasper asked.

"Oh, we will, Mr. Hale. By the eight a.m. news report, all of Cinco will know I orchestrated the capture and arrest of the city's most notorious gang, the Merchants. Led by the Slasher himself." My reflection gazed back in his polished shoes. "They'll run your mug shots on every channel. And she'll wonder where you are, Miss Redgrave."

"Who the hell is she?" I shrieked.

Good ole Bruno hauled me to my feet.

"Gianna Cross. She likes to call herself Kieran."

That was the only answer it could be. I wanted him to say it out loud.

Someone betrayed us. They told him the Merchants were coming and Adeline Redgrave would be with them.

I met Jasper's shadowed eyes.

Who?

"I'm told you're a close friend of hers. Attended Cinco University together and shared a dorm," said Katz. "What will she do to get you back?"

My muscles coiled. "If you think the answer to that is give you the ledger, you're in for a surprise. Honestly, Gianna and I aren't that close. She hogged the bathroom the whole time we lived together, and would lie about eating my food. That we both took similar criminal paths in life is a coincidence. We have nothing to do with each other now."

Katz said nothing. Hanging on to that smile, he drew his phone from his pocket and held it up for me to see. The photo was zoomed in and slightly blurred, but there was no mistaking my reddish back of the head and Gianna's frantic face fleeing the tournament with her captive in tow.

I squinted. "What am I supposed to be looking at?"

"You and Gianna Cross leaving the match together after your boyfriend here"—he motioned to Brutal—"kindly announced she possessed the ledger. You look like friends to me."

"Do we? You think friends handcuff themselves to each other and get them chased by homicidal mobs?" I clicked my tongue. "You've never had an actual friend, have you? That explains so much."

Chuckling, Katz shared a look with Bruno, shaking his head like "isn't she hilarious?"

He spun back and slapped me across the face. I hit the floor, white spots dancing in my vision.

"Hey!"

Roaring, Brutal shoved up and was jumped on by four men. They strained to pin him. Cash and Sinjin were no easier. Katz flexed all his muscle for this trap, and it was barely enough.

Saint bashed his head in his captor's face. Blood spurted on the carpet and my ankle. He took a run at Katz, but it was Jasper who got there first.

"Son of a bitch!" Hauling him around, Jasper punched the governor of our great state in the eye. "I won't be a part of whatever the fuck this is. Call the police and be done with it."

Bruno kicked me rushing to intervene. He buried a fist in Jasper's gut, doubling him over. The next hit dropped him on top of me.

"Get him out of here!"

Jasper pressed his chin to my cheek. "Obey me," he whispered. I felt something drop in my pocket.

Then, he was gone—pulled off me and forced toward the door.

"You are not a part of this, Hale," Katz bellowed, clutching his nose. "You saw nothing. You weren't here. You open your mouth and the next animal you fuck will be your cellmate and his neo-Nazi pals. Understood?!"

Katz didn't get an answer. His bodyguards had Jasper out the door and crashing down the stairs while he shouted his threats.

I stood with difficulty, meeting Katz's blazing eyes. The real sociopath had come to the party.

"You have quite a mouth on you, Redgrave."

I bit the inside of my cheek when he hit me. I spat the blood on those shiny shoes. "So I've been told. Now that you've proven what a big man you are, smacking around women with their hands bound, why don't we get back to the point? Cross won't trade me for the ledger. Whoever gave you the idea otherwise played you like a fool.

"Take out your frustration by giving me their name. Who told you we were coming?" I hissed.

"You're not asking the questions," Katz said. "I'll find out exactly what you know about Cross and my ledger. We'll have a long, in-depth discussion." Katz brushed my hair behind my ear. "If Cross does decide to leave you to me, we'll find other ways to make use of you."

My boys shouted vicious things at him.

"You're dead, Katz!" Sinjin roared. "The streets will rain with your blood. I'll cut out your heart and hang your carcass for all to see. In the name of my father, you'll suffer for your sins!"

"Bruno, call Chief Simmons. The trash is ready to be picked up," Katz said. "Follow me, Miss Redgrave. I'll show you to your room."

One of his brutes tossed me kicking and screaming over his shoulder.

"Cash! Brutal!"

The door slammed in my face.

"Saint!"

JASPER

Three men shoved me out of the house, frog-marching me past the Merchants tied and lined up on the lawn like dominoes. They were a 'roided, oversized bunch with buzz cuts, crooked noses, and pockmarks for the one wrenching my arm too far up my back.

He banged my head tossing me in the back of the car.

"Show some gratitude." Pockmark stuck his head inside. The other two climbed in the front seat, one of them digging their gun in my cheek. "The governor has kindly forgiven your assault, and breaking and entering. Be sure to vote." He strode off laughing.

The car drove away, rumbling over the dirt path, and turning south on the main road.

Cinco City was north.

I looked at my new friend and the muzzle half in my mouth.

"You don't want to do this," I said calmly.

"Shut up."

He reared to pistol-whip me. I caught his wrist, twisted, and—

"Argh!" His crunching bones echoed like die in a dice cup.

"Stop!" The driver thrashed in his seat, shouting as he yanked on his seat belt. "Let him go!"

Savagely, I bent his hand in a direction it wasn't meant to go. The gun dropped between the seats. I dove for it.

The driver twisted and the car swerved wildly. I was thrown back, but righted myself quickly and shot up.

Gun aimed at my chest, he fired.

I flung back—seizing under fifty thousand volts boiling my blood.

The man hadn't reached for his seat belt. He pulled his Taser.

Shouts leaked through my clenched jaw, louder and more desperate as black crept into my vision.

No. Adeline.

I had to get back to her.

The guard cradled his broken hand, tears running down his face. He rescued the fallen gun.

Noooo!

The butt cracked my skull, sending me into darkness.

ADELINE

The guard tossed me on the bed. Impact jarred Jasper's present from my pocket. I held still, covering whatever it was.

Light flooded the room, and I recoiled—curling in on myself as if that could get me farther away.

Whips, chains, gags, dildos. The list was endless. Nearly every device created for a sexual purpose hung on the walls. The bed itself was a twin with a stiff mattress and metal frame. Something you'd expect to find in an abandoned asylum, not in the grand cabin of a wealthy man.

My skin crawled thinking of the use this bed had been put to.

"Like it?" Katz fondled a ball gag. "I use this room for my naughty guests—which I'm partially hoping you will be." He smacked my ass.

"Do that again, I'll gut you and mail your innards to your kids!"

He laughed. "That's the spirit. You're going to tell me everything you know about Gianna Cross and her whereabouts. I've done my research. I know you're friends."

"Who told you we were coming?"

"Someone who will be paid handsomely for the service."

"Name."

"Why? You won't be getting out of here to do anything about it."

I grinned. "That's what they all said. Locks are only as secure as the men with the keys. And your flabby-bottom, ten-dollar-suit guards could barely hold down three Merchants."

"There's only one of you."

"It's cute you think that matters."

Katz slapped me again. My cheek stung. I felt the bruise forming into his handprint. None of that bothered me as much as the erection straining in his pants.

"Thank you for choosing difficult." Katz bent over me. I shouted, roughly tossing my head as he licked my cheek. "We are going to have a lot of fun together, Miss Redgrave."

"You're going to die like the worthless piece of trash you are. The world will know the truth about you, and your grand funeral procession will be two hungover cemetery workers tossing your pieces in a pine box, and dumping you in the shallow grave that'll be pissed on throughout the years till the grass turns yellow. Yes," I hissed. "I've thought about this a lot."

Katz fisted my hair, bending my head back. "Save that fire for when I come back. I'm going to see your boyfriends packaged and sent off to jail. Then, you and I will have our fun."

He slammed out of the room. I waited for the lock to click and his shoes to fade down the hall.

Scooting my knees under me, I peered upside down at the gift Jasper slipped in my pocket.

This time, I will obey you.

JASPER

Something struck my face, towing me to the surface.

"—hurry up."

"You... take over?"

"My fucking hand is broken!"

I peeled my eyes open. Two blurred figures lit in yellow light. One moved and I was hit in the face again.

Dirt.

My vision cleared on the growing pile beside my head.

They were digging.

I took stock of myself. My head pounded. The wound seeped blood. My hands were cuffed, and aches and pains riddled my body like they took a few shots while I was out.

"Shut up and bring him over. I'm almost done."

Through hooded eyes, I watched him approach clutching his arm. "Get up!" He stomped my stomach.

Eyes bulging, I shot up wheezing.

"No," I rasped. "Please, y-you don't have to do this. I won't tell anyone."

"Too late for that. On your feet."

"Please!" Tears leaked down my cheeks. "I didn't want to be here. They made me."

"Should've thought of that before." His partner threw the shovel down. "The plan was to drive you further out, dump you on the side of the road, and let you walk back to Cinco. Then you made the fatal mistake of pissing us off."

I wailed. "I was scared. He had a gun in my face! I don't want to die. Don't kill me, please. Please!"

They jumped me, grabbing under my arms and dragging me up. I thrashed around, bawling my eyes out.

"Don't do this. I have a kid," I cried. "Please, don't—"

Taser guy threw me at the grave. I tripped over my feet, falling flat on my face. They laughed their asses off.

"Don't worry about your kid," said my one-handed captor. "We'll find them. Make sure they're taken care of."

Lips curling, I pushed up on my knees. There was no way he'd find Rosie, and still the suggestion of what he'd do to her fanned the flames. I warned Adeline that Katz employed the lowest possible scum.

And they have her now.

I had to get back to her—whatever the cost.

"You don't have to do this." My feet slipped in the dirt getting up. "Just let me go like you planned."

"Kill him, Rogers."

"Get on your knees, you piece of— Wait."

My tears dried up in a blink. "Yeah, Rogers." I turned to the guard frantically patting his pockets. I waved his gun at him. "Kill me.

"Final tip," I said. "Don't bind a guy's hands in front of him and then let him fall all over you. You're just begging to lose your gun."

"Fu—"

Bang! Bang!

They dropped on either side of me, landing half in the conveniently dug grave.

I fished the key out of Rogers's pocket, unlocking my cuffs. This little detour was a needless waste of time.

Adeline was waiting for me.

ADELINE

I sat up on the bed—back against the frame and hands behind my back.

In. Out. Count of three exhale. Count of three inhale.

Great relaxation technique. It almost distracted me from the fact the Merchants were betrayed, my guys were off to jail, and the governor was making no secret of his intent to assault me when he came into this room.

Almost.

In. Out. One, two, three.

I guessed Katz would've heard the news rocking the underground and set his considerable resources toward discovering everything there was to know about Gianna Cross. Largely why I had no intention of being seen by the man until his guards were dead and he was strung up like a pinata.

I shouldn't be surprised this happened. We brought the entire gang on the job, though they didn't know the true reason we were after Governor Katz. What's loyalty compared to the hundreds of thousands Katz can drop without blinking an eye?

The door creaked open.

"Miss Redgrave."

"Satan? Is that you?"

His chuckles floated in ahead of him. "Yes. Have any sins you wish to confess?"

"I didn't vote for you."

Katz stepped inside wearing a bathrobe. It was impossible to tell if he had something on underneath. All I could see were his bare shins and feet.

I gagged looking at those hairy, pale legs. What did this man come in here to do?

"This doesn't have to be difficult, Adeline." Katz circled the bed.

"Let's stick to Miss Redgrave." I borrowed a phrase from my love. "Everyone I want to kill calls me Miss Redgrave."

"Putting on a show of bravado and tough talk to cover your fears."

One, two, three. My hands worked silently behind my back.

"Men twice your size and rap sheet started off with the same bluster. They all ended up begging me to get out of this room."

I cocked a brow. "I'm not surprised. Did you show them those pasty legs too?"

His expression remained blank as he sat on the edge of the mattress. "You're a stupid bitch. Another ignorant cunt begging to be put in your place."

It was unsettling hearing such vicious words relayed in that flat voice.

"But this doesn't have to be antagonistic. You're a beautiful young woman, Adeline Redgrave." He stroked the inside of my ankle. "If you were mine, your days of slumming it with gang trash would be over. I'd give you your own apartment, car, and a sizeable bank account. You'd want for nothing."

"Did you tell your other mistresses the same thing? Before you called people like Kieran to get rid of them?"

"Yes," he said easily. Katz finger-walked up my leg. "But the latter won't happen to you as long as you follow the rules. Be respectful. Never say no. And if you get knocked up, the brat is your problem."

"I prefer the gang trash— No, I prefer actual trash over you. Point me in the direction of a mound of rotting garbage and I'd hump that twice before I'd ever let you touch me," I spat.

Katz had reached my thigh. "Don't be too hasty. You haven't heard your other option yet. We can agree to a mutually satisfying relationship where you tell me what I need to know about Gianna Cross, and in exchange, you get paid handsomely for what you gave those thugs for free."

Anger scalded me inside and out. Katz believed his sleeping with me was some kind of gift?

"Or I take what I want from you. Violently."

The word hung in the air—no further elaboration needed.

"What's it going to be?"

Katz slipped under my dress. He tugged my underwear aside, touching my folds.

My leg flew up, kicking him in the jaw. His head snapped around and he hit the floor hard, knocking his robe open. The sad, disgusting, shit-ugly stereotype of a penis waved half-mast.

He was naked.

Katz came in here intending to give me a choice, or make it for me.

"No wonder you have to pay all of your mistresses to sleep with you. I've chosen neither. But here are your options. Walk out of this room and die later. Put your hands on me again and die tonight."

"Argh!" Katz scrambled to get up.

"What's it going to be?"

He rushed me, fist raised. I stared defiantly back.

Katz halted. "No," he hissed. "I won't hurt that pretty mouth before I've put it to use." He crossed the room and snatched something off the wall.

My hands worked faster behind my back, straining to free my binds.

"Your friends are on their way to a cell. No one knows you're here, and no one will believe them when they bleat otherwise." I spotted a glint of something metal when he turned. Katz held it behind his back as he advanced on me. "No one is coming to save you."

"Obey me."

"I don't need saving."

"Wrong again, whore." He grabbed something over my head. I didn't have to guess what it was as it came down.

The metal whip lashed my flesh, opening a dozen cuts on my leg.

I screamed. Pain seared my body, forcing out every smart comeback or taunt.

Katz shoved his second surprise in my open mouth.

"Much better."

I tried to close it but couldn't. I bit down on hard, unyielding metal.

He tied the gag in place.

"You've chosen the hard way, Adeline." His robe pooled on the floor. "You'll get what you asked for."

I screamed filthy, barely intelligible insults at him.

He whipped my thigh. "First rule: be respectful."

Tears prickled behind my eyes. I refused to let them fall.

Come on, I pleaded. *Come on!*

"Second rule."

Katz climbed on the bed. He fisted his dick, pumping as he towered over me. The other hand held the whip.

I eyed it as my hands frantically worked faster. Watching the weapon prevented me from seeing anything else. I wished it stopped me hearing him too.

"What are you, girl?" Katz pulled my hair with his dick hand, yanking me closer. He inhaled me. "White with a little something extra. I prefer the exotic ones."

He bent me painfully back, dropping the whip. "I love the colors we make when I cum on your faces."

A stupid, nonsensical thing to say, but it accomplished its purpose of leadening my bones.

Katz stroked himself in earnest, thrusting in and out of my pried-open mouth. He scraped on my teeth coming out. Each time made him groan louder.

Saint would not have his revenge. Katz would leave this room in individual crime scene bags.

"Take it, you dirty slut. I should give my new friend another hundred grand for bringing me Cross's friend, and a toy. We are going to... have a lot of fun together." His thighs tensed. "Open wide."

The binds snapped. My hand flashed, burying the knife in his thigh.

Katz howled. He dropped to his knee, cum shooting on my clothes and mattress. I pulled my legs from under him and up to my chest. I kicked, sending him flying off the bed.

"Bruno!" he hollered. "Bruno!"

Lash!

"Bruno!"

Lash! Lash! Lash!

The whip shredded his back. Bloody rivulets made a far more fascinating color on his skin than we ever could with mine.

Katz grabbed the foot of the bed, trying to crawl away.

I whipped his hand.

His scream ignited a savage, feral thrill inside me, helping overcome my violent shakes. Visions flooded my mind one after the other—a terror worse than nightmares. These were real.

Katz pushed himself up. I flung back on the bed and hooked my legs around his neck, clamping down. I ripped the gag out of my mouth.

"Take it, whore." I lashed the metal across his face.

Bruno burst inside. "Sir!"

My legs crossed and locked at the knees. Bruno pulled on me, and tightened my hold on Katz.

The governor clawed at my thighs. His lips tinged blue beneath the blood.

"Let go," Bruno shouted, tackling me.

Shoved into the mattress, he punched me in the face. Still, I held on.

Katz's slaps were slowing down.

"Let go!" He reared for the second punch.

A gunshot ripped through the noise. Shouts sounded from downstairs, followed by gunfire in rapid succession.

Pain exploded in my head. Distracted, I didn't see the hit coming.

I flopped on the bed, dazed. The horror show of sex toys spun in my vision.

Bruno pried my legs apart. He picked up his naked boss and made a run for it.

I tried to follow. Katz couldn't get away.

I stumbled into the hall, and in Jasper's arms.

"Adeline."

"Where is he?" I screamed. "Katz? Katz!"

"Adeline, what happened?"

"Stop him!"

I fought in his hold.

"He's gone."

"No!" The tears flowed now. Hot and soaking, mixing with the dirt on his coat.

"I'm sorry." Jasper held me close. "I was late. I'm so sorry, Adeline."

We sank to our knees. I cried until there was nothing left, and darkness finally took me.

JASPER

I placed the tea on the floor next to her. Adeline didn't look up.

Why do I keep giving her cups of tea like a fucking idiot?

Why? Because for the first time in my life, I didn't know what to do.

I couldn't speak even to ask for forgiveness. Adeline needed me and I was late.

It was her who should speak. She should scream. Throw the tea in my face. Bury me in a shallow grave as though I wasn't already there, crushed under heavy guilt cracking my ribs, filling my nose and mouth.

Adeline did none of those things.

My comforter swallowed her to the chin. She rested her head on the window, watching the city pulse beneath us. This was the first time I'd ever seen her look so... small.

I sat down, placing my head on the glass, but looking at her.

"Are you hungry?" I asked. "Is there anything I can get you?"

She shook her head.

I reached for the only part of her exposed, brushing her cheek. "I'm sorry."

"You've said that."

A hard edge slipped into her reply. The weight doubled.

"When I realized we were burned, I acted fast so—"

"—so you wouldn't be trotted off to jail with the rest of us," Adeline finished. "That way you could turn on Katz and free us. I know what you were thinking, Jasper, and it worked. If you were taken with Saint, Killian, and Baris, I might still be locked in that room."

My jaw clenched picturing the disgusting hole of a sex dungeon Katz had put her in.

"I didn't know he wanted you specifically."

"How could you have?" Adeline fixed on the lights passing below. "It was a trap."

"Adeline, stop."

"Stop what?"

"Acting like tonight was a string of events out of our control and no one can be blamed for it. I can," I burst out. "I should've been there! You were left alone with that man because of me."

She looked at me. "Why are you blaming yourself?"

"I got back to you as fast as I could, and it wasn't fast enough."

"It's okay, Jasper. I stopped expecting someone to rescue me a long time ago."

My chest caved in, filling with dirt. Adeline didn't sound angry. She accepted that I would not be her hero.

I found her hand through the blankets. "Next time, I'll be there," I rasped. "I'll never be late again."

"You can't promise that."

"I just did." I trapped her gaze, staring deep in her eyes. "When you need me, I'll be there."

She was quiet for a long time—those quicksand pools unreadable.

When she spoke, the final spike went through my heart.

"Why, Jasper?" she whispered. "Why me?"

I knocked the tea over crushing her to me. Adeline hid her face in my neck, crying till my collar was soaked.

Hours later, the blanket was around us both. Sun crept over the horizon, blanketing Cinco City in a cruelly beautiful day.

Adeline sat on my lap, head resting on my bare chest, and finger tracing a message on my skin. I cupped the back of her neck, my lips pressed to her forehead as I murmured sweet nothings to her.

"You changed so fast," she said softly. "One second, you were the man I'm falling in love with, the next you were standing across the divide, watching me be taken down. For a moment, I believed it, Jasper. I thought you were abandoning us to save yourself, and it crushed me into dust." Adeline drew back. "Twice I've had to feel the pain of losing you. Promise me there won't be a third."

"I promise—"

"No, Jasper." She pressed her fingers to my lips. "Don't just say the words."

I kissed her fingertips. "What more can I do? Tell me, and I'll do it."

"I need to know there are no more surprises. No more secrets. Swear there won't be another moment that I look at you and wonder who you are. Tell me that I know everything, and if I don't, then I'm ready to hear it."

I fell silent beneath her hand. The words were simple.

"You know everything, Adeline. There aren't any secrets between us."

I've lied a million times to a thousand people. None of them scraped my soul raw as every half-truth I told her—from the beginning. I should've realized then that meant something.

I knew it now. The man I am, the men I used to be, and the personas to come. They all loved Adeline Redgrave.

My gaze slid to my phone, a plastic slab on the coffee table. This was my chance to tell Adeline the truth of who I worked for. Why I joined the Merchants and why even if this truth blew up in my face, I wasn't going anywhere. This was one job I had to see through.

This is my chance.

I curled around her hand, drawing it away. My kiss was slow and sweet and rewarded by her soft moan.

"You know everything you need to about me, Adeline. The rest is details. Filler. The man I truly am," I said, "you've always seen."

"No more secrets?"

"None." *That are mine to tell.*

"Are we a team from now on? I'd like to be on the next double play."

"You will be." *Unless I get orders saying otherwise.*

"Everything I do is to protect you. I mean that, Adeline. That future I want, it doesn't make sense if you're not in it."

She moved first, closing the distance.

We kissed on the sticky remains of the spilled tea.

My phone buzzed.

"Is that her?" Adeline dove for the table. "What did she say? Where are they?"

I opened it and checked the message. "It's from Zara," I confirmed. "They just finished processing them. The notorious Merchant gang is bunking down in the cells, awaiting transfer to Cinco Penitentiary."

Adeline released a long breath. "At least they're there."

It was by promising I'd find out where they were by morning that allowed me to get Adeline back to the apartment to rest. She wanted to raze the city looking for the guys. And the governor.

Due to Katz promising to boast his capture to the press, we assumed the guys were going to the police station, and not deeper into Elmshire Woods. But you couldn't know for sure with a sociopath like Katz.

Adeline took the phone from me, reading the message for herself.

"Promise me we'll get him."

"We will kill Nicolas Katz." I knew it as surely as my heart beat and rain fell from the clouds. Katz would not live long on this earth. "Slowly, brutally, and painfully. He will spend his last hours and then an eternity in hell regretting last night."

"It's me who regrets. My father said I'd wish I never heard his name. He was right," she said. "We underestimated him."

"We were betrayed. Had to be one of the men. We'll find out who soon enough. He'll be the one who magically makes bail and then disappears."

"He's not going anywhere. When we catch whoever it was, they'll hang alongside Katz."

A mirthless smile crossed my lips. That's my girl. For better or worse, nothing kept her down.

"We have to get them out."

"Katz knows we're after him now. He won't be going out to the cabin anytime soon. Getting to him in the capitol or governor's mansion is impossible. Security's too tight."

Adeline gave me a strange look.

"What?"

"You said we."

"Of course I said we. This is no longer a one-time, break-into-the-system job." I wrapped her arms around my waist. "It's personal."

"Not just for you. If we're doing this together, you need to know this is about more than the ledger." She stopped, shaking her head. "Actually, it is about the ledger. In the end, everything that is wrong with this city and the people in it, is traced to that book."

"What are you saying?"

"Nicolas Katz paid those thugs to beat and kill St. John's father."

My eyes widened.

It was five years, two weeks, and three days to the minute since the last shock that blew up my calm mask. The words "I'm pregnant" will do that.

Adeline broke my record.

"Katz? Katz killed him?" Repeating it didn't help either. "How did you find out? When? Is this why you shoved Pais to the back burner?"

"Yes," she replied. "The truth was in the ledger. Gianna finally told us."

My mind ran off, racing a mile a minute. This changed things.

It changed everything.

"I know why you didn't tell me. Saint," I stated. "But I still wish you had."

"We've been doing all of this wrong." Adeline got up to pace in front of the windows. "I'm not blaming the guys, or you, but the reason we relied so heavily on the gang is because we didn't have you to do the recon on the governor. We need all of us on this. Especially now that we can't trust anyone else. The six of us against Nicolas Katz."

"Six?"

"Gianna."

I stood and carried her to the couch. She was throwing herself into this to distract from the night before. I wasn't about to stop her. If focusing on a problem was what she needed, then we'd discuss the murder of Katz all night and day. Still.

I stretched us out, holding her head against my chest.

It wouldn't stop me comforting her.

"Half of the six are in jail," I said. "I can call in some favors. I've got money to buy off a judge. If it comes to it, we'll break them out. In transit is best. We'll attack the prison transport."

I felt her shaking her head.

"No, Jasper. I've had all night to think about how Katz will finally get what's owed him. If the Merchants are broken out, the manhunt begins again. Alerts go wide. Katz hides in the mansion and capitol building that we can't take. Right now he thinks the only people after him are an escort and a former chef. He'll underestimate us a lot more than an entire gang."

"You said we need all of us for this."

"We do." She propped her chin under my collarbone. "We'll have to get the guys out of jail without anyone knowing."

"What do you suggest?"

"I need my phone."

ADELINE

Gianna picked up on the second ring.

"Hey," I said. "How are you? Are you still with Dad?"

"Yep. Oscar's making breakfast right now. Afterward, we're meeting up with a friend of his that can get me a fake license and passport. I said I'd die on these streets but I wasn't planning on doing it at twenty-three. We may need to get out of the city for a while. Until the heat dies down."

I picked up the second use of we. Naturally Gianna thought wherever she was going, I'd go too.

"The heat won't die down, G. People aren't going to collectively fall, smack their heads, and forget you have the ledger. If we left Cinco City, it'd be for good. And I'm not going anywhere."

There was a pause. "What happened, Addy? Are you okay?"

"No," I said honestly. "Katz was waiting for us. Saint, Baris, and Killian have been arrested along with the rest of the Merchants."

"Fucking snake," she spat. "Every time you think you've got him, he slithers away."

Bile burned my throat. I was painfully aware of how accurate that was.

"He's not getting away again," I said when I trusted myself to speak. "G, I asked you to trust me. Promised I'd think of a way to get us out of this."

"Did you?"

"I have a plan. Or the beginning of one," I said. "I'll need the ledger."

"Take it. You know where it is."

"I will but you're my glossary. Is there anything in there about the chief of police, the prison warden, or even the guy that waves hello in and out of the jail?"

"From the lawyers to the cellmates, the ledger's got something on a person in every position in our legal system. Are we planning a jailbreak?" She clapped. "Fun. It's the one law we haven't broken yet. 'Bout time."

I laughed, and secretly thanked her for making me. "Our rap sheet isn't that extensive. We've still got a few to tackle."

"But we're knocking out all the fun ones." Her tone softened. "We'll get them out, Addy. Tell me what to do, I'll help."

I hesitated. "This isn't like before, G. You don't have to drop everything for the Merchants."

"No, but I do have to drop everything when my sister needs me. That's how it works. Just because I forgot for a minute doesn't make it any less true."

"Thank you."

Jasper hooked a finger through my jeans, tugging me closer. I loved seeing this side of him. He constantly touched and flirted with me when he put on the role of Mercer. Jasper gave his affection in smaller deliberate bites. It made each time more of a treat.

"What's the plan?" Gianna asked.

I looked at Jasper. "You both might as well hear it at the same time. We're ending this once and for all."

I launched into the entire plan, leaving nothing out.

I got silence on both ends.

"Well?" I pressed. "Are you in? Gianna?"

"Adeline, the blond one deals in probabilities, right? Well, we will die if we go through with that plan. One hundred percent."

"People will die," I said. "It won't be us."

"Too much relies on variables we can't predict, Adeline," Jasper chimed in. "Someone gave us up to Katz. What if it happens again?"

"We'll know if we're given away and we'll act if that happens. This is our best chance, so are you in or out? Saint, Killian, and Baris are waiting for me."

"Can I tell Oscar?" Gianna asked.

"Uh, no. Not all of it."

"'Cause you know we're about to die," she muttered.

"Because it'll worry him unnecessarily," I corrected. "Can you handle your part?"

"You know I can."

"Jasper?" I asked.

"It'll take time," he replied, "but yes."

"Then, we're agreed."

"Agreed," they said.

DO YOU KNOW THE FEELING of working, planning, and fighting for something your whole life, and then having your goal within reach? Dangling before your fingertips and waiting to be taken. Was grabbing it everything you thought it would be?

Jasper and I stood outside the door, him waiting for me to turn the knob.

For years I sought the ledger. I've killed for it. Lied for it. Changed the course of my life to possess it.

Who was I kidding? The ledger changed the course of my life long before I was born. Every step I took was on the end of its puppet strings.

Now it will be in my hands.

"Adeline? Have you changed your mind?"

"No, we have to do this." I turned the knob. "Let's go."

A dim, empty hallway welcomed us. Security was truly dismal where Gianna chose to hide the most sought-after book in Cinco history, but in the end, there was only one right place for it.

The library was deserted this early in the morning. A few hardcore studiers and free-internet surfers ignored us as we passed by—four in total. The odds of one of them reporting back to Katz, or the many criminals after us, was slim. Even so my skin itched seeing the library worker glance at me from behind the checkout desk.

"This way," I whispered.

"Why would Gianna hide the ledger here?"

"Because." I landed on my couch. "I used to come here when I was little, and fall asleep on this couch. Most times, I wasn't alone. We felt safe here."

Peering around, no one was watching us. I flipped the cushion off the couch. A small seam cut through the fabric.

My fingers paused inches above it. All these years. All the lives lost. The clock timing my search ended. The clock to put things right started now.

I reached inside. My fingers brushed something cool.

"Someone's coming."

My moment ended.

I grabbed the book, shoved the cushion in place, and ducked out of view in the stacks. The ledger was pressed between us, with Jasper and I chest to chest like we were embracing.

The same library worker strolled by, pushing a cart. She collected a stack of books and wheeled on.

"So." Jasper clutched my hips, rocking me closer. "Is it the ledger or another book of gibberish?"

I ran my hand down the crinkled leather spine. I felt the age and wear in the yellowed pages even before I undid the clasp and opened the book.

The ledger was bigger than I expected. Nearly the size of a laptop and five times as thick. It wasn't something to casually lug around.

Or it's not anymore.

I flipped through the pages, spanning decades of owners. Small handwriting. Cramped handwriting. Block letters and cursive. Stained pages. Added pages. Each new hand added their own piece to the book that changed the fate of our city. I reached the final page, and the handwriting of Gianna Cross.

"This isn't the part where you knock me out, grab the ledger, and make a run for it, is it?" I asked Jasper.

"Nah. That part comes when we're away from the witnesses."

I shoved his shoulder. "I can't say why I feel safe with you though I should be worried about that very thing. Maybe it's because I know I can take you."

He kissed me. "I'm disturbingly interested in seeing you try."

I grinned. "We should get out of here. I saw his name. We have what we need."

Safely in the car, I asked Jasper to loop through the streets while I read everything the ledger had on Harrison West.

Gianna was right. Raul was right. From one passage I knew, the ledger changed everything.

I dialed the number for Cinco Pen.

"Hello. May I speak to Warden West?"

A light, sweet voice replied. "Your name, please, and what is this regarding?"

"My name is Judith Lightfellow calling from Cinco Memorial Hospital. It's about his wife, Kathy. I'm afraid there's been an accident."

"Oh, no," she cried. "Is Kathy okay?"

"I'm sorry, but I can only speak about this with her husband."

"Of course, I— Harrison? Harrison! The phone for you. Kathy's been in an accident."

"What?" Something clattered on the other end. "Hello? Kathy, are you okay?"

"I'm sure she's fine. Well, other than being married to a liar. Two offshore bank accounts, Harry?" I tsked. "How are you filling those up on a warden salary?"

"Wha— What's going on?"

"This is what's going on. Three men entered your prison today. You're going to grant them early release."

"Hold on a second. How dare—!"

"Do not interrupt," I sliced in. "You will see to it that they are released today while the records say otherwise. You are not going to double-cross me, alert the authorities, or speak a word about this to anyone. You will do this because I'm going to give you something you want more than whatever retribution you're dreaming up."

"And what would that be?" he snapped.

I traced a line under his name. "Your page in the ledger, Warden West. After me, no one will be able to use your many, *many* crimes against you. It's a clean slate. Are you interested?"

Silence spread through the phone.

"These men," he began, "what are their names?"

I smiled. "You've made a good choice today, Warden."

"I release those three and you give me my page. That's the deal."

"Actually, you're going to do a few other things for me too, but I doubt you'll object," I breezed. "For now, let's focus on my guys."

THE CHAIN-LINK FENCE rumbled open. I reclined on the car hood, waggling my fingers at a bemused Saint, Baris, and Killian. Jasper propped next to me—eyes unreadable behind hooded shades.

"What would you guys do without me?"

"You didn't give us a chance to find out," Killian said. "How'd you pull this off, Redgrave?"

"Warden West and I formed a mutually beneficial relationship." I jumped off the car and ran into his arms, kissing him everywhere. "Are you okay?"

"We weren't in long enough to do damage. Barely got through the cavity search before we were brought into a separate room and told we were being released."

Sinjin brushed past us.

"What are the terms of this beneficial relationship?" Killian asked.

"We..." I trailed off. Sinjin was advancing on Jasper fast. "Saint, wait. Jasper did what he did to—"

Sinjin dropped him with a single punch. Jasper didn't try to block the blow.

"I had him." Sinjin's voice was a low growl. "You got in the way."

Jasper spat blood on the gravel. "I didn't know."

I ran to get between them. Brutal hooked my waist, stopping me.

"Jasper Croix." Sinjin straightened to his full height and smoothed down his slightly rumpled suit. "Upon further deliberation, we've decided to offer you the position. You're in."

I blinked. What just happened?

"Saint?"

"He turned on us so he wouldn't be carted off to prison. Figured it out a second after he dropped to his knees, mewling like a bitch." Sinjin tipped my chin up. "Are you okay? Did he touch you?"

Lips pressed together, I looked away.

His fist balled against my throat. "Where is he?"

"Doesn't matter where he is," I croaked, "it's about where he will be. I have a plan."

"In the car." Killian kissed my hand, then my cheek, then my lips. Brutal kissed me just as gently.

I sensed the comfort the guys were pouring into me, like they sensed I wasn't ready to talk about what happened. The only part of Katz that touched me was his rotted dick scraping my teeth and I wanted to dip myself in scalding oil and burn every trace of him from me. I couldn't let myself think, let alone speak, about what would've happened if I didn't break from those binds, or Jasper didn't come back for me.

"There's something you need to know," I said as we got in the car. "Colt and Titan never made it to the cells. Jasper's friend, Zara, confirmed there's no record of their arrest."

"I saw them hogtied on the lawn with the rest," Jasper said. "Either they overpowered their guards, or they collected their money and caught the first ride out of Cinco City."

"They won't get far," Killian said. "What's this plan of yours, Redgrave? It better be overkill in every sense of the word."

"It is." The creature unfurled her wings. "Nicolas Katz will beg for death."

Chapter Ten

Five days we held up in Jasper's apartment, waiting.

We went through the plan back and forth with Killian's usual thoroughness. Once again, the probability of our deaths was put in the high nineties. Even so, the guys agreed this was our best chance.

Brutal and I lay out on the living room floor—naked under a pile of blankets. His weight was comforting on top of me as he read over my shoulder.

I tapped her name. "Bellona Alexander. Hitwoman for hire," I read. "Gianna said her life took a turn after your father's rejection."

"Who isn't in this book?"

We spent the last five days trying to answer that question and we were only halfway through. The ledger had grown into a massive tome. Everyone who ever was, is, or will be of importance had found their way into the ledger. Some of the entries weren't blackmail material. One owner had listed each rich or influential person in Cinco and attached their weaknesses.

Andrew Hudson, CEO of Organics, received a page naming his wife and three children. The scribe wrote where they worked and went to school, and how to get around security for both. It was chilling.

"Innocent or guilty, no one is truly free of the ledger," I said. "Until now. No one is going to touch Andrew Hudson's family. I hope whoever wrote this was slaughtered during the regime change."

Baris kissed just under my ear. "The news confirmed it this morning. Governor Katz leaves the safety of his mansion tomorrow."

"With a fucking limp and torn-up back."

"Are you ready?"

"My part is easy."

"No, it isn't. Your part leaves you the most exposed. Let me go with you."

I flipped over, draping my arms around his waist. Baris took this invitation to slip his hardening cock inside me.

"Oh, hello."

"Sinjin has Cash as backup," he said. "I'll be with you."

"You know you can't, Baris. You just said I'm the most exposed. Won't people notice if I'm strolling next to a man who's supposed to be in prison? This whole thing hinges on everyone believing you're behind bars."

"We change the plan."

He pushed in deep, filling me to bursting, and drawing a soft sigh out of me. I wished I could say this was the first time I simultaneously argued while making love to my guys. We've developed quite a knack for it.

Baris signed to me. My heart melted at the message.

Okay, this wasn't an argument. This was my love wanting to be there for me like he'd always been when I needed him.

And I need him more than ever now.

Baris couldn't know that I accepted the odds. I didn't expect to make it out of this. Only Gianna and I knew how this was meant to end. I told her in a private conversation away from Jasper. Like her, my fate was to die on these streets.

"We can't change the plan," I said. "You have to trust me, Baris. How many times have you walked into certain death and come back to me? I've lost count. Our story doesn't end here. Do you believe me?"

"I do." He started moving, going straight for that spot. "I'm still not letting you out of my sight."

My sigh was cut off by a moan. I knew a losing argument when it was fucking me. We could fight about this later.

JASPER

I shut the door as Adeline and Baris's discussion became heated of a different type.

"She has the ledger, but I haven't gone near it," I said. "The guys have let me back into the Merchants. Showing too much interest in the book is the red flag they're waiting for."

"In most matters, I trust your judgment," my employer replied. "In this case, I suggest you stop wasting time."

"You won't when you hear what I have to tell you. It's bigger than the ledger now. Their target is Governor Nicolas Katz."

I returned to the secret panel under the nightstand that Adeline missed in her search. My carryall lay open on the floor—half full with my passports, cash, and photos of Rosie. "He had St. John's father killed."

"This is a problem."

If I did not know that already, I would've by the tone of her voice. Years in her employ. Years of these phone calls where no matter the news, her inflection did not rise above mildly interested or annoyed. There was nothing mild about her tone today.

"You have to do something, Jasper."

"I will do something." I cocked my gun, unloading a spent casing. "Have my money ready. My contract ends tomorrow."

ADELINE

"How do I look?"

"Beautiful."

"Beautiful, huh?" The blonde strands swished back and forth. "Do you like blondes?"

"That's a trap."

I laughed. "All I'm asking is if this blonde wig should make a regular appearance. Where's the trap?"

"You are perfection personified, Adeline Redgrave," Jasper said. "I wouldn't want a single thing about you to change."

"Oooh, very good."

"Thank you. That was one of my smoother lines."

Amused, I checked myself out in his bathroom mirror. I barely recognized myself.

My copper mane disappeared under a heavy, sun-kissed blonde wig. Contacts transformed my infamous light brown eyes into the muddy brown of the masses. Wide-framed glasses slipped down my nose. I pushed them up with a pointy fake nail.

Jasper assured the guys it was the little touches that would turn me from Adeline Redgrave to—

I checked my new ID.

—Kennedy Phillips.

I didn't believe it until I saw it for myself. Katz wouldn't know I was there until it was too late.

Killian, Baris, and Sinjin watched us from the door.

"What time does Katz arrived?" I asked.

"The press conference starts at ten," said Jasper. "He'll arrive an hour early."

I looked to the guys. "You should get going, then. I'll see you when it's over."

"We will see you when it's over," Killian said. "Nothing better happen to you, Redgrave."

He made it sound like a threat.

I skipped over and popped a smooch on his lips. "I'll be careful, toy boy, as long as you four know I will drag you back from the afterlife if you die."

"Understood," Sinjin said. He helped himself to a kiss. "Let's move."

Sinjin and Cash went out the door. Brutal did not follow.

"They're going to need muscle on this job," I tried.

"They can take care of themselves."

My brows blew up my forehead. "And I can't?"

"You're not getting rid of me, Redgrave. Do what we planned. I'll be close by." He kissed me and headed out.

"Are you ready, Jasper?"

He cinched the belt on his uniform. "Please, Miss Phillips. It's Officer Normandy."

"I should feel something akin to nervousness, shouldn't I?" I checked the gun concealed in my waistband. "I heard that's what normal people feel before they eviscerate someone."

Jasper spun me, snapping me to his chest. "As it happens, normal people don't do much eviscerating."

"Hmm. Weird."

He smiled down on me. His fingers traced my lips, speeding up my pulse. They parted in anticipation. This was my life since Mercer exited and Jasper entered it.

Waiting, hoping, anticipating.

It was like when you're excited about something, and for a brief second, you forget what it is. The joy doesn't leave you. It just waits for you to remember what lit up your world.

Jasper's face changed. His smile dimmed. "Adeline."

"Yes?"

"I have to tell you…"

"Tell me what?"

"I love you. No matter what happens, I need you to know I love you."

I held his face in both hands. "I do."

Jasper nipped my bottom lip, demanding entrance. I gave it eagerly.

Our tongues entangled in a kiss that went from zero to one hundred in a blink.

He slammed me against the door, wrapping my legs around his waist. We went at each other like wild animals in sight of their prey.

Kissing Jasper was unlike anything known to man. He was confident and knowledgeable while still making me feel like it was the first time.

We broke apart eyeing each other and calculating how much time we had to make love.

"We should go." Saying the words visibly pained him. "Sorry, Kennedy. If my girlfriend catches us, we're dead."

"Girlfriend?" I bit my lip to pen a goofy smile. "Didn't know you had a girlfriend."

"I do. You got a problem with that?"

"No. No, I don't."

THE CAPITOL'S GRAND hall was packed. Reporters, cameramen, security, and workers formed a business-casual mob, taking up every seat and the three walls not claimed by the stage and podium.

I hitched my tote bag up my shoulder, searching for a free seat.

Kennedy Phillips made it through security without a problem. They checked every item in my bag, but neglected to study my fake press pass.

I'm in. Is Baris here too?

I scanned the room, but didn't see my perfect mix of broad shoulders, full lips, and quiet calm.

Baris said he'd be close by. I knew he was here somewhere—like I knew Jasper, Killian, and Saint were in place, waiting for the cue.

An empty chair peeked out from the fourth row.

"Excuse me. Excuse me," I said.

The crowd parted for me, and gave me the chance to snag my place.

"Ladies and gentlemen."

Just in time.

"Please take your seats," said an official-looking man standing at the podium. "We will begin soon. The governor is recovering, so we will limit questions following his statement."

My lips peeled back from my teeth.

Recovering. Katz wasn't so sickly he missed a chance to schedule a vanity parade. It's amazing I didn't see this man for what he was from the beginning. Another oily politician with a plastic smile and a hunger for power.

I may not have seen it before, but the entire city will see today.

I glanced at the cameras.

Live.

A hush fell on the room. Governor Katz was pushed up the ramp in a wheelchair. He nodded and smiled at the crowd, appearing pale and drawn. The bid for sympathy started right out of the gate.

All he got from me was a deep, satisfying delight watching him limping the rest of the way to the podium, holding on to Bruno and his wife, Marian. His left hand was wrapped in bandages.

"Hope it hurts, bitch," I said under my breath.

"Good morning, everyone," Katz began. "Thank you for being here today."

"Governor Katz, what happened?"

"Governor Katz, how did you receive that injury?"

Katz raised a hand, quieting the reporters. "Cinco City is a wonderful place to live. Diverse, cultured, and unique. One visit, and you can't help but find something to love. There is nowhere I'd rather live while I serve you and the people of this great state." Katz stopped to receive applause. "Even so, as much as I love this city, I am not blind to our problems.

"We lead the nation in drug arrests, overdoses, and violent crime. I've dedicated my career to fighting these issues, but I must admit, before last week, they were statistics on a page. They weren't real to me until this violence touched my life."

He paused, taking in a shuddering breath. I regretted with everything in me that he'd chosen to hold this conference inside instead of on the capitol steps. One shot and Gianna could've blown him to bloody bits.

"While vacationing in my cabin retreat, I was attacked by members of a gang known as the Merchants. I was injured in the struggle—a wound that would've been more serious, possibly fatal, if not for the quick action of my security team."

Another pause. Another round of clapping and shouts of sympathy.

"I can't begin to describe my gratitude to Bruno Morgan and the men he's trained. You are a credit to the service. The salary I pay you is not nearly enough."

He waved to someone off-stage. He was actually tearing up.

"I am happy to say, Bruno and his men subdued the Merchant gang. They are all in jail currently awaiting trial. These arrests mark a new era for me and Cinco City," he called. "It has never been more real to me what my people are facing. You have the right to feel safe in your homes. The right to walk to your cars without looking over your shoulder. Women deserve to live their lives with no fear of meeting men like St. John Bellisario, the Slasher."

The praise, flashes, and shouts of agreement were in full force.

"I vow to make these rights a reality for our home, and this is not a politician's promise. This morning I donated two million dollars to Cinco PD. We will change our city!"

The room rose up, giving Katz a standing ovation. He nodded and waved—oh so humbled by their response.

"Thank you, thank you," he said. "Now, I will answer as many questions as I can. I believe Mrs. Katz is timing me."

Marian comically raised her arm, tapping her watch. I wondered if she secretly wished the Merchants finished the job that night.

A reporter in the front row raised his hand. "Morning, Governor, I'm with the Cinco Press. Can you tell us more about your plan to battle Cinco's crime rate? Does it go beyond your generous donation?"

"Valid question," he replied. "The work doesn't end with throwing money at the issue. I'm pushing for more officers on the streets, and better training for those officers."

Hands up again.

"Governor, I'm with City Daily. Would you tell us more about what happened the night you were attacked? Why did this gang target you?"

Katz lowered his head. "I can only assume they believed I'd be an easy target, out there in Elmshire Woods alone. They were wrong."

Hands went in the air—mine highest of all.

"Morning, Governor, I'm with TheTruthComesOut dot net," I called above the crowd. "I'd like to circle back to my colleague's question of why the Merchants targeted you."

Katz squinted down at me. "All right."

"Isn't it true the Merchants came after you that night because you kidnapped and held hostage Adeline Redgrave after murdering Thiago Pais?"

"Excuse me?" Katz sputtered. "That's absurd—"

"Thiago Pais attempted to blackmail me into giving him the ledger. Little did we know, you intercepted the time of the meeting and had him *killed*"—I said that nice and loud—"to keep the ledger out of his hands. When I fled the building, your precious overpaid guards grabbed and brought me to your cabin where I was restrained, held captive, and assaulted!"

A profound silence fell on the room. The camera flashes and low murmurs of translations stopped.

"Lies!" His mask broke. "I've never seen you before in my life. Let alone heard of this— this Thiago Paid. Security? Security!"

I tore the wig off my head, letting my russet hair fly free. "Recognize me now, bitch."

The woman next to me gasped like that was the most shocking thing I said all morning.

"You ran off crying into the night when I stabbed you in the middle of assaulting me, but you were wrong if you thought that'd be the last you saw of me. You left something behind."

Katz was still bellowing for security.

I reached into my tote bag, lifting the ledger for all to see. "Any of you journalists worth your degree, will know exactly what this is. Governor Katz lied, bribed, stole, and killed for this book." I flipped off the latch. "Should I tell you all why?"

"Security! Grab her now!"

The crowd turned.

Bespectacled, pantsuit-wearing writers rushed me—falling over their chairs and sticking their camera half in my mouth.

"Miss Redgrave, is that the real ledger?"

"Miss Redgrave, is it true the governor held you captive?"

"Do you have proof of your claims?"

Security was coming for me. They swarmed with batons, stun guns, and real guns ready. The blockade formed around me wouldn't let them through.

"I have the body sitting in the morgue with a hole the size of a grapefruit in his chest. I have the marks on my wrists. I have a description of where I stabbed Governor Katz—left thigh above an oval-shaped birthmark." I narrowed on the man whose guards were trying to haul him away from the podium. "And I know the secrets he killed to protect."

I flipped to a page with Katz's name on it and shoved it at the camera. The ink truth shone stark for those watching live to see.

"From the staged drive-by that catapulted him to mayor, to the innocent man he had murdered to find Kieran, and then the wife he arranged to have raped and killed to sympathize his way into the governor's seat."

Marian Katz dropped his arm—eyes wide as she gaped at her husband.

"If you want to know how to save Cinco City, start with a change in government."

Katz broke free of Bruno. "Take her!"

"How do we know that's the real ledger?"

"What else does it say about the governor?"

"Ah!" A cry pierced the chaos. The guards were using their batons.

Panic surged through the crowd as more people cried out. They pressed in on me—pushing, hitting, shoving. I bumped into someone and knocked their camera to the floor.

"Hey!" They shoved the person next to them.

Unease crept up my spine. It was time to go.

"Is Mayor Gunderson in there too?"

I pushed on someone's back, straining to get past them. I couldn't see where the guards were coming from over the reporters' heads, but I didn't need to be around when they made themselves known.

"Miss Redgrave—"

"Give me the book!"

A hairy-knuckled hand appeared from nowhere and seized the ledger. I reacted on instinct, grabbed them, and bent their fingers back. A punch sideswiped me, knocking me into a mass of people who pushed me back.

The last thing I saw before I sunk beneath the crowd was Governor Katz wheeled out the door.

JASPER

I reclined in the swivel chair—feet tapping, arms positioned over my gun.

I had to give it to our girl. Her plan was nuts and could go wrong in a million different ways, but if it didn't, it would save us all. Might even save this ungrateful heap of concrete and grime we called home.

"This is a problem. You have to do something, Jasper."

I had no desire to be the reason it went wrong. If it was in my power, I would not be. But I had orders. I had a daughter relying on the completion of my contract, and the rewards that came with it.

Nothing mattered above Rosie. Not even me.

For better or worse, four years of waiting ended today.

Walkie feedback cut through my thoughts.

"We're on the move. Repeat, Red Eagle is on the move!" I recognized that crackly voice as Bruno's without issue. "Car. South entrance. Now."

"Roger that," someone replied.

I didn't make a move.

The parking garage was cool and dimly lit. I sat in the ticket kiosk, sharing it with the unconscious man at my feet.

A car sped around the corner, slamming to a stop before the gate.

"Raise the gate," he barked. He stuck his hand out flashing a badge. "It's an emergency. We're evacuating the governor."

"Of course. I just need to check your—"

I grabbed his arm and yanked his head out the car. I knocked him out mid-scream.

The guard joined my new friend stuffed in the box. Raising the gate, I drove the governor's car inside and parked near the exit. The door opened and Cash climbed in the front seat.

"My friend cut the security camera a minute ago," I said. "Cops will be on their way, but I assume they were already called. They'll go straight to the riot in the grand hall."

"How long?" Cash demanded. The ski mask stretched over his face.

"Bruno called for the car five minutes ago. It takes at least that long to wheel one man through the hall with a contingent of guards. They'll be out any second."

No sooner had I finished the sentence than Bruno and his injured boss blew into the garage. Two men in suits and the governor's wife followed.

"Bring her to me," Katz ordered. "Neither she nor that book leaves the building!" He smacked a hand trying to help him up. Katz stood without difficulty, obviously not as hurt as he pretended for the broadcast still streaming live.

"What is he waiting for?" Cash asked.

Katz made for the car.

Bang! Bang!

Katz's men dropped like bowling pins.

Marian screamed.

"Down!" Bruno jumped on his boss. Bending him down, he threw Katz in the back seat and spun to fire on the shooter.

I leaned out the window and fired one, two, three bullets in his back.

Bruno sank to his knees. He gurgled something—I imagined it was regret for letting his filthy fucking boss lay a hand on our girl.

"No, no!" Katz ducked Cash's gun and scrambled out the open door. He ran straight into a masked Sinjin.

I heard the butt of his gun cracking the man's skull over Marian's screeching. Silently, Cash and I got out of the car, joining Sinjin.

"P-please," Marian sobbed. She dropped to her knees, hands above her head. "Don't kill me."

"We're not here for you," I said. "We want your husband, and deep down, you want us to take him." Katz groaned on the floor. "You know he's not a man worth saving."

Marian looked at her husband. "Are you... with that woman in there?"

"We are."

"Is what she said true?"

I didn't have to ask about what. "Your husband was willing to pay Kieran to brutalize you in your own home. Anything to get the sympathy vote. You're only alive because the ruthless crime boss had a conscience."

Her face shuttered closed. "I see." She stood and dusted off her knees. "Take him."

"Run," Cash said. "Make it sound like you narrowly escaped us."

She did so, leaving her husband groaning on the floor. Cash and Sinjin hefted him up.

"I'll drive." I checked my phone. "They shut off the broadcast and it was bad enough before that. We need to pick up Adeline and get out of here."

"North entrance," Cash said. "She's supposed to text when—"

Security poured out of the building.

"They've got the governor! Fire!"

Time slowed.

Sinjin turned as Cash climbed inside the car, bent to go in after. I didn't think.

I jumped in front of him as they let loose. The force struck my chest, blowing me off my feet. I crashed into Sinjin, dropping us both on Katz.

"Kill, drive!"

The shout barely penetrated the ringing. I tried to breathe and found I couldn't. Air wouldn't go in. My last breath wouldn't come out.

Sinjin blurred around the edges.

Eyes falling shut, I let go.

ADELINE

I dropped to the floor and curled around the ledger. Jasper said there were variables I couldn't account for. The reporters boxing me in and then turning so fast wasn't planned. I was twenty feet from the door. It might as well have been miles.

Someone tripped over a chair and landed on me.

What seemed an accident changed when they grabbed the book, fighting to yank it from my hands.

"Let go!"

They flew back, toppling on the same chair. All of a sudden, I was lifted and crushed to a hard chest. "Security" read on his lapel.

"Get off me."

"Adeline." A familiar voice spoke. "I've got you. Hold on."

I dropped my head on his chest, relief filling my battered body. "I take back everything I said. I needed backup."

"Out of the way. Move!"

Baris had no trouble finding his voice, or using his fists. Hat pulled low on his face, he got us free of the clutch and was waved out by the harassed guards too busy taming the crowd to notice he wasn't one of them.

We ran for the north entrance.

"Brutal, you drive." Killian squealed to a stop and got out. "Croix's been shot."

"What?" I piled in the front seat. My heart stopped seeing Jasper unresponsive.

Brutal drove out of the lot.

A sharp turn threw us sideways. The car Brutal swerved to avoid didn't slow down for an apology. Neither did the mass of vehicles that followed—all sporting a crown somewhere on their car.

Twisting around, I held tight to Jasper's hand. "They're storming the capitol."

"They can do what the fuck they like," Sinjin said. "Adams and Third, Brutal. The governor has been waiting twenty years for this. Let's not keep him waiting."

JASPER WOKE TO TEASING fingers in his hair. He squinted at me.

"Adeline."

"Shh," I crooned. "It's okay. The vest got the bullets, but four to the chest would knock anyone on their ass." I kissed his forehead. "I'm so thankful you were wearing it."

"If I'm stealing the uniform, I might as well steal the gear." Jasper took my hand. "Where are we?"

I turned my head up to the ceiling, because there wasn't one. A gaping hole poured warm, beaming sunlight on ash and charred remains.

"Where it all started," Sinjin said. He stepped off the altar. Jasper and I sat on the last standing pew in Our Lady of the Sacred Heart Cathedral. "Hey. What you did." Sinjin clasped his hand. He didn't say more than that. Jasper nodded like he heard the rest all the same.

"Are we good?"

"We are." I helped him sit up. "We changed cars and abandoned his in an alley. The cops won't follow the rest of the trail here. Especially since they believe the only connection to this place is in jail."

"The cops won't be following any trails today." Killian secured the final rope. "Onlookers are streaming video of the capitol. It's a bloodbath. The gangsters think you're in there with the ledger, and they're not leaving without it."

Jasper pushed up, winced, and sat back down. "That's what we were going for. Less manpower to search for the governor, more time to do what you have to do."

"Hmm!"

"If you were waiting for me to start, you didn't have to." Jasper snarled at him. "Katz has been living on borrowed time. Every extra second he gets to breathe air is a crime in and of itself."

"Well said," I replied.

On the scorched steps where Paul Bellisario died, our governor lay spread eagle tied to broken chair legs sticking out of debris piles.

This beautiful, once-happy place reduced to the lonely, gutted version of its former self. Just being here filled me with pain and rage in equal measure. Men like Katz forced the ledger into existence, and then they made the innocent pay the price.

Of course he had to die here. Nowhere else was appropriate.

Brutal ripped the gag out of his mouth.

"You don't have to do this." Katz launched into pleading. "You have the ledger, I'll buy it at whatever price you name. The city knows you have it, Redgrave. You'll be under siege for the rest of—"

I crossed the room and slapped his face. "You don't get to speak my name. You're out of cute speeches and a naïve audience. This isn't a negotiation. It's a sentencing."

Sinjin moved to my side as Killian and Brutal fanned out around us. Katz's eyes rolled in his head following us.

"Twenty years ago, you sent two thugs into this church to torture Father Paul for his knowledge about Kieran. They murdered him on these steps in front of his son."

"That wasn't supposed to happen," Katz cried. "I ordered them to rough him up, not kill him."

"Because that's why people hire violent bangers." Sinjin drew his knife from its holster. "For their conversational skills."

"Wait. Think about this," Katz said, eyes fixed on the knife. "You got out of prison. You're in the clear. Why spend the rest of your lives being hunted as the men who killed a governor?"

"Why?" Sinjin stood over him. "Because I'm the son."

Sinjin plunged the blade through his hand. Katz's mouth contorted in a silent scream. His eyes bugged on me of all people.

His howl rattled the charred rafters.

"I thought I'd have the whole setup when we finally did this," Sinjin said. He stepped over the sobbing man. "You should have seen our setup. Weapons spanning the centuries. I had planned something truly magnificent for you. The man who killed my father deserved no less."

"N-no, it wasn't my fault." Katz flailed in his rope. "I'll tell you their names. Leonard and Cook! They killed him, not me."

Sinjin continued like no one spoke. "But now I'm grateful my girl's friend blew up everything I owned. It was always meant to be here, with the knife I turned on Leonard and Cook after they killed my father."

"Stop. Think about what you're d-doing."

Sinjin gestured with the bleeding blade. "Did this hand also touch my Bunny?"

"No, no, no," Katz screamed.

"Hmm. Don't know if I believe you. Just to be safe—" Saint brought the knife down, twisting viciously. I looked on in grim satisfaction.

"Where are my manners?" Sinjin curled around my waist and kissed me stupid. "Would you like a go?"

"With pleasure." I planted myself at Katz's feet. "Guys, would you be so kind as to pull his pants down?"

Katz kicked at Cash and Brutal. "You're dead. All of you!"

It was almost admirable that he was still fighting. Double the victory when they went down harder.

They shoved his clothes down to his ankles. A bandage covered his left thigh courtesy of our first meeting. His shriveled-up dick was even more pathetic, shrinking in on itself like it wanted to curl up in his body and hide.

"What makes men like you this way?" I asked. "Page after page of the wealthiest, influential people in this city using their power to corrupt. You might have actually been a good leader who transformed this city into a place people visited more than once.

"Instead, you became this pathetic shell of a man—too weak to earn anything without the help of fixers, thugs, and money, and covering that weakness by hurting those who can't fight back. Even as a disgusting, raping pig you needed Bruno to gift-wrap victims for you. Couldn't do a single thing for yourself."

"Fuck you, mutt bitch." Through tears and snot, his sneer shone clear. "I'll get out of these ropes and make you scream for the god who abandoned this church. I'll do that for myself."

My expression didn't change. "You're going the wrong way, Katz. Go back to the begging and pleading. You may convince me to go easy on you."

"You won't convince me. Two million each," he said to Killian, Baris, and Jasper. "Kill them both and give me the ledger. Rich men or wanted men. Make the right choice."

"You don't understand what's going on here, do you?" I asked. "No one's coming to save you, Katz. I'm the problem you face alone."

I stepped between his legs, holding the weapon high. Blood dripped on his shaft.

"Apologize," I ordered. "Show some remorse."

"It wasn't me. I didn't—"

The blade cut through the air. And half his penis.

"Argh!" His scream shattered my eardrums.

"I said show remorse, not make excuses. It's like you want me to do this."

Katz choked something out. Eyes rolling up his head, he fainted.

Brutal buried his fist in his stomach—a wake-up call fitting his name.

"You are excellent at your work, Bunny." Sinjin stroked my cheek and smeared it red. "We were meant to do this together. Cut the thing off. He won't need it where he's going."

"Later. If he bleeds out, the party ends too early."

I'm sure Katz wished that he RSVP'd no, mailed a present, and missed this particular party. We didn't have the toys from our dungeon, but some of the best work is made through simplicity. Katz's screams echoed in the burned-out church on the hill. The altar ran red with his blood.

"S-stop," he rasped. "Please... I'm sorry."

Nicolas Katz was a ruin.

He got mouthy and Brutal swelled his left eye shut. Another offer to buy his freedom and I gave him a matching stab wound in the other thigh. Sinjin carved the name of his victims on his chest, barring his father's name. He stopped struggling long ago—too weak even to lift his arms.

Sinjin stayed me running the blade down his leg. "Confess."

"I—" He choked and coughed up blood. "I've cheated people out of their homes and businesses. I've killed Emmanuel Webber, Joseph Saltz, and Gracie Conifer, and I've ordered dozens more to be killed. But your father, the priest"—Katz fixed his good eye on Saint—"I told Leonard and Cook not to kill him... unless he put up a fight.

"Father Paul had only himself to blame. Standing in the path of Kieran is a death sentence he earned all on his own." He lifted his head to spit in Sinjin's direction. "My only regret is they didn't gut you like the worthless bastard you are."

I held my breath, expecting Sinjin's explosion.

None came.

Face serene, he nodded. "You're welcome." The knife was taken from me.

Sinjin climbed the steps and knelt beside Katz. The governor snarled, snapping at the hand laid over his face.

"I claim your death in the name of Father Paul Bellisario."

He sliced Katz's throat in the space of a heartbeat. I clapped a hand over my gasp.

Katz's head fell to the side. He looked into my eyes as the lights went out, taking the life of a cruel and miserable man with it.

Saint's head lowered. He didn't move nor speak.

Slowly, I climbed the steps. Bending to kiss his temple, I heard, "It's over, Dad. It's finally over. You can rest."

Tears filled my vision. I couldn't say if I was crying for St. John, his father, or the book lying on the pew that shattered so many lives. I think I cried for all of us—the band of misfit toys that only worked together.

"It is over, baby." I pressed a kiss to his cheek. "You've done it."

"Almost. There's one more thing I have to do."

"Katz's funeral?" I asked as Saint moved me back. "Gianna is ready and waiting for us."

"No, not that." Saint stopped us short of the altar. Blood splatter covered his face, clothes, and hands, but the odd sight was the look in his eyes.

"Are you okay?"

"Never better." Holding on to my hips, he dropped to one knee. "Adeline Redgrave."

I froze. "Saint, what are you doing?"

He grinned that devil's grin. "What the fuck's it look like? Now, don't interrupt. I've got a whole speech."

I made a noise in my throat, my different-colored eyes huge. *How is this happening? What is happening?*

"I got into a car accident the day I met you. Swerved to avoid a kid who ran into the road and wrapped my car around a pole. They say your life flashes before you when you face death. Mine didn't," he said. "I didn't see anything. Feel anything, but a deep, coursing rage."

"Rage?" I whispered.

"Rage that after everything I've done and the man that was made of me, I would die before I met you."

I half laughed, half sobbed. "That doesn't make any sense."

"Didn't then. Still doesn't. But it's true," he said. "I died with my father that day, Adeline, and for twenty years, I thought I was looking for *him* to put it right. That was until I walked into a bathroom and a woman in a bunny costume defied me."

My cheeks warmed. "It wasn't a costume," I mumbled.

"It wasn't Katz's death I've been living for. It was a reason to care after it." Sinjin drew a ring from his pocket. A black-gold wreath band entwined with diamonds and sapphires. Blue and white.

Saint and Bunny.

"That reason is you, Adeline."

"Oh, Saint." I was shaking—tears soaking, heart racing. "I love you too."

"Will you marry me?"

"This is where I interject," Killian sliced in.

I jerked like he shot his gun off.

"I wish you mentioned your plans, brother." Killian came up to us. "'Cause I've been holding on to this for two weeks." On his palm lay a teardrop black diamond and silver band.

"Three," said Brutal. He held up a rose-gold ring lined with diamonds and band shaped into twisting laurels.

I swung to Jasper, half expecting a ring in his hand, and then shocked I had the thought. Did I want Jasper to propose to me? Did I want all of them to?

In my head and heart, they were mine in every way. I never considered the need to make it official.

"Well, looks like you're going to have to choose, Bunny," Sinjin breezed. "I'd like to point out, I'm the only one who actually asked."

"I'm not choosing between you," I cried. I took his ring, holding it against my chest as if to stop the swell. Taking a deep breath, I let it out slow. "What we're going to do is get rid of this corpse and the target over our heads. Once we do, we'll sit down"—I drifted to Jasper—"and discuss our future."

"You're our bride, Adeline." Saint uncurled my fist. He slid his ring down my finger.

Perfect fit.

"There's only one future for us," Killian said.

"And we'll wait," said Baris.

Jasper got up and hooked his pinky around mine. "For as long as it takes."

Chapter Eleven

Morning dawned on Trapp Square. Gray, damp, and darkened by gathering rain clouds. A stiff wind tickled the awnings and went straight through the people who skipped a layer getting dressed that morning.

This didn't stop us.

Trapp Square was a tiny oasis in the middle of the city. Fountains and mini themed gardens broke up the concrete. Around them were little benches for a couple of women like us to enjoy a treat from the surrounding cafés, while we watched people trickle in. Middle of it all stood the towering statue of Junto Trapp.

"Let me get this straight," Gianna said.

I was fairly certain it was her. The floppy hat, oversized glasses, and frumpy floral-patterned dress she must have gotten from a swap shop, did a great job concealing my friend's identity.

"He dropped to one knee on a bloodstained floor and proposed next to a corpse."

"It's more romantic than it sounds."

"It almost has to be."

I shoved her shoulder. "I wasn't expecting this, G. Now I have three rings on my fingers."

"And you're waiting for a fourth?"

I looked down at my hand, stroking the rings. "I don't know what I'm waiting for with Jasper. Sometimes he looks at me like he has something important to say. Then the moment passes and it's like I imagined it. The thing is, what if I am? What if I'm looking for something to be wrong to pump the brakes on us? I fell for him so hard and so fast. It almost seems—"

"—too good to be true," she finished. "The man you loved turned out to be a carefully crafted costume, but oh, it's all good—the real him is perfect for you too."

She dragged my fear out and tossed it on stage in that way Gianna does. She's always known me too well.

"Yes," I said. "It's not an exaggeration to say things rarely work out smoothly for me. What if I'm still seeing the man I want to see, and not the man he is?"

"What if you're so used to fighting, you can't tell when you've won?"

My head snapped up. I looked at her in surprise.

Gianna smiled at me. "I never thought I'd say this, but the Merchants were meant for you, Addy. The five of you together, it's right. I don't know everything about them, and maybe you don't either, but I know one thing. They love you.

"The real kind of love that drives murder-suicides, breaks sanity, and writes the tragic love stories we read for centuries to come. You're the love women lying next to their safe option wish for while he's clipping his toenails in bed."

I laughed.

"Stop waiting for the other unopened package to explode, Adeline. The only question to ask yourself is if you love him too." She tapped my hand. "Same question to ask about these rings on your fingers."

"Thanks, G." I squeezed her wrist. "I've missed this."

"You and me both," she snorted. "Your old man is driving me crazy. I've forgotten what it's like to be his student. Even a perfect shot earns a critique."

"Penance is long and hard, but it is just."

It was her turn to shove my shoulder.

"Ah! Ahhhh!"

I dropped my sunglasses in place. "Right on time."

"Was it you who bet before seven twenty?" Gianna checked her watch. "Seven nineteen. Damn, you're good."

I smirked as the woman ran past, spilling her bag's contents in a trail her poodle raced to follow.

"Help! Help," she screamed. "Call the police!"

"*Yap, yap, yap.*"

"I'll take cash," I said.

Dusting ourselves off, we ran across the square for the benefit of any eyes drawn by her screeching.

Makeup bag. Notebook. Tissue pack. Umbrella. Broken Kindle.

They led the way to our first mayor, Junto Trapp, and his new companion. He pointed to grand things in the distance, providing the perfect greenish-bronze perch for Governor Nicolas Katz.

The ropes suspended him under the arm, swaying him back and forth in the breeze. No wonder she ran screaming. Wide, staring eyes and a blood choker would turn the strongest stomach.

"The message was a nice touch," Gianna remarked.

"I thought so."

Painted on Trapp's chest were three words signed with an A.R.

Cinco Is Mine

"You go left and I go right?"

"Yep," she replied. "Let me know what you decide."

"You'll be the first."

Sucking in a breath, we let out ear-splitting screams.

"Help, it's the governor! Someone help!"

"IS THIS WHAT YOU WERE after?"

I jumped.

I was tucked behind the ledger, trying to read while actually staring at the rings. Sinjin sat at my feet. My legs were draped over his shoulders and receiving a kneading massage.

The reporter's speech penetrated.

"—live from Trapp Square. As you can see, authorities are struggling to hold the barrier and maintain calm in the wake of Governor Katz's murder."

Chelsea from Channel Ten News was pleasantly pretty with blonde-streaked brunette locks and a button nose. Neither they nor the heavy makeup on her eye and cheek hid the bruises,

"Wonder if she was at the press conference?"

My answer came quick.

"On the heels of yesterday's press conference where this reporter and others were caught in a violent confrontation, the smoke cleared only for capitol security to discover the bodies of the governor's private guard in the parking lot, and the governor himself missing. Efforts to find him were delayed by armed men laying siege to the building.

"For hours we were on lockdown, huddled in terror at the shouting, banging, and gunfire beyond the doors. Every police station in Cinco was mobilized. At five seventeen p.m., the lockdown was lifted and those trapped inside evacuated. We went home to our families believing the worst day of our lives was behind us. We were wrong."

"Hear that, Bunny? We top a violent riot and government lockdown."

We high-fived.

"The search for Governor Katz ended this morning in Trapp Square. His body was found hanging from the statue with the message, 'Cinco is mine,' signed A.R. At this time, authorities are assuming A.R. is Adeline Redgrave—the woman responsible for the capitol riot."

"Responsible? I didn't tell everyone to lose their minds and come at me like the bulls of Pamplona."

The screen cut to video of me ripping the wig off my head. I presented the ledger for all her morning viewers to see. Just in case they missed me the first time.

"Miss Redgrave claims to be in possession of a book called the ledger. Known among the Cinco criminal element, it's said the ledger holds blackmail material on nearly every person of power in our city. She certainly made serious allegations against the governor—including that he kidnapped and assaulted her. Police are forced to consider these events linked with the discovery of her initials next to his body."

"I would think so," I scoffed. "What else? Should I have drawn them a map?"

Behind her, the crowd surrounding the square grew. I heard their bellowing grow louder though I couldn't make out what they were saying.

"My colleague is live from the governor's mansion. Mrs. Katz has agreed to deliver a short statement in this difficult time."

I put the ledger down and sat up straight to hear this.

Marian Katz came on the screen, her backdrop the grand gardens of the mansion. Unlike Chelsea, her makeup sold the bit. Dark circles peppered red eyes and the slightest tinge of pink colored her nose. Unless she discovered a trace of affection for the traitorous bastard she sent off to die, this performance would be Oscar-worthy.

"Mrs. Katz," the reporter began, "in your own time, would you tell us what happened yesterday?"

She dabbed the corner of her eyes with a tissue. "It was horrible. Nicolas and I were rushed out of the building only to be ambushed in the parking lot. Seven— Possibly eight men in masks attacked us. Bullets were flying. I was terrified. Nicolas shouted for Mr. Morgan to get me to safety. The next thing I knew, I was whisked away.

"Morgan brought me to safety, told me to call for help, and returned to rescue my husband." Marian sniffed. "Neither one came back. And for him to be found like— like that. Why would anyone do this to him? He's served this city and this state faithfully for twenty-five years."

"Thank you for sharing, Mrs. Katz. Our hearts go out to you during this time."

Jasper picked up the ledger and joined me on the couch. He stroked my palm, sending shivers radiating up my arm.

It was the reverence of his touch that thrilled me. Jasper touched, kissed, and looked at me like I was the center of his world.

Something hard pressed into my skin.

"Bought it the day after our first date. I've known you were the one from the beginning. I'm just waiting for you to know it too." He brushed his lips on my temple. "There's something I have to do. I'll be back. I love you, Adeline."

Jasper walked away, leaving me with the lingering trace of his kiss and a double-band white-gold engagement ring.

"And then there were four," Sinjin said.

"You're not obligated to make trouble, you know." But my chest contracted, stealing the little air left after seeing the ring.

It was one thing to accept a proposal from Saint, Killian, and Baris. Accepting one from Jasper came with different strings. Some I couldn't see.

"Chelsea!" The shout rebounded out of the speakers.

The police lost their fight with the crowd. They trampled the barrier and flooded into the square. I could've been mistaken, but the beefy, tattooed figures running for the shaky camera weren't everyday crime scene gawkers.

"Chels, run!"

She didn't need to be told twice. Chelsea took off running, screaming to echo through the homes of Cinco City. The lens whirled, and I assumed the cameraman had tried to chase after her.

Just as quickly, he was drug back.

"Record this, boy."

There was a yelp, then red, bulging eyes and curled lips dripping such venom filled the screen, I grimaced.

"We know you're watching, Redgrave. You don't own these streets, we do. The Kings are under new management. Hand over the ledger on your own, or we burn this shit down coming after it!"

The concrete rushed to meet the camera. The news went off-air.

"Did you factor this in your plan?"

"I couldn't predict every possible outcome," I replied. "The point of flashing the ledger at the press conference was to flush out Katz and take the heat off of Gianna. They were coming for me anyway, now they have a reason."

Killian leaned on the windows. "They've seen it, Adeline. The ledger is no longer a myth or a want in the back of their heads. They know it's close by and all that's standing in their way is a five-foot-four chef from Rockchapel. He wasn't exaggerating." Killian gazed at the people below. "They will burn the city down."

"I did what I had to do," I said. "Gianna was on the run alone, and now she's with Dad. The people after her could've taken the last of my family out with one well-planned ambush. We're safe here. They'll burn the city down and then be consumed by the fire. That's when I rise from the ashes, baby. It's what I do."

Killian shook his head. "I can't decide if your overconfidence is sexy or frustrating."

"It's not overconfidence. It's just the right amount of confidence as long as we have this." I tapped the ledger. "Once the Kings, Bowery Boys, Outlaws, and the Kravets climb back into their holes, I'll use the book to seal them shut. No one can touch us, Killian."

I beckoned him over. "Sit. I'm almost done reading. About a hundred pages left."

Killian joined me, laying me out on his chest as Saint claimed my legs, and Baris banged around in the kitchen, cooking. A nearly perfect scene if it wasn't for the fact I was barely skimming, and the news broadcasted on every other channel.

"Firefighters called to the twenty-ninth precinct in Leighbridge. A gang of motorcyclists surrounded the station and threw Molotov cocktails at the windows."

"Riot police abandon Trapp Square."

"Emergency lines flooded. Reports of assaults and break-ins all over the city."

"Looting in Organics on Thirty-fourth Street result in store shut down. Other store owners following suit."

I looked up again from the third to last page, stomach tightening.

"Authorities are ordering citizens to stay indoors. Bolt the exits. Set your alarms," said Brian of Cinco Action News. "They also ask the woman known as Adeline Redgrave"—my photo flashed beside his head—"to turn herself in for her safety and the safety of the public. Men we suspect of leading the rioters have taken their demands to the internet."

A series of live videos played one after the other.

"Red Rover, Red Rover, send Redgrave on over," said a man in a skull neck gaiter. Behind him, bangers swarmed a Leighbridge neighborhood. Two carried a big-screen television.

The video changed to a panoramic of the square. A car tipped on its side next to the Trapp statue. All over, shadowed men and women trampled police tape and fallen riot gear. "This doesn't stop till I get that ledger," the videographer said. "Come out, bitch!"

"Please, Miss Redgrave." Brian and his co-host returned. "If you're watching this, turn yourself in."

"I can't watch any more of this." I crossed to the windows. "Where is Jasper? He said he had to do something and hasn't been back since. His phone is going to voicemail."

"The man has a kid," Sinjin said. "I assume he's wherever she is."

"Oh, no. I didn't think about Rosie out there. The bangers are using Leighbridge as their free television hunting ground." I clutched the book tighter. "If Jasper's trying to get her somewhere safe, I should be with him."

"You going out there would defuse the situation," Killian said, "but not in a good way. Croix knows what he's doing, Adeline. You can't leave."

"I won't go out there if I hear from him in the next thirty minutes. Jasper keeps an impressive amount of hair dye, wigs, and fake glasses. No one will know it's me. Besides, if he did get stuck between *that*"—I gestured at the television—"on the way to Rosie. He'll want us to get to her in his place."

I went into the bedroom, shutting the door on the grim news. I got comfortable in Jasper's bed and resumed reading. Without a doubt I knew, in the end, it would come down to the ledger to save us. Every secret. Every crime. Every confession. It was a layer in the armor of the new Kieran.

Brutal came in seconds after I finished the final entry—written by Gianna herself.

"Anything good?" he asked.

"Nothing good in that book, love. I need two showers after this." I shuddered. "I guessed at the secrets powerful enough to drive men to kill for it. The worst crimes I could think of, and I didn't come close."

"We'll get to them. One by one." Baris glanced over his shoulder. Over a dozen floors up and we heard the sirens piercing the night loud and clear. "Try not to think about it for now. I made lobster mac and cheese with that spinach salad you do. Eat, then we'll take those two showers together."

"My man keeps it inside most of the time, but when he speaks." I popped a kiss on his lips. "He knows exactly the right thing to say."

We met up with the guys in the kitchen. Saint poured the wine and Killian got the utensils. I went to dish out the food.

I stopped short of the serving spoon.

Days of reading, dozens of names, miles of secrets rushed through my head, and left behind one name. I rocked on my heels, physically struck.

"Jasper," I whispered.

"Sometimes he looks at me like he has something important to say."

Of course he did, and it was that he's a fucking liar.

I was wrong about him the entire time. Now he was out there, and he wasn't answering his phone.

Racing to the bedroom, I ignored the guys' calls and turned over his hiding places.

The one in the closet. *Untouched.*

The one in the nightstand. *Missing the photo album of Rosie.*

The one under the rug that I found during another snoop while he was away.

I pried up the floor panels, revealing nothing.

Passports, money, and weapons cleared out.

I sat down hard. What did this mean? Was Jasper gone? Did he get what he wanted from us and take off?

After giving me a ring.

My stomach heaved.

Was all of it a lie to keep me sweet, smiling, and asking the wrong questions?

I dove for my phone.

No, he wasn't doing this to me again. Running off and leaving me waiting for the truth. Jasper would pick up the damn phone.

I pulled up his name and my ringtone sounded off.

Gianna.

"Hey, G. Now isn't a good—"

"Addy, they're here." The cry stopped me short. "I don't know who they're with, but half a dozen bangers are outside Oscar's door right now!"

"What?" I shot up. My foot caught in the secret space and landed me painfully on my knee. "How?" I gritted. "How did they find you so fast?"

"Doesn't matter how, they're here."

"Is that Adeline?" Dad came through the speakers. "Give me the phone."

"Saint, Killian, Baris!" I called.

"Brown eyes."

"Dad, are you alright? I'm at least a thirty-five-minute drive from you, and that's not counting the riots backing up traffic."

"Forget that," he said sharply. "Wherever you are, you *stay* there if it's safe. Your old man still has a few tricks up his sleeve. I bought the apartment next to mine under another name and installed a door in the closet. They'll turn my place over while we wait."

"That'll work until they find the door," I cried. "They want me, Dad, not you. Whatever it takes to bring me running, and it worked. I'm running."

"What are you—?"

Bang! Bang!

"Oscar!"

"Dad? Dad, what's going on?"

"Don't come," he shouted.

The line went dead.

"Adeline, what's going on?" Killian asked.

"They found my dad and Gianna. You don't have to come with me, but I'm leaving."

"Don't be ridiculous." Cash drew his gun.

"I've been waiting all day for an excuse," said Sinjin. "Everyone's come out to play. This is gonna be fun."

I didn't bother to say otherwise. The streets were descending into madness, blood, and chaos. It was a wonder I kept Sinjin inside for as long as I did.

"Jasper has a weapons stash in the closet and living room. Grab as much as you can hold."

I found a backpack and stuffed the ledger and everything I needed inside. I would not be coming back.

The guys filed out the door—armed and ready. I stopped at the threshold, letting them go on out of sight.

I drew Jasper's engagement ring from my pocket and flung it as hard as I could. He didn't need to pick up the phone. There was nothing more to be said.

We were done.

THE GUYS AND I HOPPED in a borrowed car and tore out of the parking garage. Turning off O'Connell Street, Killian slammed the brakes.

A wall of stalled traffic greeted us.

"Three alternative routes," said my analytical love. "Two eventually putting us back on this road. The third taking us out to Wells Drive."

"Wells takes us twenty minutes out of the way," I said.

"Still might get us there fast—"

"Killian, look out!"

An object hurtled at the windshield.

I screamed as the trash can shattered the glass, raining cuts and blood on Sinjin and Cash.

"Whoo!"

A dozen figures in neck gaiters descended on the line of cars—shaking, battering, and tormenting the people inside. A man leaped on our hood.

"We'll have this ride, pretty boys. Climb out nice and easy—"

Killian snapped around. He fired five times in his Bandits Motorcycle Club tee. He collapsed on the trunk in front of us.

"New plan," Killian growled.

We stormed out of the car. Three men ran at Brutal carrying a bat, trash can, and a weapon that glinted silver in the moonlight. Brutal wrenched the bat from his grip and tossed it to me. I faced my fighters as he snapped bat boy's neck and threw him at trash can man.

I had a gun hanging on my hip, a knife strapped to my arm, and another gun tucked away. I could use them, but one look at these fools proved they weren't bangers. I spotted a gangster as easily as the difference between buttercream frosting and a swiss meringue. These flabby-bottom bros weren't looking for me. They were feeding off the chaos and a chance to jack expensive cars off terrified people. A bat to the head was fitting punishment.

I dented in the skull of the first idiot to run at me. Cash shot the second.

"Thanks, baby."

"What's wrong? Don't get shy now." Sinjin rocked on the balls of his feet, laughing over a body missing his throat. The three guys surrounding him backed away. One turned tail and ran.

A bottle whizzed past my face and shattered on the sidewalk.

Snarling, I went for the flaming face mask carrying the switchblade. He swiped at me.

"I."

I sunk the bat in his gut.

"Don't."

A hit to the jaw swung his head around.

"Have time."

I brought it down, cracking the bat in half on his shoulder.

"For this!"

He fell to the concrete whimpering. I finished him off.

Hopping on the hood, I brandished my bloody broken bat. "Take your asses home. Now!" I threw the piece at one of Saint's attackers, nailing him in the stomach.

They tripped over themselves fleeing.

"You're magnificent," Sinjin said, helping me down.

"Don't get yourself worked up. We don't have time for a romp."

"This is the one and only time I will agree with you. I know how we'll get through this traff—"

A noise interrupted us, making us fly to our weapons.

The lined of cars had emptied out. The passengers stood on the street looking at us, and clapping.

I stared.

"Thank you so much."

"You saved us."

"Thank you."

Sinjin slowly released his hilt. "This is new," he remarked, voicing my thoughts.

Never in my years of brutal, merciless killing did I think I'd be thanked for it.

"It's not safe on the streets right now," I said. "Please, take shelter, bolt the doors, do not come out until morning."

"Let's go," Sinjin said.

We veered down an alley with Brutal and Cash, leaving the cheering crowd behind.

"Forget the car." Sinjin was a powerful, fearless force striding through the alley in a suit blacker than night. Hades passing through the flames of the underworld. "What we need is two blocks away."

Cash and Brutal fell in step with him—cracking their knuckles, reloading ammo. My god of the sun, and my god of war.

They turned my life on its head that day in Raiden Spencer's bathroom, but here they were taking on a city on fire to save my family.

Gianna said it all. There was only one question to ask myself.

"Yes," I said. "I'll marry you."

They stopped dead.

"Feel free to actually ask me and do all you planned, Killian. Baris," I said. "But it's a yes. Of course it's a yes."

"Which one of us?" Killian asked.

"All of you. That's a crime, but we'll figure out how to break that law later." I took off past them. "We have to get to Dad and Gianna."

We came out onto the street and another logjam of cars. Seemed all of Leighbridge was trying to flee the city. Sinjin halted in front of our destination.

"Hell, yes," I said. "Saint, you're a genius."

Cash blew out the motorcycle shop windows. The four of us roared down Main, zipping through traffic.

Come on, come on, come on.

As fast as it was, I needed to move faster. If anything happened to my dad or sister, it was me who'd level this city to ash.

And where was Jasper while all of this was happening? My relationship with Mercer ended without a real goodbye. Jasper and I would go the same way.

Wind tore at me, shredding the weak warmth of my layers, and freezing my fingers numb on the handlebars. Still I kept going, leaving Leighbridge behind for the former home of the Lords: Waterford.

Traffic clogged worse nearing the expressway. Cars caught sideways, over the line, and a few tried their chances on the sidewalk. We slowed to puttering starts and stops.

Killian signaled for my attention. "Back alleys," he called. "Fifteen minutes."

If he said it, I believed him. I backed up and navigated my ride through the honking horns and raged-up drivers shouting me out of the way.

I pulled ahead of the guys, leading the way down the alley. A glimpse at the pink graffiti on the dumpster and I knew where I was. Dad and I wandered down this way one day while we were walking around our old neighborhood. We were close.

I'm coming, Dad. Gianna. Please don't stop being your incredible, indestructible selves before I get there.

I picked up speed.

"Argh! Die, you miserable bastard!"

Thud!

A force careened into my back tire, spinning me out. I veered straight at the wall.

I hit the brick—bones jarring from toe to jaw and clamping my teeth down. Searing pain in my mouth was all I knew for the split second my body flew through the air. I crashed into the wall helmet first and collapsed on a bag of trash.

I lay there dazed, listening to rats scurry to their hiding places. I couldn't move. Couldn't breathe. Agony was my world.

"Adeline? Adeline!" Baris broke through the fog. "Are you okay?"

"What... happened?"

Hands lifted me up, cradling me against his chest.

"Something got in our way," Sinjin forced out.

I didn't know what he was talking about. Then Brutal removed my helmet.

A body lay in our path—unrecognizable by the two motorcycles that ran over this speed bump. Sinjin and Cash were thrown from their bikes. Only Brutal was spared, having stopped in time.

"Shit," I breathed. "Who did this?"

"Cinco's finest will have to find out." Sinjin pushed himself up. "We don't have time to chase them up the roof." He went to his brother who groaned when he grabbed his arm.

"Killian." The initial shock was fading. A full stock of my body came away with a bruise on my forehead and a bloody lip. Killian didn't sound as good. "Are you okay?"

"Fine." Getting to his feet, his arm hung limply by his side.

"You're not fine." I scrambled out of Baris's arms.

"I am fine," he said, ripping off his dented helmet. His coat was in tatters, but I only spotted scrapes underneath. "Dislocated shoulder. Sinjin can pop it back in." He looked at the dented metal and warped wheels. "Our bikes are fucked. You go."

"Go? I'm not leaving you." I stroked Sinjin's and Cash's cheeks, reassuring myself they were okay.

"Brutal will take you on his. Go," Sinjin ordered. "We'll catch up."

"It's not safe for us to split up. Bodies are falling from the fucking sky!"

"You'll be safe," Cash said. "Save your family, Adeline."

My hands shook, balling into fists. "Right behind me." I backed toward Brutal. "You better not get one more scratch on you."

"Yes, ma'am," said Sinjin.

Brutal helped me onto his bike and secured my arms around his waist. We took off, listening to Killian's bellow as we shot out of the alley.

Brutal expertly drove through the madness. Yes, madness was the word. A thick, crushing fervor blanketed the streets of Cinco, spreading billowing miasma into otherwise ordinary people.

We dodged two men locked in a fistfight before a bagel shop. A driver rammed another to force them out of the way—screaming and honking abuse the whole way. Speeding past, I glimpsed inside a café. The staff huddled inside behind a bolted door.

The ledger has finally done it.

It's broken this city.

My father's apartment loomed ahead. I didn't need to see it to know.

"Holy hell," I breathed.

Gangsters had taken over the entire street. Kings, Outlaws, Bowery Boys, Seventh Street Gang. The different tattoos, signs, and emblems blurred.

Pop! Pop! Pop!

Hordes of men swarmed the road, crowing atop overturned cars and firing indiscriminately into shops, homes, and cars speeding to get away.

"Dad! Gianna!"

Their address had gone wide, and they'd make sure no one left with the ledger but their gang.

Brutal hooked a turn and put the street in our rearview. We jumped off the bike the next street over, pushing against the tide racing to leave.

Shoulders bumped and shoved me back. Pain burst above my eye from an elbow catching me at just the right time. Still, I kept going. Dad's place had a lush backyard surrounded by a wooden fence. If I could get over it, I'd get to them.

"Whoa!" A hand hooked me, dragging me behind a porch stoop. "Kings."

I peered over the steps, spotting what everyone was running from. The neck tats gave them away. Five or more Kings surrounded Dad's fence—gun cocked and aimed for anyone who dared to get close.

"We have to pull them away," he said. His speech was free and unhampered.

"I have an idea. Follow me."

Under cover of the throng, I broke a car's window and popped the latch. We climbed inside.

"Is there a spare key in the glove box?"

"Here." Brutal passed it to me.

I stuck it in the ignition, then we lowered our seats out of view.

And waited.

"They're okay, Adeline." He brushed my hair from my damp temple. "Have they called?"

I checked my phone and stiffened.

Zero calls from Dad or Gianna. One from Jasper.

He must've returned to the apartment and found us gone.

I erased the alert.

I asked him that night to tell me everything and he lied to my face. Jasper had nothing to say to me now.

I dialed Gianna.

"Addy."

"G, are you guys okay? I'm on your street. It's a nightmare."

"It's not better in here either." Her voice was low and muffled. "We can hear them up there, Addy. Breaking into apartments and dragging people out. This is a freaking senior residence. What kind of monsters are we dealing with?"

"All of them."

"All? How are they not killing each other?"

"That comes when I make an appearance. We have to get you both out quietly or this neighborhood will be a bloodbath," I said. "What did you mean by up there?"

"They found the door, Addy. Oscar had to break through the floor panels. We're in the crawlspace under the building," she said. "We're blind down here."

"Hold on. When I tell you, get out of there and run. Do you hear me? Run, Gianna. Do not chase after me. Don't get locked in a battle with the Kings or anyone else. Go where I told you. This ends tonight."

"Be careful, babe."

"Love you."

"Love you too."

"Adeline," Brutal said when I ended the call. "It's time."

I just noticed the street had quieted. I looked over the dash at the King thugs loitering around.

"Buckle up."

I wrenched the key. Slamming my foot on the gas, we sped toward the men.

"Hey! Stop!"

A body hit the windshield. Bullets followed close behind, spraying the windows to splinters. Another thump and a dead King dropped next to us—half in, half out the car.

I hit the brakes, checked to see who was left standing, and whipped the car around.

"Stop! Help!"

I mowed down the final four Kings, chasing one down the road and getting him as he tried to run up a stoop. He shrieked under my wheels.

"This should be a drinking game," I said. "One shot for every stupid-ass King that winds up a hood ornament. It's ridiculous they haven't learned to stop pissing me off by now."

"Too many bangers in one gang causes a dangerous increase in confidence and feelings of invincibility. The cure: a five-foot-something redhead wearing a 'donut touch my whisk' T-shirt."

I cracked a smile. "Damn straight."

Brutal pulled his gloves on and gave me a boost over the fence. I dropped behind a sourwood tree.

There was no one back here. Dad and Gianna were clear to make a run for it.

Brutal dropped down next to me.

"They're in the crawlspace under the house," I whispered.

I saw the gangs in the front street, giving over to savagery.

"The foundation is brick. They'll have to climb back up to get out."

I called Gianna and told her just that.

"We'll wait till it's quiet up there," she said. "Let us know when the street's clear."

"Good. We'll cause a diversion up—"

"Let me go!"

The building's side door banged open. Four men carried out a woman who was not a senior resident. From what was left of her torn scrubs, she was a nurse.

She thrashed in their grip, kicking off a shoe. "Get off me! Help! Help!" Her high-pitched terror was a straight shot to my chest. "Don't do this!"

One of the Outlaws fondled, then smacked her breast. "You wouldn't happen to know where our friend Oscar Redgrave hangs out, would you?" I heard him from clear across the lawn. "I'm due for a chat with his daughter. She has something of mine."

She spit in his face.

"I'll take that as you needing further encouragement."

"No!" I jumped up and a blur shot past me.

Brutal sprinted across the lawn. The Outlaws had the woman spread X on a car hood. Their jeering leader dropped his pants to laughs.

Brutal was on him before anyone could react. He kicked out the back of his knees, dropping him on the pavement. He grabbed hold of his head and chin.

"Noooo—!"

Snap.

I tripped onto the sidewalk, whipping out my gun.

Baris kicked the dead man away from him. The others pulled their guns and Baris seized an arm, yanking an Outlaw in front of him. We fired at the same time.

The Outlaw's bullet buried in his friend. Mine in his skull.

One attacker standing. Out of the dozens on the street.

"Brutal!"

The woman sprang up. Striking her captor across the face, she snatched his gun and turned it around. Her scream ripped through the street as she riddled him with holes.

"Run," Brutal ordered—a signal that went wide to the entire street.

The men jumped off the cars, out of the shops, and descended on us in all directions. One aimed at Baris's back.

"Stop!" I shouted. "I have what you want."

I ripped open my backpack and held the ledger up high.

A shock wave went through the horde, skidding them to a stop.

"The ledger. The precious book you've all been waiting for, and you won't get it by terrorizing these people." I inched back. "Come on, boys. First one to catch me, rules the city."

I ran.

Darting back the way I came, I put the phone to my ear.

"—line? Adeline, what's going on?"

"Now! Get out now!"

The hounds of hell snapped at my heels. They shouted, cursed, and fired at me. Bullets struck the ground at my feet.

I shot up the fence and vaulted over. I landed on a soft body and kept going.

Get to the main street and blend with the crowd. My mind shouted the order, spurring me on. *Lead them away from Brutal, Dad, and Gianna.*

My phone rang.

I checked it thinking it was Gianna. Jasper's name flashed on the screen.

Ending the call, I stuffed the cell in my pocket.

Heart yammering. Feet pounding. Breaths tearing from my chest. I ran faster than I knew I could.

"Give it up, Redgrave," someone huffed. "This doesn't have to be difficult."

I lifted my middle finger high overhead.

They chased me for miles.

Nowhere was safe. No one was safe.

Shop owners bolted their doors, refusing to let anyone inside. Rioters joined the mob. They howled like this was some fun game, and debasing themselves to their lowest form the prize.

I reached Panama Avenue and stopped.

Which way? There used to be old warehouses in this area. Where are they?

Every breath burned my lungs. I doubled over, wanting desperately to rest. I stopped feeling my feet and the blood filling my shoes an hour ago.

"Redgrave! She's over there."

"Give it up."

"Can't run forever."

I looked back. How was it possible the horde doubled in size? Every criminal in Cinco was after me, and they were gaining.

Going off the dimmest memory, I veered right for what I hoped was the direction of the old warehouses. I needed somewhere to hide. To breathe. To think.

My treads thundered down Panama. At the end of the street, a large square building rose above the rest.

The warehouses. I found them.

I ducked low, practically crawling around parked cars and high beams. I came out on the other side of the street. An alley swallowed me, providing shadows as cover.

There were two doors on either side of the alley. One by the dumpster and the other at the back of the building. The padlock on the door nearest me made my decision.

Plaster cracked beneath my feet. I ventured further inside, listening to the critters scattering at my arrival. I flicked the flashlight on my phone, cursing when I noticed the low battery.

That wasn't a problem I could deal with right now. First was escaping the mob of convicted murderers, rapists, and mobsters on my tail.

The old factory warehouse had been cleared of anything valuable—actually anything at all. Columns stretched from ceiling to floor. Steel beams crossed from wall to wall. And a door peeked out on the opposite side. Beside the rats, trash, and an overturned chair with three legs, there was only me.

I chose a column with "Tomorrow's A Better Day" spray-painted on the plaster. It was a surprisingly uplifting message for a desolate place.

I slid onto the floor, turning my ear to listen for "stupid bitch" or "cocksucking slut." You would've thought they were my names. They certainly yelled that more than Redgrave.

Battery at ten percent, I chanced it and called Baris, then Cash, then Sinjin. Neither one picked up.

They better be in perfect health and ready for the sex of their life when I find them. I placed the ledger on my lap, stroking its weathered pages.

"You can't have me, you dusty, ink-riddled bastard. You can take all the Kierans before, but you can't have me, my family, or my guys. A twenty-year winning streak," I said. "You're overdue to be beaten."

"—in here."

I shot up.

"She ran down this way," a gruff voice said. "She's gotta be in one of these buildings. Check in there?"

I was already off racing for the exit. I spilled out into the alley.

"Redgrave."

I plastered myself against the door, breathing hard.

"Where are you, darling? You can't hide from us. Make it easy on yourself." The croon came from the top of the street. I didn't know who it was, but they were getting close. "Give us the ledger and we won't hurt you."

Clinging to the brick, I hurried away from that slithering, soft voice.

"No," I breathed. "It can't end this way."

I halted, stopped short by the iron fence appearing out of the gloom. Barbed wire curled on top—taunting me.

"Where are you, darling?"

Facing the street, I clutched the bag strap in a death grip. If I was going out like this, so be it. I'd die looking my enemies in the eye.

"Adeline."

I whirled around.

The dark bent to allow him through, unfolding for shiny leather shoes, midnight-blue suit, and those curved full lips making every smile appear as a smirk.

"Looks like you need an assist."

"What are you doing here, Jasper?" I hissed. "How did you get here?"

"I went back to the apartment and found the place cleaned out. When you didn't answer my calls, I tracked you."

Of course he fucking did. I forgot I agreed to put the tracking app on my phone. Dangerous times called for it.

"You finally stopped here and I tried to avoid the mob by coming in the back way." He observed the fence. "That didn't work out."

"Redgrave!"

"Adeline, quick," Jasper said. "Give me the ledger."

"Come again?" I backed up. "Why the hell would I do that?"

"I thought we had a plan."

"That was before I found out Jasper's another copy of the original," I burst out, furious tears springing to my eyes. "You lied to me again."

Jasper moved forward. His smooth, handsome face reflected no worry or panic. "About what?"

I yanked out the ledger. "Joseph Lombard is *not* in this book, Jasper. He gets a mention on page one hundred along with a list of his weaknesses, but there's nothing in here that could be used to hurt him or his businesses. So what exactly has he been paying you for four years to do?"

"Not in the ledger? Wow," he said mildly. "I chose a name that had to be connected to shady shit and he happens to be the only man in Cinco who's not in the book. How's that for a lesson about lying?"

The line of my shoulders hardened. "Are you serious right now?" I forced through gritted teeth. "That's what you have to say for yourself? Oops?"

"No, I have more to say for myself but now isn't exactly the time." He flicked over my shoulder. "I couldn't tell you who I really worked for or why, so I gave you a name. Not my smartest move, but this—being here for you now—is.

"I love you, Adeline, and that's the one thing about me that's always been true. So stop asking 'who does he work for' and 'what is he hiding from me,' and ask yourself the only question that matters.

"Do you love me?"

I swallowed hard, lump lodging in my throat.

"Come out, bitch," the slithering voice called. "I'm getting tired of hide-and-seek."

"Jasper—"

"Do you?" He grabbed the bars, but his gaze reached through, trapping me in dark, swirling pools. "If they catch you with the ledger, they'll have no reason to keep you alive. Decide now if you love me." Jasper traced my trembling lips. "If you trust me."

Fury swelled in my chest and I knocked his hand away. This man lied to me, deceived me, used me, and now he asks for my only weapon against a deadly mob in exchange for trust he never earned.

All of our sweet moments together bubbled and caught fire like nitrate film. Too fast to stop. Impossible to save.

The swim under the waterfall. Bouncing in the back seat of his car. Painting each other's bodies red.

None of it was real. It couldn't be, but—

"I do," I whispered. "I love you."

"Give me the ledger, Adeline."

My body moved on its own power, placing the book in his hands.

"Hey. Hey, she's down here!"

The ledger slipped through the bars. Out of my reach.

"I'll come back for you, Adeline. I'll always come back."

"You, stop!" Thunderous footfalls chased me up the alley.

"Who was that?"

I said nothing. Just stared at the empty space that was Jasper, feeling like I should cry and finding my tears dried up.

"Who was it?" Hands hauled me around and slammed me against the bars. Over his shoulder, dozens more poured into the alley. "Where's the ledger?"

"Gone," I replied, voice dull. "He's gone."

"Argh!" His fist hurtled toward my face.

I welcomed the darkness this time. It was better than my reality.

Chapter Twelve

"**...S**he's ours..."

"...try it...I paint the...with your brains..."

"...know where to take her."

Shouts and heated words tried to reach me in my quiet place. That final, familiar voice drug me closer to the surface.

My eyes cracked open a slit. I was being carried by the arms and legs. Their grips were shackles around my limbs.

"We'll sort this out when we find who ran off with the book."

"How do we do that?"

"Take it easy. They'll come to us."

My vision blurred, and I was lost once again.

"WAKE UP, REDGRAVE."

Sharp pain split my side. I was ripped from sleep, crying out.

"Look what came out of our pinata. Wonder what else she's got in there?"

A hard smack on my ass sent me swinging. I twisted around, sweeping the three-sixty length of Trapp Square and the assembled gangs of Cinco City.

Hundreds within dozens of organizations shat out the bowels of the underground to collect in this once beautiful place. The gardens were trampled and littered with trash. Fires burned throughout the square—smoking garbage cans and the car that was overturned in the morning riots.

Heat prickled my skin, dripping sweat that mingled with blood leaking from the wound on my side—not far from the one I gave myself that day in the basement. I kept swinging, landing on the message I wrote a lifetime ago.

Cinco Is Mine. A.R.

They hung me from Junto Trapp. The ropes looped under my arms and tied to his.

This was how I died. Slow-roasted and bled like a pig.

"What did you do with my ledger, darling?"

The slithering voice attached itself to a face and knife. Tawny skin. Narrowed brown eyes. Features that might have been handsome if not contorted with malice. He fixed on me as he licked the blood from the tip.

My voice was a thin rasp. "Incredibly unsanitary."

He laughed. "I've heard about that mouth. Shame you weren't smart enough to put it to better use."

"You know me, and naturally I know nothing about a mindless peon like you. King, right?" I asked, though the tattoo made it obvious. "Got a name?"

"Name's Max, and I've graduated from mindless peon to leader of the Kings."

"Congratulations." I sent feelers throughout my body. Other than the throbbing abdomen, wrists, ankles, armpits, and face, I was fine. So not really fine at all. "The life expectancy attached to your position is one month and shortening by the minute."

"Stop fucking flirting and get on with it," someone shouted.

A beer bottle flew in my direction.

"Where is it?" Max asked.

"Isn't that why your buddies are filming this?"

They were. Dozens of phones were streaming the grand finale live. Why wouldn't they?

They were out to prove who was the true ruler of the city. Adeline Redgrave was being dethroned.

"You're hoping whoever ran off with the ledger will come running back when my torture is broadcasted for the whole city to see? Let me save you the trouble and me the pain. Jasper," I said, looking directly into someone's lens. "Bring the ledger to the square."

"Wow." Max clapped. "That was easy."

"Why would I fight you? The second the ledger makes an appearance, you'll all tear each other apart to have it while I swing above the fray—enjoying the show." I grinned. "You didn't think this through, d-did you?" I skipped a beat.

A golden crown bobbed through the crowd followed by a knit cap and silken tawny hair. The Merchants were here.

I sensed their minds working from my place of honor. They were planning how to save me, and calculating how many of them would die in the process.

The answer was all of them. And me. And more innocent people when the powder keg blew up.

"I know what I'm doing." I raised my voice to the crowd, but spoke only to my guys. "I'm safer letting this play out. It won't end the way you think."

"No, darling, it's not going to end the way *you* think. You see, we've come to an agreement." Seven men and women peeled themselves from the pack, surrounding me. "We've decided we'll share the ledger. Rule this city under one power. One organization. Many families." He lifted his shoulders. "It works for the mafia. Why not us?"

I nodded along. "Good thinking, except for one fatal flaw in your logic. The ledger cannot be shared. One of you is bound to betray the others for control of the whole pie." I shrugged right back. "It's inevitable."

"Not a concern of yours, you won't be around to see it." His blade flashed and sliced a cut on my thigh.

I bit back a scream.

"Where's this friend of yours, Redgrave? He has five minutes to get here with my book. Every minute I wait after that, I'll carve off another piece!"

Sinjin, Cash, and Brutal picked up the pace, pushing through the watchers.

Where is Jasper? You said you wouldn't be late. You promised.

"Calm down," I hissed. "Nothing more unattractive than a grown man throwing a hissy fit for not getting his way. I said you'd get your fucking book. Wait!"

My cry went out to him and my guys. Wondering if this crowd was armed to the teeth was like wondering if Governor Katz was on his own spit-roast in hell. Bullets would fly before they touched the rope.

"I will wait exactly"—Max made a show of checking his watch—"four minutes and thirty-two seconds."

Four minutes and thirty-two seconds. *Stall.*

"If you're so open to a criminal world court, why am I strung up?" I asked. "I'm willing to join. Willing to lead it actually. It makes sense since I found the ledger and—"

"—gave it up at the first boo-boo," Max finished. "I'm not sure what kind of game you think you're playing, girl, but this is the big leagues. There's no room for a disrespectful bit of skirt who spreads her legs to get her hands on things she has no business with."

"I see, so the only way I could've gotten a hold of the ledger was by stealing it off the nightstand of my passed-out lover. You want to believe that's the story. All of you," I said to them. "Easier to swallow than admitting the disrespectful bit of skirt tracked down what you've spent decades searching for. And it wasn't that hard."

"Two minutes and sixteen seconds."

I gritted my teeth, penning in a retort that was guaranteed to make him shorten the clock.

Where were the police? Riot squad? SWAT team? A city-wide uprising would spread any force thin. Even so, I'd think one or two of them would be interested in the public execution carried out by gang leaders announcing they plan to turn Cinco City into a hellmouth.

They know what you know. Confronting this crowd is a death sentence.

"Nothing else to say?" Max taunted. "Ran out of ideas after your pathetic plea to become one of us?"

"More like ran out of interest in talking to you. Give me my two minutes in silence."

The crowd heard that and let loose.

"You're going to die here, bitch."

"The city belongs to us."

"Cut off those sweet lips first."

Max raised a hand. "Five, four, three, two—"

Boom!

Flames lit the square, swinging heads around to the explosion.

Midnight blue cut across Max, and Jasper was there.

Whole, and perfect, and just in time. He tossed me the book.

"It's a shame you rejected my offer to lead the Nine Families. That's what we would've called it. Such a good name," I tsked.

Max twisted, blinking up at me.

"What you aren't understanding is I own this book, this city, and all of you. I'll decide who's fit to rule Cinco and I choose... me."

I threw the ledger, sailing it over the grasping fingertips of Max and the bosses. It smacked the metal, and fell—tumbling into the flames' open mouth. It greedily consumed the crackling pages, nowhere near satisfied with just the car.

"I will be the last owner of the ledger."

"Yes, you will." Max brandished the knife.

His head exploded.

Blood and brain matter showered everyone in the vicinity. I gaped at the mess. Then my rope snapped.

Shooting. Someone was shooting.

I swung toward the car, and quickly grabbed on to the other rope, pulling myself up.

"Adeline!"

"Adeline, let go!"

The final thread snapped and a force stronger than gravity slammed me against good old Junto and surrendered me to the roaring horde.

I would be the last owner of the ledger.

I lay on the concrete, willing myself to get up and kiss my guys as red, gushing liquid formed a halo around my body.

"Adeline, no!"

This is how I was meant to die. On the streets of my city, bringing her peace in the end of its reign of terror.

Cinco was safe.

Dad redeemed.

Soren avenged.

Gianna forgiven.

My loves free.

"Don't you dare fucking die, Redgrave." Cash's arms were around me, lifting me up. "We're getting married. We're ruling this city. Together."

"I love you," I whispered.

I closed my eyes, and fell.

Final Chapter

J*asper*

"The president sent in the National Guard this morning to return calm to the city. As you can see, many participants in the riots have been identified through video and rounded up," said the news reporter. "This help came in time to save many, but too late for the eighty-seven citizens and officers who died in the terrible violence that swept through Cinco.

"Among them was our governor, Nicolas Katz, and the woman alleged to have murdered him, Adeline Redgrave. Her death was posted live on social media when gang members tied her to Trapp statue, demanding she hand over a book of blackmail information known as the ledger. Shooter or shooters unknown fired into the crowd, killing Redgrave and others. The ensuing panic caused the gang members to scatter into the arms of authorities."

Sinjin, Killian, Baris, Oscar, and Gianna took up the living room, watching the news with grim expressions.

"You shouldn't have done this," Oscar said. "It wasn't worth it!"

"We had no choice."

Adeline walked out of the kitchen carrying a tray of steaming mugs. The bandage on her thigh and abdomen couldn't be seen under the sunflower dress. She appeared completely and wholly perfect.

As she always was.

From the doorway, I watched her set the tray down and take her seat. I stepped inside the room. They fell silent.

I'd been having that effect a lot lately.

I set my duffel bag down. *Time to set the record straight.*

"Ladies. Gentlemen."

"Jasper." Adeline rose. "Sit with me."

The hotel room was small and the furniture it came with smaller still. I budged up next to her, squeezed between the cushions, and wished it smaller. Sweet, minty perfume tickled my nose. Her warmth on my lap was as it should be. We fit together like the jagged pieces we were. Together we were whole.

She kissed me—teasing, playful, and cut short by her dad's watchful eye. Adeline recovered from the darkest day in our history, as named by the mayor.

"I knew you wouldn't approve, Dad, but Gianna's plan to fake her death was twice as dangerous," she said.

Cross threw her hands up. "Nice, best friend. Giving me up to save yourself."

She laughed. "No, I was merely pointing out that I did my best to make sure we all got out of this alive and we did. Sort of," she added. "I actually got the idea from Gianna. She said without the ledger, she might as well be tied to a pole in the square and the bloodbath broadcasted. I couldn't help thinking that if all of Cinco witnessed our deaths and the end of the ledger, the war would stop. The video of me shot by a sniper and dropped into a trampling mob got three million hits in an hour. Records show Gianna Cross and Oscar Redgrave also died when their home was attacked by rioters.

"Prison records back up the Merchants have been model inmates. We're all in the clear. As far as anyone knows, the last owners of the ledger are dead, and its secrets died with them."

Oscar grunted. "That night, it didn't look to me like you were playing scared."

"We definitely weren't playing," said Cross.

Sinjin moved to Adeline's side. He grasped her hand, stroking her black ring like the possessive man he was.

"Captain was told to spread around my general location. We thought they'd stake me out and plan a hit we'd be ready for. All we wanted was a public fight they instigated where they'd see us *die* and the ledger destroyed." She winced. "It worked out better than we planned."

"They found you too fast," Adeline said. "It was a scrambling, thrown-together plan built on the original. I got as close as I could to the square, figuring they'd take me there since none of the gangs would want the others in their territory. They'd opt for neutral ground. The final piece was Gianna on the roof. And Jasper." She rubbed my arm.

Oscar grunted. "You three took a big risk. At least the ledger has finally been reduced to ash."

"Oh." Adeline made a face. "Not quite, Daddy."

"What does that mean?"

"Part of me wanted to destroy it, then I read it," she said. "There are hundreds of horrible crimes no one has been held accountable for. To many people, the destruction of the ledger is exactly what they wanted. No one would know about the villages they slaughtered, or the unfair sentences they handed down for a bigger bank account. People like Leonidas O'Hare can't be allowed to get away with what they've done, Dad. Unlike Nicolas 'Half-Dick' Katz, I truly want to change our city."

She looked to me. "Jasper made me one ledger that passed scrutiny. I asked him to make another for our plan, but then things went wrong. I ended up running around the city with the real one, and— Well, we all know what happened." Adeline stroked my arm. "I needed him to return with the fake in time to save me. And he did."

I kissed her. "I made you a promise."

Baris, Sinjin, and Killian were out of their seats.

"Where is it?" Sinjin asked.

"Safe at my new place," I replied.

"Thank you," said Adeline.

"Don't thank him yet," Killian said.

The temperature dropped several degrees.

"Ah. So, Adeline's told you I've left a few things off my resume. Let's settle this now. I don't work for Lombard. I never did," I confessed. "The woman I work for hired me to get the ledger, and then to become a Merchant after Mercer Santos's death."

"Why?" Sinjin demanded.

I crossed the room. "I'll let her tell you that herself."

ADELINE

"I'll let her tell you that herself."

"Jasper, what's going on?"

The door swung open and a tall, willowy woman stepped over the threshold.

I could tell she made an attempt to appear casual, but the six-hundred-dollar pants and three-hundred-dollar cardigan gave her away. That's if the giant rock on her finger didn't do it for her.

Wealthy woman. Married. Pretty with dark hair streaked gray and a surprisingly soft smile. Who was she and why did she hire Jasper?

Sinjin clamped on my hand.

"Saint?" He stared at her, eyes wide with something I'd never seen. "What's wrong?"

"Aelia?"

That soft smile spread. "Hello, son."

"Son?" I repeated. "Aelia? I— I don't—"

Sinjin wasn't moving.

"Jasper, I think it's time for that explanation," I said.

"Yes," Aelia said, "it is. There is no easy way to say this, so I'll just say it. Good and bad." She lowered her head, stroking her ring like Sinjin did mine. "When I was twenty-two, I moved to Cinco for grad school. While living here, I fell in love with a young seminary student named Paul Bellisario.

"I had a strict upbringing. My father was a moralistic man and made enough money to force people into his idea of right—"

"You're dead," Sinjin hissed. "You were sick and you died."

"No, St. John—"

"Who are you?"

"I am your mother." She held her hands out, closing the distance, and Sinjin leaped off the chair. He backed away from her growling.

"It's okay, love," I murmured. I laid my hand over his chest, shielding him with my body as if I could stop what was coming. "We'll just listen. If it's too much, she'll go."

"I will go," Aelia spoke up. "If you don't want to see me again after today, I'll respect it."

Sinjin said nothing. She took it as a signal to speak.

"My father disowned me when he found out I was pregnant. I nearly cheered. I had wanted out from under his thumb my whole life," she said. "For a while, it was just you and me. My baby."

Sinjin stiffened.

"I kept you a secret from your father. Our brief romance ignited after a crisis of faith. His brother was murdered. Mugged and left to die in an alley. The senseless tragedy rocked Paul to his core. When he found his way back, I was happy for him. It was okay for me that he had his faith, because I had you.

"I loved our little life... until I found out I had cancer. Things got bad for us very quickly, St. John. You were old enough to remember. I had no health insurance. Bills were racking up. The treatments left me too sick to work. We were drowning. The week they shut off the power to our apartment, I broke down and called my father."

Aelia shook, holding tight to her ring. "He made it clear in no uncertain terms, I could come home and receive all the care I needed, as long as you did not step off the plane with me."

"You said yes."

"I said screw you and hung up the phone," she cried. "For a year, I did not speak to that man once. And during that year, I got sicker. So sick, I couldn't hide it from you any longer. The night I told you I was dying, I looked in your eyes and saw your future, St. John. Me gone and you alone.

"I was dying so that I could be with you, but that wasn't what you needed, St. John. You needed your mother. The next day, I left you in your father's church and flew home to Louisiana. I'd go through my treatments, get into remission, and then I'd be back for you. It wasn't until I stepped through the gates that my father listed his other terms."

"What terms?" Sinjin asked.

He's listening. That's a start.

"A suitable marriage for his fallen daughter. I say yes or I could forget about his money." She twisted her ring harder. "I said yes."

Jasper squeezed her shoulder.

The friendly, comforting act shocked me. Were they employer/employee? Or friends?

"Evan Benedict was a cruel, violent, controlling man. He domineered my life for six years, dictating who I saw, where I went, and how I spent my money. Still, I found a way to keep an eye on you. After Paul's murder, I booked a ticket to Cinco.

"Evan cornered me leaving the house and put me in the hospital." She raised her head. "I don't tell you this for sympathy, St. John, or to make excuses. I just want you to know the truth."

"Are you still married to him?"

"No, he—" She half twisted to Jasper, stopped herself, and turned back. "He died."

Sinjin pounced. "Why did you look at Croix?"

"Because I couldn't take it anymore. I paid him to kill my husband."

He nodded, accepting this easily.

"Once I was free, I sent you as much help as I could from afar. You had found a home by then. With Mr. and Mrs. Hunt. I sent them money to support you—determined the family you found would last. When you became... a Merchant," she said, "I hired people to follow you. Keep you safe. Then you went in search of the ledger, and I knew it was for Paul. I wanted you to succeed, St. John, so I hired Jasper."

"Santos dying complicated things," Jasper said. "The job was to help you find your father's killer, so I became a Merchant."

Sinjin pressed on me. "Why? Why didn't you fucking say? Four years, Croix!"

"You would've kicked my ass if I told you I hid the truth of your not-dead mother."

"Yes," he hissed.

Jasper held up his hands. "It's cool. I deserve it."

"No, you don't," Aelia said. "St. John, please. It was me who had to tell you the truth. Face to face. Jasper was only respecting my wishes, and to be fair to him, he asked me many times to speak to you.

"I should have. I dreamed of the day I'd see you again. But I had let that man control me. Both of them. I abandoned my only son and the consequence of that changed you." She roughly shook her head. "And that's okay. I don't judge the man you've become. I just couldn't see how that man wouldn't hate me."

"I do not hate you."

She smiled, stepping closer. "No?"

"Why would I? I don't know you. You're just a woman wearing my dead mother's face who's quietly asking for validation in abandoning me, convincing my adoptive parents to lie, and embedding a glorified bodyguard in my gang to absolve your guilt. I'll save the rage and sobbing hugs for my actual mother. The one who wouldn't come here pretending to say I'm sorry while actually asking for forgiveness. Your regrets aren't my problem."

"Sinjin—"

Her touch stayed Jasper. "I understand. I'll go." Aelia pulled something out of her purse. "I am sorry, son, and I love you more than the moon and stars." She placed her card on the table. "When you feel ready to talk, call me. I'll be there when you need me. Like your mother used to be."

Aelia quietly left and shut the door.

"Saint," I began.

He walked out. To go after her, I couldn't tell, but either way I let him be. He needed to sort this out in his own way.

I turned on Jasper. "That was the big secret, Jasper? Saint's mother." I ate the distance between us. "You're right, Saint should kick your ass. There are some secrets you don't keep."

"Just as there are some secrets that aren't yours to tell. I don't defend lying to all of you."

"So why did you?"

"Because I know," he said softly, "what it feels like to want your kid... and not deserve them."

I sighed. "Jasper, that's not true."

"It is true," he said. "I lied about something else, Adeline. It *kills* me that I'm not raising Rosie. I grew up wishing for the things a kid does with their father. Trips to the park. Learning to ride a bike. Cheesing for pictures over my birthday cake. I wanted all of that, and now my daughter is experiencing it with another man.

"Maybe this makes me a selfish shit, but Aelia offered me a million to complete the contract with an extra half million for each year it took," he said. "I couldn't say no. Money like that would change our lives. A college dropout who was only ever good at one thing, could leave the dangerous job that kept him from his kid and finally be her father."

He squeezed my hands, raven eyes wide and shining. "Can you understand that I had to do anything, *anything*, to make that happen?"

I swallowed, fighting to hold it down. "Yes," I whispered, losing my battle. "I understand."

"I knew you could." He brushed a tear from my cheek. "And it's why I don't deserve you either. A lie for a good reason is still a lie. I've earned the weariness in your eyes and the anger clenching your jaw. But I've also earned your love, and that means I'm yours for good. Ownership signed and sealed, so I better get on with making it up to you."

Jasper threaded his fingers through mine. I blinked as the mood shifted.

"I can't change the past or wave a wand and fix our broken trust, but I can take that huge duffel bag full of money and split it with my girl and partners. I can move us into the penthouse in the sky that I just bought, and get started renovating the space on the bottom floor that will be Restaurant Redgrave."

I hiccupped on a sob.

"I can get custody of my daughter, quit contract work, and live on my terms. Ruling a city with the woman I love is first on the retirement list." Jasper drew out the ring I tossed away. I stopped breathing as he dropped to one knee.

"I can put this ring on your finger and promise for as long as I live, the only lies I tell will be about surprise vacations, baby weight, and that you don't snore."

My laugh was light and breathless. "Goodness, Jasper. What is with you guys choosing the most inappropriate times to propose?"

"We've never done this right. We kidnapped you, then fell in love. You plotted to kill us, then saved our lives. We began on the wrong foot and ended up where we needed to be." The ring slid where it belonged, and where it would always stay. "We're talking about starting the rest of our lives together. Of course I have to do it wrong. Why mess with what works?"

"Damn," Gianna said. "I think you've gotta say yes, girl. To the money and penthouse at least."

I giggled, heart filling with so much love and happiness, it burst in my chest. Yes, everything about this was wrong, and that's what made it right.

"Yes, Jasper. I will marry—"

The door banged open.

Saint filled the entrance, knife white-knuckled in his grip. "We said something about an ass-kicking?"

"Excuse me, love," said Jasper. "We'll pick this up in a second."

"—you," I finished as they flew at each other.

I sighed. Yes, that's what the proposal was missing.

Blood.

Still, this was the start of our new lives, and I wouldn't have it any other way.

One Year Later

"SO, THERE'S REALLY a kid in there?" Saint poked my mountainous belly. The baby kicked back.

Saint, Killian, Baris, and Mercer gathered around me on the bed—or I should say, my stomach. They'd been fascinated by the little bundle of life I was growing since I showed them the three positive pregnancy tests. I thought they couldn't get more overprotective and was laughably proved wrong.

"Feel like mine?" he asked.

"She tap-dances on my bladder for fun, so I'm definitely getting some Bellisario vibes."

"Nah," said Killian. He rested his cheek on my swollen abdomen. "She's mine."

"She's mine," Rosie cheered. "My little sister."

"That's right, Rosie," Jasper said. "No matter what, she's your little sister. You going to look after her?"

"Yes!"

My head lay on the pillow in her lap. Rosie loved combing and braiding my hair, and I loved spending this time with the sweet little girl. Just us.

Custody on weekends is what the Bakers and Jasper agreed to, but the difference in him since she'd permanently come into our lives couldn't be hidden. No one could say Jasper Croix was empty now.

I reached a hand out to my husbands. Yes, my husbands.

Each ceremony after mine and Saint's was illegal in all fifty states. But you know what? So was murder, extortion, and running a criminal organization. Marrying the men I loved was at the very bottom of my crimes, and I didn't regret it for a second.

"Help me up," I said. "I've got to get my seven-month-pregnant self down to the restaurant. Big night tonight."

I got up, intending to go down by myself, and found four men and a six-year-old following me into the elevator. I burrowed into Baris's side, thinking how much our life had changed since that day on the roof. He kissed my forehead like he shared the thought.

We plunged from the elevator to the bottom floor, opening right up to my restaurant, Cabernet. Named in honor of the bottle of wine that brought me and my guys together.

I chose a mix of cozy and high-end. Leather booths and soft lighting. Warm red tones in the wallpaper and cherry floors. Prints of Cinco on the walls. It was everything I imagined my restaurant would be and more.

I closed in on the door, smiling as the clanging pots and pans, shouting sous chef, and sizzling aromas hit my senses. *Welcome home.*

Jasper broke off to set Rosie up with crayons and a coloring book at the table. Killian, Baris, and Saint followed me inside.

"Odette, you're on the roast pork and mushroom dressing. Davis, the chicken kiev. I'll handle the crostini. Knox, you're doing the eclairs. Who's on my stuffed salmon?"

"I am," I said.

"Boss." My sous chef, Ricki, kissed both my cheeks. "Shouldn't you be resting?"

"No," I said, giving my guys a pointed look. "If I don't get out of that bed, I'll be rocking sores. Besides, tonight is a special night. I have to make sure everything is perfect."

"I understand. Oh." She flicked to the guys. "Boss, Boss, and Boss, Diego's in the back for you. There's a territory issue between the Beast Boys and the Twenty-Ninth Street gang. Diego did some checking and found out the Beast Boys are stocking guns in their warehouse, readying for a fight."

I sighed. "Their boss, Timothy, is a hothead. You say his haircut looks stupid and he's scrambling for a gun. I warned his ass if he couldn't behave, we'd replace him with someone who can."

"We'll take care of this and be back in time for dinner," Sinjin said.

It wasn't a problem we were talking about this in front of my chefs. They all worked for me in both capacities. Ricki could debone a duck in the same time she could fillet a man.

"Thirty minutes on your feet," Killian warned, following the guys out. "Then, rest. I don't care if the damn salmon burns."

I shook my head fondly. "Yes, my love. We'll be fine. See you in an hour."

The guys took off and I was left to chop, peel, and listen to reports. A multitasking challenge when you're pregnant and standing in front of a hot stove, but no one said running an empire would be easy.

A year had passed, and Cinco City was a different place. The secrets of the ledger had been revealed.

All across the city, CEOs, judges, politicians, and financiers were hauled out of their offices in cuffs. Gang leaders found themselves running a prison crew.

The ledger truly was destroyed. In the name of saving my city, I drained it of its power. The secrets people killed and died to protect were out.

In these twelve months, the crime rate dropped forty percent. Our Lady of the Sacred Heart was rebuilt. And from what I could tell, the governor who rose to take Katz's place was a good man with a solid plan to improve the city and our state.

That's not to say we suddenly became a utopia. More men and women than I could stomach bought their way out of prison sentences with fines and probation due to their high-priced lawyers. We still had gangs in every borough, and I used a false name so no one would know Adeline Redgrave rose from the dead.

Still, I liked to believe people walked a little safer at night, and that one day, my daughter would bask in the good side of Cinco—and only take a stroll through the bad when it tickled her fancy.

An hour later, the food was done, the guys were back, and I was holding Jasper's and Saint's hands as we welcomed our guests.

"Love what you've done with the place, Addy." Mrs. Hunt hugged me. "Look at you, you're beautiful."

"Thank you, Margot. Please, sit, drink, and feast on appetizers. Everyone should be here soon."

"Don't mind if I do," said Killian's father. "Come, son. Tell your old da what you've been up to."

Killian went off with his father, launching into his studies at med school.

One after the other, the Hunt clan poured in. All the brothers, sisters, nephews, nieces, and—

"Addy!" Kaylee threw her arms around me, kissing my stomach. "I missed you."

"I missed you too. Sit next to me because I've got to hear absolutely everything that's happened since I last saw you."

She ran to snag our seats.

With the arrival of the Hunts, everyone else soon trickled in. Edie and her sister. Dad and his new girlfriend. Gianna and her new boyfriend, Cade. I actually kinda liked him.

"Babe, we need to talk about the property we're moving on this weekend," she said as she hugged me.

"The warehouse?" I asked.

"Nope, the daycare." She pointed at her flat stomach. "We've got to send our kids somewhere."

My scream rattled the china. "Oh, G, I'm so happy for you."

"Thank you. We're out-of-our-minds excited." Gianna gazed up at Cade adoringly.

He was still growing on me, but one thing was for sure, Gianna no longer questioned that love was real.

Captain rolled in and smooched my cheek before anyone could stop him. He hurried away cackling. His days of living on the street were over with his well-paid position as my informant, but some things you just can't change.

"Adeline." Ryan came in with a bottle of wine in one hand, and Mateo Rivas's hand in the other. That the bitter rivalry between them was sexual tension suddenly made so much sense. "What's on the menu?" He went right into the kitchen to find out.

Last to arrive was Aelia Brooke, her kind second husband, Simon Brooke, and their two daughters. Saint didn't react to the kiss on his cheek, but she was here, and they were trying. That was more than enough for today.

Saint whipped around on the two girls, Gemma and Iris. "Children?!"

They ran streaking through my restaurant, shrieking glee. Saint met them a grand total of one time when he went to visit his mother's hometown. Naturally, that was all it took for them to fall in love with him. Saint had a way with kids and I couldn't wait to see him with our daughter.

Together, we sat down—eating, drinking, laughing, and sharing. A beautiful scene like I imagined in those hallways, thinking of the family inside and pushing down hopes I'd ever have my own.

This was almost like I imagined. Kind of, but not quite.

Baris wrapped his arm around me, feeling the exact moment our daughter kicked.

"I love you," he whispered.

What we had was so much better.

Keep In Touch

Join Ruby's mailing list for news, teasers, and more: https://www.sub-scribepage.com/rubyvincentpage
Join Ruby's Facebook Reader Group:
https://bit.ly/3bNuCOq

ABOUT THE AUTHOR

Ruby Vincent is a lover of mysteries, suspense, and paranormal romances, but after taking a fun foray into contemporary romance, she found her love of saucy heroines, bold alpha males, and weaving a tale where both get their happy ever after.

www.ingramcontent.com/pod-product-compliance
Lightning Source LLC
Chambersburg PA
CBHW022103310726

48972CB00007B/1865